PRISONERS

PRISONERS

A Jewish Guard in a
Nazi POW Camp

BURT ZOLLO

ACADEMY CHICAGO PUBLISHERS

Published in 2003 by
Academy Chicago Publishers
363 West Erie Street
Chicago, Illinois 60654

First paperback edition 2010

© 2003 Burt Zollo

Manufactured in the U.S.A.
ISBN 978-0-89733-600-0 (paper)

Library of Congress Cataloging-in-Publication Data

Zollo, Burt.
  Prisoners / Burt Zollo.
      p. cm.
  1.World War, 1939–1945—Prisoners and prisons, American—Fiction.
2. World War, 1939–1945—France—Fiction. 3. Americans—France—
Fiction. 4. Germans—France—Fiction. 5. Prisoners of war—Fiction.
6. Jewish soldiers—Fiction. 7. Antisemitism—Fiction. 8. France—Fiction.
I. Title.

PS3626.O44P75 2003
813'.6—dc21

                                        2003001845

For Lois and our family

CHAPTER 1

TECHNICAL SERGEANT FOURTH Class Stuart "Sandy" Delman flapped his long arms and stamped his large feet. After twenty minutes, the cutting December night air had penetrated his heavy overcoat, his green fatigues, his winter underwear. Typical, he thought: hurry up and wait. He heard the repetitious commands of the bored, tough MPs, "*Mach schnell, mach schnell.*" Move quickly. The defeated Germans, traumatized by their capture, did what they were told as they were hustled from the train station to the stockade.

Along with other cage wardens—part of the POW compound's American cadre—Delman's job tonight was to direct the shivering enemy troops to one of the nine cages within the barbed wire fence. It circled what had been rolling farmland seven miles south of Le Mans.

Delman thought the snow-covered camp wasn't what it seemed. Its exterior was a façade. From the nearby two-lane road, you saw only the compound's uniform headquarters buildings, its wooden watch towers, and its heavily gated entrance manned by armed Belgian sentries. The enclosure appeared secure, well-organized, properly military.

But away from the road, the camp's true character—its chaotic squalidness—was exposed.

Except for its headquarters, it was a wretched, helter-skelter conglomeration of tents and ramshackle shelters. And POWs continued to arrive. There were too many of them, too few jailers, and an awful paucity of supplies.

The camp's endless misery bred endless rumors. The least believable, Delman hoped, was that the horrors of the prison were intentional, that the Allies were out to kill the Germans however they could, in combat or in a stockade. What difference did it make? Who cared?

Delman did. He returned to his cage. He thought, We're not here to slaughter Germans. That doesn't mean we care about them; it means we care about ourselves more. There's a difference between a warrior and an executioner.

He listened without sympathy to the POWs' gripes. They were too crowded. They were freezing. They were hungry. And you're the lucky ones, Delman thought. New arrivals got the leftovers, scraps of rations and tentless dugouts. They survived in body-length holes in the frozen earth, some insulated with cardboard, some covered with canvas shelter-halfs. And some, with little protection, were no different from open graves.

Delman thought, Let the Germans suffer. Let them suffer the way they made the world suffer. Let them suffer nightmares about the deadly, low-flying American P47s—the Jabos the Germans called them, the hunter aircraft—and the lethal salvos of U.S. synchronized artillery. But don't kill them here.

After his new POWs were checked in, Delman walked around his pyramidal tents to make sure flaps were secure. That's when he heard the expletive. Shouted out to make sure he heard. And in English. To make sure he understood. To infuriate him, maybe to destroy him.

It was starting again. They knew about him, this Jewish football player. They knew that, as a cage warden, he'd slugged a foul-mouthed POW who had hurled an invective at him. The story was as much a part of the compound's scuttlebutt as was Sergeant Perry's growing score with local women.

Delman wasn't surprised to hear another German curse him. What surprised him—annoyed him—was his own reaction, his rising temper, almost beyond his control.

He couldn't let it happen again—attacking another POW who had the gall to mock him. This time, Delman knew, his punishment would be severe. He wouldn't escape with a wrist-slap, a reprimand, a cancellation of a weekend pass.

He recalled the advice he'd received from the camp's commander, Colonel Nelson. "Pinch yourself, hard, until it hurts. Concentrate on that hurt, that pain. Let it overwhelm the psychological pain you feel when you hear their insult."

Delman had followed instructions. He pinched his thigh, his arm, his midriff. He pulled and twisted his own flesh as if he were trying to remove it. Nelson's prescription didn't work. Delman couldn't cauterize his wound.

When he heard the profanity, nothing could stop the rush of his anger. It was fueled, in part, by his father's hatred, which was fueled by *his* father's hatred. Delman had heard their stories of persecution so often he could repeat them, word for word. They were his family's tradition and also his family's shame, at least to Delman. Why hadn't his father and grandfather—two large, strong, quiet men—fought against their persecutors instead of hiding their hostility, their hatred?

Instead of fighting, Delman's father, like his father before him, ran. Delman's grandfather ran from country to country, from Russia to Poland. Delman's father ran from continent to continent, from Europe to America. And, even there, his father continued to run. Not from his persecutors, but from his identity, his Jewishness. He said he wasn't running, he was assimilating.

When Delman became a popular high school varsity football player, his father said, "Now you're truly an American." But Delman refused to play football on Rosh Hashanah and Yom Kippur and his refusal was reported by the press. Delman was surprised that his personal decision had become public knowledge. There were many well-known Jewish athletes, from Barney Ross to Hank Greenberg, from Nat Holman to Sid Luckman, who didn't hide their faith. But, his father said, they didn't flaunt their Jewishness, either.

Delman was even more surprised when a variety of colleges offered him unexpected incentives to study and play when he graduated from high school. Especially because he wasn't a quarterback or a fullback, only a guard, although a big, fast and nearsighted one who could play his position without his glasses. He chose Northwestern—in spite of its Jewish quota—because of its journalism school.

"Maybe I learned how to run so fast from you," he kidded his father, who got the joke but didn't like it. Delman meant it to be funny but realized too late that his humor could be mistaken for ridicule.

"It was a different time," his father said. "Let's see how brave you are—parading your Jewishness—when you get in the real world."

Delman stealthily checked each tent in his cage. Eavesdropping, he was careful not to hit the tent pegs or the tight ropes pulling the canvas upright. He waited for a repetition of the curse or giveaway sniggers.

When he heard the expletive, he looked through the tent flaps and located the blasphemous POW. Confronted, the German admitted he was the one who cursed, but he didn't cringe. He was doing his duty, fighting the enemy, baiting him. He rose and faced Delman who removed his Army-issued steel-rimmed glasses and carefully placed them in the right pocket of his long overcoat.

Then, staring at the POW, Delman floored him. With one punch. No warning. No left to the body. Only a single round-house right into the German's startled face. He went down, blood dropping from the nose broken from the full impact of Delman's fist.

As soon as he struck the POW, Delman knew he'd be brought before the camp's commander, Colonel Ellsworth Nelson, a Chicago detective. Most of the camp's American personnel were policemen who had received Military Police training at Camp McCoy, Wisconsin.

Delman liked Nelson. In fact, most GIs liked the balding, laid-back light colonel who could have been a double for the Allies' supreme commander, General Dwight David Eisenhower. Unlike most officers, Nelson wasn't impressed with his rank.

He considered the military—especially its pomp and inbred protect-your-ass mentality—as a necessary evil. Most of the time he wore enlisted men's green fatigues and returned salutes with a perfunctory wave of the hand.

According to the camp's Table of Organization, Nelson should have had an executive officer. His had been transferred and Nelson never replaced him. He felt as comfortable with NCOs as with officers. But, as Delman discovered, Nelson was a civilian at heart, an iconoclast, an original.

Take the Colonel's secret informers—POWs, GIs, probably some of the Belgian security guard—who didn't miss an opportunity to squeal. Each of the Colonel's rat-finks, Delman thought, worked like an overachieving tabloid gossip columnist. Small revelations generated small compensations—a few cigarettes, a few squares of Hershey, a month-old copy of *Yank*. Expose a serious act of chicanery and the Colonel's rewards were bountiful: a weekend pass, a carton of cigarettes (your choice), a bottle of Scotch (the Colonel's choice).

His largesse enabled him to stay on top of the camp's burgeoning black market—as well as other, more imaginative corruption. No small feat, Delman thought, considering the tented city of 10,000 Germans was getting bigger each day of the Allied advance. Without the Colonel's informers, it would have been difficult to maintain control.

When it came to his own men's offenses, the Colonel was lenient. He probably figured, Delman thought, that away-from-home boredom would prove deadly without some minor crimes. So he overlooked the extra rations of booze and cigarettes certain officers and Non-Coms finagled, the women they hustled in and out of their barracks and, sometimes, even their larger exploits. One officer was notorious for sending a jeep home—in pieces. Each cosmoline-coated part was mailed parcel post to a different address. Within a year, a dismantled jeep waited to be assembled at a split-level in Miami. But certain acts stretched Nelson's tolerance.

Entering the Colonel's office, Delman knew his offense was serious—he wasn't offered the baby Tootsie Rolls the Colonel kept in a bowl fabricated from an artillery shell. Nelson's office doubled as his bedroom. He had another in the officer's quarters, but when he worked late he bombed out on his office's narrow cot.

His metal desk was bare except for a single ominous manila folder. Behind him was a beat-up table that held his thermos of coffee, books—including some about central France—and photos of his dark-haired wife and their two boys sporting Cubs' caps.

Delman sat down on one of the three wooden chairs facing the desk. A large map of France, its slick surface careening the morning sun into Delman's eyes, was behind the Colonel. The location of POW camps, supply depots, and the Allied advance were marked with colored dots and arrows.

"You hit a POW again," the Colonel began.

"I'd do it again," Delman said.

"He called you a name," the Colonel said.

"He cursed me," Delman confirmed.

"He called you a dirty Jew."

"This time I was also called a kike."

"The Germans," the Colonel said. "They've got your number, haven't they?"

"I doubt if a German would have the guts to curse me," Delman said, "let alone know the word kike, unless he was put up to it."

"By whom?" the Colonel asked.

"The Germans aren't the only bigots in this camp."

"You're being wasted here," the Colonel said, leaning back in his swivel chair, resting his feet in their scuffed combat boots on the desk. "You belong in the infantry. Then you could let out all your anger with an M1."

"Transfer me," Delman said.

"Whether you've been set up or not, this is the second time

you hit a POW," the Colonel said, lowering his boots, glaring at Delman. "I've warned you before. We do not—let me repeat, *not*—hit POWs, whether they're asking for it or not. Curse them. Make them dig holes. Order them to clean shitty honey-buckets. I don't care what you make them do. But you do not hit them."

"I officially request a transfer to the infantry," Delman said.

"I wish I could," Nelson said. "I'd love to get rid of you, Delman. You're a royal pain in the ass. But unfortunately they don't want limited service GIs with 20/400 vision in the infantry. Not even expert riflemen. Not even big-name football guards. And don't think you're the only celebrity here.

"One of our POWs is Sacher, probably the greatest race-driver ever. You're known in the United States. Sacher's known all over the world. But fame's forgotten here. It's unimportant. That's why you were transferred to me and became an MP. And, regardless of how big and tough and famous you think you are, you'll stay an MP. But I'm going to transfer you, Delman—straight to Sergeant Mueller's supply tent."

"What I know about supplies couldn't displace one of your Tootsie Rolls."

"Sergeant Mueller knows all there is to know about supplies," the Colonel said. "He's known and respected far and wide. He's got a working network of NCOs, young and old, regular Army veterans and draftees, who will do anything for him. Sergeant Mueller's been a supply sergeant for longer than you've been alive. How long's that, Delman?"

"Nineteen years."

"You're younger than I thought."

"I enlisted."

"Sergeant Mueller hates enlistees as much as he hates fuck-ups," the Colonel continued. "He's regular Army. He has five hash marks. He figures enlistees joined up to avoid the draft."

"I joined up to kill Germans."

"You probably did, Delman," the Colonel said.

"Who'll take over my cage?"

"That's my worry."

"How long do I have to work for Mueller?"

"It's Sergeant Mueller, Delman. He earned every one of his six stripes. You'll do whatever Sergeant Mueller tells you to do—without complaint. That could mean wiping his ass, polishing his boots, or picking up after the POW who works for him."

"I'm a sergeant," Delman said.

"Were," Nelson replied. "Were. Now you're a buck private."

"For striking a German who cursed me!"

Colonel Nelson rose. "I'd advise you to say thank you and leave before I lose patience and give you what you deserve."

Delman drew his body to attention, saluted, and did a smart about-face.

The Colonel waited for what he had ordered and, not hearing it, shouted, "Delman!"

"Thank you, Colonel!"

"I don't want to see you here again," the Colonel said, "Abuse one more POW and you'll be court-martialed. That could mean imprisonment. That would follow you the rest of your life. You hear me, private?"

"I hear you, Colonel."

"Dismissed."

*   *   *

Delman, back in the enlisted men's bunkhouse—a Quonset hut with wooden double-tiered bunks and a black wood-burning stove—figured his predicament was typical of the Army: SNAFU, Situation Normal, All Fucked Up. He pulled himself up on his narrow upper bunk and attacked his straw-filled mattress—as if he were striking Colonel Nelson or himself—before he fell back against it. A private again! And, even worse, to work for Mueller, Sergeant Mueller!

Delman respected the Army veteran. But he didn't like him and he didn't trust him. While Delman savored Mueller's endless stories about the peacetime Army, its perks, its comforts, its isolation from the stresses of civilian life, he knew Sergeant Curt Mueller was as German as his name. He admired German efficiency. He praised German culture. He read German books. He never said a critical word about a Nazi.

Delman thought, The military invests thousands of dollars to train me to be a rifleman, a grunt, to kill Germans. It puts me through thirteen mean weeks of basic. It teaches me to kill with an M1, a carbine, a BAR, a bazooka, a bayonet. In the movie theater at Fort McClellan, Alabama, it shows me films documenting the rise of Nazism. Hitler's staged rallies. Germany's blitzkrieg. Deutschland's systematic persecution of Jews.

The master race. The Germans. Our enemy. The Army teaches me to hate them. Yet when I strike a German POW for sneering at me, I—not the POW—am reprimanded, demoted. And now, working for Sergeant Mueller, as German as the POWs, I'll be taunted, demeaned, by the enemy I was encouraged to hate, to kill.

Delman cursed Mueller and Nelson and the Army and, most of all, himself. He savaged his flattened mattress. I should've left when I had the chance, he thought. I should've accepted an honorable discharge when the Army was trying to phase out "limited service."

He recalled his physical examination, sitting naked in front of a young, bored doctor who studied his file and finally asked, "You have migraines, private?"

"No, sir."

"A bad back? Maybe you hurt it playing football. If you have a recurring sports injury combined with your poor vision, I don't see how you can go into combat. I'd recommend you for an honorable discharge."

"I don't have a recurring sports injury. I don't have a bad back."

The expert rifleman became an inexpert clerk-typist. He was transferred from the infantry to the Military Police and, once overseas, assigned to the overhead cadre of the POW camp. A week after he arrived at the ugly tent city, he became a cage warden. His assignment was created by the heavy influx of POWs and the favorable commendations in his personnel file. A college student. Leadership qualities. Foreign language skills. Chose to remain in the Army. Since the POW camp's T/O called for cage wardens to be sergeants, Delman was instantly promoted.

His demotion was just as rapid. As was his humiliation. Sergeant Mueller didn't look at Private Delman when he reported for duty in the supply depot, a series of connected tents.

"Talk to Heinrich," Sergeant Mueller said, clipping his fingernails. "He's in the back."

"He's a POW," Delman said. "A Kraut."

"You'll do what he tells you to do."

"A German's going to tell an American what to do!"

Mueller slowly finished his last finger, blew on the metal nail clipper, and leaned back so he could look up into the angry face of the curly-haired, burly ex-sergeant.

"Got a problem with that, private?"

Early that morning, Delman had been a sergeant. At breakfast in the large noisy mess hall, smelling of powdered eggs and bacon grease, he had called Sergeant Mueller by his first name, Curt. Mueller called Delman by his nickname, Sandy. Now Sergeant Mueller was turning over his cashiered compatriot, his fellow GI, to the enemy.

Delman told himself it was wrong, crazy, cockeyed—making him work for a POW—but it was better than a court-martial. He slumped through the long darkened corridor of tents. He felt disoriented. He would be tortured by the enemy he learned to hate, the enemy who considered Jews less than human, the enemy—the German—who now was Delman's fucking boss.

CHAPTER 2

DELMAN WROTE DAILY in a three-ring 5"x 7" black notebook he'd bought at Chandlers, a bookstore near Northwestern's Evanston campus. Delman's English professor, poet Robert Mills, said the only way you learn how to write is to write.

"At first, you'll hate it," he said. "Then it'll become your friend and, finally, your addiction."

At first, Delman did hate it. Just as he hated his morning exercise, especially the push-ups. But he became stronger, the muscles in his arms and shoulders more defined. Maybe, he thought, the same would happen to his writing: he'd see some results, he'd gain a journalist's skill.

He sent at least five journal pages home in addition to his weekly letters. The system worked: it became a habit and, at the same time, forced him to write his parents who deposited his journal in an empty typewriter-paper box he'd left on his closet shelf.

On December 6, 1944, he wrote in his journal: "I never heard about my application to OCS, Officer's Candidate School. Maybe I should write Senator Brooks. I've been reclassified because of my vision. Instead of 745, I'm 405. I'm no longer a nearsighted infantry rifleman. I'm a nearsighted clerk-typist.

"I'm being transferred to a POW camp. This war gets crazier all the time. For thirteen weeks they trained me to hate and kill the enemy. Now, I'll learn how to care for him and feed him.

"I've learned you have to be self-sufficient. You can't depend on anyone else. You're alone. Your friends are either killed or transferred.

"What you are, regardless of what they call you, is a serial number. I'm 16146055. It's on your dog tags that you wear around your neck until you're discharged or killed."

*   *   *

Colonel Nelson leaned back in his chair, his feet on his desk. He felt exhausted. Delman did that to him. Delman was an idealist, a moralist, and, as he told him, a royal pain. Now that he left, the Colonel reached for Delman's personnel file.

He had intended to use it as a prop, maybe a threat when he met with Delman, as if the file could reveal more about Delman than Delman. But the Colonel had become so involved in reprimanding the cocky ex-sergeant that he had forgotten about the file.

Nelson balanced it on his stomach as he thumbed through it. There were the usual contents. Biographical information. Evaluation reports. What was unusual were the numerous newspaper clippings. Articles from the Fort McClellan *Chronicle*, the newspaper for the Alabama military base where Delman completed his basic training.

The first clipping Nelson read described the arrival of Fort McClellan's latest celebrity, Delman, the football guard. A second article reported that he, and a featured Hollywood actor, had completed their training and were shipped out. Delman's name appeared first.

Other clippings were articles written by Delman for the *Chronicle*. One was about the perils of crawling on your belly carrying an M1 through the obstacle course, a notorious part of basic training. Another described the conversations of GIs waiting in the base's telephone exchange to call home.

That's what we need here, Nelson thought, a camp newspaper. Delman could be the editor. Only one problem: unless he wrote it in German, its circulation would be too limited.

The Colonel folded his hands behind his head and wondered what was next for the feisty Delman, his glasses falling down his nose, his big body still growing. He's a heavyweight, Nelson thought. Maybe next time he'll take on two Germans. Why not? Delman, provoked, had already taken the bait twice and was caught twice. As bright as he was, he still had plenty of maturing to do. And the Germans knew it. Maybe he could be set up again.

When you threw "Jew" at Delman, you threw a dagger. And when you threw "kike" at Delman, you threw a machete, an ax. Among Jews, "kike" was the ultimate curse. No self-respecting Jew could do any less than strike his tormentor but Nelson knew some Jews didn't react. Like some NCOs attacked by officers, they hunkered down, refusing to dignify the criticism or the profanity by responding. They let the slur slide off their bodies like repellent slime.

But, the Colonel thought, not Delman. He's a fighter. Maybe part of that came from the basic training he received. The other part? Perhaps from his family, his heritage. Together, Nelson thought, they gave him his pugnacity and his pride. Delman, the Colonel was convinced, was a throwback. An angry Old Testament Jew.

Nevertheless as commendable as his behavior might be in civilian terms, it was disastrous in the military. And the Germans knew it. Did they set him up or was someone else involved? Either way, although the Germans had to be surprised when he struck them—Germans considered Jews sheep—Delman's belligerence played into their hands. Every time he threw a punch, he became the victim.

The Colonel focused on a new file folder he was handed. "Delman's replacement?" he asked First Sergeant Clayton Bosworth.

"As you requested, Colonel," Bosworth answered. "Corporal Waddell. He's new. Now he's detailed to move POWs from the train station."

Nelson quickly checked Waddell's credentials. Early twenties. Single. High school education. A Texas cop, mostly desk work. Drafted.

"How does he stack up against Delman?"

"No one stacks up against Delman," Bosworth reported. "He ran the best cage in the camp. He was tough but he was fair. He never backed down. He made sure you knew who was in charge. But Waddell's a fast learner."

The sound of someone shouting angry orders in bad German broke through the thin walls of the prefab headquarters building. Nelson turned to look out the window.

"Waddell, sir," Sergeant Bosworth said.

The American corporal, darting back and forth like a sheep dog herding its charges, kept the bedraggled Germans moving up the dirt road from the railroad spur.

"Where do we put them?" Bosworth asked. "We need more tents, everything. And our rations are down to nothing."

Colonel Nelson approached the map on his wall. He jabbed at the red pins west of the camp.

"There, there, there and there," he said, "Supply depots. Plenty of them. But you notice I don't say *our* supply depots. They've got everything we need. Tents. Blankets. Clothes. Rations. But it all goes to the front. Right past our nose. Via the Red Ball Express. I know how they think and, if I were in their boots, I'd think the same way. Why worry about POWs? So they freeze! So they starve! Who gives a shit! As long as they're dead. The damn MPs at the POW camp just want to coddle the enemy."

Nelson looked at Sergeant Bosworth. "Maybe they're right," he said. "Let someone even punch a POW and he's in trouble."

"Delman knows better," Sergeant Bosworth said.

"For Christ's sake, sergeant!" The Colonel shook his head. "Delman's nineteen years old. He's a kid. He's a rifleman. He was taught to kill Germans, not to coddle them."

"His second offense," Bosworth answered. "He's smart, maybe too smart for his own good. The trouble is he's a Jew. Jews shouldn't be cage wardens."

Nelson glared at his first sergeant. But Bosworth didn't back off. He liked to shock, to test, to argue. Like some baseball players, managers: they liked the victim role, it gave them a cause.

It's comfortable to be a Non-Com, Nelson thought. They always have justification: they aren't appreciated, utilized. Even though they're asked to give advice, they aren't expected to make important decisions. It's easy to be tough, he thought, to be inflexible when you don't have serious responsibilities. That's left to officers; they're paid to make decisions. NCOs are paid to be cop-outs; it comes with the stripes. And Bosworth probably never saw a Jew before he joined the Army.

"If anyone deserves to push around Germans," Nelson said, "it's Jews."

"If you say so, sir."

"You're some piece of work, Bosworth."

"Yes, sir."

Push any American Non-Com far enough, Nelson thought, and they drop 'sir's' like hand-grenades. You think a private dislikes officers? He fears them, for good reason. An NCO resents them. He's seen them bare-assed. A Non-Com'll say he does everything for his officer and what does he get in return? Not even a thank you. A Non-Com does all the work and receives no credit, no respect. He's also convinced he's underpaid—an abused underclass.

"What about Waddell, sir?"

The Colonel wasn't impressed with the corporal's credentials but he had decided a long time ago that he would leave minor decisions to Bosworth. It would give him a taste of authority; he would suffer some responsibility, get an idea of what it meant to be an officer.

"Your decision, sergeant."

Sure, Bosworth would make some mistakes. But he would save Nelson time. He had to take risks; you didn't have a choice if you were understaffed.

"I'll give him Delman's cage," Bosworth decided. "Do we promote him to sergeant? If we do, there's no way Delman'll get his stripes back. That's what you want, isn't it, sir?"

Nelson returned to his chair, leaned back and studied his

first sergeant. Short, slick-haired, looking-for-a-fight Bosworth. Always ready with an arrogant quip, a loaded question.

It was a given, Nelson thought: Americans resent authority. Subordinates express that resentment through head shrugs, smart-assed grins, and not-so-subtle innuendo. It's American to be brazen to your superiors. Nelson put up with Bosworth's sarcasm because he knew a replacement would be no better.

"Let's see if Waddell can handle the job," the Colonel said, "before we talk promotion."

"You like Delman, don't you, Colonel?"

"You don't let up, do you, Bosworth?"

"I don't understand, sir, why Delman's not getting a court-martial."

"He could be back in college," Colonel Nelson said, "like the rest of his fellow limited-service goldbricks. He could've lied about a bad back, a trick knee, an ingrown toenail. Delman refused to play that game. He chose to remain in the Army. He asked me to transfer him to the infantry."

"Why didn't you, sir?" Bosworth asked.

"He's lost without his glasses."

"So you took away his stripes," Bosworth went on, "and gave him to Mueller."

Bosworth had him there, Nelson thought. The Army made you do what you didn't want to do. Nelson tried not to lose his temper. He reached into his desk drawer and pulled out a cigar. A Perfecta Garcia. He slipped off its cellophane sleeve, bit off the cigar's end, flicked his Zippo lighter, and puffed four times before he was ready to react to Bosworth's latest challenge.

"In this man's army, sergeant," the Colonel explained, "the first thing you learn is to cover your ass. I can't risk protecting Delman again. But I don't have to crucify him."

"Mueller'll take care of that, sir."

* * *

Awakened in the middle of the night by the sound of gunfire, Nelson hurriedly pulled on his trousers and stepped into his boots as he grabbed his loaded carbine and ran toward the commotion. Searchlights, manned at the lookout towers by the rugged Belgian security guards, turned the POWs' intended escape hatch into a grotesque daytime tableau.

In the foreground were two bloodied POWs, their hands upraised as the Belgians prodded them with their rifles. In spite of their wounds, the Germans didn't cringe. One had a head wound, probably from a rifle butt; the other, a bullet wound in his calf.

In the tableau's lower background was the accordion-like tangle of barbed wire cut from the perimeter fence. In the upper background a third POW was dead, melodramatically draped over the top of the fence, his bullet-torn body impaled on the killing barrier's wicked stilettos.

"It had to be sudden, spontaneous," Nelson told Captain Roland, the security force commander. "This escape."

"Why do you say that, Colonel?"

"I would've heard about it," Nelson answered.

"From your spies," Roland said. "Your informers."

"We've had this argument before," Nelson said.

He liked the young, pragmatic, English-speaking Belgian, a career officer who regarded the war with brutal simplicity. Like Delman. You killed or you'd be killed. He had no patience with half-measures.

"I don't do business with POWs," Nelson explained again. "I use them."

"They say you've created your own Gestapo," Roland said.

Nelson bristled. "How do you respond when you hear that?"

"I say you don't need spies," Roland answered. "I say you

can get all the information you want if you make it clear to the Germans you'll kill them if they refuse to answer your questions."

"Escapes could tear this place apart," Nelson replied, side-stepping another argument. "I learn about escape plans before they begin. I abort escapes. Do you think your company—as good as it is—could contain all the Germans we have here if we had constant escape attempts? But why this one—without planning? An aberration?"

"They're starving." Roland answered. "They're sick. They're wet and cold. They think anything will be better than staying here. What have they got to lose? Furthermore, it's drilled into them that if you're captured, you must try to escape."

"Leave the body on the fence until tonight," Nelson ordered. "As a warning. Put the other two in solitary after you clean them up."

"Shoot them," Roland said. "That's the way to stop escapes."

"Solitary," Nelson repeated.

"There'll be more attempts unless you bring in tents, blankets, clothes, food."

"I fight for supplies every day," Nelson said.

"There'll be more attempted escapes."

"Maybe Paris will listen," Nelson said, "when some of them are successful."

CHAPTER 3

DELMAN SLOWLY APPROACHED his prison within a prison—the bleak supply tent. As a cage warden, he had been in the tent—really a series of tents telescoped into one another—many times but never had paid much attention to it. Now, as an inmate, he studied the site of his punishment.

It resembled a long dugout boat. Its entrance was in front, like a landing craft. Its sunken top, due to the snow and ice that froze and weighed it down, was concave. Nearby were pre-fabricated headquarter buildings. Toward the camp's center were barracks and mess halls. Outhouses were up a small hill near the motor pool. Beyond that were the ugly rambling cages, surrounded and divided by barbed wire.

Delman moved his double gloves along the top of the tent, tossing aside slabs of snow and ice, so he could separate the tent's flaps and enter Sergeant Mueller's empire. Delman pushed his way inside, and moved toward a black pot-bellied stove, its sweet-smelling heat wafting against his face, the only part of him that was uncovered. Before his glasses fogged up, he caught sight of a long counter and, behind it, the desk where Sergeant Mueller was bent over a thick pile of requisitions.

"Reporting for duty," Delman said. He whipped off his glasses and rubbed them against his overcoat's cold sleeve.

Mueller was too occupied to look up. He inclined his head toward the rear of the tent.

"See Heinrich," he muttered.

Delman replaced his still slightly fogged-up glasses and saw Mueller's POW kneeling on the bare ground, rolling up a side panel. Light slowly entered to expose the tent's contents: precisely piled canvas, rope, and folded cartons along with open barrels containing a variety of supplies, from tent pegs to gun parts.

The POW was dressed for the clammy colder portion of the tent, far from the stove. He wore stained gray pants, a tattered, fake fur flight jacket with a white "POW" splashed on its back, and a peaked wool cap Delman thought he might have lifted from some dead American.

My many-layered boss, Delman thought. He wondered how long he would have to take orders from the rancid POW and how far he'd go to make Delman's life miserable. After all, the German only had to answer to Nazi-loving Master Sergeant Mueller who, Delman was convinced, felt a moral obligation to torture any smart-ass ex-NCO who had the hubris to attack a POW—not once but twice.

"Heinrich?" Delman began.

The impassive German stopped what he was doing, rose, and confronted the American.

"Josef Heinrich."

"Delman."

The German's square, gaunt, lightly bearded face tightened. Delman could see he was trying to recall why he was facing this taciturn soldier. Delman, not about to make life easier for any POW, offered no clue. He waited for the German to remember what Mueller had told him about a trigger-tempered cage warden who'd been demoted to private.

You're my sentence, Delman was about to say, you're my daily punishment. But Heinrich's memory clicked. Not flinching from Delman's glare, the German found a yellow-handled broom and, with a half-smile, presented it to Delman.

"I'd suggest you take it—and use it," the German said in clear English, without even the suggestion of a German accent.

Delman's first inclination was to show his resentment. He considered remaining immobile to force the POW to do what no POW did in the compound, take the initiative, order an American soldier to sweep up.

Then Delman remembered another time he was handed a broom. It was Hell Week for the pledges of Northwestern University's Tau Delta Pi chapter. Delman, with twelve other pledges, had reported to the fraternity house on tree-lined Orrington Avenue, not far from NU's Evanston campus. It was six a.m., a week before the new semester. The pledges' job was to clean the frat house from top to bottom. Their supplies included postage-stamp-sized rags, worn toothbrushes, broken pieces of laundry soap, and toy buckets. Delman laughed and was immediately attacked by several of his fellow pledges.

"What's so goddamn funny?" Herb Gottlieb asked. "I didn't join this famous fraternity to be a goddam janitor!"

"At least a janitor's got decent supplies," Alex Weiss said. "Look at what we've got—shit!"

A few of the fraternity's senior members, carrying their rectangular wooden paddles engraved with the fraternity's Greek letters and the member's name, suddenly stepped into the living room where the pledges had gathered.

"Line up single file," "Hunkie" Levin ordered the pledges, "and assume the position."

That meant, Delman recalled, you were about to be whacked. To prepare for your ordeal, you bent forward and grabbed your genitals, carefully raising them out of the way.

The members, with Levin leading the hitting squad, proceeded to slap their paddles against the upraised asses. Most hazing was done quickly, even lightly, except for Levin. He was notorious for the power of his sadistic slams.

Two of the pledges refused to participate. They left the line, the frat house, and the opportunity to become paying members of Tau Delta Pi.

"What do you think?" Ed Matanky asked Delman. "Who needs this?"

Delman wouldn't reveal why he needed it. He had no real friends. As much as he questioned fraternity life, he thought it might lead him to what he had never had, a genuine friend.

"Hell," Delman replied, the first of the new candidates to
be invited into the fraternity because of his athletic fame, "you
knew what you were getting into when you accepted. Why
chicken out? If you hate this so much, do away with it when
you're a member. It's too late now."

No different with Heinrich, Delman thought. If he'd wanted
to avoid his present punishment, he could have requested a
court-martial. It was too late now to stiff the POW. Delman
accepted the broom.

The POW's position was no less sticky than Delman's. For
all Heinrich knew, Delman could be dangerous, ready to slug
any German who showed any courage. If Delman attacked two
POWs—whatever the provocations—wouldn't there be as much
reason, if not more, to hit the nervy POW who was ordered to
harass him? And maybe it went beyond the POW. Maybe, Delman thought, he would prove unwilling—maybe even unable—
to accept authority. Maybe he was another spoiled American
who made a fetish of his independence, his individualism.

Furthermore, Heinrich might think any American in
Delman's situation—demoted in rank, taking orders from the
enemy—would eventually explode. Being publicly abused would
become too much. He would feel obligated to prove his courage
by repeating his crime. That's what Delman feared most. That he
would lose control, that he'd surrender to the resentment inside
him. He knew he might say something that was meant to be
funny but that would seem arrogant and he, as well as Colonel
Nelson, his surprising savior, would be pilloried.

Watch yourself, Delman thought. Drop any feelings of
self-righteousness, any misplaced fury at the unfairness of your
sentence. You broke the rules. The Colonel did what he had to
do. And he was being amazingly lenient.

Delman repeated to himself, Don't give them the satisfaction
of seeing you lose control. As long as they don't sneer at me, I'll
stand it. I'll survive their heckling, their dirty tricks, their cruelty.
I'll even accept their commands, maybe not without anger but

without violence as long as they don't savor my punishment with too much relish.

He was beginning to sweep the dirt floor when he heard Mueller, from the front of the depot, shout, "Delman!" He looked up through the telescoped tents. Silhouetted against the front tent's opening stood the sturdy, compact body of a screaming Mueller.

"On the double, Delman!"

He trotted through the tents to stand in front of the sergeant, who had resumed his seat.

"This is where you sweep, Delman. Not back there, where you can't be seen but up here, where everyone can see what happens to a smart-ass who likes to hit POWs."

"Whatever you say, sergeant."

"After you finish doing whatever I say," Mueller said, pulling off his paratrooper boots and flinging them at Delman, "you polish these. And I mean, polish them, soldier. I want them to glow like glass."

Delman almost flung the black boots back in Mueller's face. But he caught himself and pulled the boots against his body.

"Help me get into these replacement boots," Mueller ordered. "Get down on your knees, Delman. Hey, I like you there. From now on, you never—I mean *never*—stand above me. If I'm seated, you're kneeling. I saw that somewhere, some king wouldn't let his subjects rise above him. Good idea. Just remember that, Delman. I'm your king."

Delman placed the paratrooper boots on the ground and grabbed the combat boots. He spread their tops wider, first the left and then the right, for Mueller to insert his feet.

"Something you want to say, Delman?"

Mueller's looking for a way to sandbag Nelson, Delman thought, to force him to do what he's reluctant to do, to court-martial me. Delman, now sure of what was happening, held his temper.

Mueller wouldn't be put off. "C'mon, Delman, don't tell me

you wouldn't like to throw those boots in my face? You'd like to punch me out, wouldn't you, private? Knock me unconscious. Just the way you beat up those two POWs too afraid to fight back. That's when you like to attack, isn't it? When you know you won't be hit back?"

For the first time, Delman grasped the scope of his sentence. He wasn't simply being assigned to the supply tent to work for Mueller and Mueller's POW. Delman was to suffer, to be humiliated, debased, to become Mueller's entertainment.

And, what's more, Delman thought, Mueller will be able to torture me with impunity. Mueller's a friend of First Sergeant Bosworth. If I dare to go to Nelson to gripe, I'll be confronted with his first sergeant, uncompromising Bosworth, who'll deny me access to the Colonel.

It was 1700. Delman took a deep breath. He'd got through his first day of punishment. Heinrich had been marched, along with other POWs wearing white armbands, back to his cage. Delman stored his broom, straightened cartons, meandered to the tent's entrance.

Mueller, disregarding Delman, leaned back in his chair, stretched, groaned and rose. He leaned down to straighten the file folders he kept symmetrically arranged on his neat desk. He had a phone and that—along with a proclivity to write letters to his friends—kept him in touch with his network of gossipy NCOs. He walked to the nearby counter and removed a stray requisition.

He turned to Delman. "Close up at 1900. Make sure all tents are secure."

"Will do," Delman said.

"And you can open at 0700," Mueller said. "When I arrive, I expect to see this place in perfect order. Spic and span. Inside and out. You got that, Delman?"

He nodded. By making certain I stay late and arrive early, Delman thought, Mueller makes certain I'll miss mess. So I'll be forced to scrounge for chow. What could be better than cold scraps, burnt meat, bottom-of-the-pot beans, soggy cabbage, hard bread, and bitter coffee?

He watched Mueller stop at the nearby four-holer, the outdoor latrine used by everyone working in the area except officers. Delman had returned to the warmth of the stove when he heard Mueller call him from the four-holer.

"This place stinks," Mueller announced when Delman arrived. "It's putrid. Cobwebs. Torn newspapers. Slime. Spiders. I want it cleaned up, Delman, from top to bottom. Scrub each shit hole. Get down on your hands and knees, if necessary. Clean every crevice. Use a nail file if you have to, a toothbrush. That's your assignment. And, Delman, it better smell like roses when I return here in the morning. Or you'll be on permanent honey-bucket detail."

"Like roses," Delman replied.

Delman could see Mueller wasn't pleased. He probably expected opposition, some visible anger, a sarcastic rebuttal. Besides having to remain late and open early, Delman now had to clean up the stench-filled latrine. But he refused to argue. Maybe, he thought, I've stumbled on a way to fight the Nazi, to survive my sentence. I don't complain. I accept my new chicken-shit existence. I appreciate it. I embrace it. It's better than a court-martial.

After Mueller left, Delman carried brushes and a bucket of soapy water to the four-holer. He'd been lucky. He'd never before pulled latrine duty. In fact, his necessary visits to the latrine always were hurried. The smell, the darkness, the bugs repelled him. He broomed off the cobwebs, stepped on fleeing spiders—some big and black—and scrubbed the wooden seats. He brushed the walls, ceilings, and door.

He was careful to breathe through his mouth so he wouldn't inhale the latrine's stench. He threw lye into the excrement-coated holes and dropped some along the bottoms of the wooden toilets where brown slime oozed out.

He recalled Mueller's command: make the latrine smell like

roses. He needed some type of deodorant. Some spray. Some disguise. He searched the tent, starting at the front near Mueller's desk, to see what he could find. He discovered a few crates of new weapons, wrapped in cosmoline, several boxes of soap and brushes, a large barrel holding individually wrapped condoms. But, except for the laughable inventory, the name of the supply tent remained a misnomer. Its supplies were mostly flattened boxes and empty crates.

His search was interrupted by the funereal sound of a plaintive trumpet from the cages. Delman stepped outside and looked toward the cages to see security troops removing the ripening body of the impaled POW. The daytime transfer was meant to be a warning. But the POWs' military dirge changed the message. Momentarily, Delman was surprised by the POWs' concern for another war victim. Then he realized that the dead soldier was not being mourned, he was being used, exploited by the Germans to show they weren't afraid of their captors.

Delman was no longer appalled by seeing the dead. When he landed in Normandy, he'd been shocked by the sight of American corpses. Later, he was repulsed by the enemy dead. He'd seen them frozen by the ugly winter, some with their arms grotesquely manipulated to point toward the front. They were freaky markers, deformed guideposts.

Soon, like most soldiers, Delman distanced himself emotionally from the horror. Seeing a dead human was like viewing a dead animal—you were distressed, not destroyed.

Delman knew Colonel Nelson wouldn't let the POWs' arrogance go unanswered. Another less compassionate commander might cut back on the Germans' already meager ration, but he didn't think Nelson would do that. Instead, he'd revoke some privileges, maybe prohibit music for a week or a month. Brazenness wouldn't be tolerated but it wouldn't be used as justification for another cruelty.

Delman knew the incessant war within the camp would
never end. The POWs would parade their disdain, their occasional daring. Their captors would display their power.

He returned to the smelly latrine and propped open its door.
He tore snow-wet branches from a bent pine, spread them on
the latrine floor and stood up a row of them against the wall.
Perhaps the pine branches would counter the slimy stink of
the four-holer. Then he went back to the supplyless supply tent
and sat on a pile of cartons. He thought of dictatorial Mueller and impassive Heinrich. How had it happened? How had
the enemy, the Curts and Josefs, suckered him into becoming
another POW?

CHAPTER 4

"IT'S THEIR SECRET plan," Willy Wanger said, his German fast and rolling, wrapped in his dirty overcoat and torn blanket. "They don't have room for all of us in this Godforsaken stockade so they're slowly starving us to death."

The whining barber, perched on top of the wooden double-bunk he shared with Heinrich, exposed his emaciated body.

"Look at this—you can count my fucking ribs. How do you stay so fit? Don't tell me. You get extra rations. Why don't you, for a change, think of somebody else? Is it asking too much to bring me back some lousy crackers, some soggy beans, anything? I tell you, if you don't get me some food soon, I'll wind up with those rotting corpses piled up behind Cage Three."

Heinrich thought Wanger had it right. They were starving the POWs. With more Germans being shipped in every day, rations had been decreased. Portions always were small—now they were minuscule. Could supplies be that sparse—or were the Americans solving the problem of overcrowding by killing POWs?

They had not only cut down on rations. They had stopped erecting new shelters. Why weren't there more tents, some pre-fabricated huts? Why stick new arrivals in unprotected holes in the frozen ground?

Escape was the only answer. But no answer for timid soldiers, no answer for Wanger. The griping barber, typical of all griping enlisted men, preferred the miseries of prison to the dangers of combat. Forget your duty, your Fatherland, your comrades. Wanger always put his stomach first. He knew rations were stored in the mess hall, not the supply tent. But he thought Heinrich could scrounge food from Mueller. He did manage to get Heinrich occasional work in the officer's mess where he was able to wolf down leftovers. But to try to slip them out was too dangerous. He was frisked by the rough Belgian sentries every time he entered the officers' mess and every time he left. Heinrich had explained the tight security procedures to Wanger again and again but he refused to listen.

"K rations," he pleaded. "Get me some K rations. American K rations. Their fucking plastic cheese. At least it would bind me. I'm not alone. We all have dysentery. And you have to wait in line, shivering in the cold, before you can even get into their disgusting latrine. Believe me, this French hole's ten times worse than one of our concentration camps."

The POW compound had a small hospital. Crowded beds. German doctors. Limited medical supplies. Some POWs spent all their time on sick call. But Heinrich shared the opinion that the hospital was a sop. It allowed self-righteous Americans to pretend they were humanitarians.

He adjusted his white armband—his passport out of his cage—on his right sleeve. He rubbed his hand over his shorn head, and he slumped on his bunk in the damp, cold, over-crowded tent.

Bunk on top of bunk. Plus more POWs, wrapped in coats or blankets, sleeping on the tent's frigid bare ground. Not even cartons or boards as barriers against the winter cold. Heinrich knew the Americans—even the enlisted men and Non-Coms—had all the comforts. He'd seen their barracks. They had stoves. Firewood. Lights. Hot water. Soap. To the victors, Heinrich started to think and then he caught himself. Germany, Hitler said, was destined to win and Heinrich never—not for a second—doubted him.

He thought of his easy life before he had entered combat. He thought of his handsome, dignified father and his stately, glamorous mother. They were famous as the ideal Aryan couple, blond hair, fair skin, and slim, tall bodies.

On his few weekends at home—when he took a break from his university studies in Munich—he liked to watch his parents prepare for their evening ritual, one of their parties or a party given by one of Hitler's elite. They would brush their clothes and carefully check each other's appearance before leaving their Berlin apartment.

His father, known for his business acumen, worked closely with Hitler's financial advisers. His mother, active in numerous charities, sometimes represented Germany in matters of protocol. But, most of all, Heinrich saw his parents as adornments, ornaments, adding beauty but little substance to the war effort.

Exactly what Heinrich didn't want to be. He did what he could to diminish his own attractiveness. He wanted to keep his tall body gaunt so he tried to curb his healthy appetite. He cut his hair short. He kept his face bristly too, by shaving every other day. He wished dueling still was in fashion so he could sport a saber scar.

As soon as he graduated, he entered the army. When he became an officer, he volunteered for combat. He became a member of Hitler's elite, the Waffen S.S., the Reich's most fanatical fighting force.

Now, disguised as an enlisted man, he wasn't dismayed. His capture was unfortunate, but he refused to consider it a defeat. It was another challenge and he welcomed challenges. Challenges were a way to test his courage, to improve his character. He knew what he was. A devoted, fearless German. And he knew what he had to do. When the opportunity came—and he was certain it would—he'd be ready.

He kicked off his muddy boots. His two layers of threadbare stockings had been repaired so often they were bundles of bulges. He tore them off and furiously scratched his peeling toes. Now his fingers, like the rest of his body, had a fishy, repugnant smell. His weekly cold-water shower did not expunge his odor. All the POWs were gamy. Part of the problem was that each POW had to provide his own soap. Few had any. Heinrich had only shards. He felt below his bed to make sure the few pieces he had liberated from the supply tent were still safely wrapped in a torn towel.

He ran his hand along the ground below his bunk. Where was his towel? He fell on his hands and knees and peered under his bunk's wooden slats. Again he ran his hand over the cold dirt. The towel was gone. Who took it? It couldn't have dissolved.

"Someone stole my soap," he said, shocked.

He'd taken a risk when he cleaned out a carton a few weeks ago—the last supply delivery Sergeant Mueller received—and hid soap shards in his jacket pockets. Now his prized pieces of processed fat had disappeared. He ran his hand a third time along the dirt. The towel, the soap, had vanished.

Only sleazy Wanger, who always watched Heinrich's comings and goings, could have known about the hidden soap. Heinrich rose. He stood next to his reclining scruffy bunkmate.

"Something wrong?" Wanger asked, turning to face Heinrich.

"My soap's gone," Heinrich replied.

"What soap?" Wanger shook his head.

He turned away, but Heinrich pulled him around. None of the other POWs interfered—at least a fight in the tent's close quarters provided some relief from the long cold night.

Heinrich could smell the barber's strong foul breath. Wanger, seeing Heinrich's discomfort, smiled and carefully blew straight into the furious, offended face of his bunkmate.

"You pig!" Heinrich yelled.

He grabbed the front of Wanger's jacket and pulled him down from his upper bunk. Together, they struck the dirt floor. Wanger wildly swung his arms and hit Heinrich on the right cheek. The glancing blow sparked Heinrich's anger. He smashed his fists against the barber's odorous mouth, his dripping nose, his startled eyes.

"You're killing me," Wanger yelled, "you fucking fag!"

"You fucking thief!"

Desperately, Wanger retaliated and struck Heinrich on the throat causing him to gag. Heinrich pulled himself up and delivered two powerful kicks to Wanger's ribs. As he tried to rise, Heinrich followed with a looping uppercut.

Wanger fell over, groaning, bringing up his knees to his chest to ward off more blows. His moans infuriated Heinrich who tore apart Wanger's bunk. He shook the barber's overcoat and blanket. Heinrich's torn towel with its soap scraps dropped to the ground. He quickly gathered up the soap in the towel and stuffed it into his pocket. Wanger continued to groan as he slowly pulled himself back into his bunk. He wrapped the overcoat and blanket around his body and turned away from Heinrich.

"You win," Wanger muttered. "I'm too weak. You know it's true—they are starving us. They want us to die."

"Food goes to the front," Heinrich replied, disgusted with Wanger. Bad enough he was a thief but he also—like too many of the defeated Wehrmacht troops—fabricated his own self-serving, stupid theories. Anything to avoid blame for his own sorry refusal to do what any good German POW should do, plan to escape.

"We need food," Wanger persisted. "Food and heat. Or we'll all be dead."

He turned around again, looking down at Heinrich. He had layers of pants and shirts below his flight jacket and stained pants.

"I'm frisked when I arrive," Heinrich explained, "and frisked when I leave."

"You look fat," Wanger said. "What did you have to do to get Mueller to feed you and give you all those clothes?"

Heinrich rose and glared at his dirty-minded tormentor. Who needs a disgrace like this? Momentarily—a sudden insight—Heinrich knew how the demoted American sergeant felt when he was provoked, when he was cursed.

"At least steal some rifles," Wanger said. "They must have rifles in your sacred supply tent. And rifle parts, too. And ammunition. Rifles and ammunition. Wouldn't that help your big escape plan?"

Wanger's sarcastic rifle-talk, Heinrich believed, was intended to assuage his guilt. He wanted to maintain the phony veneer of the good soldier, nothing else. Like too many ordinary German soldiers, the bleeding barber was a craven fraud. In spite of the cold, the dysentery, the paucity of food and medicine, he didn't want to escape. He would think about it, talk about it, but he would never risk it. He would rather starve—perhaps believing the war would end soon—than fight.

"Remember how we were when we first came here?" Wanger sat up, his legs over the side of his bunk. Heinrich knew what he was doing: trying to get Heinrich to forget the towel, the soap, their fight.

"Escape—that's all we thought about. How we would escape from the simple Americans. Now all we think about is our stomachs. Everyone but you. God, what I'd give for some bratwurst, some sauerbraten."

"Your stomach," Heinrich said, "runs your life. If you keep listening to it, you won't have any life left."

But it's hard not to think of anything but food, Heinrich thought, when you never have enough of it. Even women, he thought, take second place to food when you're constantly suffering hunger pangs. But he thought of women as he stumbled through the mud to the latrine. Then he realized that he wasn't starving like Wanger and too many of the other half-dead POWs. But thinking about women was self-defeating; it led only to masturbation. He had to overcome his constant hungers, Heinrich thought, and concentrate on his escape. That's what was important, that's what must consume his thoughts, not Wanger's sauerbraten, not his own growing desires.

But why? He was safe, yet he felt guilty. He confronted his guilt every day, every hour, every minute and he felt ashamed he was still a prisoner. He'd been trained to resist, to fight, to escape if he was captured. He said to himself, "My time will come."

Inside the latrine, he latched its flimsy wooden door. He carefully pried loose a board near the third hole and stuck his hand into the crevice. He touched the cloth package he had placed there a week ago.

He pulled it out, unfolded it, and found neatly folded francs. He had gotten them from an officer in exchange for an unopened pack of Lucky Strikes he had won from Sergeant Mueller in their weekly card game.

He continued to unwrap the cloth to check his hidden cache of cigarettes. More winnings—thank you, Sergeant Mueller. Heinrich counted them. Eight. Eight cigarettes, enough for more barter when his escape plan was set. He slowly refolded the stiff cloth over the cigarettes, over the francs.

There would be more card games, more cigarettes. He was not certain how he'd use them. Perhaps to bribe a civilian for information. Or for food once he was away from the camp, on his return to combat. That would happen. He was as sure he would fight again for Germany as he was that he would find a way to escape his daily drudgery.

He stomped on the floorboard to make sure it was even. He unlatched the door and strode confidently back to his tent. He would escape. It was his duty, his obligation.

He knew his job in the supply tent was an opportunity, maybe a test. He would have to exploit it, perhaps steal rifle parts, piece by piece, as Wanger suggested. Then, assuming he could assemble a weapon, he'd have to secure ammunition. Another problem. How much easier it would be to accept his imprisonment, relish his safety, and wait for Germany to win. That was the ordinary soldier's choice, not his.

Heinrich remembered what his leaders had always said: Germans are the master race, the future is ours. That belief was his engine, his catalyst, and, like his hidden francs and cigarettes, his secret reserve. He had the creativity, the ingenuity, the desire. Now, he had to have the patience.

Every Friday he played casino with Sergeant Mueller. They sat at his desk in the supply tent and spoke German. Heinrich's winnings were rations or cigarettes. Sergeant Mueller's winnings were souvenirs made by POWs commissioned by Heinrich. Mueller's favorite was an engraved ashtray fabricated from an artillery shell.

Almost as much as he enjoyed his winnings—and he suspected Sergeant Mueller threw many games his way—Heinrich enjoyed their conversations. The muscular unsmiling American sergeant spoke of his military life before the war, of the women he knew, the family he despised, the country he loved, the NCO friends he made, even the unusual NCO network he created.

"It started with baseball," Mueller had explained. "We loved the game but we always got the Major League scores too late in the Army daily, *Stars & Stripe*s, because of delivery snafus. Sometimes we'd get two or three issues at the same time. So I contacted my friend who worked at the paper's Paris bureau. He'd pick up scores from AP or UP right after a game ended. He'd get them to me by walkie-talkie or phone, I'd relay them to a nearby NCO, he'd relay them to another NCO and so on. Pretty soon we were relaying daily messages throughout the ETO about everything, including the war. Sometimes we sent V-mail to alert fellow NCOs what to look for. I truly believe we know more about what's going on than the OSS and FBI combined."

Heinrich, if only for an hour once a week, escaped from his dull, gray, monotonous, wearisome life, each day worse than the last. He waited eagerly for those conversations. But he didn't like his last talk with Sergeant Mueller. That was when Heinrich was told he had to devise new ways—"be creative," Sergeant Mueller ordered—to make Delman sorry he had ever touched a German soldier.

"He must live to regret his actions," Mueller explained.

I may live to regret mine, Heinrich thought. He almost complained but stopped in time. He had learned, more from his own military service than from being a POW, that you didn't question authority. You accepted commands. You did as you were told.

"Give him dirty work to do," Sergeant Mueller continued.

"I've got him cleaning latrines. Figure out something else to make him miserable. Use your imagination. What do POWs hate to do—most of all? That's what you should order Delman to do. The worse, the better. He deserves to suffer for what he did."

Heinrich wondered what Delman had done. Hit his enemy when he was provoked? Heinrich found this latest charge ironic. He was ordered to punish his captor for an offense Heinrich found inoffensive. Why were Americans so intimidated by conventions and rules? Who was to say what was right, what was wrong in war?

Did Americans think their enemies treated American POWs kindly? If so, they were naïve. Naïve and confused.

Not our troops. We've learned from our wars, Heinrich thought. We've gained from our experience. That's why, as sick and hungry as we are, we are realistic: we know what we must do to win. And I know what I must do to win. Right now, Heinrich thought, I must escape.

CHAPTER 5

SERGEANT MUELLER WAS flabbergasted. His dark slab of a face, topped with the prescribed half-inch of black tuft, began to turn fire-engine red. His gravely voice, increasing in volume, was a drum roll announcing Delman's imminent execution.

"You of all people—an ex-sergeant who beats up POWs! You're telling me you'll lead a convoy driven by POWs to bring back supplies from depots that don't even acknowledge my requisitions! Either you're pulling my leg, Delman, or you're bucking for a Section Eight."

"I don't beat up POWs." Delman stood in front of his seated boss. "I hit two Nazis who cursed me."

Delman realized a prisoner shouldn't argue with his immediate superior, especially if he's also his parole officer. But Delman had to escape from the supply tent. Mueller's hostility was on the rise. He'd gone well beyond the Colonel's sentence. Mueller was improvising—devising new, demeaning projects—to increase Delman's daily punishment. And he was encouraging fellow-German Heinrich, overlooking his POW status, to do the same.

Lately, they seemed to have a fixation on latrines. First was the four-holer near the supply tent; now other latrines, according to the two Nazis, demanded Delman's immediate and scrupulous attention. And, to add to his discomfort, he was ordered to re-use—which meant clean—the sticky, stained, long-handled brushes he used to swab off filth leaking from the wooden commodes.

Delman knew he had to be careful. He couldn't complain. Mueller was known to have a temper and, already, Delman had provoked him. When he ordered Delman to go into the nearby woods to get firewood for the supply tent's stove, Delman took a detail of POWs along to help him.

"You know damn well I didn't mean you should get POWs to find wood!" Mueller screamed. "I didn't need you to put together a detail of POWs. Hell, I could've done that myself. I meant for you, Private Delman, to get out there alone and find some fucking wood. You knew damn well what I wanted, what I meant."

"My mistake," Delman said. "From now on, I'll get the wood myself. No detail of POWs."

"It's too late now," Mueller said. "Thanks to you and your POW detail, we've got enough fucking wood in this supply tent to last through the next five winters."

He glowered at Delman. He strutted around the tent. Then, without another word, still staring at Delman, he whipped off his short mackinaw. He dropped his wide body to the tent's hard ground and proceeded to do push-ups. Five, ten, twenty, thirty of them. Fast, effortless, gruntless push-ups.

Delman, startled, almost laughed. Fortunately, he caught himself as well as Mueller's message: when you're about to explode, do something, anything, to short-circuit the surge. The more physical the better. The movement of the muscles cools off the emotions. You relax. Falling on your stomach to do push-ups beats slugging your antagonist.

Mueller, at last taking some deep breaths, rose. He'd worked off his rage. He stopped as quickly as he started. He threw on his mackinaw. He brought his stubby legs forward, and stood in front of Delman, daring him to speak. Delman remained silent. But he kept his unblinking eyes locked with Mueller's. It was another test. Mueller always had another test for Delman.

Okay, Mueller, he thought. You're an animal. You're a bull. You've developed a novel way to expunge your disgust. Congratulations. I'll remember your theatrics. I'll recall them the next time I feel myself going over the edge.

Delman also would have to emulate Heinrich's method of holding his own with superiors—stay calm, show respect. Once

Mueller sat down, Delman started to talk, quickly forgetting Heinrich's final example—keep your mouth shut.

"Sending convoys to supply depots isn't a new idea," Delman said. "I know that. I know we've got enough trucks but not enough drivers. My only thought was to use POWs to drive the convoy. What s wrong with that, sergeant?"

Delman, watching Mueller crack his knuckles, tried to imagine what was racing through the supply sergeant's crafty head. Officers were paid to think. Non-Coms were paid to react. Privates? They were paid to take orders. Period. The last thing Mueller needed was a smart-assed private who thought the sergeant couldn't see through his self-indulgent scheme.

"I'll tell you what's wrong, Delman," Mueller said. "Your plan'll get you out of camp, away from me. That's its whole purpose, isn't it, to let you escape from me, from Heinrich? Only you're forgetting one thing, Delman. You're forgetting that your idea will encourage POWs to escape. Once out of this stockade, they'll feel challenged. They'll feel impelled to make a break.

"And there's more, Delman. Escapes lead to gunfire and gunfire leads to deaths. Your convoy can turn into a death trap. Our own men could be killed. Americans and Belgians. And how many trucks would you take? Five, ten, twenty? The whole scheme's too fucking dangerous. It's not worth the risk. It's a long shot that's not worth taking."

He could be right, Delman thought. But he also could be exaggerating the danger because a POW-driven convoy wasn't his idea.

"There'll be guards on the convoy," Delman persisted. "I don't think a POW's going to risk his life when the war's winding down."

"Think again," Mueller said. "You're talking about soldiers. German soldiers. Real soldiers. Disciplined soldiers. They're trained to escape."

You lousy Nazi-lover, Delman wanted to say, you've fallen for the Aryan mumbo-jumbo. You won't admit your stiff-necked

German soldiers, real soldiers, disciplined soldiers, have found
a home here, that they're as ready to make a break as you are
to go to OCS.

Mueller's face slowly began to turn fire-engine red again.
Why, Delman wondered, why's Mueller so dead set against my
brainstorm? Then Delman realized: it's because it is my brainstorm. I'm invading his turf. This great idea should've been his,
not mine.

Delman looked past Mueller and saw more straggling
columns of Germans—their Wehrmacht uniforms torn and
dirty—being marched into the compound. "We can't even feed
and clothe the prisoners we've got," Delman said, "and look
at them, they keep coming in every day. We've got to do something." He knew his next words could sound wrong, conceited,
but he didn't know how else to put it. "Sergeant, the convoy's
your idea, not mine, no strings attached."

"You smug college shit," Mueller said. "This might come as
a shock but I don't want anything to do with your cockamamie
convoy. I wouldn't touch it with a ten-foot pole."

*   *   *

Mueller had to abort Delman's convoy idea before the private
found a way to present it to the Colonel. Bad enough Delman
might go over Mueller's head and show him up, but the Colonel
might even listen to the private. For some reason, Nelson liked
Delman. Long ago Mueller had stopped trying to figure out why
people did what they did—why, for example, officers liked one
GI and not another.

All he knew was that Delman was lucky. He should have
been court-martialed the first time he attacked a POW. Not giving him his proper punishment had led to a second offense—and
again, as if he hadn't learned a lesson, the Colonel had waffled.
No court-martial. Another lenient sentence. Another serious
mistake.

Mueller seldom distrusted authority but he had serious misgivings about Colonel Nelson. He was popular, he was smart, but he misunderstood—no, he disliked—the military. His casual throw-away salutes revealed his disdain. Nelson had a civilian reaction to everything military that was dead wrong. The Army needed its salutes, needed its medals, needed its caste system as much as it needed the latest weapons and the deadliest ammunition. As much as Mueller needed his NCO network and a steady always-available woman like Denise.

He had to devise a plan to counter Delman but he couldn't force himself to sit down and think. He could think clearly only while he was talking. He had to discuss his problem with someone, preferably another regular Army lifer who also resented all the new officers and GIs who thought they could run the war better than experienced regular Army soldiers, better than Ike. He tried calling some of his peers in nearby Angers but he couldn't get through.

On his way to visit Denise, Mueller stopped at the small overheated NCO club, with its tiny bar, faded travel posters and nearby outdoor urinal. As he had hoped, Sergeant Anthony Perry, his shaved head as bright as his broad smile, was sitting impatiently at a back table nursing his second bottle of beer. In charge of the motor pool, Perry tapped his grease-lined nails on the plastic table.

"Just the man I want to see," Mueller said, carrying his bottle of beer to Perry's table.

"Take a load off." Perry grinned, bouncing his big body around. He seemed unable to sit still.

"Got a problem," Mueller began. He took a long gulp of beer and then explained Delman's plan. "I've got to stop him."

"Not a bad plan," Perry said, "if it works."

"Delman just wants to get out of camp, away from me." Mueller explained that Nelson had assigned Delman to Mueller and that Mueller had put his POW assistant, Heinrich, in charge of the blowhard Jew.

"Delman's getting some of his own back," Mueller said. "Heinrich and I've got him humping pretty good."

"I'd say you've done a real job on him," Perry said. "Putting a POW in charge of Delman should've been enough to shake him up. You can be one cruel son of a bitch. No wonder he's come up with his plan. He wants to get as far away from you and your POW as possible."

"Maybe I'll confine him to the camp," Mueller said. "That'll take care of him."

"You mean he gets out at night, he gets passes?" Perry said. "Hell, he's getting off easy."

"Too easy," Mueller agreed. "Too damn easy." Mueller liked Perry. He was an all-American extrovert, always the life of the party, tough, outspoken, sometimes even reckless. In fact, he would have had as many stripes as Mueller if he hadn't been caught with women in his quarters—not once but twice—and also taken off to nearby cities without proper credentials to visit fellow womanizers. Perry and Delman had that in common. Both made the same mistake twice. Both were rebels, anything to be different. Perry with his shaved head and Delman with his crazy scheme.

"That's what I'll do," Mueller said. "I'll confine Delman to the post."

"I've got an idea," Perry said. "Get Delman to hit your German officer. That would do it. Then the Colonel would have to throw him in front of a court-martial. He couldn't duck his responsibility again."

"What German officer?"

"Your POW assistant," Perry said, "that's who. What's his name? Heinrich. Josef Heinrich. Everybody knows Josef Heinrich's a fucking German officer. Probably S.S. or Gestapo. He's masquerading as an ordinary soldier. He thinks he won't be noticed if he's a grunt instead of one of Hitler's ordained. Then it would be easier for him to escape. I tell you, Curt, he's too damn clever to be another rifleman."

Perry always turns conversations around to make me uneasy, Mueller thought. He's jealous because I outrank him—six stripes against three—even though we've both served the same time. Heinrich's no more an officer than Perry. Clever? Sure, Heinrich's clever. But that's because I encourage him to be clever. I give him ideas—I give him his head.

"I'll make a case that Delman's not doing what he's told," Mueller said, overlooking Perry's attempt to change the subject, to center their conversation on the POW instead of where it belonged, on Delman. "I told him to clean up latrines and he didn't. They still stink."

"You're going to confine him to the post because of a stinking latrine?" Perry said. "What makes you think that'll keep him from leading his crazy convoy if the Colonel buys his idea?"

"It's the best I can do for now," Mueller said. "I can only go so far. I still have to remember it was the Colonel who gave Delman his easy sentence."

"Not so easy," Perry said, "with you and your German officer hassling him."

"I got to run," Mueller said. He rose from the table, taking a last gulp from his bottle. "Keep your nose clean, Perry."

Mueller walked around the club to his drafty jeep, raising the collar of his officer's coat against the December wind. He touched the musette bag next to him that contained Denise's gifts—cigarettes, candy, silk stockings—switched on the ignition and started to roll. Soon he was speeding past the barbed wire, past the Belgian security troops. He wasn't going to worry about Perry and his accusation about Heinrich. And he sure as hell wasn't going to worry about greasy Delman. Not now. He wasn't going to let any demoted, smart-assed, ex-NCO Jew spoil his evening with Denise. He'd nail the son of a bitch tomorrow.

CHAPTER 6

"DEC. 26, 1944—I received a Christmas present from Mueller. Gift-wrapped scouring powder. My reward for doing so well with four-holers. He's all heart. He transferred me from my old barracks to the Belgians. One of their soldiers, Jacques Clary, tried to make me feel welcome. He may be the buddy I need. I guess I'm still the big ungainly kid searching for a friend.

"I can get along during the day without a close friend. Nights are different. Then you want to talk, to visit, to review what happened, what might happen. That's when you need a friend.

"The convoy's my last chance to get out of here, even briefly. Of course Mueller intends to stop it. It will invite escapes, he says, it will result in the deaths of our troops. That includes me, which, somehow, he overlooked.

"To make sure I don't forget I'm being punished, I heard he's going to add to my sentence by confining me to the post. I better get moving."

*   *   *

Delman was the only one awake in the barracks. He checked his watch. He had another ten minutes before he had to get up. Half of the Belgians had left for duty; the other half were asleep. Staring at the ceiling from the least desirable top bunk, Delman recalled a similar aloneness. When he was twelve, an only child. He'd hungered for a friend, then as now. He recalled he wanted to consider his parents' friends, but they were too busy to spend time with him. And there were no other candidates. He blamed his loneliness on his size.

44

He was too big, too fat, too awkward. His size intimidated other boys his age. So he decided to create a friend. He'd get a two-wheeler, pretend it was a horse, and name it Tony, after movie star Tom Mix's horse. He'd have his friend.

But a bike was expensive. He couldn't ask his parents for it. They were always fighting over money. His mother said money was to spend; his father said money was to save. They seldom agreed about anything.

When Delman learned he could get a bike if he sold enough magazine subscriptions—for *Liberty, The Saturday Evening Post* and *Colliers*—he became a secret businessman. Every day after school he'd pull his sales kit from under his bed. First, he'd make sure his canvas bag's contents were complete. He checked his sample magazines, subscription blanks and sharpened pencils. Then, with the white bag over his shoulder, he'd begin his route. He solicited every apartment in every walk-up in Rogers Park, a middle-class Chicago neighborhood fronting Lake Michigan.

The hulking twelve-year-old developed a routine. He'd go into each building as if he lived there. He knew salesmen weren't welcome. When no one was watching, he'd ring doorbells. One at a time. He'd wait patiently in the small tile-floored vestibule for a voice. Regardless of what the voice said, his reply was the same. "If you subscribe to one of my magazines, I can win a bike. It'll cost you only a few cents a day. Buzz me in and I'll show you my magazines."

The conversation usually ended there. Occasionally, he'd be surprised to hear the welcome sound of a buzzer unlatching the downstairs door. He would dive to open it, rush upstairs, two steps at a time, wedge his appealing face through the apartment front door with a metal latch securing it, and his urgent sales pitch would begin.

After nine months of after-school visits, Delman got his bike. A resplendent two-color Ranger. Balloon tires. Leather seat. Chrome handlebars. Glistening fenders.

When his mother saw it, she berated his father. She called him cheap; she whistled her "cheap" tune. She said their son, instead of playing outside with other kids, spent nine months begging at neighbors' doors because his father was too cheap to buy him a bike. She whistled. His father dismissed her whistle and her words. He shook off her anger. He said his son wasn't begging. He was selling. He got his bike because he showed initiative, courage, and perseverance. He was a born entrepreneur. Delman heard them attack each other. Back and forth, a crescendo of invective. He usually turned them off. He was hurt by their constant arguing. But this time he listened. At times, they talked about him, the boy he thought displeased them, the boy he thought they overlooked. Now, he was startled to learn what they never said to him—they were proud of him. Maybe they even loved him, but their words were so rapid, so heated, he couldn't be sure. He wondered, could parents be friends?

He didn't know about that—and he didn't know about them. He didn't know if he could trust them. He did know about his bike, his manufactured friend. He ran his fingers over its hard body. It was here and it was real.

*　　*　　*

Delman dropped from his bunk, quickly dressed, brushed his teeth, washed and went to the latrine. When he left it to unbutton the supply tent, he decided he'd have to figure a way to outflank Mueller's carefully assembled shock troops—most of the compound's NCOs. They were primed to continue to punish him, to squash his crazy convoy concept, to keep him away from the Colonel. They wanted to make it clear they shared Mueller's opinion that his punishment was too light.

He knew how they felt. He even understood Mueller's anger, although Mueller didn't realize the convoy he despised might save a couple of his precious Germans from freezing or starving to death. Wasn't that something? Or was Mueller so angry—both because of Delman and the rumor about Heinrich—that he couldn't think straight?

Delman believed Mueller's logic was as irrational as it was inflexible. Since he considered Delman wrong for striking POWs, he considered that anything Delman thought of had to be wrong. It was the best example of Mueller's unique brand of deductive reasoning. Delman knew he had also caught the brunt of Mueller's frustration caused by his running disagreement with the rest of the NCOs. They thought he was being exploited by Heinrich. They said his favorite POW was a phony. Delman had overheard Bosworth making the case.

"Your POW's masquerading as an ordinary soldier," Sergeant Bosworth said. "He's an officer. Look at him. The guy's smart. He's well-educated. And he looks like an officer. The way he carries himself. And he doesn't tell the other POWs what to do. He orders them. But what's more compelling, they respect him. They accept his leadership. He gives an order and they follow it. Whenever they have a problem, they go to Josef Heinrich to solve it. I tell you, Curt, your boy's an officer in disguise."

"Why would he do it?" Mueller asked. "Why would he pretend to be another ordinary soldier?"

"To avoid the extra security around captured officers," Bosworth said. "They're kept together here in one well-guarded cage. By pretending to be what he isn't, Heinrich's in a better position to escape. With his white armband, he can come and go as he likes. Then there's your supply tent where he thought he could pick up stuff to help him escape. Little did he know you didn't have any supplies."

"I say it's bullshit," Mueller said. "It's speculation. It's bullshit, that's all it is."

But unable to disprove the rumors, unable to counter with facts of his own, Mueller became increasingly angry. Increasingly frustrated. He was left with only one course of action: to take it out on a scapegoat. And what better scapegoat than Delman, one of a long line of scapegoats?

Delman thought it was proper he was getting hit by Mueller's double-barreled hate, for who he was and for who Heinrich wasn't. Hell, it was perfect military logic. It made no sense at all.

When Delman learned the Colonel had stopped POW music for two weeks—because of the now famous trumpet dirge when the body was removed from the barbed wire—he had his cover story. His subterfuge for asking for an audience with the camp's commanding officer. But how could he steal past Sergeant Bosworth, sitting outside the Colonel's office? Bosworth was the stolid gatekeeper, the protector, the enforcer. But he found his answer. It was simple. He'd get past Bosworth by entering with the Colonel.

But to do that, to know exactly what time the Colonel returned to his office, Delman had to get a fix on the Colonel's daily routine. Delman spent the next day studying the comings and goings of his commanding officer. He timed Nelson's morning exit from his office. He timed Nelson's daily inspection of the cages. And he figured out exactly when the Colonel was returning to his office. That would be the time to intercept him, to create a diversion, and then to walk with him into his office.

Delman's investigation uncovered a surprising footnote: the casual Colonel liked playing the martinet. He played his unfamiliar role well, with Patton-like aplomb—he even had the General's strut down pat. Using a swagger stick, the Colonel looked like an experienced British sahib, followed by his fawning entourage, who appeared to be awed by his exaggerated theatrical gestures. The Colonel's posturing had a point. It said, "We're in charge." He dramatized the Allies' dominance. He demonstrated to the POWs that the camp's cadre, as small as it was, operated with confidence.

Delman s plan was simple: interrupt the Colonel's return to his office. Use his POW music ban to pique his interest. Finally, accompany him inside, passing the formidable Bosworth. It sounded simple. Delman knew it was dangerous. Mueller could have beaten Delman to the Colonel and warned him that the demoted private had some scheme in mind. If that happened, Delman thought, his convoy idea was finished. All he could do was move rapidly and hope his plan hadn't been aborted by a preemptive Mueller strike.

He didn't see leaving the supply tent as a problem, even under Sergeant Mueller s constant scrutiny. Delman would carry his bucket, brushes and scouring powder with him. Mueller would assume his lackey was maintaining the cleanliness of the camp's outhouses. Heinrich was another problem. He was more alert than Mueller, maybe because he was more deceptive. The suspicious German could upset Delman's logistics. To deflect him, Delman did his frenetic best to look busy. He discovered constant problems—out of the tent—that demanded his attention. He replaced new rope for frayed tent ties. He repaired tent pegs damaged by the cold. He reinforced deteriorating seams. And he did that most important Army task of all, policing the frozen area around the tent, removing cigarette butts and candy and gum wrappers.

On R Day Plus Two (that is, two days after Mueller soundly rejected Delman's brainstorm), Delman placed his brushes and cleaning supplies off to the side and, with a brisk salute, interrupted the Colonel's stroll back to his office from his morning inspection.

"Delman," the Colonel said, returning the private's surprisingly professional salute with a casual two-finger swipe at his overseas cap, "you must be sick, saluting like a soldier. Or has Sergeant Mueller put the fear of God into you?"

"Yes, sir," Delman replied. "I've learned what it means to be a proper soldier in this man's army."

"I bet," the Colonel said, continuing to walk toward his office. When he saw Delman following him, he paused. "What's up, private?"

"You stopped the music, Colonel."

"I did what?"

"May I explain?" Delman said, moving forward so quickly that he almost pushed the Colonel into his office.

Sergeant Bosworth rose behind his desk as he saw Delman hurry past him, but Nelson's nod returned the reluctant sergeant to his chair. Delman had got past his first obstacle. He followed Colonel Nelson inside, closed the door and stood at attention.

"The POWs," Delman began, "are calmed by music. As we are, sir. The POWs look forward to concerts. They love spontaneous sessions. Take away their music and you take away sunshine from their lives."

"I didn't know you were so poetic," the Colonel said, leaning back in his chair, "and so concerned for the welfare of our prisoners."

"By punishing the musicians, sir, you're taking jobs away from one of the most creative and possibly dangerous groups in the camp."

"You're serious, aren't you, Delman?"

"When I was a cage warden," Delman said, "I thought of getting some of the more creative POWs, including the musicians, to start a cage newspaper. It kept them occupied. It was more than busy work."

"I remember those obscene newspapers," Colonel Nelson said.

"We printed them by hand," Delman said. "The longer it took, the better."

"Where are you going with this, Delman?" Colonel Nelson said.

"POWs," Delman explained, "must be kept busy or they'll do something you don't want them to do."

"Thanks, Delman."

"One more thing, sir, if I may?"

"Make it fast, private," the Colonel said. "I know this has to have a point."

"Another way to keep them busy, sir . . ."

"Quickly," the Colonel said.

"Yes, sir," Delman answered. "Another way to keep them busy is to let them drive our trucks in a convoy that we'll send to supply depots."

That stopped the Colonel. "Elaborate on that, private."

"Sir, we need supplies—desperately." Delman was no longer standing at attention. He was leaning on the Colonel's desk. "As I understand it, we haven't sent a convoy out to supply depots because we can't spare GIs to drive the trucks. We've got the trucks but not the drivers. So why not, sir, use POWs as drivers? I could lead the convoy, along with a few guards. I bet a face-to-face appeal to NCOs dishing out supplies at depots would get results. Like tents, blankets, clothes, maybe even rations."

"Hold it, Delman."

The Colonel rose and walked to the window where he stood, unmoving, for several minutes. Delman, drawing himself to attention, thought, Let him see it's worth a chance, let him agree that as risky as it is, it deserves a try.

"You're suggesting," Nelson said, turning to face Delman, "we let Germans drive American trucks to supply depots behind our lines?"

"Yes, sir."

The Colonel returned to his chair. He picked up a pencil and worked over a pad of paper. Was he figuring how many trucks could be spared? No problem there, Delman thought; most weren't used for anything except taking cadre to and from Le Mans.

Or was he figuring how many POW-drivers were available? Delman thought, We've got enough POW-drivers to move a company, a division, the whole fucking army. What's he doing? Finally, Nelson raised his head.

"So obvious, so simple," the Colonel said. "It's a possibility, Delman. What've we got to lose except a few POWs?"

"Yes, sir."

"Anything else?" Nelson asked.

"We could disguise the POWs as American solders, sir. It would be just another convoy driven by GIs. And if they try to escape and our guards shoot them—kill them—it would be acceptable. Dressed in American uniforms, the POWs would be considered spies."

"Too complicated," Nelson said. "I think the idea's not to get the POWs killed. Otherwise, who drives the trucks back here?"

"I stand corrected."

"Your idea's a possibility, Delman." Nelson rose and paced in front of the map. He studied it. He turned back to Delman. "No masquerade's necessary. The POWs will drive as POWs. We'll need guards, maybe a mechanic and a leader."

"I can handle that job, sir."

The Colonel said, "It would provide you with a nice way to get out from under Sergeant Mueller's thumb, wouldn't it, Delman, if you led the convoy? And there'd be no POW telling you what latrine to clean."

Delman returned to standing at attention.

"What else have you thought about, Delman?"

"We'd select drivers who are family men."

"Less likely to try an escape," the Colonel said. "Good thinking, Delman. A convoy driven by POWs. It's something I'll have to discuss with your immediate superior, Sergeant Mueller. I assume you've discussed this with him."

"Yes, sir," Delman replied.

He saluted. He did an about-face. He left the Colonel's office hurriedly, before he could ask the next question, "What did Mueller think of it?" As he passed the glowering Bosworth, Delman nodded. He hoped his face wasn't a giveaway, that it didn't reflect his optimism, his belief that the Colonel would buy his idea.

CHAPTER 7

DELMAN STOOD NEXT to his bunk pulling on his heavy over-coat.

"You must have a regular girl," Jacques Clary said. He sat on the bunk across from Delman.

"I only wish," Delman said.

"You go into Le Mans every night," Clary said.

"Mueller's going to confine me to the post," Delman said, "so I'm taking advantage of my freedom while it lasts."

"What do you do?" Clary asked.

"You mean when I'm not cleaning latrines?" Delman said, "I work in the supply tent for the two Nazis, Mueller and his POW."

"No, I know that, I mean what do you do when you go into town?" Clary asked. "You don't have a girl. You can't be sitting at the Red Cross all the time. You must visit prostitutes."

"Most of the time I just wander around. You get sick of sitting in the Red Cross. I get so damn restless."

"You're looking for a girl," Clary said.

"I suppose so," Delman admitted.

"No prostitutes?" Clary persisted.

"There's this one girl," Delman said, "who kept talking to me at the Red Cross."

"And?"

"We went to her room a few times, but she never asked for money."

"Did you offer her any?" Clary asked.

"I was afraid I might insult her."

"Did she look like a prostitute?"

"How do you tell?" Delman said.

53

"I will ask my girl if she knows somebody." Clary rubbed his round face. "It is different when you can find a nice girl. You go into a home. You become part of a family. You feel like you did before. And you still find time to be alone. You speak French?"

"Like I speak German," Delman said. "I understand it—but I have to think before I speak. But don't trouble yourself, Jacques. I know Mueller is going to confine me to the post."

"Why hasn't he?"

"I don't know," Delman said. "Maybe he's counting on me getting into trouble so he can push for a court-martial this time around."

"What is that saying about rope?"

Delman smiled. "He's giving me enough rope to hang myself." He liked Clary.

"What will you do if you are confined to the post? There is nothing to do here."

"I keep looking for books," Delman said, "in English."

"I will ask my girl," Clary said. "Her parents are teachers. But where could you read? The light in here is terrible."

"You're right about the light but I'll find a place."

"A girl, books, and a lamp," Clary said.

"In that order."

"I know what you did and why you did it. I think your punishment is too severe. I think working for a POW is too much. Perhaps that's why Mueller has not confined you to the post."

"You don't know Mueller," Delman said.

He retrieved his bucket and cleaning supplies from where he'd left them after yesterday's visit with Colonel Nelson. Trudging back to the supply tent, he thought the slow-falling snow had some value. It cloaked the camp, it softened its ugliness. The compound might even appear welcoming to the droves of newly arrived POWs. He glanced at the latest contingent being marched to their cages and wondered if they'd be as docile as their comrades in the stockade. Or would a Heinrich arise to encourage them to join him in a revolt?

"Why don't they try to take over the camp?" Delman re-membered asking Clary.

"No leaders," Clary replied. "That's why they are segre-gated."

"Simple arithmetic shows they could make a break."

"Now we get the young and the old," Clary said. "They do not want to escape."

"A mass insurrection could be successful. They already outnumber us more than a hundred to one."

"And the odds in their favor keep increasing," Clary said, "but they are afraid to try anything. In spite of their orders to escape. And they are relieved to be here, to be away from the killing."

All newly arrived POWs seemed in a daze. They had been defeated in combat and now they were defeated by the cold. They hungered for a warm haven the way Delman had hungered for a real friend before he found Clary.

"Besides," Clary added, "they think the Americans will take care of them. You are the world's richest nation. At the least, you will see they are provided with the basics—food, clothing, blankets, tents.

"They've got it all wrong," Delman had said. "They'll be lucky to get out of here alive."

"Why?"

"Supplies go to the front."

"There's this rumor," Clary had said, "that it's more than that. That it comes from General Eisenhower's hatred of the Germans, that coming here is a death sentence."

*   *   *

Delman pushed open the latrine's wooden door. The pine limbs he'd put there to reduce its stench were shriveled. He replaced them with fresh boughs he threw on the dirt floor. He knew he could not stop his demeaning duties until the convoy was on its way; Mueller would never relent. He left the latrine for the supply tent. He opened it and went immediately to the potbellied stove to light the wood chips wrapped in paper he had stuffed in it the previous night. When it flamed, he added some logs. The front of the tent was already warm when Sergeant Mueller arrived.

"Sergeant," Delman said, greeting him.

There was no return greeting. Not even a nod. Mueller paused as close to the stove as he could get and rubbed his hands together. He never acknowledged Delman. Then the sergeant sat down at his desk and soon was immersed in compiling some sort of list. Delman could see him putting names on one side of a sheet of paper, numbers on the other.

Heinrich soon arrived. He greeted Mueller, did not even glance at Delman, and began a count of the limited supplies in the tent. He proceeded carefully, looking into empty crates, counting empty cartons, making marks on a pad of paper attached to a clipboard he carried with him.

Delman was suspicious. To find both of his tormentors preoccupied was unexpected. It had to be an act concocted to make him anxious, to convince him his great convoy concept had been rejected.

Had the Colonel talked to Mueller about it? Delman knew Nelson acted quickly. If he were taken with the idea, he'd be propelling it forward. Delman refused to be dejected. He wasn't going to give Mueller the satisfaction of asking about the Colonel's reaction. He dismissed his captors as they dismissed him. He placed his cleaning supplies in a corner. He put new tent pegs in his pocket and located a mallet. He walked outside and began to replace pegs split by the cold.

"Back in here, Delman," Mueller suddenly ordered.

Delman stopped working and returned to face the master sergeant.

Mueller looked up. "I'm putting together a plan for our convoy."

"Our" convoy! It took a moment before Mueller's statement registered. Then Delman realized his idea hadn't been rejected. Mueller's and Heinrich's lack of greeting was a typical Mueller ploy.

"Our convoy!" Delman wanted to cheer, to celebrate but he saw Mueller was waiting for him to do something, anything, that would give the supply sergeant a reason to ridicule the idea. Delman said nothing.

"POWs driving our trucks," Mueller said. "But the Colonel's convinced our situation's desperate. At least he's got that right. So he's going to risk it, a convoy driven by POWs. Even though it's custom-made to let POWs escape. And if the trucks get stuck—a bad tire, a frozen engine—the POWs could be jumped by the French. We could lose lives, we could lose equipment. In fact, we could lose the whole fucking convoy—trucks, drivers, guards, the works. That's where you come in, Delman. It's your idea—so maybe you should lead it. I have to decide if I could spare you."

Not me, Delman thought, I'm indispensable. Who else could polish your boots and scrub your latrines? But a better punishment might be for me to lead the convoy. If you're right, Mueller, if it's as dangerous as you say, who better to lead it than expendable Delman?

He wanted to tell Mueller, You've got it backwards—the convoy will be successful. POWs won't try to escape, the well-tended trucks won't break down, and the French have more important things to do than watch the road for trucks driven by POWs.

"How many trucks?" Delman asked.

"Eight," Mueller replied, "if Heinrich can find enough POWs willing to risk their necks. Not many, but if it works, the Colonel's talking about twice that amount next time around."

"Heinrich?"

"Your right-hand man," Mueller explained, "You need someone who can speak German and French and English."

Your spy, Delman wanted to say, your patsy. Delman could get along in both languages—but he decided not to protest. He needed Mueller on his side and if taking escape-prone Heinrich would keep Mueller from opposing the convoy, Delman would make the best of it.

"I'm also seeing about getting some Belgian guards," Mueller said, "to make sure the Frogs you love so much won't attack our convoy."

"You're all heart," Delman said, unable to resist the opening even though he realized he'd fallen into another Mueller trap.

"Wisecrack with me, Delman, and you'll find yourself holding the shit end of the stick. But play it straight and maybe I'll see you get your stripes back."

Clever, Delman thought. Rank was necessary for the convoy's commander. He had to be at least equal to the NCOs who ran the supply depots, the ones who could order Red Ball Express supplies transferred to Delman's convoy.

He wondered if he should suggest to Nelson that a battlefield commission was warranted, that getting supplies—and an officer might make the crucial difference—was worth the flack Nelson would receive if he gave Delman a gold bar. Maybe they weren't in combat but they were fighting for survival. There was only one problem, Delman realized: it was the enemy's survival.

What was wrong with a humane act during a war? Why not? Why couldn't some morality exist? Besides, if the word got out that the Americans were going out of their way to take care of their POWs, wasn't it possible the enemy would think twice before mistreating their POWs?

Or was he being foolish, self-serving? Wasn't a reprieve more than he deserved? Wasn't escaping the camp—and Mueller—sufficient? Delman knew he had to be realistic. He had only a single hope: that Nelson's personal T/O for convoys driven by POWs allowed a sergeant to be commander.

*   *   *

There were no secrets in the compound. Heinrich's bunk was a listening post, like sitting in a bar or restaurant back home, the German language swirling around him. He sat on its wooden slats, wrapped in blankets, Wanger's stench wafting down from his upper bunk, and heard the latest rumors from passing prisoners, both inside and outside the tent.

"They're talking about a convoy," a POW told him, "to get supplies before they're all trucked to the front. And it'll be driven by us. They've got the trucks but not the drivers. So they'll use us to drive. It's the football player's idea."

"So the French can kill us," Wanger said. "But, at least the drivers will be out of this fucking hole. Anything has to be better than starving to death here."

Heinrich wasn't surprised when he learned what the Americans might do.

"Typically American," he said. "Who else but Americans would trust enemy troops to drive your trucks behind your own lines? That's what makes them likable."

"Likable?" Wanger said, "You mean crazy."

"They think the best of others," Heinrich said.

"They're crazy," Wanger repeated.

"It's the kind of crazy I like," Heinrich said.

He thought it was a true reflection of America's democratic spirit. Now all he had to do was exploit it. Later, he pretended surprise when Sergeant Mueller told Delman his convoy idea had been approved.

"I want you to make up a list," Mueller ordered Heinrich, "of ten reliable, experienced POWs who could drive trucks. It's a risky assignment and drivers will receive extra rations along with cigarettes. As you heard, Delman will probably lead the convoy and you'll go as his right-hand man."

Let it happen, Heinrich thought. But he knew nothing was certain until it happened. If Delman was the leader, he wouldn't want the POW who bossed him to be his "right-hand man." But, more than likely, he wouldn't have a choice.

Another rumor was that drivers would wear American uniforms. Heinrich thought it was a reaction to what the Germans were doing in their Ardennes offensive, disguising Germans as American soldiers to infiltrate their lines. If the Americans set up POWs as spies—that's what they'd be considered in enemy clothes—do-gooders like the Red Cross would condemn the ploy. There'd be a scandal and the American military, except for the warrior Patton, feared scandals. It would never happen.

Mueller made it clear he wanted POW drivers who wouldn't try to escape. He didn't put it that way, but told Heinrich, "Select soldiers who are smart, who won't cause any trouble, who won't make me sorry I trust you."

Heinrich knew Mueller, unfortunately, had little to fear. Few of Heinrich's current comrades had the courage to do what they were trained to do—escape. They were like pitiful Wanger, ready to complain, unwilling to do anything else.

Heinrich didn't want Mueller to discover the timidity of the German soldier. Let Mueller be nervous. Let him think I'm the only one who could keep the drivers in line. That would encourage him to insist I have some authority in the convoy.

Heinrich knew he might have to risk an escape alone. Fellow officers would have joined him—but they were in a different cage, better guarded. Without their superiors prodding them, German soldiers, once captured, showed little inclination to return to battle. Heinrich realized he was now paying for his masquerade. But he thought it a fair trade-off. If he hadn't pretended to be an enlisted man, he'd never have the opportunity to leave his prison.

What he had to do now was to plan his escape. Mueller wanted him in the jeep with Delman, if only to make him suffer. But that was the worst place to be for an escape, under his captor's nose. Heinrich had to figure out how to get into one of the trucks at the rear of the convoy.

He also had to accumulate more winnings from Mueller. Cigarettes and francs. Both would help his escape. When he visited cages to find drivers, he'd look to barter. Who knew what he'd find. A pistol? Never. The Belgians and Americans were too careful: they frisked and frisked and frisked. Yet he liked to think the impossible might happen. The mere thought of securing a weapon excited him. He could almost feel the delicious pleasure of pushing it into Delman's over-fed body.

CHAPTER 8

"You're going over Sergeant Mueller's head!" Sergeant Bosworth shouted.

Bosworth yelling? It was rare. The Colonel shot out of his office to see who was causing the uproar. There was Delman—unblinking, cocksure, his bespectacled face tough and tempting, a student daring a professor to zing him—hanging over Bosworth.

"It's okay, sergeant," Colonel Nelson interrupted.

With a fast, irritated head motion, Nelson signaled Delman into his office. This is exactly what Nelson didn't need. Not now. Not another distraction. And not, above all, Delman. Nelson hurried him into his office.

"Sit down, Delman. And not a word, not a sound until I finish what I'm doing."

The Colonel dropped into his desk chair. For the first time in a month, he could see the person across from him. His paper mountain, his Everest created by his procrastination, had been eliminated. It finally had overwhelmed him and he'd gone on an all-night cleaning spree, burning most of the wasteful meaningless documents issued by frustrated desk-bound officers.

Nelson studied jumpy Delman. Hunched forward, hands clenched, head bowed. The Colonel guessed he was consciously pushing down his impatience, forcing himself to obey but afraid he couldn't remain silent much longer. The Colonel held up his hand before Delman's pained face.

"One more minute," he said.

Nelson was determined to stall the torrent of words that infuriated Bosworth and now was about to descend upon him. Before opening the dam, the Colonel wanted to check the two piles of documents in front of him, all that remained after last night's paper purge. To his right, his "action" pile. He quickly signed the memos to the appropriate officers at TPM headquarters, requesting—in some cases, demanding—medicine, food, clothes and tents. Next to his signature, he added exhortations:—"Urgent, absolutely vital, must have, third request."

To his left, his pile of "read now" documents. The depressing report about the camp's rising death toll. The usual inaccurate list of arrivals. The latest ration order: POWs were to receive the minimum under Geneva rules, 1,000 calories a day, half the amount given to American troops. Nelson knew he'd have to cut even these paltry allocations in order to feed new arrivals.

Finally, he returned to Delman. "I don't know why I keep saving your stupid ass," Nelson said. "Why were you bothering Sergeant Bosworth? Wait, let me guess. Sergeant Mueller appropriated your convoy idea."

"Yes, sir," Delman replied. "According to Sergeant Mueller . . ."

"Enough." Colonel Nelson broke in, fed up with privates disregarding regulations; showing no respect, ready to tell a Colonel what to do. Some military, he thought, the perils of a citizen army.

He recognized he was the cause of Delman's latest mistake. In fact, Nelson was certain his attitude, his behavior, infected every member of his cadre. He inspired a civilian mindset. Except for the few Army regulars, his cadre emulated him. He knew his cavalier attitude about military procedure had boomeranged. Delman believed he could rebel without restraint. Because the Colonel never pulled rank, Delman thought he could disregard it. Berating a first sergeant—even patronizing a master sergeant—became acceptable.

"Colonel," Delman said, his eyes straight ahead. "I'm bothering you at the wrong time."

"There's no right time," Nelson said.

He wasn't appeased. The trouble was obvious. He'd made

a common error. He assumed braininess and maturity went together. Not so. Delman, as smart as he was, had a lot to learn,
a lot of growing up to do, emotionally.

At least he was focused, concentrating on the convoy. But
there was a downside—he overlooked everything else. He disregarded military protocol and forgot about tact and common
sense. He gave absolutely no thought to how his behavior was
viewed by Mueller and Bosworth. And he also failed to see how
he had compromised Nelson.

"I adopted your risky convoy idea," Nelson said, "only
because I've run out of options. And, in spite of your dismal
record, I was going to put you in charge because the convoy
was your idea. Now, I'm not so sure. Charging in here without
clearing it with Sergeant Mueller!" Nelson shook his head.
"Christ, Delman, look around, think before you act. Don't you
know Bosworth and Mueller are friends?"

"It won't happen again," Delman said. "Mueller has . . ."

"Sergeant Mueller," the Colonel said. "Delman. Stop and
think what you're going to say before you spout off. It's Sergeant Mueller."

"Sergeant Mueller," Delman quickly repeated. "Sergeant
Mueller forgot who came up with the idea to have POWs drive
the convoy."

"Wrong," Nelson said. "He didn't forget. He knows the
score. Ideas are a dime a dozen." The Colonel straightened
the papers on his desk. Slow down, he told himself, relax. He
now lowered his voice and spoke slowly, clearly, letting each
word—he hoped—ring through Delman's stubborn head. "It's
what you do with ideas that counts."

"I can lead the convoy," Delman said.

That was better. That was much better. Nelson had had it
with accusations and ambiguities. Delman had said all he had to
say. He was confident. He had dropped his momentary campaign
against his immediate superior. He now had said precisely what
Nelson wanted to hear.

And Nelson wanted to believe what he heard. He wanted to put his trust in intelligence, sensitivity and daring. He wanted to prove that he, a colonel, could give individuality—in this case, Delman—a chance without wrecking the entire military establishment.

Yet how could he expect Delman not to be confused? If he forgot to give an NCO's rank before his name, he was reprimanded. If he talked too loud, he was reprimanded. And if he fought for what he originated, he was reprimanded. What was his choice? To be tactful? Indirect? To become a manipulator? Nelson thought: pretend what you're not. That's it. Delman will become a Mueller. He'll dissemble and he'll succeed.

The Colonel had thought Delman, after losing his stripes, might subdue his rebellious tendencies. But he remained cocky, an adolescent prima donna. Nevertheless Nelson admired Delman's resilience, his courage, his refusal to become another faceless, timid GI cipher.

"What do you want me to do, sir?" Delman asked.

"I want you to shut up," Colonel Nelson said, "that's what I want you to do. Stop trying to prove you're smarter than the entire U.S. Army."

He reached into his crowded desk drawer, pushed aside snapshots from his wife, felt what he was looking for and tossed staff sergeant stripes at the surprised Delman.

"You're not getting your old stripes back," the Colonel announced. "You're getting boosted. Promoted. Thanks to, of all people, Sergeant Mueller. He's able to disregard your smart-ass actions and think of the job that has to be done. He says you must outrank the NCOs you'll confront when you lead your convoy to supply depots.

"One last thing. We won't give you a promotion and then demean you. Your sentence, your punishment, ends as soon as the convoy begins. No more cleaning latrines—or Sergeant Mueller's boots."

Nelson saw Delman's shock and, for the first time, considered Mueller's motivation. The supply sergeant hated Delman.
He hated his celebrity, he hated his size, and he hated his faith.
Add to that Delman's actions—striking Mueller's beloved Germans—and you had an individual who incorporated in one
single repugnant form, everything Mueller despised.

Then why would he urge his colonel to let Delman lead
the convoy? Why say Delman should not only get his stripes
back—but be promoted? Why insist his punishment cease as
soon as the convoy starts?

Perhaps, thought Nelson, Mueller, convinced the convoy
will fail, wants to continue to punish Delman, to make him suffer. That suffering would increase if he was built up and then,
finally dropped when the convoy collapsed. And, maybe, the
worst would happen. Maybe Delman wouldn't return; maybe
he'd be killed.

But why, Nelson wondered, would Mueller put Heinrich in the
same death caravan? A ploy to disguise Mueller's real plan? Would
he sacrifice Heinrich to get Delman? Or was it a mistake—like
Delman's thought that POW drivers should be dressed as GIs?

That was a possibility. There was another. Mueller wanted
to please Heinrich, and believed that, eventually, he'd remove
himself from the convoy. He'd escape.

Whatever the reason, Nelson believed that the real conun-
drum was Mueller himself. Was this regular Army NCO, this
sweet-appearing veteran devious and subtle and Machiavellian?
Could avuncular Mueller really be a secret manipulator?

Nelson watched Delman examine the stripes he'd received.
He'd been a T/4 and now he was a staff sergeant. He'd been promoted. He also had been humiliated. How would he react?

"Thank you," Delman said.

At least he's practical, Nelson thought. He didn't toss the
stripes into the nearest wastepaper basket. Or into my face. He
didn't let his emotion get out of hand. He didn't let his disgust

with the severity of his sentence turn him into a cantankerous
cynic.

Nelson pushed back his chair, handed Delman a pad of paper
and a pencil and walked to the map on the far wall.

"These colored pins," Nelson began, "represent supply depots. Write down where they are—what roads they're on, what
towns they're near. You won't be able to stop at a gas station
to ask directions. You have to consider every single detail. You
want as few surprises as possible."

"Yes, sir," Delman said, "that's why I took the chance to
come here, going over Sergeant Mueller's head, to discuss some
of those details."

He can't stop, Nelson thought. But his enthusiasm might
pull him through. It's possible this nineteen-year-old student, this
big-name football player who, finally, had a worthwhile job to
do, might just have both the courage and imagination to lead
a band of POW-driven U.S. Army trucks across the center of
war-torn France. Yet the crazy convoy concept was less a risk
for Nelson with Delman leading it. Like the POWs who'd drive
the trucks, he was expendable. Nelson hated to admit he shared
the Army's prevalent attitude—save your own ass first—but if
the worst happened, the Colonel knew he was covered.

*   *   *

"What additional details do we have to discuss?" Colonel Nelson
asked when Delman returned to his office the next day.

Delman, Nelson thought, believes he's back in college. He
thinks he's performing before the student group he gathered to
help him pass Poly Sci I. And, what's worse, I've become his
friendly professor.

"The guards," Delman said. "How many? Will they have
orders to shoot if there's the slightest provocation—or will they
be encouraged to give a warning first? What if a driver's shot?

What happens to his truck? Should we take an extra driver along? What if a truck has to stop? Should we halt the convoy and take the chance we'd be ambushed? What about—"

"Slow down," Nelson said.

But Delman couldn't stop, he talked faster.

"Should we try to contact supply depots first? Or is it better to startle them, to ambush them? Would they be intimidated by a bigger convoy? And—"

"Stop!" the Colonel ordered. "You've made your point. You've thought it through. Report here after noon mess and we'll discuss all your questions."

"Yes, sir," Delman replied, saluting, doing an about-face and leaving.

Nelson, exhausted by Delman's litany, was relieved to see him depart. The Colonel wondered if he'd ever been that enthusiastic, that loquacious, that pedantic, that young.

Nelson called Bosworth. "Find Captain Roland. Tell him I'd like to see him as soon as possible."

The slim Belgian career officer stood rigidly at attention, his slit-eyes straight ahead, his body stiff, until Colonel Nelson said, "Roland, pull up a chair."

Roland's strict adherence to rules and regulations pushed Nelson into heightened casualness, exaggerated camaraderie, just to break down the Belgian's formality. Nelson slid a package of Old Golds on his desk toward the security guards' commander.

"I've decided to move ahead with the convoy," Nelson said.

"It will be dangerous," Roland replied, taking a cigarette, nodding thanks, lighting it.

"I don't have a choice," Nelson said.

"Unless you accept the situation as it is," Roland said.

"I can't do that," Nelson said, "and live with myself."

"What if the rumor's accurate?"

"That we're supposed to kill them here?" Nelson said.

"Those aren't my orders."

"How many trucks?" Roland asked.

"At least eight. More later, if it works. I need a guard in front, in back and in the jeep with the convoy's commander, Sergeant Delman."

"The football player. I thought he'd been demoted."

"He's been resurrected."

"Shouldn't you have a mechanic along? Your Sergeant Perry? He also could drive a truck if a driver's lost."

"Good idea," Nelson replied.

"Then perhaps two guards would do. My best are Privates Clary and Trabert. They're friends. College students. Intelligent. Well-trained and tough."

"Two guards will do," Nelson said.

"When will it leave?"

"As soon as possible."

"I hope it works," Roland said as he left.

The addition of Perry was perfect, Nelson thought. He'd give the convoy maturity. He'd be able to take care of any necessary roadside repairs; Delman wouldn't have to depend on POWs.

And, if Mueller—assuming he was as deceptive and as manipulative as Nelson was starting to suspect—had concocted some sort of elaborate, sinister scheme, the motor pool chief's presence could be the monkey wrench that would wreck it.

*   *   *

Sergeant Mueller drove to the edge of Le Mans where he'd rented a small, one-bedroom apartment for Denise. It was far enough away from the camp not to cause a problem, yet close enough so every night Mueller could fill up his metal mess kit with an extra portion of the evening's meal and bring it, still warm, to his mistress.

Like most of the women he'd bedded and boarded, Denise worked behind the perfume counter of a local department store.

Mueller had met her by following a routine so well established he'd stop refining it. Mueller thought its consistency—it always worked—was his finest achievement.

He always started the same way. He would visit one of the city's major department stores where he would check out the clerks selling perfume. If they pleased him, he'd look for the department's manager. Once he found him, Mueller would begin his cigarette ploy. In the case of Denise it worked perfectly. "I have a question for you," Mueller began as he tapped out a cigarette for himself. Then, watching the manager's eyes—if he was a smoker they never left the package—Mueller tapped out a second cigarette and offered it to the manager, who accepted the cigarette, slipped it into his breast pocket, and explained, "If you don't mind, I'll save it for after dinner."

Then Mueller tapped the package again and held it temptingly in front of the manager. They all wanted more.

"Please," Mueller said.

"Thank you," the manager replied.

Having established some rapport, Mueller said, "Perhaps you can assist me. Do you have an attractive clerk who could help me select some perfume? A clerk who speaks English."

"Of course."

"If she's single, I think she'd be more helpful for the gift I have in mind."

"I have just the person for you," the manager said.

Mueller was then led toward a single attractive clerk who spoke English.

"Miss Boudreau," the manager said. "We have a customer who needs your expertise. And if there's anything I can do, sergeant, please see me before you leave. Thank you again."

Mueller turned to the woman. "I'd like some perfume, let's say the kind you might select for yourself."

Miss Boudreau smiled and slowly made her selection. She showed Mueller a bottle of Chanel Number 5 and then dabbed some of the perfume on her wrist. "It's subtle but long lasting," she said.

Mueller bent forward, sniffed, raised his head to smile at her and sniffed again. He nodded. "Very nice. Please gift wrap it for me."

Next, Mueller followed his usual practice. It never varied. He waited outside the department store's employee entrance to present the gift-wrapped perfume to the woman who had sold it to him.

"Miss Boudreau," he said, as she was leaving the store.

"Sergeant Mueller."

"The perfume you were kind enough to select for me," he said. He presented it to her. "It's for you."

He watched all the rapid changes in her small, attractive face: surprise, suspicion and, finally, amusement.

"How charming," she said, but she didn't take his gift.

"Please," Mueller said, moving the package closer to her. "No strings attached. I promise you. My only request is that, perhaps sometime during the next week, you'll let me see you again. Only to walk you home. Nothing more."

He hurried away. A few days later he was at the store when it closed.

"I wondered when you'd return," she said.

"I have less than an hour before my truck returns to camp," he explained.

When they arrived at her apartment building, Mueller kept his distance. He said, "May I see you again—perhaps next Tuesday?"

As always, he kept their first date casual. A visit to a local cafe. He learned she was thirty and, after a difficult divorce, had decided to return to Le Mans where she was born, even though her parents had moved to Casablanca. Mueller told her he would never return to his home. That, in fact, he joined the army to escape it.

It was still early when they returned to her apartment building. Following his tested approach, he did not stand close to her.

He made sure he appeared respectful, considerate.

"Dinner Saturday?" he asked.

As always, he made a dinner reservation at the city's best hotel restaurant. He provided the hotel's chef with prime steaks—secured from Mueller's mess sergeant in exchange for two cartons of cigarettes and a bottle of bourbon—and condiments. He'd obtained enough for both his dinner and that of the chef who, in appreciation, made certain Mueller and his guest were well treated.

"That was wonderful," she said. "I didn't know such food still was available. You must have provided it. Even our best restaurants can't obtain such fine cuts of beef."

She passed his final test. She was intelligent.

"You're very observant," he said.

"Let me supply the coffee and dessert," she said.

They returned to her one-bedroom apartment.

"It's not much," she said. "But it's clean and quiet and private. And it's close enough to the store so I can walk when it's not too cold."

"And you have a bathtub," Mueller said.

She smiled. He could predict what she would say and what would happen after he emerged naked from the bath, and found her waiting for him. Before the next morning, he gave her the present he'd taken with him—silk stockings.

He'd been with Denise almost four months. His affairs seldom lasted longer. He knew their relationship was nearing its end. Once more, he'd have to visit another department store.

Perhaps Denise knew of someone else. He didn't want to hurt her—but it was an idea. He was getting tired of his routine, regardless of how well it worked, and having his current mistress suggest a replacement involved a certain element of daring that appealed to him. He'd have to give it more thought.

CHAPTER 9

"JAN. 3, 1945—I may lead the first American convoy driven by POWs in the ETO—European Theater of Operation. Which means we'll try to get supplies to prolong the lives of our POWs. Their single aim is to escape, rejoin their outfits, and try to kill us.

"If Colonel Nelson lets Sergeant Mueller get his way, Heinrich will be my right-hand man. A perfect guy for the job. A genuine Nazi. All he wants is to escape.

"According to *Stars & Stripes*, Hitler will fight to the last German. At that rate, we may end up with more of the enemy than the Wehrmacht. That assumes our convoy's successful so we can keep them alive.

"And this on top of the rumor that our secret mission is to keep our POW population down. By any means possible. Does any of this make sense?"

*   *   *

"He's piling it on," Clary said, "while he can."

That's exactly what Mueller was doing, Delman thought, getting in extra licks before the convoy started.

"I'm naming you our official fireman," Mueller had told Delman. "But instead of putting out fires, you'll start them."

"I'll do what?" Delman asked.

"You'll keep us warm," Mueller said. "You'll start with the stove in your barracks. You'll fill it up and light it. Then you'll do the same in the other barracks, the officer's mess, your mess and, finally, the supply tent. And you'll do all this every morning before reveille."

Delman knew Mueller's latest order meant he'd have to get up two hours earlier than usual. It would take that long, at least at first, for him to go from place to place, find the wood, light it, and make sure it stayed lit.

Mueller's order assured Delman of a long day, maybe eighteen or nineteen hours. He wasn't happy with it, but he wasn't destroyed, either. He knew he could function with five hours of sleep. More was better but not necessary. He had learned that when he was a thirteen-year-old at a summer boy's camp where his roommate was Alfred Shultz, who was as tall as Delman and also wore glasses. Shultz immediately told Delman, "I'm here for fun so I'm not cleaning this room. If you want it clean, you better clean it yourself."

There were daily room inspections. Dirty rooms resulted in a variety of graduated punishments, from demerits (which reduced your award opportunities) to no desserts to not going into Minocqua, the nearby town.

Delman told Shultz he had to do his share. He refused, which led to a loud argument and a louder fight, campers yelling as they gathered around the wild-swinging pugilists. Counselor Larry Rolnick, a biology major from the University of Wisconsin, broke it up and said if there was another fight they'd both be sent home.

Every morning Delman made the beds, swept the room, cleaned the sink, put away their clothes. To do everything and have the room ready for morning inspection, he rose at 4 a.m., two hours before the recording of an out-of-tune trumpet woke the camp.

Shultz did everything he could to exasperate Delman. He dropped candy wrappers on the floor. He squeezed toothpaste in the sink. He put a dead chipmunk in Delman's Keds.

Delman hated Shultz as much as his daily morning labor but discovered he could handle it. He got by with less sleep. He cleaned their room every day. He stopped talking to Shultz and learned he didn't need him. It was a momentous discovery:

Delman could get along fine by himself.

When Rolnick found out what was happening, he tried to switch roommates but none of the other boys wanted to have anything to do with Shultz. It was bad enough he didn't help to clean his room—he didn't clean himself. He smelled.

The last night of camp was award night. Steak, french fries, corn on the cob, apple pie à la mode, a few speeches, some humor, and the long-awaited awards. Those who were outstanding in sports and arts and crafts received large "I's" to sew on their sweatshirts. There were also special awards for the most improved camper, the most enthusiastic camper and, the highest award, Honor Camper. He was the camper who excelled in a variety of activities but, most of all, displayed an outstanding character.

Rolnick nominated Delman. He said Delman showed maturity beyond his years. As the climax to the award dinner, the Honor Camper trophy was presented—to Delman. As Honor Camper, his name was engraved on a large trophy that was displayed on the fireplace mantel in the mess hall. Delman also received a small replica to take home.

Before he left camp, he walked up to Shultz and gave him the replica, announcing, "I wouldn't have been named Honor Camper without you. Every time you look at it, I want you to remember what I think of you. You are," Delman took a deep breath because he'd never used the adult expression before, "one rotten son of a bitch."

Delman liked to recall that moment. The birth of his self-confidence, of his self-esteem, of his independence. After that, he believed anything was possible; there were no limits to what he could do—or take.

He also knew he couldn't risk showing even the slightest disgust with Mueller's latest ploy. Telling him off could keep Delman off the convoy. Once again, the supply sergeant revealed his malevolent sense of humor with another gift, this time an alarm clock. Delman added the clock to his sleeping paraphernalia. He slept in his shorts and a T-shirt and, as nights got colder, added socks. In case of a drop in temperature, he kept his winter underwear nearby. He used them as his pillow and a place to bury Mueller's not-so-funny gift, the small, round-faced, four-legged alarm clock.

Besides being the only person in his barracks with a clock below his head, Delman probably was the only soldier with sheets. He found them in a torn bag at the bottom of a carton of tools in a forgotten corner of the supply tent. He was afraid they were used to wrap the dead so he washed them several times before he put them on his bed.

He also appropriated extra blankets. Three on top and one, doubled up, on the bottom, below his mattress. It gave him more warmth and prevented him from feeling his bunk's wooden slats. His mattress—a long bag stuffed with straw—didn't help. It was as flat as the clothes Delman kept in the bottom of his duffel.

As soon as the alarm clanged, Delman punched it off. Stepping out of his warm bed onto the cold wooden floor of the freezing barracks was no different, he thought, from a cold morning shower. He hated both. He forced himself to move rapidly, sliding past snoring Clary in the lower bunk. He reached into his duffel for heavy pants and the wool shirt his mother had sent him, and hurriedly pulled them over his winter underwear. He added one more layer, a fatigue jacket, and then slipped on a second pair of socks before he stepped into his clammy combat boots.

He jogged to the outdoor latrine and returned to splash cold water on his face. He was awake. His eyes grew accustomed to the dark. He could see his breath. He'd start his assignment within his own barracks. He shuffled toward the stove and piled logs in it. He found matches in his pants pocket, next to his condoms. Once the logs caught, he put on his overcoat, two pairs of gloves, a wool cap and went outside to begin his fireman's route.

The morning, as early as it was, wasn't that dark. It still was enough to mask the ugliness of the buildings—and the frozen mud. The moon was almost perfectly round. The air was raw and a heavy wind blew the lightly falling snow straight into his face. When he reached the other barracks, he had to use his flashlight to find its stove and logs.

"What the fuck are you doing?" Delman heard.

He moved his flashlight to the angry face of one of the mess sergeants. He sat up in his bed holding an M1.

"I'm here to light your fucking stove," Delman said. "Sergeant Mueller's fucking orders."

"Well, hold it down," the chef said. "We're sleeping here. And don't forget the fucking stove in the fucking mess hall."

"I wouldn't miss it for the fucking world," Delman said.

"Up yours," the cook said.

"You act like the convoy's going to be paradise," Clary had said.

"It will be," Delman had replied. "Without Mueller and Heinrich, it will be paradise."

With all his stoves blazing, Delman unbuttoned the stiff side panels of the supply tent. It would be an hour before Mueller arrived, at least a half-hour after that before Heinrich joined them. For once, Delman didn't dread the arrival of his captors.

His new stripes changed his outlook. He didn't want to admit the military's manufactured class distinction affected him, but for the first time since he'd been assigned to the supply tent, his anger had disappeared. He felt upbeat, positive.

Stripes were power. You were more than a dogface. You had some authority, some control. That helped him as he watched Mueller swagger toward him.

"Morning, sergeant," Delman said.

"Get those fucking stripes sewn on properly," Mueller said, pulling off the staff sergeant stripes Delman had tacked to his overcoat. "Do things right or not at all."

Mueller's always offended by my appearance, Delman thought. He thinks I'm too relaxed, too casual, too confident. And some of his resentment's caused because I had a single good idea. And not even a new idea. Only a slight alteration of a familiar routine, one truck lined up behind another and another.

"Everyone has ideas," the Colonel said. "It's what you do with them that counts."

To Delman that meant ideas were changed, embroidered. Their origins were unimportant. Maybe that was the basis for Mueller's anger. Perhaps his ideas had been so altered over the years—probably usurped—that he felt justified trying to do the same with Delman's idea.

Mueller tossed the ripped-off stripes back at Delman with a second packet of staff sergeant stripes. Delman wondered if Mueller was assuming he was making an even exchange, his stripes for Delman's idea. If that's what you think, Delman felt like saying, think again.

"Get those sewn on your shirts and jackets," Mueller ordered. "Get your ass over to the tailor shop. The POWs'll sew them on for you. Go ahead, do it now."

Delman was pleased to get Mueller's stripes—but why the tough words? He always had to be tough, unbending, a perfectionist. He always had to display his superiority. No, it was more than that; Mueller had to throw his power at Delman, like the stiff punches Delman threw at the two Germans who, Delman was sure, had been set up to curse him.

"After you're done with the tailor shop, get your ass back here," Mueller ordered. "We'll get together with Heinrich and figure out how to get the right drivers for the convoy."

The convoy. Delman caught that. Not *your* convoy. Delman knew the meeting would be another test. Who would select the drivers? Delman tried to fathom Mueller's reasoning. It probably went this way—Mueller didn't believe Heinrich was an officer so he believed he wouldn't try to escape.

And one Mueller blind spot led to another. He would try to impose Heinrich's selections on Delman, never believing what Delman saw as apparent: Heinrich's drivers would, at the least, help him escape. And, at the most, they'd take off, following

Mueller's trusted Nazi as they left the empty trucks, laughing at Mueller, shooting at Delman.

When he went to the cages to get his stripes sewed on, Delman would have the opportunity to see which POWs could become his drivers. He wasn't about to leave the selection solely up to Heinrich and Mueller. But how do you select the right drivers? He decided he'd better ask the Colonel.

Sergeant Bosworth no longer tried to halt Delman's entry to the Colonel's office. Maybe, Delman thought, the hostile gatekeeper had become resigned to Delman's easy access, although he had to believe Delman's time would come; his convoy would collapse.

Nelson, on the phone, nodded to Delman to sit down. When he hung up, the Colonel's face was colorless. "Headquarters. The Theater Provost Marshal. The TPM. They couldn't care less about our rising death toll. They told me not to worry—we're capturing as many Germans as we're burying."

"I'm sure you're aware of the rumor," Delman said.

"That there's a conspiracy that we're here to kill POWs?"

"As long as no one finds out," Delman said.

"Bullshit," the Colonel said. "Sure we're killing them—but it's not intentional, there's no conspiracy."

"Would you know?" Delman asked. "Would you really know if there was a conspiracy?"

Then he realized that maybe even the Colonel was a POW— subservient to the TPM, manipulated by the boss of the MPs who worked in the lush suburb outside of Paris—and that the Colonel didn't realize it. Or if he did, he refused to admit it. To himself and, especially, to Delman.

"What brings you here?" the Colonel asked.

"Sergeant Mueller said we've got to think about drivers," Delman said. "The ones who'll be in the convoy."

"And?"

"I've been thinking about what we want in a driver. It's a given they should be experienced truck drivers and know English. I also think . . ."

"Wait," Nelson said. "How are you going to check their truck driving skills? You know as much about driving a truck as I do. It can't be easy and what happens when the trucks are full? How fast do you go without breaking an axle or ripping a tire?"

"A driver's test," Delman said.

"Given by someone who knows trucks," the Colonel said. "Captain Roland suggested we add Sergeant Perry to the convoy. He could give the test. He could be on the convoy. In case you have something mechanical go wrong, you'd have the best guy available. You have a problem with Sergeant Perry?"

Delman knew he had one more stripe than Perry and that Perry was a friend of Mueller's. The motor pool boss, with his shaved head and equally smooth talk, was known as a wild, obsessive womanizer. He also was an artist with trucks and jeeps. He'd protect Mueller's interest. He'd also protect the convoy, if only to save his own ass.

"No problem, sir," Delman replied.

"Continue," the Colonel said.

"I thought we should look for drivers who are family men; they'd be reluctant to escape."

"You've said that before."

"No disrespect intended, sir, but I'd want drivers who don't buckle down to officers."

"Explain."

"Sergeant Mueller expects Heinrich to be my right-hand man, and everyone knows Heinrich's an officer who has one goal—to break out of here."

"You can't prove he's an officer," Nelson said, "but let's assume he is. You think he'll lead a revolt? If so, why hasn't he tried anything?"

"I've been working for him, sir. I know him. He wants out of here. He's been waiting for the right opportunity. He'll figure the convoy's it. I wouldn't want other drivers intimidated by Heinrich."

"Sergeant Mueller only suggested Heinrich," the Colonel replied, rising behind his desk, beginning to pace. "Nothing's set."

Delman didn't want to say anything to jeopardize his chance to lead the convoy. Perhaps having Perry on the convoy—both to maintain the trucks and to watch Delman—would eliminate the need for Heinrich. He could see the Colonel, upset after his phone call, was on edge and Delman's reference to the rumor didn't help. He recalled the Colonel had told him to shut up before when he was too outspoken. He decided this was a good time to apply that advice.

Nelson stopped pacing and sat down. "Do what you have to do but make sure, along with a driver's test, every driver gets a physical. Most of the POWs are too exhausted, too weak, too sick to handle a truck. They'll pretend otherwise to get out of here, to get more rations. You can't afford something unexpected happening to one of your drivers. You don't want surprises."

"Yes, sir."

He saw the meeting was over. He saluted and left.

"I want your convoy to succeed," Colonel Nelson called after him.

Of course, Delman thought. But why say that? Are you feeling guilty? Are you thinking that you'll get credit if the convoy succeeds but, if it fails, I'll be the one to blame? Is that why I was chosen to lead it?

*   *   *

Delman had stayed away from the prisoners' cages where, formerly, he had spent each day. Now, as he returned on his way to the tailor shop, he was startled by the growth of the compound—more barbed-wire enclosures had been added to house the flood of captured Germans.

Tents and make-shift quarters—utilizing materials scavenged from Le Mans—made the new cages look like a shanty-town, one tent on top of another. The meandering line of poorly heated workshops, most under tin and canvas roofs, reminded Delman of hurriedly repaired, bomb-damaged homes.

During the day, the camp was a hectic, busy, damp, ramshackle workshop. Bundled-up POW look-alikes, in wet-smelling layers of ragged uniforms stamped with huge white "POW"s, shuffled through their repetitious tasks. You heard only the humming of conversation, the banging of tools.

Delman's first stop was the barber shop. POW barbers, except for their scruffiness, seemed little different from the barbers Delman knew at home. Except here their chairs were immobile. But their procedure was familiar. As soon as he sat down, his barber draped a cloth over Delman's shoulders and pinned thin paper around his neck. His scissors began a speedy clip-clip against his comb quickly travelling through Delman's hair.

Delman rubbed the two-day growth on his cheeks and chin and said, "A shave, too." Now that he could occasionally leave the supply tent, he decided he'd no longer shave himself. He'd enjoy the luxury of having a POW soap his face, stroke away his whiskers. He never failed to wonder when the straight razor slowly glided over his vulnerable throat, if the barber was tempted to do more than shave his enemy.

But the barber proceeded carefully and concluded with a wet towel wrapped around Delman's smooth face. As the barber bent, placing his hands against the towel, Delman could smell his sour breath. The towel, Delman thought, should be hot and steaming. But hot water was a luxury, limited to that boiled on the stove. A brush of powder ended the shave before the hair-laden cloth was whisked off.

Delman paid the barber a cigarette for each service—one for the haircut, another for the shave—and looked at him for the first time. He was thin, his eyes dark and sunken in his lean face, but perhaps he was stronger than he appeared.

"Hear about the convoy?" Delman asked.

"Yes," the barber replied.

"You like to drive one of the trucks?"

"I know how to drive trucks. But I'm a barber."

"You'd get more rations," Delman offered. "You have a family?"

"Three children."

"Don't you want more rations and cigarettes?"

"Rations," the barber said pulling up his clothes, showing his bony body, "that's what I need. Look, you can see my ribs. But when the convoy's over, would I continue as a barber?"

"I guarantee it," Delman said. "Of course, you'll have to pass a driver's test."

He withdrew a small notebook and pen from his shirt pocket. "Your name and cage number," he said.

"Wanger," the barber replied. "Cage six. And there's a soldier making ashtrays who was head of our motor pool. I don't know him too well—but they say there's nothing he doesn't know about cars and trucks. He's famous. He raced cars all over Europe."

"Sacher," Delman said. "I've heard of him."

"Sacher," the barber repeated, "like the torte. Tell him I gave you his name."

Delman proceeded through the factories. The tin roof was supported by makeshift columns of found steel and wooden tent poles ingeniously held together with wire and rope. Inside, POWs leaned over wooden tables fashioning ashtrays, lamps and wall decorations out of spent shells.

Delman walked along bent rows of chilled, intense Germans, only their fingers uncovered. One stove barely lessened the cold; light came from between tin slats, raised side-vents, and an occasional naked bulb hanging from dangerous-looking overhead wiring.

"Sacher?" Delman asked in English "Sacher, the Sacher who ran a motor pool?"

A lean, narrow-faced POW wearing a wool cap, looked up. "I'm Sacher."

"There's going to be a convoy," Delman said, "to pick up supplies. It'll be warm in the trucks. We could use a driver who knows trucks. You'll be well fed."

Sacher didn't hesitate. "I know trucks. All kinds of trucks."

"You a family man?" Delman asked.

"Two children."

"I hear you're famous," Delman said, "the world's best race-driver."

"That's stretching it," Sacher said.

"Your two children," Delman asked, "how old are they?"

"Five and seven," Sacher said. "No, three years older than that. That's how old when I saw them last."

"You going to make racers out of them?" Delman asked.

"It's a good life," Sacher said, "although tough, but what isn't? And they're both good with their hands. But it's up to them." He pulled out a frayed wallet and withdrew their photos.

"They look like great kids," Delman said. "You like officers? Just between the two of us."

"Fuck officers."

"Your cage number," Delman said.

Sacher replied and then, more animated, pointed to the man across the table from him. "He's a good driver and . . ."

"No," interrupted the man. "I'll stay here. I have a family to worry about."

"Cigarettes," Delman said.

Sacher smiled. "Ramer's his name. Same cage as mine."

In another workshop, POWs were crafting bookends, picture frames, boxes, and a variety of novel decorations. Other factories were repairing shoes, tents. There was a small book bindery, a leather factory and even a model shop, manned by officers who made miniatures of tanks, cars, planes, boats and ships.

The largest workshop manufactured and repaired clothes. Delman was carrying his shirts and jackets. A POW asked him what he wanted done. He showed his stripes. The POW measured each shirt and jacket, marked it with pins and began to sew.

"This afternoon?" Delman asked.

The POW nodded, his head bent, concentrating on his sewing. What were you, Delman wondered, before you were drafted—your own boss where you ordered Jewish tailors around? Or did you create uniforms for Von Runstedt and Rommel and the higher-ups, the dressed-up theatrical elite?

"Can you drive a truck?" Delman asked the tailor.

"Yes, sergeant. For cigarettes?"

Delman noticed his fingers, sewing on the stripes, were nicotine-stained. Delman asked if he was married and the German nodded. Delman added his name to his growing list.

Delman returned to the supply tent. He checked the names he had secured and thought about the POWs he had interviewed. They could have been Americans. Individually, they seemed no different from the people he knew. Even the ones who bought his magazines when he was a kid. But it was together, as a nation, as a herd, that they became what they were. Terrors of the world. Pillagers. Bigots. And vicious, show-no-mercy killers.

Delman had the names of ten POWs who—for extra rations and cigarettes—were willing to risk their lives in a first-of-its-kind convoy, guarded by trigger-happy Belgians and led by an American sergeant known for slugging POWs.

They'll get something tangible in return. What will I get? Escape from my prison, my captors. Is that enough? Is that worth the risk I'll be taking? Delman, warming his hands over the stove, knew it was too late for such questions.

CHAPTER 10

SITTING IN HIS office, Colonel Nelson couldn't forget Delman's question, "Would you know if there was a conspiracy?" The reinstated NCO was too smart, Nelson thought, too discerning. The straight answer was that Nelson might not know if there was a conscious plan to kill captured Germans.

But he couldn't believe anyone—any American or any of the Allies—would tolerate such a plot. He looked at his first sergeant, comfortable Bosworth who liked to ask tough questions.

"Sergeant," Nelson said, standing in front of Bosworth's desk.

Bosworth was startled. He immediately jumped up and stood at attention.

"Sir."

"As you were, sergeant. I was thinking that you see everything I do. All the memos, all the orders. You know as much about this camp—probably a hell of a lot more—than I do."

"Sir?"

"How does it add up to you?" the Colonel asked. "I mean all these deaths. We keep losing more POWs every day. You've heard the rumors that we're killing them on purpose. What do you make of that?"

"You're asking my opinion, sir?"

Nelson nodded.

"Maybe we should go into your office, sir," Bosworth suggested.

He closed the office door once the Colonel was seated behind his desk.

"Sit down, sergeant."

86

Nelson studied his first sergeant. He enjoyed being asked his opinion. He looked proud. He was preening. Nelson would have to remember to ask Bosworth's opinion more often.

"Tell me what you think."

"I've heard the rumors and I've seen all the orders," Bosworth said. "I think the TPM's at a loss. They don't know what to do. That's why they don't answer you. They keep trying to meet your requests, but all they've got are orders to get more supplies to the front."

"What orders?"

"From the front, sir. From Ike. His staff. They want to win the war. That's all they think about. Supplying the troops at the front. They come first. They're the priority. Not us. We're an afterthought, if even that."

"No conspiracy?" the Colonel asked. "That's what we want to believe, isn't it, sergeant?"

"We don't kill prisoners," Bosworth said.

"Or we don't get written orders to kill prisoners," Nelson said.

"Are you saying, sir," Bosworth asked, "that what we're running here is a death camp?"

"I sure as hell hope not," the Colonel said. "Not intentionally."

Nelson didn't want to believe the decimation of POWs was intentional. He did want to believe his superiors in the omnipotent Theater Provost Marshal were either weary of his complaints or simply didn't give a damn about POWs and the poor slobs who were under orders to care for them and feed them. The TPM's silence, their indifference, made him question his own concern. Why worry about the Germans? Did *they* worry about the people they humiliated, dominated, murdered? But he thought, aren't we better, aren't we more compassionate, aren't we more humane?

"Thanks, sergeant," the Colonel said. "Dismissed."

Nelson stood up and began his restless pacing. Why couldn't

he get the TPM to discuss what was happening? He was left with no choice but to continue his constant, tiresome pressure—official requests, unofficial telephone calls, leaning on friends he knew from Officer's Candidate School—if only to assuage his own guilt.

*   *   *

"We should castrate him!"

Officer Donald Frank's reaction to the pederast who had attacked one boy and was terrorizing the whole school was typical of everyone in the suburban police station. Nelson didn't favor Frank's solution, but not a single officer expressed the slightest sympathy for the pervert. That he could be a typical suburbanite, maybe the guy next to you at a Little League game, didn't lessen his crime. He probably mowed his lawn on the weekend, took his wife out on Saturday night, and left every morning at the same time, five days a week, to commute to his office.

The fact that he looked normal and acted normal didn't mean he was normal. He was sick, Nelson thought, and what he did was sick. Even the older, single officers who had seen it all, felt a special aversion to the crime. But those police who had children—particularly those who lived in the area and had boys—could discuss little else. The pederast was free and they had to get him before he molested their sons.

Nelson, then an officer, was alone in his squad car. He was cruising on Lake Avenue, a through street close to all of the schools, when he heard the report. A suspicious man with a boy was seen in the parking lot behind Hillcrest Grammar School.

Nelson pushed down his accelerator, flipped on his lights and siren, and raced to the school. Another police car, its lights flashing, already had arrived. Nelson jumped out of his car and ran toward the other patrol car. It was Frank's, muscle-bound Frank who worked out each day with weights and paraded shirtless in the locker room to show off his muscled stomach and huge biceps.

"You pervert," Nelson heard Frank scream, "you fucking bastard!"

On the other side of his car, he was attacking a man kneeling in front of him who offered no resistance. As if he wanted to be punished. His head was bloodied. He slowly slid to the ground. Frank kicked him again and again. First, in the rib cage. Then in the head. Finally, in the balls.

"Enough," Nelson called, running toward his fellow officer. Nelson grabbed Frank from behind. "Enough," he repeated. "You'll kill him."

"See about that kid," Frank said, "over there."

"Don't hit him again," Nelson said.

He left Frank to run to the small boy standing in a nearby doorway. He was trembling. Nelson examined him. He saw his shirt was unbuttoned but he seemed okay.

"Did he hurt you?" Nelson asked.

The boy shook his head.

"Did he do anything to you?"

"He unbuttoned my shirt," the boy said. "Then the policeman came."

Nelson turned to see a woman leaving a parked car. She held the hand of another small boy. It was Frank's wife and son.

Frank was astounded. "What are you doing here? I don't understand."

"We missed the school bus," his wife said, "so I drove. Then I saw your patrol car."

"The pervert," Frank said. "I got the pervert."

Nelson lifted the beaten man to his feet. He moaned. His face was cut and bleeding and his left eye was puffed and closed. His clothes were torn. One shoe had fallen off.

"You could've killed him," Frank's wife said. "I saw everything. So did your son. I've never seen you like that. I've never seen anyone beaten like you beat him. You never stopped beating him."

"He's a pervert," Frank said.

"Jimmy saw you," she said. "I wish he hadn't seen you. I better take him to his room."

Nelson piled the beaten man into Frank's car. He was leaning against it, vomiting and gagging.

He wiped his face. Finally, he raised his head and looked at Nelson.

"I can't believe my wife was here," Frank said. "What a time for her to drive up. She said she saw everything. Did you see how Jimmy looked at me? God, he'll never forget what he saw."

Nelson never forgot what he saw. A double tragedy. If he'd arrived before Frank, if the school bus had arrived a few minutes later, the tragedy might not have occurred. But timing and coincidence were part of tragedies.

At least Frank attacked the right man. Lucky for Frank. His victim confessed and was punished. His family suffered. But, if it was any consolation to them, to him, he was sick. But the other tragedy was Frank's. His behavior. It shocked and offended his wife and traumatized his son. Neither would forget what they saw. The tragedy was that Frank did it to himself. He went beyond his mission, his orders. He exceeded the boundaries of his command. His job was to investigate, apprehend, prevent—not to judge. And, most certainly, not to punish.

Understanding where Frank went wrong—and the importance of concentrating, focusing on your job, only that—enormously influenced all of Nelson's later work. He knew his job was tough. He knew he could not anticipate what would happen. But to take what you did beyond its boundaries was to take it too far. If you did that, you became what you were against.

*   *   *

The Colonel, sitting at his desk, was surprised when Sergeant Bosworth called, "Look out your window, Colonel. The Engineers have arrived."

Nelson couldn't believe it. After all of his requests to expand the camp, someone had taken him seriously. He had been calling the same number so long, he never expected someone to pick up the phone and reply. The Engineers would build more cages. They'd relieve some of the camp's terrible overcrowding.

Nelson saw a convoy of mud-splattered trucks pull alongside his headquarters. Sergeant Bosworth already was outside, saluting the Engineers' young shavetail who had to be the unit commander. Nelson was struck by the second lieutenant's cocky bearing. The casualness of his return salute, the self-confident slouch, the way he wore his overseas cap. He looked like Delman. Only Delman never made it to OCS. He should have studied engineering, Nelson thought, instead of—what was it?—English or journalism.

Sergeant Bosworth had stepped into the cab of the lead truck to direct the convoy to the area where more cages could be constructed. The lanky lieutenant, his gold bar glistening in the winter sun, strolled into Nelson's office.

"Lieutenant George Taylor," he said, saluting, "with orders to build you five new enclosures, sir."

"Cages," Colonel Nelson said, returning his salute, aware of his explosive reply, "and you're supposed to construct ten—not five! That's what I hope you mean. Sorry, Taylor. Sit down. I didn't mean to shout at you. But it's been a career trying to get you here. And now I'm not even receiving half of what I need, what I requested."

"Yes, sir," Taylor said, unruffled. He handed over a folded, single page he took from an inside pocket. The order read, "Five enclosures are to be built."

"I need twenty," Nelson said, his voice rising. "I requested fifteen and I figured I'd get ten. My disgust has nothing to do with you, lieutenant. But, damn it, five lousy cages is a sop, a put-down. How the hell am I supposed to take care of these hundreds of new POWs arriving every day! Wait. I've got the answer. We should set up firing squads to kill them! Why drag out the process!"

He could see Taylor wasn't moved. He reacted as if the Colonel was slightly demented, a confused, crotchety griper. The lieutenant's annoyed look said it all: he had had it with behind-the-line officers who thought what they were doing was important when only combat, killing the enemy, was important.

He's very young, Nelson thought. He's uninformed. He might think differently if he knew that this POW camp—in spite of our best efforts—is a killing machine. He probably would like that. We might even gain his respect.

But now, Nelson feared, the smooth-cheeked officer—probably a "C" freshman from some unknown, throw-away engineering school before he was drafted—would say, "There's a war on, Colonel. Get out of my way, I've got work to do. I have to return to the front where the action is." Nelson wanted him to leave, to get out of his sight. He didn't need any more proof that what he was doing was worthless. He already despised Taylor's haughty attitude, his patronizing half-smile, a sprightly teenager eager to escape his doddering elder.

"Sergeant Bosworth will see you and your men are fed and quartered," Nelson said impatiently, eager to get rid of him. "If you need anything, anything at all, see me."

Evidently, the Colonel's offer wasn't appreciated. Two days later, Sergeant Bosworth delivered Taylor's unexpected message. "He doesn't like the way he and his men are being treated," Bosworth reported. "He expected something for his work."

"Here I thought he was in the army," the Colonel said. "I should've realized he was a contractor, a mercenary who expected to be paid in what—booze and tobacco?"

"That's about the size of it, sir," Bosworth replied.

"Tell that son of a bitch to report to me immediately," the Colonel said.

The shavetail calmly disregarded Nelson's order. His rank, as well as his indignation, meant nothing. After working for a second day, the youthful commander nonchalantly packed his wares, ordered his men to get on their trucks and, without a word of explanation, left.

Sergeant Bosworth reported to Nelson. "The Engineers have taken off, sir. They erected one cage."

"One fucking cage!" the Colonel screamed.

He considered calling the TPM. But he knew his strident complaint would only antagonize his indifferent superiors. They'd reply he was lucky to get what he got.

Or, Nelson thought, maybe they'd be surprised Taylor had been here at all. Maybe his arrival—the construction of even a single cage—was either a mistake or a little entrepreneurship by the young lieutenant. It was possible his innocent appearance masked his unbounded hubris.

Why, with all of Nelson's demands for more food, more clothes, more tents, did he receive the construction of a single cage? It was at the bottom of his priority list. Perhaps, Nelson began to believe, the tall officer saw a quick way to pick up some easy loot. A slight detour behind the lines. A few days of construction. But, getting nothing, he left.

"I'll get him for this," Nelson said. "Somehow, I'll get Lieutenant George Taylor back here and he'll build the additional cages I need."

"I hope you do, sir," Bosworth said.

"I will," Nelson said, "that's a promise. One way or another, I'll get smart-ass Lieutenant George Taylor back here."

Nelson stormed from his office to check the new cage. Capt. Roland had preceded him. They studied the construction. At least the Engineers did a passable job. Nelson pushed at the wooden columns anchoring the barbed wire and looked up at the two additional watchtowers.

Watchtowers! Nelson shook his head. He knew the empty perches would remain empty. They represented another unsolved problem that he, unlike his superiors, couldn't disregard. He needed additional troops to control the hordes of POWs that arrived daily. Once he had hoped getting extra cages would accelerate his request for more troops. Now he knew the Army didn't work that way. It was too logical. The Colonel wanted to rail at Captain Roland, but he knew the intense Belgian was as frustrated as he was.

"This overcrowding," Captain Roland said. "One more cage is better than no more cages. But POWs will continue to live on top of each other. And you know what that means. More sickness. More deaths. We don't have enough medicine. It's the same old story. We need more of everything. Tents. Blankets. Medicine. And, most of all, food. If something's not done soon, they'll try a mass escape. And, with our limited troops, it could be successful. We simply don't have enough guards. Those I have are exhausted. They'd be incapable of preventing an outbreak. Colonel, I've said this before, but I have to say it again. We're going to have a catastrophe on our hands if something isn't done quickly."

"The more I complain," Nelson said, "the worse it gets. Ike and his generals—like the German General Staff—want POWs to disappear. We already have them on a starvation diet." He looked at Roland. "Maybe they want them to escape. Maybe that's the plan. Then we can kill them with just cause."

"You're doing all you can," Roland said. "As you requested, I held a few surprise inspections. They don't know when we might hold a few more so maybe we're aborting some escapes."

"And I keep moving suspected ringleaders to different cages. That might help, too."

"Those rumors you manufacture," Roland said. "I like the latest one, that more security forces are on the way."

"Do they believe it?" Nelson asked.

"It throws them off balance whether they believe it or not."

Back in his office, Nelson talked to Bosworth.

"The convoy," the Colonel said. "It's our last chance to get supplies unless we turn this place into a cemetery. I like what the TPM told me. Don't worry, they said, we're capturing as many as you're burying. Nice. You better get Sergeant Mueller over here. We've got to get the convoy on the road."

*   *   *

Delman stood in the supply tent, in front of Mueller's desk, and pulled out his list of candidates who'd agreed to be drivers in the convoy. He read their names.

"You know them?" Sergeant Mueller asked Heinrich.

"None of them," Heinrich said. He stood next to Delman. "My list is better. I can vouch for each of my selections. I live with them. They're from my cage. We'd work as a unit."

"What about that, Delman?" Sergeant Mueller asked. "Doesn't it make sense to select drivers we know?"

"I don't know them," Delman said, "and I wouldn't rely on a bunch of POWs from the same cage. I went out of my way to select drivers from different cages, POWs who don't know each other, who couldn't be hatching some escape plot together."

Heinrich laughed. "What escape plot? We've found a home here, our war's over."

"You're admitting Germany's lost the war?" Delman asked.

"I'll vouch for every one of the men I selected," Heinrich said.

Sergeant Mueller leaned back in his chair. He took a long and vigorous stretch and then rose from behind his desk.

Mueller circled them. Like a referee, Delman thought, sizing up the combatants, studying their techniques, keeping score. As he returned to stand behind his desk, his hands holding the back of his chair, Delman believed he could read Mueller's thoughts. The convoy's a bad mistake—but the Colonel's for it. So I'll do everything possible to see it's well organized and properly staffed. I don't want to be blamed when it falls apart.

"What about that, Heinrich?" Mueller asked. "You believe Germany's lost the war?"

"Why would you ask me such a question, Sergeant Mueller?"

After that reply, Delman believed Mueller couldn't support Heinrich. His refusal to answer Mueller's question was too transparent. Yet the German probably believed his mentor would accept anything he said.

Not this time, Delman thought. I've got the Colonel's ear and Mueller knows it. If he showed favoritism—bigotry's a better name for it—he'd be found out. Revealed. Exposed.

"I'll talk to the Colonel," Mueller said.

It was the only option Delman hadn't considered.

"After all," Mueller said, looking at Delman, "the Colonel should make this decision. That's why he's an officer. He's been trained to make such decisions. He's been trained to handle the tough ones. It's not my job. I'm only an NCO."

CHAPTER II

"HEY," SERGEANT PERRY said, "how about visiting your old barracks?"

Delman, kneeling, opening the supply tent's flaps as he was about to complete his daily fireman's duties, looked up into the smiling face of the exuberant, likable motor pool chief.

"Hey," Delman replied, "how about coming inside?"

Perry always greeted Delman effusively, but that was the way Perry greeted everyone. He was the compound's fun-loving optimist, always eager for the day to begin, its most colorful storyteller, and its most notorious womanizer.

His reputation became even more complex when he began the first of his monthly parties for kids. He said it was about time the camp did more than accept the largesse of the good people of Le Mans. They co-sponsored, with the Red Cross, weekly dances for servicemen. And the city also had a program that brought soldiers—mostly officers, Perry had to admit—into Le Mans homes on a regular basis.

So Perry, always the host, reciprocated for the camp. He convinced the owner of one of the local movie houses to make it available to Perry one Saturday morning a month, free of charge. With the help of the Army's special services, he obtained movies—mostly cartoons, Westerns and musicals—and found a teacher who provided on-the-spot translation. He got off-duty soldiers to be ushers. And, somehow, he also provided fresh, butter-rich popcorn for the kids that they greedily downed with cokes while they watched the films.

Clary, acting as one of the ushers, told Delman that Perry welcomed the kids in French no one understood. "But he was so happy," Clary said, "so funny that the kids couldn't stop laughing and applauding. Then he retired to the darkened booth with his young female projectionist."

"I'll warm up the tent for you," Delman said, as he led the compound's impresario into the cold supply tent. He placed paper, kindling, and firewood in the black stove, removed his double gloves and lit the paper. Within minutes, heat began to displace some of the tent's frigid morning air.

"Great!" Perry said.

Looking into his smiling face, Delman knew his presence, whatever the reason, would warm up the tent faster than the firewood. Yet, much as he was drawn to the man, he remained suspicious. Why had he stopped over? To get to know Delman better since they'd both be on the convoy? To show that NCOs were NCOs, regardless of their length of service, regardless of their backgrounds?

Delman didn't think so. He watched the smooth-pated sergeant remove his gloves and rub his hands together close to the stove, its kindling now crackling, its damp logs sizzling.

"This is terrific," he announced, smiling again at Delman.

How could he be suspicious of such a cheerful character? But he was. In fact, he doubted if Perry's appearance was as spontaneous as it appeared. His visit could be a ploy he engineered with his fellow military careerist, Sergeant Mueller.

Delman was certain that if the Colonel asked Mueller and Perry why they continued to go after Delman, he could repeat their answer, verbatim. They'd say, in ringing unison, "Delman should've been court-martialed for slugging two POWs. He got off too easy." But Delman believed that was their rational reply reserved for questioning officers. Their real resentment was emotional. They felt Delman got a light sentence because he was a college celebrity, a Jewish football star.

Delman knew there was even more that rankled them: the Jewish football star had become an instant NCO. An overnight metamorphosis. Mueller and Perry, like the good Army regulars they were, despised such sudden changes, such "battlefield" promotions. What right did these newcomers have to get instant authority? And the extra pay that went with their stripes, especially when regular Army men had to struggle for theirs, moving up gradually, first one stripe, than two, then three or more, and over several years.

The fact that instant NCO Delman had lost his stripes as fast as he got them didn't compensate, didn't lessen their anger. They were always sure that he would find a way to get them back. When he did, their resentment had to double.

So they were out to get him, and Delman was certain that was why Perry was now warming his hands in the supply tent. He and Mueller knew there wasn't much time left before Delman's sentence would end and he would be out of their control. Delman could see the two veterans sitting over their beer in the NCO club plotting his misery. He could hear crafty Perry suggest some surprising scheme and cautious Mueller responding, his cackle rising as Perry's inspiration grabbed him.

"Okay." Delman said. He decided he'd be Perry's straight man, reply to his earlier invitation. "Why should I visit my old barracks?"

"Pussy," Perry said. "We've been enjoying pussy there almost every night. Right on your old bunk. Up to now, I've been going to Tours. Got a friend near there, Lippy, who's got a harem of girls. I mean nice girls who are so deprived. But now I stay here."

Count on Perry for an original approach, Delman thought, right in keeping with his favorite subject. Up to now, Delman's sex life—or lack of it—was off limits. But leave it to Perry to exploit Delman's most serious deprivation.

Sneaking women into the compound wasn't new; what was new was using sex to increase Delman's angst. Since his most recent punishment—confinement to the post—he hadn't seen a woman. Unlike the Americans, the Belgian security forces wouldn't dare bring a female to their barracks.

Perry, perpetually horny, had to know how abstinence kept
Delman on edge, how frustration turned each irritation into a
major trauma. The only surprise, thought Delman, was that his
enforced state hadn't been exploited earlier. But Perry's graphic
description of mass sex taking place on Delman's straw-filled mattress had to be phony, a clever fiendish device to add to Delman's
discomfort. His bunk was right out in the open. Even though pri-
vacy was virtually non-existent for enlisted men, Delman couldn't
believe his barracks was the site of an open orgy.

Then why create such a story? Why try to get him to visit
his old barracks? He had his answer the same morning.

"You're falling down on your job, Delman," Sergeant Mueller said as soon as he entered the supply tent, only minutes after
Perry left. "I checked some latrines this morning and they were a
mess. You're so busy with your crazy convoy, you're not paying
attention to what you're supposed to be doing."

Delman knew the latrines were clean. Maybe they didn't
smell like roses but they had a distinct pine aroma. He had
worked at them, just as Mueller was now working on him to
get him to argue.

"I'll get to them right away," he said.

"Not good enough," Mueller replied. "No more wandering
around this post. No more freedom of movement in this camp.
From now on when you're not working here, in this supply tent,
you're confined to your barracks and the mess hall. Period."

It was too neat, Delman thought. Perry's lewd description of
what was supposedly happening on his old bunk immediately
followed by a new Mueller mandate. Tempt the kid, Delman
could hear Perry say, build him up, get him excited, then squash
him. That was their game, Delman realized. Their obvious purpose was to get him to disobey their latest order. They wanted
to be able to go to the Colonel and say his convoy commander
had sacrificed his command. He had disobeyed orders. He had
to be replaced.

Delman realized they had to be desperate to try something

so outrageous, so transparent, so dumb. He wasn't going to be intimidated by such an obvious hoax. He'd simply follow all their orders, without complaint, and know that it wouldn't be long before his revenge, his convoy, would be on its way.

The day before he was confined to the post, the restriction before the last one, Delman had met Jeanne Barr. Clary's girl had arranged a double date but at the last moment plans had to be changed because Clary had to pull guard duty.

"See her anyway," he told Delman. "You won't regret it and she's looking forward to meeting the famous football star."

"You sure?" Delman asked.

"Do it," Clary said.

"You are a friend," Delman said.

So, carrying flowers for Jeanne and a carton of Chesterfields for her parents, Delman rang their apartment bell. He was greeted by Jeanne, her older sister, Charlotte, her younger brother, Henri, and her parents. She introduced all of them as she buried her face in the flowers.

"I love them," she said, clearly delighted.

"And for you and your wife," Delman said, giving the cigarettes to Mr. Barr, a large man as big as Delman, who was wearing a heavy turtleneck sweater and carrying a soccer ball.

"Thank you," he said, tossing the ball to Delman. "I like American cigarettes. We heard what a famous football player you are so we thought we would see for ourselves."

"What you call football," Delman said, turning the ball in his hands, and then throwing it back to Jeanne's father, "we call soccer. I've never played soccer."

"Glad to hear it," Mr. Barr replied. "Henri and I against you and the girls."

"Mrs. Barr?" Delman asked.

"Too cold and slippery for me," she replied.

"I hope your soccer's not as good as your English," Delman said. "I don't like to lose."

"I never lose," Mr. Barr said.

"You can use any part of your body to move the ball," Jeanne said, "except your hands."

He looked at her. In spite of her heavy jacket, she looked feminine and pert.

"I give up," Delman announced.

They played on a nearby street that seemed devoid of cars and people. Bushel baskets were the nets. Delman thought they made up their own rules as they kicked, blocked, passed, and laughed at his confusion. At the end, exhausted and tired—mostly from laughing—he surrendered, even though his team was ahead.

Mrs. Barr had hot chocolate and cookies waiting for them. "Winners receive second helpings," she decreed, "before our concert."

After second servings for everyone, the Barrs brought out their instruments. Charlotte and her father had violins, Jeanne a viola and Henri a cello while Mrs. Barr sat at their grand piano. They played Mozart. Delman was impressed. He couldn't hear any mistakes, and he enjoyed their enthusiasm. Following his long applause, they returned to their hot chocolate and he put down his cup to go to the piano.

"What do we have here?" Mr. Barr asked.

"More Mozart," Delman said.

He played a sonata he'd studied and even surprised himself that his memory, if not his fingerwork, held out. Long applause plus several "bravo's" continued after he returned to his chair. Jeanne bent over and, with great care, kissed him on each cheek. She left to help her mother and sister clear the dishes.

Before the family said their good-byes, Mr. Barr told Delman, "You're everything Jacques said you were and more. You must come again."

Delman, left alone with Jeanne, didn't linger.

"My truck will leave soon," he said. "This is the best night I've had in Le Mans. I forgot what it means to be with a family. Thank you."

She opened the door for him and he didn't know if he should kiss her. She raised her head so he carefully reached around her and let his lips lightly touch hers. He felt her body move toward him so he opened his lips, slowly flicked his tongue and let his hands slide down to encircle her hips.

"No," she said, pulling away, startling him.

"I'm sorry," he quickly apologized.

"You go," she said, pushing him through the door that was hurriedly closed behind him.

Standing outside their apartment, he was appalled at what he had done.

"Damn," he said aloud, "I didn't mean to do anything. It just happened."

He ran to the truck feeling like an awkward high school kid leaving his first date, unsure if his behavior was as offensive as he feared. He had to see her again but he decided he had to talk to Clary first.

*　　*　　*

Right after he graduated from high school, Mueller enlisted in the army. He couldn't wait to escape his broken family, his domineering mother, his weak father, his crazy brother, his promiscuous sister. If he hadn't enlisted, he'd be stuck working in the family gas station and he would never leave Springfield. He didn't know what he wanted—only what he didn't want. No filling gas tanks, cleaning windshields, checking oil. No crawling under cars. He hated working in the gas station with its constant gas fumes—reminding him of the smell of his house with gas always escaping from the stove—as much as living with his mixed-up family.

He was inducted at Camp McCoy and stayed there, learning how to be an MP. At first, he despised Army discipline. It was the same as home, always being told what to do, where to go, what to wear, how to act. Yet he enjoyed his classes—the

lectures and blackboards—and, most of all, the tests, because
he did well.

After a year, he had accepted the discipline. Others thought
for you. You were without responsibility. And, more important,
you were without your nagging, demanding, belittling family.
There were no obligations; no heartbreaks. He didn't write his
family and they didn't write him.

The Army was peaceful. There was no tension if you accepted its rules. And if you were as restless as Mueller, you
liked its mobility. Wherever you were sent—another camp,
overseas—you had your own space, your own food, as ordinary
as it was. your own clothes, as ugly as they were, and more free
time than you could use.

He enjoyed the Army's routine. You knew what you had to
do. Its demands were simple. What's more, you were rewarded
when you did something right. Mueller realized he'd never been
rewarded before—only criticized. He liked the rewards, he liked
the stripes. The more you had, the more money you made. And
Mueller discovered he liked money, spent little of it—except for
necessary items in the PX, necessary sex at brothels near the
base which he seldom left. He began to accumulate what he'd
never thought he'd have: his own nest egg.

He liked the safety of the Army base and he had no curiosity
to take him far from its comfortable confines. He would visit the
PX, eat a pint of chocolate ice cream at a time, enjoy a first-run
movie at the base theater, treat himself to a big Sunday breakfast
in the base's cafeteria.

Mueller re-enlisted again and again. He counted his days by
beer bottles, Army stripes, battle ribbons. He discovered how,
with a little effort mixed with a little savvy, you got ahead. Above
all, you had to be patient. More than anything, the Army demanded patience. And if you followed the rules—some unwritten
but there if you watched and listened—you progressed.

Mueller learned you didn't buck the system, including its
cosmetics. You made your bed so tight that a quarter dropped

on it would bounce. You shined your shoes, your brass buttons, your rifle, and you made the inside of your foot locker look like a well-organized department store. You showed respect for your superiors, especially the NCOs. They were to be emulated. Your goal was to become an NCO. NCOs had power but not the power of the officers, who were the elite, the show-offs, the college boys.

You learned to be careful. You stayed within regulations. No shortcuts without permission. No squeezing an extra hour for a weekend pass, no taking an extra day when you were on furlough. You cultivated the long view. Unlike short-term en-listees or draftees who would come and go—as the wars came and went—you were in for the duration. In twenty years, you'd be retired, living on your pension keyed to the pay received by the rank just below yours.

Finally. you did your best to avoid making decisions; you'd leave that to officers. If you were forced to make a decision, you'd do it with advice. You'd check regulations, check the wishes of your immediate superior. You'd check, check, and double check.

*   *   *

Mueller paced in the supply tent. In spite of his caution, he had to make a decision about the convoy; he had to select its drivers. He studied the stove as if he could find some answers there. Then he walked through the corridor of tents and, finally, back to his desk. He paused, waiting for some revelation. None came. He resumed his pacing. He needed to talk to someone, to discuss the pros and cons of each list, Heinrich's and Delman's. He couldn't wait any longer. There wasn't time. He had to make a decision now. Without advice. Not the way he liked to operate but, according to Bosworth, the Colonel was getting antsy.

What list of POWs was better—no, safer for Mueller—Hein-rich's or Delman's? The Colonel should've made the decision,

Mueller thought, but Sergeant Bosworth had told him again and again that Nelson expected NCOs to handle details.

Mueller wanted to go with Heinrich's choices. His solution, using POWs he knew and lived with, made sense. No surprises. Better control. And Heinrich in the convoy would be watchful, cautious, and under obligation to his mentor.

On the other hand, Delman's logic was irrefutable. If Heinrich was looking to escape, his list would be totally self-serving. Delman was smart. That's how Jews got along, Mueller thought, looking ahead, coming up with an approach that always seemed so obvious, so natural but, usually, was unexpected.

Mueller had to admit he often forgot that Heinrich was the enemy. POW was stamped on his clothes—and in his mind—but Mueller felt closer to Heinrich, a fellow German, a fellow Christian, than to clever Delman, American or not. However, if Heinrich did try to escape, and if his escape was facilitated by Mueller-approved drivers, the supply sergeant's career could be hurt. Maybe ruined. And how would he explain helping a German, maybe a German officer at that, although he refused to believe the rumors about Heinrich.

But if Mueller went along with Delman's selections, as repugnant as that would be, he'd risk nothing. He'd be out of danger. Delman was Colonel Nelson's boy and if his drivers proved inadequate, it would be Delman and the Colonel's fault, not Mueller's. He stopped pacing. He slumped at his desk.

"Shit," he said aloud, "shit, shit, shit."

Colonel Nelson, working at his desk, accepted Mueller's salute with a brisk touching of his fingers to his forehead. God, he thought, why do these regular Army types put so much stock in military folderol? They're worse than rigid clergy with their inflexible rituals, or at least they're not that different. Military rules and traditions become sacred. Especially to Army careerists. The salutes, the giving and accepting orders, the commands from on high, the obedience to superiors are all part of their religion—the Army.

When Perry or Mueller enter your office and you're slouch-
ing in your chair, they're in a sanctuary. Their stiffness continues
until you figure out what's wrong and tell them to be at ease,
sit down. But, unknowingly, you've stepped into their trap.
That's what they want to hear: your disdain, your blasphemy.
It marks you, if not as the enemy, as the thoughtless short-term
visitor, the civilian in military clothing, never to be trusted, the
unsophisticated laity. They gain a feeling of superiority.

"Sergeant Mueller, I want the convoy moving now," Nelson
said, "What's holding it up?"

"I've got my drivers lined up, sir," Mueller responded. "Sergeant Delman wisely picked POWs who don't know each other so
they won't try anything. Unlike Heinrich's candidates and . . ."

"Let's talk about Heinrich," Nelson interrupted. "I know
you want him on the convoy and you don't buy the rumor that
he's an officer."

"That's what it is, sir, strictly a rumor."

"Is he worth the risk, Sergeant Mueller? Also it gets a little
sticky, doesn't it, having a POW who's been bossing Delman
around installed as his right-hand man?"

Mueller paused for only a moment. Than he said, "Heinrich
will not be on the convoy, sir."

"How soon can you get it rolling, sergeant?"

"Day after tomorrow, Colonel."

"I'll see them off," Nelson said. "Make sure you inform me
of the time of departure. That's all, sergeant."

*   *   *

Mueller met Perry at the NCO club that night.

"You did good," Mueller said, putting down two bottles of
beer on the small, round table, "setting up Delman. Pussy on
his old bunk. I like that."

"Thanks," Perry said, taking a gulp. "I even told him about
Lippy in Tours. I talked to him. No sweat. I used your technique,

sending a letter to Lippy so he'd be prepared when I called. But we were too cute—trying to get Delman excited and then putting the screws to him right away. Bad timing. Too soon, too obvious. And Delman's smart. He's got to be on to us."

"Let him know we're on his case. He'll think a second time before he slugs another POW."

"Is that what this is all about," Perry said, "protecting POWs?"

"At least you're on the convoy," Mueller said.

"You mean Heinrich isn't?"

Mueller took a long swig from his bottle. "I didn't push the Colonel to get Heinrich on the convoy as long as you're on it."

"You mean the Colonel didn't want Heinrich on it," Perry said. "That's it, isn't it?"

"The Colonel wants me to let him know when the convoy's ready to take off," Mueller said. "I think he's got some sort of ceremony in mind."

"The convoy won't be a cakewalk" Perry said, "but I gather the Colonel thinks it's important."

"We're forgotten here. Nobody wants POWs. Ever take a look at my empty supply tent?"

"What else is new? How come you're not with Denise tonight?"

"I'm not like you," Mueller said. "I got to recharge my batteries now and then."

"That line I gave Delman," Perry said, "about the pussy on his old bunk? You know, it's true. Every fucking night."

Mueller lifted the bottle to his mouth. He took another swig and gave a long look at Perry. Then he laughed.

"Don't you wish," he said.

CHAPTER 12

"YOUR LONG HORSE face," Willy Wanger said, "is even longer than usual."

The wizened barber, wrapped in his dirty blanket, sat in his bare bunk above Heinrich.

"What's wrong?" Wanger continued, leaning down. "Wait, I know. Your comrade, Sergeant Mueller, took care of you again. He cut back on your secret rations. Am I right? Or is it the heavy underwear he gave you—it's squeezing the blood out of your balls?"

If you didn't look at the malicious grin on Wanger's flaccid face—if you only listened to his incessant ravings—you might even laugh. His voice, his delivery, his off-color remarks reminded Heinrich of a loud-mouthed vaudevillian whose coarse humor was based on ridiculing—often insulting—his amused but uncertain audience.

To appreciate Wanger, you had to be broad-minded and strong-stomached. He'd say anything. Heinrich thought he was the most vulgar, obnoxious human being he'd ever met, smut incarnate. Even in his carefree pre-war days, Heinrich had been uneasy with dirty jokers like Wanger. He never had the ability, or the willingness, to step back from himself and laugh. He took himself and everything else too seriously, too personally, too intensely. What had his father always said to him?

"Loosen up, Josef. Don't be a prig. No one likes a stuffed shirt. Enjoy life."

So Heinrich tried not to be offended by Wanger's filthy drivel and his blathering sarcasm. Heinrich kept repeating to himself, "He's trying to be funny." But, in spite of the license he granted

the scurrilous barber, he couldn't consider him anything but
gross and repulsive, like a Jew.

"My list of drivers," Heinrich said, "to drive the convoy.
It was rejected."

Wanger, his hands in his tangled, unwashed hair, pretended
to weep. "My heart breaks for you, poor Heinrich. With all
your ass-licking, all you wound up with was shit. What a bad
taste that must have left in your busy mouth. And you think
my breath stinks!" He laughed uproariously. "But I bet you're
still in the Jew's caravan."

"I've also been rejected." Heinrich replied.

"How tragic," Wanger said. "No wonder you look like a
lost sheep. No, a lost horse, your face dragging in the dirt. Don't
tell me you're surprised? Did you really think they'd go with a
POW's list? Hell, in spite of your high-and-mighty airs, in spite
of what Sergeant Mueller thinks of you, you're a lousy POW,
you're the enemy."

Heinrich had to rid himself of Wanger. He had had enough
of his nasty boorish prattle. Heinrich pushed himself away from
the barber—it was like rising from a steamy, sticky, malodorous
quagmire—and walked between bedrolls and blankets and torn
cartons to the center of the tent.

"Those of you who I talked to about the convoy," Heinrich
called, waving his arms toward his gaunt body, "please, gather
around."

Slowly, the men he'd recommended as drivers ambled toward
him. They showed no spirit, no enthusiasm, no concern about
Heinrich's news, whatever it was. Apathetic, worn out, they
dragged themselves like wounded animals, as if their capture
had depleted their energy, drained their lifeblood.

"I did my best to get you on the convoy," Heinrich said,
"so you'd get some food and cigarettes and get out of this lousy
camp."

He tried to catch their eyes but most of them looked away,
or down, or through him.

"But what I did wasn't good enough. We're all off the convoy. They rejected me and they rejected you. I'm sorry if I built up your hopes."

No one said anything. Heinrich looked at the recent arrivals along with the long-time sufferers. They seemed indifferent to their rejection. It occurred to Heinrich that he was the only one who saw the convoy as an opportunity, a possible exit from imprisonment, and, at its worst, a brief but welcome break in the tedium of their enforced routine.

"Is there anything you want to say?" Heinrich offered.

"I've got something to say," a POW close to Heinrich replied. "If you got such an 'in' with the supply sergeant, get us some firewood."

"And another stove," a POW interrupted. "One that works."

"Get us some food," came a shout from a third POW.

"Yes," several other men shouted, chanting the word, "Food! Food! Food!"

It became louder, a chorus.

"You think we cared about the convoy?" one of the POWs said. "We only cared about the convoy because it meant food."

The chant began again, "Food! Food!"

"At least we're safe here," called a POW on the way back to his bunk. "The fucking convoy could be a death trap. I've been shot at enough."

The rest of those gathered around Heinrich nodded in agreement. Some laughed—cynically, disgustedly, more snorts than laughs—as they drifted back to their beds. Heinrich watched and then, disappointed in them and in himself, returned to sprawl disconsolately on his bunk.

It was clear, he thought: whatever he did, he'd have to do it alone. The rest of them would be satisfied to remain prisoners of the Americans for the duration. They'd freeze in their drafty, unheated tents, they'd chant "food, food," they'd continue to complain about everything. But they would do nothing to escape from their miserable but safe prison.

"You bastard," Wanger said, suddenly serious, sliding down from his upper bunk to sit next to Heinrich. "All you ever think of is yourself. You've gotten extra clothes, extra rations, even a mattress cover you stuffed with straw so you didn't have to get slivers on your ass from these rotting wooden slats."

He pushed his face so close to Heinrich's that he felt the spray of Wanger's angry spittle and smelled the acrid odor of his empty belly coming through his non-stop mouth.

"You ever think I'm starving?" Wanger asked. "You ever think that even a lousy can of beans would help? All you think about is Josef Heinrich, high-ranking officer in disguise, intent to do his duty for the Fatherland."

"Shut your mouth!" Heinrich whispered.

"Everybody knows you're an officer!" Wanger said, more loudly. "You think you're fooling anyone? Did you see how they all came over when you gave them the word? You think they'd act that way for an ordinary POW? They were taking orders from their superior."

"Bullshit," Heinrich said.

"Maybe you've got the Americans hoodwinked," Wanger continued, "but not us. And if you don't start taking care of me, I'll make sure the Americans learn who you really are. And don't think I can't do that. I can and I will if you don't do more than think only of yourself. That's a promise. And won't that put a crimp in your secret escape plans. Won't that make your protector Sergeant Mueller think a second time about taking care of his ass-licking POW. Believe me, I'm not making idle threats. Ever think that I cut the hair of American NCOs and officers every day? Move your head down so I can tell you my little secret."

Heinrich didn't move. So Wanger raised himself up to press his dripping lips against Heinrich's ear.

Wanger whispered, "I'm on Sergeant Delman's list to be

a driver. That's right. I was cutting his hair and he wanted to know if I could drive a truck. So Wanger the barber'll become Wanger the driver. And there's more. I gave him the name of other POWs who could be drivers. Including Sacher."

"Sacher," Heinrich said. "Sacher the racer? He's here?"

Heinrich recalled newspaper articles about Sacher that dissected his popularity. What gave him such appeal? Part of it was that, in many ways, he seemed no different from any other lower middle-class German. The crowd liked his regular-guy personality, his cockiness, and his daredevil courage. In spite of his car's occasional mechanical failures, he always seemed to have a game plan that was composed equally of surprise maneuvers and last-turn wins. Always modest, he never took sole credit for his team's success. He made sure everyone recognized he was competing in a team sport and, above all, it was the team—not Sacher—that deserved credit.

"Delman listens to me." Wanger backed away from Heinrich's ear but continued to whisper. "That's right, me, Wanger, I'm now Delman's confidant, his trusted source for all the dirt about POWs. I told him about Sacher and he got Sacher to drive in his convoy because of me. So if you don't start paying me attention—and getting me some rations—I'll give Delman what he'd love to get, confirmation of the rumor that you're really a fucking S.S. officer."

Heinrich didn't believe anyone was on to his pose. But now, whether Wanger was lying or not, something had to be done. He had to shut down the whining, babbling barber whose humor had turned vicious. Wanger could hinder, maybe even prevent, Heinrich's ultimate escape. His constant yapping had to have some effect. Wanger was no longer only an annoyance. He was a danger. Stealing Heinrich's soap was the beginning, a minor misdemeanor. Now Wanger was capable of committing a capital crime, squealing to the Americans. And his first offense, which started it all, as trivial as it was, still rankled as much as this latest threat.

That memory propelled Heinrich's hand into his mattress. He rummaged through the mass of dried stalks and found nothing. He couldn't believe it. Where was the cloth that contained his soap? Slowly Heinrich rechecked his mattress' innards, inch by inch.

Still no cloth, no soap; Wanger had done it again. The shards of processed fat, so carefully wrapped in a cloth and hidden in the straw-filled mattress cover, were gone.

Heinrich had had enough. He had kept hoping that the barber would change, that he'd stop his whimpering, that he'd work with Heinrich, not against him. Instead, he'd become more obstreperous, more deceitful, and more threatening now that he, if his claim could be believed, had a direct line to Delman.

Heinrich had to put himself first, his escape first, his country first. He had to be as ruthless as he was when he decided to postpone his marriage.

He had been engaged to Elsie Meyer, a spectacularly beautiful, notoriously headstrong and constantly busy actress, the daughter of one of Austria's most famous artistic families. Her father was an acclaimed concert violinist, her mother, a former prima ballerina, was the director of Vienna's most successful ballet troupe.

When Heinrich announced that he was going to enlist, that he had to join the Wehrmacht—"it's time I do more than give lip-service to my beliefs"—Elsie responded quickly. "We'll get married right away," she said.

"No," Heinrich said, "we'll marry later, after the war. What if something happens to me?"

"Nothing's going to happen to you," Elsie said in her usual assured, assertive manner. "Besides, we both want a family. The war may go on longer than we think. We'll marry before you complete your training."

"After my training and after the war," he said, "when we can make sensible plans."

Thanks to his father's influence, Heinrich trained near Berlin where Elsie shared an apartment with another actress who was often away so Elsie and Heinrich lived together when he did not have to remain on his base.

Heinrich was sure they must have talked about their future, or at least Elsie talked, humorously, incessantly, about their upcoming marriage and their life together. But all he could remember was their rising passion—everywhere, exhaustively, constantly, creatively—from the moment they entered her apartment in the evening to their early departure, exhausted, the next morning.

When Elsie's mother told him, "We must make wedding plans now," he knew Elsie didn't take his objections seriously. Why would she? For so long she had heard Heinrich's talk about enlisting but never doing it; why should she believe he wasn't, once more, giving only lip service to delaying their marriage?

How to oppose her without hurting her? He told her mother he wanted a small wedding, instead of Elsie's plan for a large one. He said he wanted it at his parent's Berlin apartment, not in the massive ballroom Elsie had chosen in Vienna. He opposed everything Elsie wanted, hoping he could bring her around to his way of thinking. But she refused to take his objections seriously.

"Aren't we wonderful together?" she said. "It will be even better when we're married!"

Frustrated with Heinrich's obstructions, Elsie's mother wrote to his parents: "Please let me know your schedule and Heinrich's. I'm eager to complete plans for the children's wedding as soon as possible."

Heinrich felt pressured. Elsie's mother had become as forceful as her daughter. Even his parents made light of his protests, "the normal fears of a young man about to take on the responsibility of a wife." He had to initiate some dramatic action to postpone the wedding.

There always had been rumors about the heritage of Elsie's parents. Creative people always faced the suspicion that somewhere in their history, there were Jewish ancestors. Heinrich, seeing his ploys to postpone the marriage discounted, was desperate. He hired a private investigator to explore the background of Elsie's family and checked with him daily, urging speed. "I need your report within the week."

The investigator saying, "My research is fragmented at best," concluded that "It's possible the Meyers—if you go back far enough—are Jewish."

Heinrich confronted Elsie with the report.

"Is it true?" he asked.

"Is it true you're investigating my family?" she replied. "Why would you even consider such an awful thing? You're a fucking bastard!"

"You're a fucking bitch," he countered. "I found your diaphragm in the bathroom. Is that your plan—to get pregnant and force me to marry you?"

"How could you think such a thing?" Elsie replied, "First, your investigation and now this accusation! What are you thinking?"

"I'm thinking of what I want," he replied, "and what I want is to enter the Wehrmacht unencumbered. I want to fight for my country, not worry about my wife. Don't you understand that if I'm married, I won't be the soldier I must be? You'll make me too careful, too reluctant to take risks. I'll be thinking of what I owe you instead of what I owe my country."

She was shocked. But it was not the shock he anticipated. Instead of pleading with him, throwing her body against his to remind him of the passion he'd be without, she attacked.

"To investigate my family," she said, "to accuse me of trying to trap you and now saying I'll stop you from being the soldier you should be! Josef Heinrich, you're nothing but a stupid, pompous ass!"

She struck him across his face. He was startled, overwhelmed by her words, suddenly full of guilt but, at the same time, angered by her slap. He struck her back.

"You pig!" she screamed. She tore at him, scratching his face, ripping his shirt, kneeing his groin.

He pulled Reichsmarks out of his wallet and threw them at her.

"This is all you get from me," he screamed, "you ungrateful whore! I don't want to see you again."

She never called him, nor did she write him. Yet he was certain Elsie would return to him, that her fury was an act, a pretense, a way to hide her disappointment. She would realize she couldn't live without him and that he loved her; after all, he never released the damaging report about her family.

*   *   *

"Maybe I can get you a can of beans," Heinrich said to Wanger. "Look, meet me in the latrine in one hour. Let's check our watches. Now. One hour. And don't let anyone see you. I'll try to find a can of beans for you. Don't lock the latrine door. Just wait there for me."

"You'll bring me a can of beans," Wanger said.

"I'll try," Heinrich said, "in one hour."

Heinrich went to the latrine, locked its door, and pulled up the floorboard. He removed it. He saw it contained several nails. He feared using that end against Wanger's head. There'd be too much blood. He turned the board around so he could hold the other end, but he thought the board could slip and the nails pierce his skin. He would have to risk the nails going into Wanger's head. He leaned the board against the inside of the latrine, away from the door.

He quickly slipped outside to wait for Wanger, who soon came trudging into the darkened outhouse. As Heinrich had instructed him, Wanger didn't lock the latrine door. After waiting a few minutes, Heinrich backed into the latrine and pushed the eager, trembling Wanger aside to latch the door.

At that moment, Heinrich considered strangling Wanger. It could be done silently. Or could it? As frail as Wanger was, he was a fighter. He would fight to save his life. He might even

escape. And, escape or not, he might scream, although the latrine was far enough from the tents so it was unlikely he would
be heard. But if his scream wouldn't be heard, neither would
the sound of the board hitting his skull. Heinrich decided his
original plan was the best: he'd use the floorboard.

"My beans," Wanger demanded. "I'm starving. Give me
the fucking beans."

Without hesitation, Heinrich found the board, raised it
above his head, and crashed it against Wanger's skull. Heinrich
caught Wanger before he fell to the ground and quickly moved
back from the body. He didn't want the dead thief's blood stain-
ing his boots.

But was Wanger dead? Heinrich wasn't sure. He checked
Wanger's pulse, his breathing. Heinrich still wasn't certain. He
could hit him again but he didn't need more blood. He knelt
next to the body, put one hand over Wanger's mouth; his other
hand pressing Wanger's nostril's together. For several minutes
Heinrich remained immobile, listening to his own breathing.

Finally, he rose. He realized Wanger had been starving. He
felt practically weightless in Heinrich's arms. He shoved him
into position so he could slide him, feet first, into a mattress
cover he had secreted under his overcoat. He used rope to tie it
securely above Wanger's bloody head.

Heinrich rubbed his boots again and again over the blood
that had dripped on the latrine floor. He replaced the floorboard.
He slowly lifted the door's latch, and checked to make sure no
one was around. He lifted the bound body and easily carried it
to the nearby woods, where he kicked aside wads of leaves near
a clump of birch to deposit Wanger on the bare ground.

He pushed more leaves and branches around the corpse. He
knew the body would be consumed by wild dogs that scavenged
the area. All that would be left would be a skull, bones, and the
torn remnants of the mattress cover. He doubted Wanger would
be missed. His empty bunk would be quickly filled by one of the
new POWs. But if anyone noticed Wanger was gone, he would

assume the emaciated barber, like so many of the POWs, had died and that his body had been removed during the night.

If, somehow, his skeleton was found, it would be disregarded. Another war casualty, another body. There was no way, Heinrich was certain, anyone could trace Wanger's death to him. Besides, he thought, he'd be away from the compound shortly, he'd escape. He had to manage, somehow, to get on the convoy. But, if that proved impossible, he would find another way out—and he was certain he'd find one before anyone found Wanger.

CHAPTER 13

"Jan. 11, 1945—I finally have a genuine friend, Jacques Clary, one of the Belgians. He's not like my draft-dodging boyhood pal Larry Bayer but who is? Larry writes he's so exhausted with twelve-hour days in a tank parts factory he's down to bedding only three girls.

"He doesn't fool me. He exaggerates his prowess to add to my frustration. And it works. Especially now that I'm confined to my barracks—except when I work and eat. But even when the convoy takes off I won't be free.

"We're all POWs. The Colonel's controlled by the TPM, Mueller and Perry by their prejudices and pensions, the Belgians by their culture—military and non-military—and Heinrich by his history and hatred.

"I try to take the long view. Larry is safe and comfortable and a guilty observer. I'm a guilty participant, more careful than before (who likes to clean latrines and shine boots?), but still rolling with my lot, trying to save lives but the wrong ones.

"Ask me in a year—assuming I'm around—if I'm glad I'm Delman instead of Bayer. Now, you do what you have to do and you get by as long as you keep the anger at bay.

"POWs keep pouring in. Little do they know we're getting our revenge with leaky tents if any at all, bad sanitation, minimum medical care, and starvation rations. Weather keeps our planes grounded so the Germans continue their unexpected offensive."

* * *

Delman, shouldering a musette bag, walked briskly toward the
motor pool. Trucks, jeeps and command cars—along with the
vehicles in Delman's convoy—were lined up outside the pre-
fabricated building that, in spite of the cold, had its large, sliding
doors slightly cracked to combat the smell of oil and gasoline.
The Belgian guards, Clary and Trabert, had lined up the convoy's
drivers on the side of the building away from the searing wind.

Delman was dressed in layers: winter underwear, two shirts,
a fatigue jacket under his mackinaw, and double gloves. He
stood in front of his drivers. They had to be as sad and smarmy
a menagerie of bedraggled soldiers as he'd ever seen. They may
have passed Sergeant Perry's driver's test but Delman wasn't sure
they'd last through the convoy's first day. They looked exhausted,
skeletal, some wobbling as they tried to stand at attention. All
of them were trembling from the cold.

Delman was afraid they'd fall asleep once they got comfortable in their warm cabs. And, even awake, would their reflexes
respond to the rough roads? Hell, Delman thought, they could
be trying to avoid a pothole and smash into one of the over-
turned vehicles pushed to the side of the road by the advancing
Allies.

He'd have to discuss with Perry how long you could expect
such exhausted men to drive the big trucks before they started to
have accidents. One mishap could lead to another and, eventually, Delman could see his entire convoy piled up like a crashed
train, telescoped into itself. He knew they'd want a break every
ten minutes, but they would have to survive for at least two hours
at a stretch or the convoy wouldn't return until the war ended.
Delman realized he'd already made a serious miscalculation: he
hadn't considered how his drivers' deterioration, their obvious
frailness, would slow down his trip.

Eight regular drivers and numerous replacements waited for
his inspection. This was the first time he had seen them since
he signed them up in their frigid work stations. Then, they'd
been seated, working over their benches. Now, standing up,

they appeared more emaciated than he remembered, their faces alarmingly thin, their eyes bleary and sunken.

And some of those on his original list—he remembered one fast-talking barber who gave him the names of other candidates, including the race-driver Sacher, his prize catch—weren't around. Perhaps they hadn't survived their incarceration during the mean winter. Delman glanced at Clary and could see he shared Delman's low assessment of their crew.

"Some master race," Clary said, approaching Delman. "They're a disgrace to their uniforms. And I remember how they always looked down their haughty noses at the rest of us. Now they're the misfits, willing to do anything for a scrap of food. Except for that racer."

Delman knew the guards, both university students from Brussels, looked forward to their new assignment, a welcome respite from their monotonous daily duty. He also knew they enjoyed annoying the hated Germans, especially those whom they considered weaklings, those who went out of their way to cooperate, exchanging servility for a cigarette butt.

The guards were too severe, Delman thought, too ready to rough up the POWs if they were slow to obey. Delman believed in discipline but not in cruelty. He was afraid the guards' mistreatment could backfire, that they'd aggravate the POWs into rebellion. He respected the Belgians' attitude but he didn't want them to be the cause of an uprising, regardless of how minor it would be considering the sad condition of the Germans.

"Show you're in control," Delman told Clary and Trabert, "but don't pick on the POWs. No poking your rifles in their bodies just to show you're the boss, as much as they deserve it."

"They're swine," Clary said. "You can't trust them for a minute."

In spite of his youthful, almost pudgy appearance and his baby face, Clary was tough. He nodded as Delman spoke in favor of showing some restraint but his behavior, and that of Trabert, told Delman he had to watch his guards as closely as he watched his drivers. But, at the same time, he listened to their warnings. He realized the POWs, as feeble as they appeared, were still dangerous. He knew if anything went wrong, he'd get the blame. And he was talking about lives, not just the Germans, but the guards and Perry.

"Frisk them," Delman ordered, "and pile up their packs."

They all carried everything they owned with them. They were afraid they'd be moved without their paltry belongings or that they'd be stolen if they were left behind when they were on the convoy. But they could be hiding weapons and ammunition in their tattered packs.

"They'll take what they've got on their backs," Delman ordered, "nothing more. See their stuff is covered so they can retrieve it when they return. If you find any POW with anything even resembling a weapon, he's out."

The guards went down the line, carefully patting down each POW.

"What about this?" Clary asked.

He handed Delman a homemade nail file. The German who had it protested vigorously, claiming the small metal instrument wasn't a weapon.

"Back to your cage," Delman ordered.

The POW stood his ground, whining his innocence. Delman studied the nail file. He held it in his hand as he'd hold a dagger, a bayonet. The file was small and had little heft. But it was long enough to punch out an eye, sharp enough to rip open a throat. Delman thumbed the complaining POW out of line. To replace him, Delman signaled for one of the substitute drivers, one of the stand-ins he ordered to be available. Six candidates, less experienced than the first-line drivers, pushed each other to get to the front of their line. Delman was convinced they weren't thinking, as he was, that the convoy would mean a reprieve from the camp, even briefly. Nor, like a Heinrich, were they thinking of it as a way to escape. All they wanted, Delman believed, were the beans and cheese and cigarettes.

A weak shoving match broke out. Elbows grazed jaws, boots banged shins. As frail as they were, the POWs struggled to display their toughness. Punches were thrown. Names called. They thought the more combative they appeared, the better their chance to replace the rejected driver.

"Break it up," Delman impatiently shouted.

Clary tried to separate the POWs, too busy hitting or defending themselves to pay attention. They were lost in the struggle. Finally, Trabert fired a shot into the air and the fighting ceased. The POWs backed off. Delman, disgusted at the brawl, pointed to the least belligerent POW.

Sergeant Perry rushed from the motor pool at the sound of the gunfire. "Everything okay?" he asked.

"We're just about set," Delman said. "I was thinking of putting one guard in the first truck, another in the middle and let you bring up the rear. You'd act as a guard and you'd also be able to help any truck that dropped out."

Perry exploded. "I haven't been in charge of our motor pool for a year to be turned into a fucking security guard. Here I am, going out of my way to help you, giving driving tests, getting people to replace me while I'm away, and you're saying I should sit with a loaded M1 on my lap to guard your crazy parade! Hell, I'd drive a truck before I'd ride herd on your brainwashed POWs."

Delman was startled that the usual easy-going Perry would erupt over his job in the convoy. Maybe he saw it as another demotion and he had had enough of those. Delman knew he couldn't waffle or he'd instantly risk reducing his authority, his credibility. Perry gave him an out, his last frustrated peroration. Delman decided to take him literally.

"Okay, you'll drive," Delman said. "I'll put a guard next to you. The second guard will be posted in the center of the convoy. I'll cover the front."

Delman realized Perry was taken aback so he jumped in with a question to change Perry's focus, to derail his accelerating temper. "What do we do to fight our drivers' exhaustion?" Delman asked. "Tell me. They look beat."

Perry paused. Delman wondered if the surprisingly touchy Army regular would erupt himself right off the convoy.

"Take it slow," Perry said. "Don't act like you're the Red Ball Express. And make plenty of piss stops."

Delman nodded. Perry could be the most important person on the convoy or the most dangerous. Delman figured that, as Mueller's friend, Perry would like to see the convoy flop, another disaster promoted by the mistaken Colonel who was taken in by the crafty Jew. But, like Mueller who never stopped thinking of his pension, maybe Perry would be cautious and think a second time before he provoked a fight with Delman.

He turned to the POWs. "The new driver who was chosen as a replacement," he said, "you'll be with me. You'll drive the jeep. Sergeant Perry will drive the last truck."

Delman took a long look at his bedraggled, miserable crew, the deliverers, the salvation of their fellow prisoners. If he had known the sorry state of his rescue operation, he wondered if he would ever have pursued it.

"You guys look great," he announced. "You make a man proud. Board your trucks."

*   *   *

As soon as he believed his convoy might become a reality, Delman had started to scrounge for what he thought was necessary cargo, supplies to enable the convoy to be self-sustaining. He squirreled away tents, blankets, and clothes in back-of-the-tent crates. When the convoy was "go," he revealed his stash to the supply sergeant.

"Pretty sure of yourself, weren't you?" Mueller said. "What you've got's okay for starters. I'll put together the rest, including gasoline, and stuff you could barter."

"Barter," Delman knew was a euphemism for "bribe." Sup-

ply requisitions had produced nothing. So, according to Sergeant
Mueller, liquor and cigarettes would be used to get the supply
depot cadre to give Delman tents, blankets, clothing, and rations.
This was based on the assumption he could convince them that
accepting loot for supplies for POWs wasn't against the war
effort. Or against their high moral standards. They still might
be laboring under the misconception that it was the military's
job to kill Germans, not to save them.

"I don't get it," Delman said to Mueller. "You're telling me
we have to bribe to get supplies. Who owns them? I thought
supplies were for all of us, even the lousy POWs if we want
them to survive so that, eventually, we could exchange them for
American POWs. Is this the way your army operates?"

"My army, your army, every fucking army," Mueller said,
"and it's no different from the way any business operates. You
take a customer to dinner. A bribe? You give gifts to customers
on holidays. A bribe? One customer leads you to another. You
thank him with baseball tickets. A bribe? Hell, that's reality.
That's the way business is conducted."

"Hold on, Sergeant Mueller. With all due respect, it's not the
same. In business you're dealing with your own products, your
own company, your own money. That may seem a minor point
but it's the crux of the matter. Your Army's confused. The Army
didn't earn the supplies they control. They were given those supplies by taxpayers. No officer or NCO, wherever he is, has the
right to sell what he doesn't own to the highest bidder."

"Wrong," Sergeant Mueller said. "You've got a lot to learn
about the Army, Delman. Once you control anything, it's yours.
Possession is one hundred percent of the Army's law. If you've
got someone eager to get what you have, it's yours to sell. And
you sell it to the highest bidder. If the Red Ball Express is bidding for supplies we want, you've got to bid higher. That's why
you'll be traveling with beaucoup barter."

Delman thought of discussing the concept—whatever was
sitting in your truck or your tent or your barracks was yours,

yours alone, to sell, to trade—with Colonel Nelson. But, like everyone else, the Colonel probably took such Army chutzpah for granted. If you can't stop it, you accept it. Delman guessed such exchanges of U.S. Government-issued property had been going on since the Revolutionary War. Old George probably got his wooden teeth in exchange for rifles he appropriated.

Maybe the taxpayer could force a change if he knew what was happening but he was blind-sided. Delman, not wanting to endanger the convoy, sighed, felt guilty, and surrendered. Like all sleazy soldiers before him, he went along. Corrupt? Absolutely. But, as Sergeant Mueller said, that was reality. That was the way business was in conducted in the Army.

Delman checked his mackinaw's inside pocket. It was there he carried copies of supply requisitions—listing what the camp requested—that had been submitted several times but never filled; an order signed by Colonel Nelson that verified an NCO had authority to command the convoy, and a map in a water-proof envelope, marked with the supply depots west of Le Mans and the best routes to reach them.

The departure morning turned cold and wet. Hail mixed with snow pelted the waiting POWs, Americans, and Belgians. But the miserable weather didn't deter a sprightly overcoated Colonel Nelson, trailed by Sergeants Bosworth and Mueller, who arrived to see the convoy off.

Nelson was buoyant. If Delman didn't know better—he remembered the photos of the Colonel's family—he would have thought Nelson had recently got laid. Or was it that Delman was so horny, thanks to Perry, that getting laid, except for the departure of the convoy, seemed the only reason for cheerfulness on such a drab, cloudy, miserable day?

He hadn't seen the Colonel this positive, this confident, for weeks. It was contagious. Delman responded with his own smile and a crisp salute that was returned with equal brio.

The Colonel's visit, Delman realized, was meant to be a tes-timonial to Delman's leadership. The Colonel didn't want any

POW to fail to recognize that Delman, in spite of his notorious history and his youth, had the Colonel's blessing.

His visit also gave the lie to the Fuehrer's claim of German racial superiority. The convoy's pure-bred Aryan drivers would not only be working for mongrel Americans but they'd be led by the worst mongrel of all, a Jew.

"Take no unnecessary risks," the Colonel told Delman. "Even Germans are more important than your trucks. If it comes to a choice between the two, opt for lives. That's an order, Delman."

"Yes, sir."

"You've got two weeks to pull this off, no more," Nelson continued, "and I'm confident you'll be successful. If this wasn't such a fucked-up army, you'd be a lieutenant. Unfortunately, all I can promise is that I'll keep trying to get you one of those little gold bars."

Forget the bar, Delman thought, getting out of this prison's reward enough. Although, he thought, he wouldn't mind becoming an officer, getting his own liquor ration and enjoying better living conditions. But leading the convoy was all he wanted now. He didn't like the two-week timetable. One week, two weeks, three weeks—more or less, what did it matter? Why a deadline? You're short-sighted, Delman wanted to say. He thought that the sooner he returned, the sooner he'd take out another convoy. That was motivation enough. But he didn't want to argue. He just wanted to leave.

He saluted and said, "Thank you, sir."

"One more thing, sergeant," the Colonel said. "When it comes to the trucks, turn to Sergeant Perry. He's a first-rate mechanic. You can trust him."

He's about as trustworthy as Heinrich, Delman thought. But he'd already tried to cultivate him by asking for his advice. Delman thought the Colonel, who made few mistakes, was sometimes mistaken about people. He trusted Sergeant Bosworth, he trusted

Sergeant Mueller and now, it appeared, he trusted Sergeant Perry.

"Finally," Colonel Nelson continued, "I've got something for you, Delman."

The Colonel turned to Sergeant Bosworth who presented him with an ornate wooden box. He lifted its cover and withdrew a German Luger.

"Take this with you," Nelson ordered. "It's poetic justice. It'll impress your drivers. I hope you don't have to use it, but if you do, it's oiled and loaded. It's my gift to you, sergeant. Sort of a replacement for the commission I haven't been able to get."

Delman was moved. Maybe the Colonel, if not a friend, was close to it. Or was he simply feeling guilty about sending Delman on a questionable, dangerous mission? Certainly the Luger would show Perry who was in charge and, Delman thought, maybe that's one of the reasons for Nelson's gift. The famous weapon also possessed some obvious irony, some obvious symbolism.

When the Colonel left, Delman made a final check of his convoy. He studied the sad-sack drivers in their cabs, the guards Clary and Trabert, and disgruntled Perry in the last truck. Delman moved a few steps back to address his group.

"We'll be driving in two-hour stretches. Stay close to the truck in front of you. I don't want any other vehicle getting into our convoy. Stay awake. If you feel sleepy, honk. We'll stop the convoy. I don't want a single accident. If you fail to follow my orders, you'll be returned here. That's a promise."

For the first time in the Army, Delman was in command. He thought of the time he'd completed basic and was passing in review in front of the camp's general. The day was bright, his unit paraded to a Sousa march, and Delman felt proud. He waited for that same feeling to return. He felt the same excitement but concern had taken the place of pride.

He stepped into his jeep and tapped his driver. He wondered which POWs were planning an escape but then he remembered the Luger on his hip. It, along with his carbine, helped.

He turned to watch his trucks. Finally, he thought, I'm out of here. At least no more demeaning daily chores. Instead, he had more serious responsibilities, the lives he now controlled, including that of his newest antagonist, Sergeant Perry.

CHAPTER 14

PERRY MOVED HIS well-muscled shoulders up and down, swiveled his large, shaved head on his short neck, and cracked his thick fingers, one by one, still keeping one hand on the steering wheel. He unsuccessfully tried to dodge the holes in the uneven road as the convoy pulled out.

"Sorry about that," he said to the guard next to him as the truck bounced. "It's been a while since I navigated one of these fuckers. I repair 'em, I don't drive 'em."

He knew the two-ton, six-by-six, ten-wheel truck would rattle his bones before the convoy was over. Well, at least he wouldn't be alone, although he wasn't sure the kid next to him spoke English.

"What's your name?" Perry asked.

"Private Jacques Clary, sir."

"Drop the 'sir.' We reserve that for officers. I'm a sergeant. How old are you?"

"Eighteen, sergeant."

He took a good look at the baby-faced Belgian and realized, with a shock, that he was old enough to be the kid's father. They're all kids, he thought, as the convoy started to move away from the motor pool.

Even more discouraging was the fact the convoy was being led by another kid, Delman, who, in spite of his size, was an inexperienced teenager. But he also was smart and not averse to sticking it to Perry if he thought the motor pool chief was out to get him. And Delman hadn't wasted any time. Perry hadn't wanted to start up with Delman but he was damned if he was going to be a guard as well as the convoy's mechanic. He spoke up when he had to, when Delman tried to show his authority.

So Perry became a driver.

Either way, he thought, he was going to be imprisoned in a bucking, rough-riding truck for longer than he wanted to be. With its POW drivers looking and acting half dead, it was going to be a long, long haul.

From the first time he had heard about the convoy, Perry had thought it was a mistake, a disaster in the making, a loser from start to finish. And here he was busting his ass, carrying a repair kit with plenty of parts, bringing up the dumb caravan's rear, watching for stragglers, real and phony.

He was where he didn't want to be. All because the Colonel had a severe case of the guilts. According to rumors, all he ever wanted to do was to get the fucking war over as quickly as possible and, to him, that meant being an infantry officer.

Sergeant Bosworth told it best. The Colonel wanted combat but his timing did him in. A qualified officer was needed to take over this camp just when his class graduated from OCS. Who better to handle the hard, lousy job than a tough Chicago cop?

When Nelson heard he might be transferred to the Military Police so he could run a POW camp, he yelled and screamed that he'd enlisted to kill Germans, not baby them. His superiors were so impressed with his noisy outburst that they immediately put the transfer through along with a hefty promotion.

It didn't take Nelson long to explain what he said, or at least what he meant: "I never equated babying the Germans with burying them. Something got lost in the translation. I wanted to kill the Krauts but I didn't want to murder them." What the Colonel meant was that it was okay to kill the Germans in combat but not in a POW camp. Not by starving them, not by failing to provide decent shelters and not by denying decent medical care.

What shit, Perry thought. He believed Ike had it right. He said the only good German was a dead German. Who cares how he was killed? The convoy was a reach, Perry believed, an impossible one. Somehow, Delman, this college teen, this varsity football player—big deal!—hit the Colonel with the convoy concept when he was feeling his guiltiest and couldn't get supplies through normal channels

Concentrating too hard on the Colonel's dilemma, Perry let his truck drift and, almost too late, heard the Belgian yell, "Watch out, sergeant!" Perry stomped on the brake and the clutch and hurriedly down-shifted. The nose of his truck almost collided with the tail of the one in front of him.

"Thanks, kid," Perry said. "I owe you one."

The trouble was, Perry realized, Delman was leading the damn convoy in the wrong direction—away from the entrance. Instead of taking the exit road near the motor pool, he opted for the cruddy road inside the compound. Relieved that he hadn't hit the truck in front of him, Perry started to laugh.

"Don't you see what Delman's doing?" he said to the Belgian. "He's making a fucking farewell tour of the cages. He's taking a bow for his great rescue mission even before he's left the fucking camp."

Finally, the convoy exited the compound.

"About time," Perry muttered. He took a deep breath and pushed back in his seat. The convoy, now out of the camp, still was crawling along. Perry had urged Delman to take it slow but he didn't mean for him to limp along in his lead jeep. At this rate, the trip to Tours, usually a few hours, would take a full day.

But the kid would learn. Perry had to admit he liked Delman's attitude; receptive, tough, and full of hate for the Germans. No pretending what he wasn't. Perry thought he was the same. He didn't hide what he was. He was proud of his reputation. He was out for a good time and the Army, as he boasted to all the new draftees, was made for it. You had to know how to handle the Army. You had to know how to turn its rules in your favor, how to carry out orders for your own benefit and still do your job while you kept pompous officers off your back.

But it was Mueller, Perry thought, who went by the book and

got to be a master sergeant. Yet he was relegated to an empty
supply tent with a staff of two, an arrogant POW and a departed
Delman. Twice-demoted Perry, with only three stripes, supervised a ten-man motor pool and was now seeing the countryside.

That's what Perry liked about the Army. It was unpredictable. It was irrational. If you stayed out of trouble, it was yours
to manipulate, maybe not to control, but to tailor in your
favor. Just as he intended to manipulate Delman. In the Army,
Perry believed, you could make your own world and it could
be a safe one. If you played it smart, you could avoid serious
problems, you could avoid combat, and you could even avoid
accountability.

Perry thought of Army life as a game, like a pinball machine.
He was always ready to tilt it, Mueller seldom was.

Delman had pulled the convoy over to the side of the road.
At least the kid had listened. He wasn't rushing. Just as well.
The POWs had no endurance. Half of them looked finished.
And they'd just started.

When they stopped, Perry almost slid his truck into the one
in front of him. The road's slick, narrow shoulder, nothing but
frozen earth and sloping at that, was dangerous. He pushed open
his truck's heavy door and practically fell out of the cab. Too
much sitting in the same position for his old legs. He'd have to
figure out how to move around more, to stretch his legs while
he was driving. He didn't want to look as old as he felt.

"Stay here," he told Clary. "I'm going up ahead to see what
our intrepid leader's up to."

Delman had spread a map on his jeep's hood and signaled
Perry to join him.

"Here's the route Sergeant Mueller marked," Delman said,
tracing the red line with his gloved finger. "First, Tours. We're
not that far from it. Then, depending what supplies we get,
Angers and Rennes."

Perry leaned against the jeep, pulled out his pack of cigarettes and offered one to Delman who shook his head. Perry

tapped out a Camel. Delman thinks he's Patton, Perry thought, assembling his forces to rout the enemy. War. That's what it does to the young. Gives them a high, a moment of excitement, of importance. As bad as everything is, they're learning, it's new, it's an adventure. That's how "glory" got mixed up with war. As if what Delman's doing will make a mark, will be remembered.

But, Perry thought, what am I doing that will be remembered? That's why he thought his philosophy—enjoy every day, don't take yourself too seriously, play the angles, take some risks—made more sense than Mueller's cautious, go-by-the-book shit.

"This convoy," Perry said, "it's the biggest thing in your life, isn't it, Delman? Your first command. You're finally where you're supposed to be, leading your own hand-picked outfit, taking it to the enemy."

"Some hand-picked outfit!" Delman laughed. "A bunch of POWs, alert, strong, eager for action. Hand-picked Nazis, that's what they are. What more could you ask for?"

Perry smiled. "You know, kid, you may have a future."

"Kid." It reminded Delman of his father's nickname, "The Gambiner Kid," after the small village where he was born, the youngest of nine children. Gambin was in Poland, near the Russian border. Like many small border towns, its population fluctuated wildly, depending on what country ruled it. Finally, with his grandfather leading the retreat, the Delmans—Americanized from their Polish name—fled Gambin to escape the Russian army which regularly swooped in to force males to replace soldiers killed in one clash or another. The Delmans, along with their shtetl's other Jewish families, had had enough and left for America.

The Russian army's regular rampages left a mark on Delman's father. He developed a lifelong fear of the military. He would see a uniform, hear a bugle, even watch a military parade and freeze or shake, reacting physically to a childhood past he could barely recall.

When the U.S. entered World War I, his father was drafted. A high school graduate (the first in his family) with a useful specialty—he was men's clothing buyer for Mandel Brothers, one of Chicago's largest department stores—he was given three stripes and assigned to the Quartermaster Corps at Fort Sheridan. Just as quickly, he was dispatched overseas and transferred to the infantry. With little training, he was given an Einfeld and thrown into combat. He spent four months recovering from his wounds. He was discharged with a permanent limp, his left leg two inches shorter than his right.

He applied for a disability pension but his claim was rejected. According to the records, he hadn't been wounded. The Army claimed he had spent his entire service career in the Quartermaster Corps at Fort Sheridan.

Like his father, Sandy Delman distrusted authority, knew it was unreliable, often cockeyed. Especially his father's authority. That's why Delman disregarded his father's warning about the Army. "Go in the Navy if you have to," his father advised, "but avoid the Army, at any cost."

Now, as he stepped into his jeep to lead a convoy driven by POWs, he reconsidered his father's other favorite declaration: "All armies are crazy." At least the old guy had that right.

The convoy, finally picking up speed, approached the outskirts of Tours. It was getting dark. The Belgian guards had warned Delman that if the POWs were going to try anything, it could happen when they entered a city. There'd be more traffic, more buildings, more crossroads. All would suggest to the drivers—if they had any inclination to cause trouble—more opportunities for escape. It would be easier for them to make a run for it, to cause confusion, maybe even to find places to hide.

Delman checked the frigid countryside and saw no one eyeing the convoy. He wondered what the French would make of POWs driving American trucks. They were used to the Red Ball Express hurtling down their roads but they'd never seen a convoy like Delman's.

Suddenly a tractor, with two farmers aboard, broke into the convoy and, just as quickly, left to turn into a side road. If the tractor hadn't departed so rapidly, the convoy could have been divided; a truck could have escaped before Delman or a guard realized what was happening. He wondered if the same idea had occurred to one of the drivers. Perhaps he saw that neither Delman nor the guards reacted fast enough, that if his truck dropped far enough behind the vehicle in front of him, letting other traffic get in the way, the entire convoy could be disrupted, and escape was possible.

Delman couldn't take the chance that such an incident could take place again. He quickly ordered his driver to speed up and run the jeep next to the slow-moving trucks.

"Close it up," Delman called, rising in his seat, signaling each driver. "Get closer to the truck in front of you. Move up!"

He would have to make sure the guards kept the trucks close together. Then, he thought, I better count the trucks. They crossed a bridge over the Loire River and Delman was able to look back and count the trucks in his convoy. Six! It had to be a mistake.

He saw the road ahead was clear and ordered his driver to move to the side of the road. As the jeep stopped, Delman signaled for the convoy to continue: he had to make another count.

"Six," he repeated to his driver. "Get to the front of the convoy and look for a place where we can stop. I've got to go back and look for the two missing trucks."

The realization that his convoy was coming apart—that his first command could become a disaster—struck him with such force, that his body, like his father's when he regarded the military, started to shake. But, unlike his father, Delman wouldn't have any of it. He forced himself to stop trembling.

When the convoy halted, Delman jumped from his jeep and rushed along the convoy to make sure the trucks behind him were close to one another.

"Bumper to bumper" he called, running along the side of the road. "Turn off your engines."

He told Trabert, "Two trucks are missing. Including the one with Perry and Clary. I'm going after them. Don't let anyone get out or leave his truck until I return. Not for any reason."

Trabert nodded and Delman hurried to his jeep. All I need, he thought, were those farmers in their tractor returning to attack our POWs while they're taking a piss. Delman ordered his driver to make a fast U-turn and speed back to search for the missing trucks.

He guessed what had happened. A truck dropped out. But why? To escape, a mechanical problem, a flat tire? Then, Perry at the rear with Clary next to him, stopped to help. And rather than go after Delman, they opted to wait for him. That was what Delman wanted to believe and he wasn't going to consider any other possibility.

Within a few minutes he saw the missing vehicles off to the side of the road. He didn't see anyone in either truck. He grabbed his carbine and, as he approached, released its safety. He walked slowly and relaxed only when he saw Perry and Clary standing over a sick, heaving driver. His pants were stained. As Delman got closer, the POW's stink reminded Delman of the latrines he had cleaned.

"I'll show you the trouble," Perry said, leading Delman to the back of the first truck, its tailgate down. Delman saw the carton of C rations. Its flaps had been ripped open. Inside, hidden among its contents, were three empty bean cans.

"The son of a bitch couldn't control his hunger," Perry said. "He must've got into the rations before we started out."

Clary looked at the two American NCOs. "What's surprising," he said, "is that not more of them have done it. Breaking into the rations. They're starving, you know."

Delman knew. Food was in short supply. And it would remain that way even if the convoy returned full of supplies. The

Allies simply were capturing Germans faster than they could be properly housed or fed.

Right now, the problem was the sick POW. Delman looked at his drained face, his head drooping, his apparent shame. Delman's anger abated. The POW looked more like a defenseless victim than a conniving aggressor.

"He'll have to be punished," Delman said, almost regretfully, "and sent back to Le Mans. Put him in my jeep. I'll drive it and my driver can drive the truck."

"You should get another driver," Perry said. "As good as you are, don't consider driving a jeep yourself and leading the convoy at the same time. It can't be done. You'll be asking for trouble. The POWs will be on to you, believe me. Look, we're only a few hours from camp. Get another driver. Mueller can truck one here and take the sick son of a bitch back with him."

"Good idea," Delman said.

He knew it made sense and he wanted to trust Perry, but he also knew he'd have to be careful. Perry was Mueller's friend and their ultimate aim was to undercut Delman and show his crazy idea up as the disaster they believed it was.

But Delman did need another driver. Perry was right. Mueller could send one in a truck that would return the sick thief back to camp. But who would Mueller select? Heinrich?

Would the cautious supply sergeant risk sending him? It would be out of character. Unless, Delman considered, that all of this—the thief raiding C rations discovered by Perry—was part of a plot.

Unlikely? Sure, Delman thought, but it was unlikely he'd fall for Germans baiting him a second time. And it was unlikely he'd be punished by the very person who set him up—if Delman's suspicion was correct. Wasn't Mueller just the guy to say, "Let's take down the Jew"?

Delman had listened to career soldiers like Mueller and Perry long enough to learn they savored creating such convoluted traps. Why? For the hell of it. To break up the monotony of their everyday lives. Mueller and Perry, Delman thought, lived for such machinations.

But what other choice did Delman have? He needed another driver.

CHAPTER 15

HEINRICH HEARD ABOUT it from Rudy Keifur, a big, lumbering, recently captured, older POW, assigned to work with him in the supply tent. They were being marched from their cages to begin their day's work.

Sergeant Mueller was supposed to get three new POWs to work for him but he refused to accept more than one. "Three!" he complained. "I don't even need Heinrich. There's nothing to do. Why would I need another three? Maybe one more, that's it, assuming the convoy's more than an exercise."

A late winter blizzard attacked the camp. The POWs and a single guard, their caps pulled down over their faces, clumped through the thick heavy snow. The swirling gusts of wind threatened to uproot the creaking buildings, the suddenly billowing tents, the fences, particularly the new one erected by the engineers, that was already wobbling in the erratic storm.

Keifur talked to Heinrich. "You hear the latest about the convoy? One of the drivers couldn't control his hunger. Gorged himself on stolen beans and got sick. He's being brought back here and a replacement will take his place."

Suddenly alert, Heinrich said, "My last chance."

"For what?" Keifur asked.

"To get on the convoy," Heinrich said and then decided to risk it. "To escape."

"Don't wait for the convoy," Keifur said. "Escape from here. No sense waiting. Don't postpone it. Suicide's suicide."

Another big-mouthed weakling, Heinrich thought, another know-it-all defeatist. An older version of the ersatz soldier who uses cynicism to hide his cowardice. He's glad he's been captured.

And, as uncomfortable and hungry as he is, he's ready to suffer if he can sit out the rest of the war, rationalizing his fear, forgetting his duty. But, Heinrich thought, I'll use him. He'll help me devise the best way to get Mueller to drop his caution, change his character, make me his replacement. Keifur can help me.

"I have to figure out," Heinrich began, "how to get Sergeant Mueller to select me as the replacement."

"It's his decision," Keifur asked, "the supply sergeant's?"

They had left the group of POWs who worked outside their cages and trudged unguarded to the almost-obscured snow-covered supply tent.

"I never thought I'd have another chance to get on the convoy," Heinrich said. He pushed off the snow from the tent; it was so heavy, it took several swipes. "It's still the best way to escape."

Keifur answered with a sneer, a laugh. "There's no best way. Their guns'll still be trained on you."

"What did you do," Heinrich asked, grunting, removing his gloves, blowing on his hands so he could untie the ropes that held the flaps together, "what did you do before the war?"

"Owned a restaurant," Keifur said, helping Heinrich. "A restaurant and a beer garden. Always had more people than I could handle. I was going to enlarge it and open one or two more when the war started."

"You're a little old for this," Heinrich said.

"Too damn old," Keifur said. "That's what I told them."

"You were working in a mess hall . . ." Heinrich started to ask.

"When the Americans overran us," Keifur said, finishing the sentence. "First artillery, then planes and, finally, the fucking tanks."

They got the ropes loose and slowly rolled up the flaps. This was Heinrich's new job, opening up the tent each morning for Mueller, now that Delman was where Heinrich wanted to be—on the convoy, out of the camp. Keifur imitated Heinrich's technique, carefully folding up another flap. He followed Heinrich inside.

"You get along with Sergeant Mueller?" Keifur asked, looking around the tent.

"He's German." Heinrich replied, "as German as we are. A German in an American uniform. The kind of German you'd feel right at home with in your beer garden. Guzzling beer. Singing songs. We play cards together once a week."

"So why didn't he put you on the convoy?" Keifur asked.

Heinrich pulled the flaps up higher, from the inside of the tent this time, and watched light drift into the tent as light seemed to drift into his mind. It became clear to him what he had to do: figure out exactly where Mueller was most vulnerable and then attack.

"Why didn't Sergeant Mueller put me on the convoy? Because he saw it as too risky. Delman came up with the idea for the convoy, so the Colonel chose him to lead it. And Delman worked for me. That was his punishment, to work for Mueller who turned him over to me. Delman's a Jew. He hates everything German. Mueller assured me I would be on the convoy as Delman's right-hand man. Except the Colonel didn't approve. You've got to understand Sergeant Mueller. He's a career NCO. As much as he may want to help me, he doesn't take chances."

"I know the type," Keifur said.

"I think he feels guilty," Heinrich said, "and I've got to play upon that guilt, enlarge it, make him feel so guilty he'll do anything to rid himself of the feeling. Including making me the replacement."

"What makes you think he feels guilty?" Keifur asked.

"He avoids me," Heinrich said, "he avoids making eye contact with me, he goes out of his way to keep his distance. He's feeling guilty. What else could it be?"

Keifur wandered around the tent, brushing off his overcoat, removing his cap, knocking the snow off it against his gray pants.

He seemed intrigued with Heinrich's dilemma.

Keifur's clothes looked familiar, Heinrich thought. Shabby, dirty, partially torn but familiar, like the officer's clothes he threw away and exchanged for the coarse uniform he found, that scratched and didn't fit but hid Heinrich's rank, aided his masquerade.

"Your clothes," Heinrich said, "they look good."

"Found them," Keifur said. "Some officer must've thrown them away. A little beat-up and snug but still better than the shit I was wearing."

"Sergeant Mueller knew I wanted to go on that convoy," Heinrich said, returning to the reason he was cultivating the blustery POW. "I didn't hide how much I wanted to be on that convoy."

"Maybe that's why you were left off," Keifur said. "You were too eager. Maybe he figured you were looking to escape. Why else would anyone want to go on the convoy?"

"Food," Heinrich said. "Food and cigarettes."

"But he knew," Keifur said, "you had food and cigarettes, thanks to him."

He's smart, Heinrich thought, he's enjoying himself, he likes to solve problems. He must've been a good businessman. He considers the angles, the details. He knows what's important.

"So what are you saying?" Heinrich asked.

"You have to have something else," Keifur said, "some other overriding reason to convince Mueller to select you as a replacement."

Heinrich found his ax and rubbed his thumb over its edge, testing its sharpness. He reached toward the logs Delman had piled up.

What other reason could he use to show Mueller why he had to get on the convoy? It had to be compelling, dramatic, a life and death reason. He concentrated—focusing on the problem—as he used the ax to draw long, thin curls from the log he'd selected. Keifur handed him a torn page from an old newspaper and Heinrich wrapped it around the shavings and stuffed it into the stove.

"I have to get on the convoy to save my life," Heinrich said. "Someone's trying to kill me and if I can't get on the convoy, if I don't get away from them, they'll kill me."

"Why?" Keifur asked. "Why are they trying to kill you?"

"I work here." Heinrich said, "in the supply tent. They don't know it's empty. They think there's food here and cigarettes and extra clothes and that I should share it with them. If I don't . . ."

"Now you're talking," Keifur said. "It's starting to make sense. He should stick you on the convoy to save your life. But why not just move you to another cage?"

"He's in charge of the convoy," Heinrich answered. "It's his. He controls it."

"That might work," Keifur said, "but what happens when you return from the convoy?"

"Chances are," Heinrich said, "I'd be put in another cage. My old place will be taken by another POW. That's why the drivers had to take all their belongings with them. They'll go wherever there's room."

"It's worth the gamble," Keifur said.

Heinrich struck a match and let it engulf the paper. He was so caught by what he was thinking—what Keifur had triggered—that he almost burnt his finger. He quickly shook the match out. He was standing still, listening to the kindling sputter and crackle when Sergeant Mueller entered the tent.

Heinrich quickly approached him. He moved close to the supply sergeant so Keifur wouldn't overhear their conversation.

"I heard you're going to select another driver," Heinrich said, "to replace the one who's being returned today. I must be the replacement driver. I know trucks, sergeant, I do, and I need to be on the convoy to get out of here. Could I show you now, before you make your selection, why it's important you choose me?"

"Not now," Mueller replied. "I've got other things to do."

Heinrich touched Mueller's arm. "Please. I'm not exaggerating. It's a matter of life and death that I get on the convoy. Please. Come to my cage with me now. It won't take long. And then you'll understand."

"Right now?"

Heinrich nodded. "Keifur can be trusted while we're gone. Please. It won't take long."

Mueller stopped to tell a guard that Keifur was alone in the supply tent as he followed Heinrich to the latrine in his cage. He opened its flimsy door, and pointed to the floor.

"You might be able to see where the floor was roughed up," Heinrich said. "You might be able to see where somebody kicked it and rubbed their shoe over the boards to hide the blood."

Heinrich had Mueller's attention. Up to now, the supply sergeant seemed confused, resentful at being pulled out of the supply tent to rush to a shit-stained latrine in Heinrich's cage.

"The day the convoy left," Heinrich said, "I was forced in here at gunpoint along with my closest friend, Willy Wanger, the barber who slept above me."

"Gunpoint?" Mueller said. "You're telling me your fellow POWs had guns?"

"One of the four POWs who forced us in here had a small pistol, a P.P.K.," Heinrich said. "They knew I worked for you. They thought I could get them food. They demanded food. I kept telling them there wasn't food, or much of anything else, in the supply tent. They didn't believe me. They threatened me. They said they'd kill me if I didn't bring them food. They brought me here—along with Wanger—as a final warning."

"The stink in here," Mueller said. "Let's go outside."

"They didn't waste any time once we got here," Heinrich said. "They held the pistol against Wanger's head. They killed him, just like that."

Mueller went back into the latrine. Heinrich pointed to the spot. Mueller dropped to his knees, removed his gloves, wet his fingers and ran them over the floorboard. He saw, below the dirt, dark red stains.

"Blood," he said, looking at Heinrich. "I can't believe it, Germans killing Germans."

"Over here," Heinrich said, leaving the latrine and leading the supply sergeant to a clump of nearby birch. Heinrich kicked aside branches and leaves to expose a mattress cover. He held open the end of it that had been ripped so Mueller could see what it contained.

"Christ!" Mueller said. "A fucking bloody head."

"Dogs must've gotten to it," Heinrich said. He slowly pulled the cloth over the torn body.

Heinrich followed Sergeant Mueller, his head lowered, as he walked slowly to the supply tent. Inside, Mueller paced while Heinrich added more logs to the fire in the stove. Keifur remained in the last tent.

"I caused that," Mueller said, "that half-eaten body, that bloody head."

"You?" Heinrich said.

"You should've been on the convoy in the first place," Mueller said. "If I had done what I should've done, the murder of your friend might never have taken place." He stared at Heinrich. "You're telling me it still could happen to you, aren't you? That's why you put me through all of this."

"They want food," Heinrich said. "They're starving. They think I could get it for them. They won't believe anything else, regardless of what I say. They'll kill me."

"You may escape them now, going on the convoy," Mueller said, "but what about when you return?"

"When the drivers left," Heinrich said, "they took all their belongings with them. When they return, they'll be put in different cages, where there's room, not necessarily the cages they left."

"So when you return," Mueller said, "you might be put in another cage. It's a gamble, isn't it. I could try to get you transferred to a different cage right now."

"Too obvious." Heinrich said. "You'd be showing your hand. Your favoritism would be obvious. But if I return from the convoy, my being put in a different cage would appear routine. I'd be like the others."

Mueller repeated, "It's a gamble."

"One I want to take," Heinrich said.

Mueller came close to Heinrich. He thought the sergeant was going to embrace him. Instead he paused and awkwardly patted Heinrich's shoulder.

"I'm sorry about your friend," Mueller said. "Get your belongings together. The truck'll be here soon."

*   *   *

"I'm not going to bother Colonel Nelson with my decision about the replacement driver," Mueller told Bosworth.

Mueller traced a stubby finger down his beaded beer bottle as he and Sergeant Bosworth sat in the NCO club that the two of them, along with Perry, had created although there were few NCOs in the camp.

"We didn't bother him about starting this club," Mueller continued, trying to convince himself he had done the right thing, "and he's never said anything about it. You told me he wants NCOs to exert their own authority, to make their own decisions, to come to him only when we're not sure what to do."

"He's got enough on his mind," Bosworth replied, "with POWs dropping like flies, without worrying about who drives in the convoy."

Mueller returned their empty bottles to the bar and brought two full bottles back.

"He keeps fighting the TPM," Bosworth said.

"Why?" Mueller asked. "Why doesn't he leave well enough alone?"

"He says we're not in this camp to kill the enemy," Bosworth said. "He says that's Nazi thinking."

"So what does he think we're doing?" Mueller asked. "Hell, why does he think we're not getting supplies?"

"Priorities," Bosworth said.

"Winning," Mueller replied. "Any way we can. The TPM's realistic. They want to win this fucking war. Who cares how you do it as long as you do it."

"You don't murder POWs."

"Not that again," Mueller said. "Killing's killing. No one will ever care what happened here."

Bosworth took a long gulp. "So what did you do?"

"I've sent a truck with the replacement driver," Mueller said. "I've sent Heinrich. The truck'll go where the convoy's spending the night, the Tours supply depot, and it will return with the sorry son of a bitch who broke into the rations."

"I thought you were smart not to have put Heinrich on the convoy in the first place," Bosworth said. "Why send him now?"

"He's earned it," Mueller said.

"You know what they say about him."

"I don't care what they say about him," Mueller replied. "I'm not going to be swayed by a fucking rumor. I'll make up my own mind."

"I'll tell you this," Bosworth said. "The Colonel won't like it."

"I know the Colonel won't like it," Mueller said, "but what I want to know is if the Colonel will do anything about it?"

Bosworth ran his fingers up and down his cold beer bottle. "Every morning he sees more Germans coming in—and every night he sees more going out, feet first. He's not going to worry about who drives in the convoy."

Chapter 16

"You're up early," Sergeant Bosworth said.

He placed the Colonel's mug of steaming coffee on his crowded desk.

"Too early," Nelson said, sipping it gingerly.

He had made the mistake once of complaining to Bosworth that his daily morning coffee was tepid. Now he knew it would scorch his mouth if he wasn't careful.

"Tell me, sergeant, what do you write your wife? Mine's always complaining I don't tell her what's going on."

"They don't really want to know, sir," Bosworth replied. "If you told them the truth, what really goes on around here, they'd say you were putting them on."

Nelson didn't pursue Bosworth's provocative remark. Instead, the Colonel picked up his wife's latest letter.

"Listen to this," he said. "'Confide in me and please don't write me about the weather. I don't care about the weather. I care about what's going on with you.'"

"I get that same letter," Bosworth said, "at least once a month."

"How about that entrepreneur of an engineer," the Colonel asked, "who left because we weren't giving him booze for his efforts?"

"Good for starters," Bosworth agreed.

"What else?" Nelson asked.

"The convoy," Bosworth said. "Germans, led by a Jew, driving American trucks. That's worth a few laughs."

Nelson took a long look at his lean first sergeant, his hair slicked back, a suave George Raft in uniform.

"Funny as hell," Nelson said.

He leaned back in his chair and rubbed his fingers over one of the pencils Bosworth sharpened for him. The Colonel showed a proclivity for sharpened pencils so Bosworth gave them his steaming coffee treatment: the Colonel received a fresh batch of pencils each day, their points sharp as needles. Everything Bosworth did had a get-even quality, a nasty, smart-assed edge.

"Then there's food and drink," Bosworth said, "another uproarious subject."

"Food and drink?"

"How the POWs are starving," Bosworth said, "but how our officers never fail to get their liquor ration."

"I can't tell you what a help you've been, sergeant."

"Any time, Colonel."

As he considered his first sergeant, Nelson's hand drifted to his bristly face. Like all of the officers and most of the NCOs, he no longer shaved himself, but visited the POW barbers. He noticed that they had upped the price for a shave. Now it was two cigarettes. Should he write his wife about that or would she ask, rightfully he knew, who's running the store?

He looked at the blank V Mail he intended to use. What should he write? He'd never been good at confiding, especially about himself. Nor was he good at even talking about his work, either as a detective or now, as a warden, undertaker and promulgator of crazy schemes. And what would happen if that craziest of schemes—Delman's crazy convoy—failed?

"Bosworth," he called. "Bring me everything I've written to the TPM."

He examined the file and realized that half of his notes had gone to the same person: his old OCS friend Nagel, now an aide to the TPM's commanding general. First, Nelson had sent a short memo—using the news that one of their fellow candidates had been killed in action—as a reason to resume their friendship. Nagel immediately replied with a brief, heartfelt note. Next, Nelson had sent Nagel a cartoon about the war—how women were now even acting as traffic cops—that his wife had clipped

from one of the Chicago dailies. Nagel hadn't replied right away
but later returned the favor with a cartoon that *his* wife had sent.
This prompted Nelson to suggest they should get together—to
swap more cartoons and stories—and Nagel agreed, but did
not set a time or place.

Nelson dated the V Mail to his wife and wrote, "I keep thinking about the last time we took the kids to the Oak Street beach.
Remember how clear it was? How we saw the Gary steel mills
across Lake Michigan? I love that beach. And that weekend at
the Wisconsin Dells. Especially that twilight Indian ceremony.
We've got to do that again."

Nostalgic recollections were not what she wanted. She
wanted facts, specifics, details. She wanted to smell the blood.
If he sent her an hourly report of his daily activities—maybe his
marked-up calendar pages—she'd feel better. He had considered
doing that, but she would never be able to decipher his hasty
scrawls, and, besides, his notations were too revealing: he didn't
want to parade his disillusionment.

He reread the last memo he had sent Nagel, mentioning British
reports that the Germans were killing Jews, gypsies and political
prisoners inside its POW camps. It took a few weeks for Nagel to
reply. And then he sent no memo, but only a poor aerial shot of a
German POW camp in Poland showing huge excavations. On the
back Nagel had jotted, "What do you make of this?"

Nelson studied it again. He had thought that it showed the
Germans were constructing one or more huge buildings for their
prisoners. But now, studying the photo, he realized he didn't
see any piles of prefabricated roofs or walls. Only the gigantic
hole in the ground.

"Christ!" he exclaimed. "It could be a mass grave. The
bastards could be slaughtering their POWs!"

He couldn't believe even the Germans would be that blood-
thirsty. There had to be another explanation. He looked at his
unfinished letter and stuffed it in a drawer. He'd finish it later. His
disgust with what he was doing—what he saw each day—was

making him more frustrated, increasingly restless. He left his desk and stood at his window. He couldn't concentrate on any single project very long, especially a letter home. Those took two days to write, sometimes more.

He wandered back to his desk, circled it, and then sank into his chair. He had learned about Mueller putting Heinrich on the convoy and wondered why he would take such a risk? Only one reason: Mueller didn't think it was much of a risk. He probably figured the Colonel wasn't going to start an argument with one of his NCOs about something as trivial as what POW drove in the convoy.

Nelson got up and went to the window again. He assumed the convoy, even if successful, wouldn't be able to bring back enough supplies. It was a typical back-of-the lines Army project, created out of frustration, producing little, going nowhere. And more convoys would face more problems as the Allies' advance continued. The front would get more supplies, his camp would get more POWs and, now needing more supplies for more POWs, his camp would get less.

That left him with a single option, the only one he hadn't tried. He'd confront the Theater Provost Marshal—commander of all U.S. POW camps—face to face. He'd do the unthinkable. He'd plead his case in person. No more phone calls to non-committal officer friends, no more requisitions that were never filled, no more sleepless nights because of an increasingly troubled conscience working overtime.

He called Bosworth. "Get Mueller over here."

*   *   *

Mueller got the thumbs-up sign from Bosworth when he passed the first sergeant's desk to enter the Colonel's office. So Mueller wasn't worried that his unexpected order to report to the Colonel was caused by sending Heinrich to the convoy.

With that out of the way, Mueller actually looked forward

to being called before the camp's commander. Anything was preferable to biding uneasy time in his empty supply tent or visiting the overcrowded cages. Each time Mueller saw them—as he did when he went inside for a shave or to check on one of the ashtrays he was getting made—he confronted one of the effects of war you didn't consider. The misery of existence for the least important survivors, the forgotten POWs, on both sides. What he saw—the lack of concern for the enemy—made him question his own career.

But then he thought it was to prevent exactly such indifference to suffering and to the ugly panoramas displayed in the cages—thousands of dehumanized men trying to survive in mud and cold and their own filth—that there was a military. Most people out there, and that probably included the idealistic Nelson, didn't realize the Army was, above all, a force for peace.

Standing in front of the fast-aging Colonel, Mueller couldn't resist going through the motions he knew drove the commander crazy. These civilians better learn—Mueller thought as he snapped and saluted and kept his eyes straight ahead—that all the folderol they hated unified an army, particularly when what it was doing seemed dead wrong.

"Sit down, Mueller," the Colonel said, so restless, so angry, so frustrated he had to leap up from behind his desk to look out the window, to pace a few steps and then return to his desk, facing Mueller. Finally, he understood the pacing of the big cats in the zoo cages.

"If I remember correctly, sergeant, you spent some time with the Theater Provost Marshal."

"Two weeks, sir, to help them get their files in shape. I know something about the Dewey Decimal System."

"We're going to Paris," Nelson said. "We're going to have a little dialogue with the sons of bitches who refuse to send us supplies. What do you think of that?"

Mueller didn't answer. He knew the truth would only exasperate the Colonel. He had to find out for himself that the power he enjoyed in the camp would not transfer to Paris. It would be a wasted trip. It would also be a dangerous trip. You don't confront your superior face to face when you know your prior attempts to get more supplies have failed. The Colonel was asking for trouble. But Mueller wasn't going to tell him that and he hadn't seen Paris for several months and getting away from the monotony of the camp, even for a brief time, would be a tonic.

"What I'm trying to figure out," Nelson went on, "is it better to make an appointment or just show up?"

"The latter, sir," Mueller answered, without hesitation. "If you called, they could order you to remain at your post."

"We leave at 0600 tomorrow," Nelson said. "Having my supply sergeant along with me will show them I'm serious. You'll drive. Arrange for a jeep. We'll drive back the same day. You know exactly where the TPM's located?"

"St. Cloud, sir, right outside Paris," Mueller replied. "I know exactly where it is."

"At 0600," the Colonel repeated. "That should get us there in mid-morning. Dismissed."

Well, what d'you know? The Colonel's starting to act like a colonel. Fast questions. No "thanks for your advice." Authoritative. Military. He's getting the hang of it, Mueller thought, but that didn't stop him from putting Nelson through another fast salute before he left.

Back in the supply tent, he telephoned his friend Sergeant Love. He was part of Mueller's NCO network and was in charge of TPM's files in St. Cloud. "Curt," Love replied. "Got the copy of your letter to the guys along the trail of your convoy. What's up?"

Mueller said, "Top secret. I'm coming your way tomorrow morning with my colonel. He's going to make a personal plea for supplies. I'll drop in if I can."

"It'll wind up being a face-off between two colonels," Sergeant Love said. "Your colonel and Pomerantz. Look, I got the stuff you wanted for Denise. In case we get together, bring your booze. Hope to see you."

*   *   *

Nelson barely noticed the empty recaptured city as they drove through it to TPM headquarters. It was another frigid sunless day. Speeding Allied vehicles—trucks, command cars, jeeps, plus a variety of sedans with special plates and flags—didn't reduce the grandeur of the handsome Parisian boulevards. But Nelson gave them short shrift; he was trying to think of the best way to confront his superiors.

They arrived at the guarded gates of the Military Police nerve center in St. Cloud. Blank-faced armed MPs rigorously questioned Nelson's lack of written orders. He bluffed his way past them and directed Mueller to park in front of the large tree-surrounded residence that could have been an embassy. It was huge and impressive.

Stopping to stretch after leaving his jeep, Nelson saw more camouflaged Army command cars with stars on their license plates. He climbed a long staircase to the entrance where armed MPs, sporting SHAEF shoulder patches, colorful braids, and gleaming white helmet liners, presented arms. Nelson snapped a return salute and checked to see if Mueller, who trailed behind, was suitably impressed.

Inside the three-story building, the rich marble floor and ornate plastered walls were polished and pristine. Some poor privates, Nelson thought, probably busted their asses daily wondering if this was why they were drafted—to keep the MPs' palace suitably scrubbed and shining. A tall staff sergeant manned a desk in a center alcove backed by Allied flags. A large oil landscape covered one wall and smaller framed artifacts— mostly heraldic insignias—climbed the wall along an adjoining wide staircase. Evidently, the Germans hadn't confiscated all French art.

The headquarters was too neat, Nelson thought, too immaculate, too Hollywood. It reminded him of a movie set from a World War I film. Any moment he expected to see an American general and a captured German general descend the staircase, arm in arm. He wanted proof that the war touched this unreal oasis. What's needed, he thought, is mud on the floor, feces in a corner, urine stains on the wall. The thought made him aware that he had to use the latrine and he realized this miniature palace probably came equipped with flush toilets, a forgotten blessing. If he could use one—after knowing only dank outhouses—the trip would be worth it even if his mission failed.

He told the NCO his immediate need was a bathroom and he was directed to one off the main hall. Inside, he was awed by its cleanliness, its bar of perfumed soap, its ornately framed floor-to-ceiling mirror and, most impressive of all, its glistening white flush toilet that the Colonel used with vast relief and unbounded pleasure. Like coming home, he thought, shaking off his last drops. After buttoning his fly, he joined Sergeant Mueller who was talking to the NCO. He rose hurriedly and stood at attention as Nelson approached. God, Nelson thought, we're all martinets.

"General Littleton," Colonel Nelson said, naming the TPM.

"As I was telling Sergeant Mueller," the NCO replied, "the General will be in conference all week."

"Major Nagel," Nelson said.

"He's with the General," the NCO said. "May I suggest Colonel Pomerantz? He's in charge of administration for POW camps. Third floor, Room 304, second office to the right of the stairs. I'll let him know you're on your way."

Evidently Mueller had told the sergeant the reason for their visit. Nelson had wanted to avoid Pomerantz, the officer who had stonewalled all his efforts to get supplies. Now, the Colonel had no choice. He took the stairs two at a time with Mueller struggling to keep up. On the third floor, Nelson thought he'd wandered into General Motors' corporate headquarters or, more appropriately, Citroen's. Except for the sudden rattle of typewriters, the plush headquarters was quiet. Nelson was struck with its size as well as the Army's obvious attempt to maintain its appearance. Offices that in pre-war days must have been bedrooms and sitting rooms, were carefully numbered.

As Nelson approached Room 304, he began to understand why his requisitions, his memos, his arguments, went unheeded. Headquarters personnel were isolated from the war, physically emotionally, totally. How could they avoid it, working in this plush building near Paris? How could they be expected to grasp the intensity of Nelson's desperate need?

Did they even know that an overcrowded hell-hole of a stinking camp, full of traumatized, starving, lice-ridden POWs, was only a few hours away? In their insulated world, they probably thought the war's misery was confined to the front, to combat, never to the behind-the-lines sinkholes that the TPM, in all its wisdom, supervised with little care and complete indifference.

"Colonel Nelson," a corporal said from his front desk inside Room 304, "Colonel Pomerantz's expecting you. Please go right in. If you wish, I'd be happy to show Sergeant Mueller around."

"Stick close, Mueller," Nelson ordered. "I may need you."

Inside, the two colonels shook hands. Nelson knew Pomerantz by reputation. Nagel had told Nelson that Pomerantz nurtured an unrelieved hatred for the Germans and, after learning about the walking skeletons in concentration camps, was determined to give them back what they'd given his fellow Jews. With the TPM's tacit approval, he had cut back on the already meager supplies for POWs under U.S. control.

"I was wondering when you'd show up," Pomerantz said. "I've been keeping a record of your memos." He waved a thick file he had on his desk. "You've been busy, Colonel. I know you're trying to do your job . . ."

Nelson interrupted. "Except my job isn't to kill POWs.

That's what I'm doing. That's what you're doing by withholding supplies. Perhaps you should visit us and see, firsthand, how your policy works. It's a death sentence."

Arthur Pomerantz, Nelson knew, had been one of Patton's best officers. After earning several Purple Hearts, he had been transferred to the TPM on temporary assignment. He wanted to return to Patton. Wide-shouldered, square-headed, with his short haircut and paratrooper boots, Pomerantz resembled the Prussians he hated.

"You're putting me on," Pomerantz said. "Right? You don't like these fucking Germans any better than I do. You know as well as I do that we're not here to pamper them."

"I need rations," Nelson said. "I need shelter halfs, I need blankets, I need clothes, I need medicine. I've stopped counting how many POWs die every day and I can't even estimate how many more will die if I can't get more supplies for my POWs."

"You mean your Nazis," Pomerantz boomed, rising behind his desk.

Nelson stood up to face him.

"Some of them," Nelson replied, "but do you really think the children and the middle-aged we're now capturing are . . ."

"Nazis?" said Pomerantz, finishing the sentence. "If they're not, they're no better than Nazis. Maybe they didn't 'Heil Hitler' all over the place but they didn't denounce him, either. Did any of them do anything to stop him?"

"Did any of us?" Nelson asked.

Pomerantz glared.

"I understand," he said, returning to his chair, "you've sent a convoy, driven by POWs, to scrounge supplies."

"A gamble," Nelson said. He pulled up a chair and sat down. "Maybe a gesture. I don't know. I had to do something. Perhaps to prove that I'm not as bad as your Nazis."

"I like it," Pomerantz said. "It's a gutsy call. But your convoy could be doomed. Since deGaulle led his Free French through

Paris, they think they're free to kill any German."

"There are armed Belgian guards and armed GIs on that convoy," Nelson said.

"You think they'll have a chance against a countryside full of armed French looking for revenge?"

"I sent out a convoy, doomed or not," Nelson said, "because you gave me no choice. You think you know what's going on in POW camps. But you don't. Spend a few days with me. You'll see we're also running concentration camps."

Pomerantz leaned back in his chair. "What you need—maybe what you want—is a transfer. Isn't that really why you came here?"

"To what outfit?" Nelson asked. "Graves Registration? That's where I excel."

"So what do you want?" Pomerantz asked.

"Visit my camp," Nelson said.

"Your camp!" Pomerantz mimicked. "Your camp's not alone. I've visited POW stockades all the way to Metz. Supplies are going where they're needed—to our troops at the front. And don't give me any of your 'holier than thou' shit. We do what we have to do with what we have. And I don't have to feed and clothe fucking Nazis."

Nelson stood up. "That's it?"

"Unless you want out," Pomerantz said, "out of your unit, away from your Nazis. I'm serious about a transfer. You look spent, tired. Maybe it's about time you left your concentration camp."

It was tempting. Perhaps for the first time, Nelson realized he was as much a prisoner as any of his POWs. And now, unexpectedly, he'd been given a reprieve, a way out, a chance to escape. But he would carry the guilt of his leaving, letting some other sucker suffer his burden. Accepting Pomerantz's offer would be the ultimate cop-out.

For a moment, Nelson thought of turning around and departing without another word to Pomerantz. But he knew

everyone had his own agenda, everyone was fighting his own
war. Nelson reached out his hand to Pomerantz.

"Thanks for your time, Colonel."

"Holier than thou," Nelson thought as he walked downstairs. That got to him. He had admitted that his supporting
Delman's convoy might have been a gesture. And, admitting that,
wasn't he as wrong as Pomerantz? And why, Nelson thought,
did I bring Mueller with me? To show him how compassionate I
am while I send off a convoy that Pomerantz says is doomed?

Downstairs with Mueller, Nelson knew he was risking lives.
He cared little about the POWs but he did care about Delman
and Perry and the Belgian guards. SNAFU, he thought, that's
what it is and I'm stuck in the middle of it.

CHAPTER 17

IT WAS DARK when Heinrich, stiff and cold, his worn musette bag over his shoulder, climbed down from the truck. One of the Belgian guards—unnecessarily rough, Heinrich thought—hurried him into the unheated, dimly lit Quonset.

Before he could adjust to the sudden change from the noisy, bouncing vehicle to the silent, cylinder-shaped hut, he was in front of Sergeant Delman. Heinrich's former charge, the celebrity football player who refused to be cowed by Mueller's efforts, seemed more amused than angry that Heinrich, Mueller's surrogate, was the replacement driver.

The perpetual anger that creased Delman's face when he was sweeping the tent, cleaning latrines, and starting fires was, if not gone, at least diminished. He looked taller, stronger, more intense. It must be his confidence, Heinrich thought; he had what he wanted, his own command, his own out-of-camp project that he controlled without anyone interfering.

"Why is it, Heinrich," Delman asked, "that I'm not surprised to see you?"

The POW had spent the drive from the Le Mans camp to the Tours supply depot considering this meeting, wondering if Delman would still resent him as much as Mueller still resented Delman. And would he see Heinrich as a pawn—or as a manipulator? Maybe Delman was so impressed with regaining his stripes, so self-satisfied because his idea had been accepted, that he didn't care about the POW who replaced the POW. Now the target of Delman's unwavering scrutiny, Heinrich believed that was unlikely. Delman was invigorated, reborn, in charge. Overseer of every detail. He was relishing his first command

and savoring the reversal: he was now the boss of the POW who had been his boss.

Heinrich knew what he did now—and how that was perceived by Delman—was all-important. If he could get the convoy's commander to reduce his resentment, his suspicion, his surveillance might also be lessened. If the opposite occurred, he would have failed to exploit his last best chance to escape. Above all, he had to strike the right balance—not too subservient, not too proud—to convince cynical Delman he wasn't dangerous.

"I'm here to drive," Heinrich said, "nothing else."

"I'm here to get supplies," Delman replied, "nothing else, unless someone tries to escape. Then we shoot to kill."

"I won't give you any trouble," Heinrich said.

A few days ago you hustled for me, Heinrich thought, now I'll hustle for you. He glanced into the silent hut with its sleeping bodies snoring on narrow cots in spite of three lit bulbs dangling from the ceiling. Security foremost, over everything else, the Americans' constant preoccupation.

He thought: why couldn't you be generous and erect a few of these machine-made barracks in your POW camp? You're so Germanic, so close to us in thought and behavior, yet you crowd us into leaky, unheated tents or freezing uncovered mud-holes when you have these pre-fabs coming off your manufacturing lines like chips off a log.

"Search him," Delman said to the guard.

Heinrich raised his hands and held his temper. The round-faced Belgian padded him up and down with unexpected force. First the front, then the back. Next, Heinrich was ordered to lower his hands and give the Belgian his jacket. He felt its pockets, its lining, its collar and, finally, hurled it back at Heinrich.

"Your pockets," Clary said. "Empty them on the ground."

He used his rifle like a pole to unfold the crumpled handkerchief, move the greasy comb, open the folded money. He reached down to pick up the leather wallet and withdrew its packet of photos. He examined each snapshot and then sailed them, one by one, a kid tossing cards into a hat, except he was aiming at the wallet on the ground.

"Pick up your stuff," he ordered Heinrich.

He did as he was told, but slowly, he wasn't going to be hurried by the officious soldier as he gathered his photos and replaced them in his wallet. He knew the guard was trying to get him to react, but he refused to be coerced by, of all people, a petty Belgian private.

"Your bag," Clary said. "Hand it over."

Heinrich presented his officer's musette bag. He had thought earlier of discarding it—fearing it would suggest what he didn't want to reveal—but he saw ordinary soldiers in officers' garb carrying equipment they were never issued. Everything became everyone's on the battlefield, if you weren't queasy about taking from the dead.

So he kept his own musette bag. Now the guard held it at arm's length, like a repugnant dead animal, and dropped it in a waste container.

"That's everything I own," Heinrich complained.

"Sergeant," Clary said to Delman who hadn't wanted to interrupt Clary's hard-nosed inspection.

"We didn't allow any drivers to bring their belongings with them," Delman said. "Since you're a replacement, we'll make an exception."

The Jew was smart, Heinrich thought. He was making a gesture, being the kind American, the considerate captor, and why not? What did he have to lose? Being magnanimous underlined the sea change that had occurred: their roles had been reversed.

Clary retrieved Heinrich's bag, opened it and dumped its ragtag contents. He kicked through its rolled-up shirts, its torn winter underwear, a hairbrush, a toothbrush, a notebook, several letters, pencil stubs, a towel wrapped around soap, cigarettes. The Belgian felt the bag, inside and out. He looked inside. Then he threw it at Heinrich who quickly swept his belongings into it. He thought of saying "thank you," but he realized anything he said, just as anything he did, would be misunderstood. Intentionally. He said nothing, closed his bag, and drew himself to attention.

Clary directed Heinrich down the corridor between the facing rows of cots. He tried to see who the sleeping POWs were, but the guard pushed him along—rapidly, harshly poking his rifle against Heinrich's bony rump. They found an empty cot. The guard nodded and Heinrich sat down. He removed his boots and pushed his bag under his head. He pulled up the two blankets at the foot of the cot. He rested his arm on his forehead to shield his eyes from the bulbs' glare and watched the guard take up a position on an empty cot opposite him.

It's never too early to start getting even, Heinrich thought. He looked at the guard, threw off the blankets, and sat up. He stepped into his boots and laced them. He saw that the guard, now alert, was pointing his rifle at him.

"What do you think you're doing?"

"The latrine," Heinrich said, rising.

"You son of a bitch," the guard said. "You had to wait until I got settled. Out the door and to your right."

Heinrich shuffled to the door with the irate guard behind him. He sat down on the cold wooden seat. He was chilled but not as cold as the guard who waited for him outside, facing the frigid blast of the winter night's wind. Heinrich sat quietly, prolonging the guard's discomfort, until he began to tremble.

"I hoped you fell in," the guard said when Heinrich emerged.

He didn't look at the Belgian as he was returned to the hut, to his cot, to thoughts he hadn't had since he'd been captured. He pulled up the blankets and for some reason—perhaps his small act of defiance against the arrogant guard—thought about his wild sister. He hadn't seen Hannah, ten years his senior, since he enlisted. The last time was when, dazzling as usual, she was dancing with high-ranking Wehrmacht and S.S. officers at one of their parents' balls. Hannah had inherited her mother's beauty and her father's strength. No, Heinrich thought, not true. His mother was equally strong but, unlike her rambunctious daughter, she didn't flaunt her power or her beauty. From her mid-teenage years, Hannah did. She became one of Europe's most publicized models. She was spectacularly photogenic. She was on the covers of twenty-nine European magazines—their mother kept count—and was the center of numerous advertising campaigns, lauding the benefits of everything from automobiles to diamonds to tobacco. She made herself accessible—to photographers and to men, as long as they were powerful. However, her less than discreet affairs with leading Nazis and German and Italian industrialists disturbed her father.

"You told Heinrich, my little brother," he heard his sister answer their father, "that he should live, not be a stuffed shirt, a prig. I heard you and I followed your advice."

"Advice for Josef," their father replied, "for my son, not for my daughter."

"So following your advice," she said, "your son becomes a man and your daughter becomes a whore."

"I would never call you that," their father replied. "Never. That's your opinion, your epithet, your stigma."

Heinrich hadn't seen it that way, the difference between a man and a woman, the difference between a son and a daughter. He thought they both put the emphasis in the wrong place. What was important was Germany, the Fatherland, not the individual.

"In spite of what father thinks," Hannah told him, "I know what I'm doing. I'm through with modeling. I'm tired of being used, of being told to sit this way, sit that way, move your head up, move it down, give me more cleavage, give me more leg. Now I'll use others."

She became a photo editor of a small Berlin magazine, then the fashion editor of a French magazine and, finally, the editor-in-chief of a new Austrian publication. But the war changed her plans. Her magazine's publisher became Goebbel's deputy. The last Heinrich heard about Hannah was that she had been put in charge of the propaganda ministry's publication division. The right place but for the wrong reason. Hannah's defiance was misdirected. She thought only of Hannah. She should have thought of Germany.

*   *   *

Delman awoke before sunset. He could see his breath in the Quonset's cold air. He forced himself out of his cocoon of blankets. He was the first to brush his teeth, throw cold water over his head, and use the latrine. When he returned, he nodded to Trabert, already dressed, cleaning his rifle on his cot at the other end of the hut. He came over to speak to Delman. "The new POW says this place's paradise."

"I wouldn't talk to a POW," Delman said, "unless you're giving him orders."

Trabert said, "He talked to me."

"He should only speak when he's spoken to. I'd tell him that the next time he tries to talk to you."

"I'll do what you say," Trabert replied, "but what's your point?"

"Heinrich's the bastard I worked for. He's masquerading as an ordinary soldier. He's an S.S. officer who's out for only one thing, to escape. Anything he does has a purpose. Maybe he's hoping that the one brief exchange with you will make you reluctant to go after him. You'll think of him as a human being instead of an enemy soldier."

"If he's thinking only of escape," Trabert said "he could be searching for another POW to go with him, to help him. Two's better than one. They'd help each other, be more objective in their planing, determine together how to create a distraction so, if the worst happens, at least one escapes."

"You're right," Delman said. "Tell Clary and I'll tell Perry, that we should keep an eye on Heinrich and any driver he seems to be spending time with. And if Heinrich suddenly tries something that even looks like an escape, shoot the bastard. Don't hesitate. Now, why don't you wake up everyone while I see to breakfast."

Delman liked Trabert, but he didn't seem as bright as Clary and not as tough. He had liked what he saw when Clary searched Heinrich and his belongings. Delman knew the two Belgians would keep him alert and maybe Perry, too, although he didn't trust the motor pool chief. If anything happened to Delman, Perry would be the logical person to take over the convoy. But that's never going to happen, Delman thought. Before he left for the depot's mess hall to arrange breakfast, he wanted to brief Perry, who was still asleep. Delman shook his cot and then Perry's massive shoulder.

He sat up quickly.

"I have to talk to you," Delman said.

"Give me a minute," Perry said.

He stretched, scratched his shaved head, and reached into his shirt pocket and pulled out a package of Camels. He bounced out one cigarette, lit it, and took a deep puff.

"That's better," he said.

Perry's awakening gave Delman time for a second thought. Rather than give him an order, Delman decided to flatter him and seek his advice.

"I did what you suggested," Delman said, "and got a replacement for our sick thief. He arrived last night. Who do you think Sergeant Mueller sent?"

"Heinrich," Perry said.

Delman realized Perry knew who Heinrich was and what message his arrival carried. But Perry, Delman also realized, wasn't going to criticize Mueller, not to Delman, not even by a shrug or a glance. He took another puff of his cigarette.

Delman would be as diffident as Perry. "I'm going to see if I can arrange breakfast. The guards have orders to shoot to kill if Heinrich or anyone else tries to escape. I'm thinking of putting him in the middle of the convoy—with Clary sitting next to him. Trabert'll be with you, in place of Clary."

Perry blew smoke rings into the cold air. "Is Clary tough enough?"

"He's tough enough," Delman said.

"He doesn't look tough enough," Perry said.

"Heinrich'll find out just how tough he is if he tries anything."

"It's your call," Perry said. "But why switch them around? Why not leave Clary where he is—and put Trabert with Heinrich?"

"Heinrich's been talking to Trabert to get him to consider Heinrich as another friendly, humble POW. He's up to no good. I don't trust him."

"Because he was your boss?"

"Clary patted down Heinrich when he got off the truck, and went through his belongings with a fine-tooth comb. I saw some sparks fly between Clary and Heinrich. Clary's tough enough. And I want Heinrich to know that I'm on to his tricks, like his talking to Trabert."

"Maybe he was just talking to him," Perry said. "Maybe you're being a little paranoid."

"A lot paranoid," Delman said.

"You know," Perry continued, "I think I spoke too soon about having a guard with me."

"How do you mean?"

"If I have a guard in my truck and have to stop for any reason," Perry said, "the rear of the convoy's left unguarded. But if you put a guard in the truck in front of me, the rear of the convoy's covered."

"Interesting idea," Delman said, "but having you bring up the rear with a guard gives me a feeling of security. You can see what's happening. If you have to stop, you let me know and then we could decide what to do."

Delman thought, I don't trust you, Perry. You're Mueller's friend, not mine. In spite of your seeming goodwill, you're under suspicion. You're wily and you're experienced. Trabert sitting next to you has double duty: watching the convoy and watching you. That's the way I want it.

*   *   *

Delman's got the makings of a good leader, Perry thought. He's not afraid to accept new ideas—and not afraid to reject them. He's decisive. Perry took a deep drag of his cigarette and watched the two guards prod the sleeping POWs. Mueller's smart, too, Perry thought, so why did he send Heinrich?

Maybe as a reward. He liked the German. Simple as that. And maybe Mueller was parading his authority since it was known he backed down once because of Delman, pulling Heinrich off the convoy, and he sure as hell wasn't going to be seen backing down a second time. Delman could have complained to Perry about Mueller's selection. But, instead, the kid said he ordered guards to shoot to kill if the German tried anything. That said it all. No anger, just a statement. If Mueller wanted to play hardball, the kid proved he was ready.

Perry field-stripped his cigarette, threw the blankets off, and stepped into the combat boots he left under his cot. Shit, he thought, you could freeze your ass off here. He saw the stove, with wood next to it, but no one had started it. Typical. No orders, no action. He wondered if Delman could talk the kitchen into feeding the Germans. He doubted it. We've become pariahs, Perry thought, because we use POWs as drivers. What's even worse, we've become their fucking nursemaids.

*   *   *

Delman was glad to feel the warmth of the mess hall. In spite of sleeping in his clothes, he felt chilled. He walked toward a private who was preparing powdered eggs.

"I'll be bringing in my group," Delman said. "How soon before you're ready?"

"You the convoy that came in last night?"

Delman nodded, found a clean mess kit, held it in front of the soldier and leaned against a counter as he gulped eggs along with a piece of bread he tore off a loaf.

"Coffee?"

The private nodded toward a large vat in the corner and Delman found a cup.

"Where's your sergeant?" Delman asked.

"We just got a new one," the private said. "From the 106th. That's the outfit that just got clobbered."

Delman said, "My drivers are POWs."

"You got POWs driving your trucks?"

Delman carefully sipped the hot coffee. "We'll put them at that table over there."

"I don't know about feeding Germans," the private said. "You better clear it with the mess sergeant."

Delman knew he had to move quickly. He doubted if an NCO from the battered 106th, the victim of the recent Wehrmacht surge, was going to be happy about feeding the enemy. He finished eating, pulled off another piece of bread, and started to leave when the mess sergeant arrived.

The private wasn't taking any chances. "He's got POWs he wants us to feed."

"We came in last night," Delman explained. "They're driving our trucks. I'd like to bring them in here for breakfast."

"Am I hearing you right?" the sergeant said. "You got POWs driving your convoy?"

Delman knew what was coming. He figured being assertive was his only chance. "I've got to move fast—so I'll bring them in right now."

The sergeant held up his hand. "Not here. Not while I'm in charge. I don't feed fucking Germans."

"Your call," Delman said.

The sergeant didn't reply, so Delman took four loaves of bread, challenged the sergeant with a long look, and turned to leave.

"I'll feed you and any other GI you got with you," the sergeant said, "but no fucking Germans."

"I understand," Delman said.

What he didn't understand was his own reaction. He was ready to curse the mess sergeant for his belligerent attitude. When did Delman become the protector of POWs? And why? Because the convoy, already more confusing than he ever thought it would be, was his idea? Was that it?

CHAPTER 18

"JAN. 12, 1945—I underestimate everyone. Including the Colonel. I figured a Chicago cop, even a detective, wouldn't be carrying a high IQ. Tough, sure, but not clever and definitely not subtle.

"Wrong. Nelson's sharp. Take the Luger he gave me. I thought his whole point in presenting it to me was symbolic, to show I was in charge. That was only part of it. The other part finally dawned on me. The Luger was meant to be practical, to wake me up to the convoy's danger. Nelson was saying not to underestimate the POW drivers, to be prepared to use the handgun. Now with Heinrich here, I understand the message.

"I told Trabert, Clary and Perry to shoot to kill our replacement driver if he tries anything. I don't blame the Colonel for sending Heinrich here. He probably didn't know anything about it. I do blame Mueller. The whole setup's perfect for him. If anything happens to me, Perry can take over, exactly what Mueller wants. In fact, everything fits together so neatly, I'm wondering if there's some way Mueller could have choreographed the whole thing."

*   *   *

Sergeant Bosworth stepped out of headquarters when the Colonel and Mueller returned from St. Cloud.

"Hope it was a successful trip, sir," Bosworth said, saluting.

"Don't count on it, sergeant," the Colonel replied, slowly unfolding his cramped body from the jeep, flicking two fingers against his overseas cap. "Any coffee inside?"

"I'll bring you a cup right away, Colonel," Bosworth replied, watching him slowly, sullenly stretch and then trudge toward his office. Bosworth, leaning on the jeep, checked with Mueller.

"How did it go?"

"He didn't say much on the way back," Mueller said. "He sure as hell wasn't happy."

"He's never happy."

"If you ask me," Mueller said, "he's got the wrong idea. The TPM's got bigger worries than a POW camp."

"You should sit where he is," Bosworth said, "for one day. Hell, if anyone should appreciate how few supplies we get, it should be you."

"I tell you what I think," Mueller said, turning off the ignition. "I think he's trying to justify Delman's crazy convoy. That's what I think this is all about."

"You should get out of your supply tent and visit the cages."

"I'm always visiting the cages."

"How far inside do you go? You talk to the cage warden, you sit in his office. I mean really go inside those zoos and see for yourself how we treat your precious Germans. We're killing them."

"Bosworth," Mueller said, turning on his ignition, looking up at the first sergeant, "you're being hoodwinked by your colonel."

*   *   *

"Stack those cartons," Mueller ordered Keifur, "and get those barrels in a straight line."

He was no Heinrich, Mueller thought, but if he was going to be stuck with another POW, he was going to use him to straighten up the supply tent. Heinrich, as smart as he was, had let it go to pot; everything was disorganized.

"The POWs in my tent should see what you got here," Keifur said.

"What we got here?"

"Nothing," Keifur explained. "You've got nothing except mountains of cartons and half-empty barrels. They think you're hoarding food in here and clothes and blankets."

"Why do they think there's a convoy?" Mueller asked. "Everything goes to the front."

"They think the convoy's a sop to the Jew. They don't believe what they don't see."

"I can understand that," Mueller said. "I didn't believe Germany was sending kids to fight, let alone older men, until I got a look at the latest contingent of prisoners."

"Old men like me," Keifur said.

"How old are you, Keifur?"

"Too old to be here," Keifur said.

"Forty?"

"How about fifty-four?"

"Start in the last tent," Mueller ordered, "and move forward. I want to see this supply tent straightened up and swept clean when I return."

He tightened the waist string of his fatigue jacket and buttoned up its front. Then he tied and buttoned a second jacket over the first. It was cold out there and it would be cold visiting the cages.

"I'm going to tell the guard to watch you," Mueller said. "I have to check some of the cages."

"You don't have to talk to the guard," Keifur said, smiling. "I'm not going any place. I'll stick around until you get back."

"Funny man," Mueller muttered.

He left the supply tent and trotted toward the barbed wire enclosing the cages. May as well get some exercise while I'm at it, he thought; besides, you get warm running.

"Go and see how they treat your precious Germans," Mueller said aloud.

He pulled the two jackets tight around his compact body.

The wind never let up. What they needed around here, he thought, slightly puffing from his run, were some mountains to break the cutting wind ripping across the flat, uncultivated farmlands.

What did Bosworth think I did all day, sit in my tent and mope the way Nelson probably did? So what if I didn't go into the cages. I'll take care of that now.

At the first cage, he nodded to the guard, who swung open the gate. Inside, Mueller looked for the cage warden and, finding no one, approached the large tent near the cage's entrance. Inside, he saw crowded bodies, some looking dead, some shuddering from the cold, and a few preparing to go to their jobs. There should be more space between their sleeping nests—rags, dirty clothes, dirtier blankets, and torn cartons. There had to be rodents here somewhere, field mice, maybe rats. Could the POWs be eating them? Was it that bad?

Disgusting, he thought, so many Germans sleeping so close, breathing each others' foul air, smelling each others' putrid excretions. These were soldiers, German soldiers, human beings. It was repulsive the way they were forced to live, like the swine the French called them.

He moved some of the blankets and clothing, trying to even out the space between each sloppy nest. The POWs, afraid to stop him, began to retrieve their overcoats, their blankets, their warming rags, their shields from the raw cold as the American continued his busy work. They began to shove and then they turned on each other. Their whispers increased into rumblings and curses. Mueller remembered what had happened to him at the concert he attended last week in one of the cages.

He'd been invited by Heinrich, who saved Mueller a seat in the front row, not far from where Heinrich played his trumpet. However, until he took his seat—and even after he had—Mueller had heard the undertone of complaint, first only a sound, then, as it became louder, the clear, angry words.

"Why is the American pig intruding into our concert? What

does he think he's doing here? Why is he sticking his fucking face into the little enjoyment we're able to scrape together? If you want to be accepted," came one brazen sentence, louder than the rest, shouted, as were the others, in German, "then give us some food, some clothing, some decent shelter. If you don't, we'll know you're another phony American pretending to be concerned about your POWs."

Mueller knew the POWs didn't think he could understand them. That was why they were so brazen. But he knew German as well as they did. He grew up on German. German was his native language. "Stop it!" he had ordered, in German. "Who do you think you're cursing?"

He hurried from the tent and stepped into the frozen swamp of pup tents and makeshift shelters where the most recent batch of sodden POWs had clawed out the hard ground so they could find some warmth. He hadn't known it was this bad, this primitive, this repugnant. No wonder they're dying, he thought: it's their easiest escape.

He had planned to visit all the cages, pretending to see what supplies were needed. But one tent, one cage, one swamp was all he could take, all he could stomach. Rushing away, Mueller almost knocked down Colonel Nelson who was making his own tour of the cages.

"Sir," Mueller said, surprised, apologetic.

"Visiting the battlefield, sergeant?"

Mueller didn't want to say it was worse than he had imagined. He didn't want to reveal he had never gone into the POWs' tents—even though he would often stop at the cages to see the Americans in charge—or that he'd avoided the swamp of covered holes where the latest arrivals suffered.

"It's bad, sir."

"It's hell," Nelson said.

"Any word from St. Cloud, Colonel?"

"Damn right," Nelson said. "We showed them who's boss.

They're sending us more prisoners. We sure threw a scare into them, didn't we, Mueller?"

The sergeant pulled himself erect and saluted. But the Colonel had left, already on his way to another cage.

*   *   *

Heinrich pushed away the blankets. He sat up and looked at the POWs still asleep in the frigid hut. Neither the still-burning electric light bulbs nor the morning light interfered with their sleep, probably the first restful night they had since their capture.

Which one will escape with me, he wondered, which one's strong? And how will I find him? He tried to talk to the prisoner in the next cot but the belligerent guard across the aisle would have none of it. Then Heinrich recalled Wanger had told him about the racer, Sacher. Perhaps he was in the next cot. And perhaps, after all, slimy Wagner's miserable life had not been wasted. Heinrich tried to whisper to the nearby POW.

"Shut up," the guard said. Then he shouted, "Out of bed, all of you."

Along with the other Belgian, he hustled the shivering POWs to the outdoor latrine. When they were finished, the guards herded them back to the hut and its stained wash basins.

The guards never let up. "Hurry up," one of them said. "What do you think this is—some sort of spa? Move your asses."

Heinrich, already at a sink, stuck his haggard face below a faucet. He groaned as the icy water hit his skin. Without soap, he tried to scratch away the caked dirt on his hands and face. He threw water over his bristly, itchy scalp. He disregarded the guards' commands and methodically blotted his crumpled handkerchief against his weary face, his spiky head, his rough, cracked hands. At the same time, he whispered to the POW at the next basin.

"You," Clary said, "you, the new driver. Keep your big fat German mouth shut. No talking, not a single word unless I give you permission. Is that clear? Now, remove yourself from the sink and let someone else get in there."

"Big fat German mouth," Heinrich said to himself. I'd like to rip your big fat Belgian mouth right of your weak pudgy baby face. To have to take such garbage from an ordinary soldier—and from a second-rate nation at that.

But Heinrich stayed silent. He didn't dare do anything to compromise his position, to make him more of a target than he was. He had to become invisible. The less attention he drew to himself, the better. The guard, receiving no reaction from Heinrich, switched his attention to the other POWs.

"When you leave the washroom," he ordered, "make a single line in front of your cots."

He enjoys pushing people around, Heinrich thought. He stood still as the guard frisked him, roughly slapping his hand up and down his body. He watched the other guard check the cots: he ran his hand along the bottom of each one, around its blankets and then down where the hut's wall met the floor.

What were they searching for—homemade bombs, hidden ammunition, what? As if the POWs could have something in their possession or in their cots that the guards missed during their earlier inspection. Assume the guards did know what they were doing. They were experienced, they were tough, even the friendlier one, and they were always searching. Exactly why?

Heinrich was sure their constant suspicion was motivated and reinforced by their suspicious leader. Delman trusted no one. His busy mind was always reviewing every detail. Like most Jews, he had animal cunning. It was said—in fact Heinrich's sister conducted research on the subject—that Jews were sub-human.

Gross? Vulgar? Yes, but subhuman? Heinrich wasn't certain. He did believe Delman was uncouth, uncultured, insensitive and now, because of his new job, stupidly pompous.

After their latest search, the guards ordered the POWs outside to board the trucks. Heinrich straggled. He had to find the one POW who would escape with him. He believed it would be the race driver, the famous race driver, but where was Sacher?

Heinrich knew the POW who helped him would be risking his life. And if he stayed alive, he might be caught, punished, and denied the wonders of the convoy: sleeping inside on a cot, getting ample rations, washing with running water, escaping the daily drudgery of the stockade. But those comforts were meaningless to a committed German who recognized his duty, who was convinced the Third Reich would win, who hadn't been seduced by the safety of imprisonment. That one brave, good soldier—still eager to fight for the Fatherland—would make up for all the cringing, craven Wangers.

Heinrich had no regrets about his old bunkmate. He was worthless, a burden, and would have interfered with Heinrich's plans. But Wanger's questions, as self-centered as they were, did provide Heinrich with some intellectual stimulation. Heinrich missed their discussions. But he realized that in the Wehrmacht, as in the POW camp, most soldiers were too exhausted to do more than accept orders and complain. Not Heinrich. He still felt vigorous, mentally and physically.

Yet as much as he missed his family, his university, his pleasant life before the war, he knew you had to empty your mind of the past. No longer were you a son, a brother, a student, a civilian, an individual. You were a soldier, submissive with your superiors, aggressive with others. You had to narrow your focus—act quickly, decisively, and lethally.

Now Heinrich had to determine how he would hide from the guards while he searched for his fellow risk-taker. Suddenly, he knew what to do. He pretended to drop his jacket. He used it as a screen, to hide the grab he made at the sleeve of the nearest POW.

"I need your help," Heinrich whispered.

At that moment, the more hostile guard raised his head and

swung his rifle around like a cobra, feeling movement, discerning sound. The POW wrenched his arm from Heinrich's fingers and kept walking. So close, Heinrich thought—smarting from his near success, annoyed by his necessary rejection.

Out of frustration, he kicked out his boot. He knew it was stupid, impetuous, as soon as he did it. Inadvertently, he tripped the same POW. To break his fall, the man reached out for the unyielding, frozen, rock-strewn ground and bloodied his partly gloved hands. The baby-faced guard materialized.

"My fault," the POW said quickly, pulling himself up, not looking at Heinrich. "Fell over my own feet."

The POW gave a slight bow to the scowling guard and limped toward his truck. He's the one, Heinrich thought. Could he be Sacher? Heinrich had only seen photos of him but that was long ago. The POW didn't give Heinrich away; he didn't even look in his direction.

He's the soldier I need, Heinrich thought. He'd cause a distraction, create chaos and, if necessary, risk his life so I could escape.

"Heinrich," Delman called from his jeep. "You're driving the fourth truck."

He looked at the Jew. The young hero, one foot outside the jeep, the commander, eager for battle. What a laugh, Heinrich thought, leading a tired group of the enemy to collect supplies—for whom? The enemy! Delman deceived himself. He believed what he was doing was important.

How will you feel, Sergeant Delman, Heinrich thought, when your easy, behind-the-line war disintegrates, when your grand dream of returning with trucks crammed with proof of your cleverness will be shown up for what they are, part of a comic act in your theater of the absurd?

"The fourth truck," Heinrich repeated.

He climbed into its cab. He thought: I have to find a way to speak to the POW I tripped, to brief him about my plan, to arrange a signal so at the opportune moment we'll be ready.

A Belgian opened the cab's passenger door and was about to drop his heavily clothed body next to Heinrich when Delman called him. He joined the other guard and Perry to distribute breakfast—hunks of crisp freshly baked bread—to the POWs. A welcome change from the C and K rations.

Finally, the baby-faced Belgian slipped back into the cab. Heinrich knew it was Delman's doing, closeting him with a guard. A warning, making sure he knew he was in a box, wrapped by Delman, to be opened only at his command.

Nor was Heinrich surprised that the Belgian next to him was not the guard he'd talked to earlier. Watchful Delman understood what Heinrich had been doing. The American recognized Heinrich's ploy—maybe the same one he would have used—and countered it.

"Let's go," Delman called.

Heinrich turned on the ignition and slowly pressed down the gas pedal as he closely followed the truck in front of him. Perhaps he would escape in this truck. He glanced behind and saw jerry cans, ration cartons, and piles of clothes. Well, thank you, Sergeant Delman, he said to himself, you've thought of everything.

CHAPTER 19

ALL OF THE TRUCKS lined up, single-file, in the hangar-like supply depot that smelled of hay and manure. It could have been a stable, Delman thought, or an indoor polo field. He left his jeep and, with Perry, closed the depot's huge sliding door. Delman inhaled the aroma. What was it? Wet cartons, wet wool, or forgotten deposits from horses or cattle? He wasn't sure. Maybe, he thought, I'm smelling the corruption here, the payoffs that grease the transfer of supplies.

The depot was divided by a long counter. In front, the interior road for vehicles dropping off or picking up supplies. Behind, long well-marked aisles of supplies piled high on metal shelves. A smiling, slope-shouldered, round buck-sergeant left the counter and shuffled forward.

"Where you from?" he asked.

Except for a few civilians working in the rear of the massive store, he appeared to be in charge.

"Le Mans," Delman replied, handing him requisitions.

The NCO checked the documents and then traipsed along the convoy, peering into the cabs. He returned to stand in front of Delman. Then he discovered Perry.

"You old bastard," the buck-sergeant said.

"Good to see you, old buddy," Perry replied, as they embraced.

"Don't tell me you got fucking POWs driving your trucks," the NCO said, astounded.

"How about that," Delman said.

"How come fucking POWs are driving your trucks?"

Delman had it with unnecessary questions. First, the officious mess sergeant and now this ass of a fleshy NCO, standing

183

nose to nose with Delman. But, he realized, the NCO was true to Army tradition. Like Perry, he was probably regular Army. He believed, because he was in charge of distribution at the depot, that he owned the supplies. They belonged to him. He had elevated his routine job into one of decision. When the officer in charge was away, the NCO made the play—he decided who got what.

Delman stared at his pockmarked face, his droopy eyelids and considered pulling rank. But Delman wanted supplies and this lump of an NCO had the power to pull it off, to make Delman's convoy a success if he held his temper. "I'm carrying cigarettes," Delman announced, "cigarettes and booze."

"Well, what d'you know," the rotund NCO said. "That should entitle you to something. You want to show me your loot?"

So this was negotiation, Delman thought. He looked at Perry who gave him a half-smile, a raise of eyebrows, a wink. Delman felt like kicking ass, not bowing and scraping to this flabby supply jerk. Why don't I pull out my Luger, Delman thought, and order the flab of an NCO to fill my trucks? He'll do it, I'll take off and if he or Perry complains, I'll say the guy was asking for a bribe and I answered in a way any upright, Jack Armstrong-type of clean American boy would answer.

Only one problem. Regular Army veteran Perry, probably used to other NCOs collecting their shakedown dues, had jumped into a truck and emerged with armsful of Old Golds and Camels and a bottle of booze in each hand. And, just as quickly, the gangster of an NCO returned to stand behind his long counter and patted it with his fat hands. Perry obliged, lining up the cartons in front of the two bottles of Scotch.

The NCO wasted no time. He scraped the cartons from his counter into a waiting box the way a cook scrapes his grill. He carefully lifted the Scotch into the box and hurriedly put his loot out of sight. Then he signaled one of his waiting gofers to bring over a different carton that he placed in front of Delman.

"Here you go," the NCO said.

Delman ripped open the carton's top to find cans of lye. Probably good for the four-holers, he thought, but the last thing he needed. "Clothes, tents, rations," Delman said, "that's what I need."

"'That's what I need,'" mimicked the NCO. "This is what you get."

Delman looked out at the supply depot, crowded with cartons and crates, folded tents, piles of clothing, blankets. And what does the bastard give me—lye! To think I have to bribe this stupid asshole—and for what?

"Something wrong, soldier?"

Delman vaulted the counter and grabbed a handful of the NCO's fatigue jacket when he heard Perry call, "Attention," and then a question from a new voice that Delman couldn't decipher. He didn't let go until he heard the question repeated.

"What's going on here?" a first lieutenant asked.

"Joking around," the NCO replied, "sir."

"Your convoy?" the lieutenant asked Delman.

"Yes, sir."

"Our supplies are for front line troops," the lieutenant said. "Your orders, sergeant."

As the officer studied them, Delman reached under the counter, closed the flaps on the carton that contained the cigarettes and Scotch and hoisted it on his shoulder.

"What've you got there?" the lieutenant asked.

"It's theirs, sir," the NCO said.

The lieutenant took a long look at the NCO. He returned the orders to Delman. "You leaving?" he asked Delman.

"Right now, sir," Delman replied, depositing the carton in his jeep.

He saluted and nodded to Perry who glared at Delman, paused, and, finally, helped Delman open the huge door. They returned to their vehicles and Delman told his driver to move out. The trucks followed the jeep out of the depot, past the camp's buildings, including the Quonset where the convoy had spent the night.

They drove away from Tours. Even when the city was far behind them, Delman could smell the depot's repugnant odor. He was convinced the offensive smell wasn't solely from hay or manure or wet supplies.

*   *   *

As long as you keep your sense of humor, Perry told himself as he brought up the rear of the convoy, you'll be okay. You'll avoid getting that most dreaded mark against you, a Section 8 discharge, a sign of your instability, maybe even of your craziness.

In his younger days, the possibility of going off the deep end—and getting caught—was real. Perry's trigger-temper was famous, as explosive as a bazooka shell slamming into a nearby target and without a warning whoosh. His reaction to frustration had always been sudden rage. Noisy rage. Breaking heads rage. No more. After losing his stripes several times, getting close to a court-martial once and closer to spending time in a stockade, Perry learned to pause, take several deep breaths, and accept a basic, indisputable fact of Army life: nothing went according to plan.

Once he accepted that, a Section 8 discharge became only a metaphor, never a reality, never even a threat. He learned how to laugh at his own foibles, his own fears, his own fuckups. He became a true believer: the unexpected always happened in the Army.

He recalled telling Mueller, "If you made arrangements for R & R in Switzerland, it was absolutely certain you'd be transferred—or given some assignment that demanded immediate action—exactly when your furlough was to begin."

Mueller nodded. He knew. He, too, believed. All career soldiers learned that a devil lurked behind the most desired, elaborate hopes. He was out to crush you, to conquer you, to destroy you unless you had the ability to back off, look at yourself, and laugh. Perry had hoped to have at least one free night in Tours. Without Delman telling him what to do. Without the angry Belgians. Without the servile POWs, except for Mueller's replacement.

Perry had discovered that Lippy, the NCO who supervised the supply depot, had a stable of available women. Thanks to his creative record-keeping and his ability to trade Army staples for such prized gifts as silk stockings and lingerie, Lippy developed a following of willing locals. "I told them about this big, deep-voiced, shaved-head American sergeant," Lippy said, "who was a laugh a minute. They can't wait to meet you."

But touchy Delman, always on edge—now there's a guy ripe for a Section 8—had to grab a handful of Lippy when an officer was around. So, instead of being shacked up in Tours, Perry was in and out of the untouched city faster than you could say Errol Flynn.

It was all a question of attitude, Perry thought. He could have gone berserk when he saw Delman reclaim Lippy's loot. Every pack in those two cartons of returned cigarettes represented a lay. Lippy, if nothing else, met his markers. Instead, Perry laughed. Who would've thought the kid would have the balls to take back his barter with Lippy hanging over him and a lieutenant breathing down his neck? Lippy had met his match. Delman, always cocky, was in his prime.

At least, Perry thought, he'd been able to talk Lippy out of two walkie-talkies, something that should've been SOP for the convoy. How could Delman in his jeep know what was happening at the convoy's rear without something like the hand-held radios?

The Colonel knew that, Delman should've known that, and it had occurred immediately to Perry. He'd discussed it with Mueller, who said he'd been trying to secure the communications link for months. But, like a lot of other supplies he requisitioned, the front lines got priority and the POW camp got nothing. Perry's only fear was that, like a lot of Lippy's merchandise, the walkie-talkies he received were inferior, maybe even damaged. He'd have to field test them with the kid, to handle that test carefully. Delman, always working with a short fuse, might mistake such a discussion as a rebuke, Perry saying, "How come you didn't get these for your convoy?"

Perry didn't need that. He didn't want to start any kind of a running battle with Delman. He had learned what it was to buck authority, especially when it was a four-eyed zealot who liked to punch out Germans. Furthermore, he and Heinrich provided a mix that was too explosive.

Give me soldiers, Perry thought, with one aim, to see the fucking war end as soon as possible. Not guys out to prove something and, above all, not a Nazi and a Jew.

*　*　*

"Get over to the side of the road," Delman told his driver. "Let our trucks pass us. I want to check them out."

As his jeep drifted to the rear, Delman waited to see Perry. He wasn't surprised when the motor pool chief, in the last vehicle, shook his head to let Delman know he thought his hurried departure with empty trucks was a mistake. I don't deal with slimy NCOs, Delman would've told Perry if he'd done more than thrown his big, restless body into his cab and grunted his disgust. Delman knew what Perry would say. "You're leaving the depot with nothing! You grabbed your barter and ran. Now what, you asshole?"

"Let's get back to the front of the convoy, Ramer," Delman told his driver.

Maybe I'll do the same thing again, Delman thought. Maybe I'll have another disgusting encounter. Maybe I'll face another slippery, calculating thief of an NCO and another indifferent officer who were looking for payoffs for disbursing supplies they didn't own, who never considered the consequences of their chiseling—time wasted, lives lost.

He could always return to Tours if he didn't have any better luck in Angers or Rennes, the two other places Mueller marked on Delman's map. After all, he thought, my job's to secure supplies, not squander barter. Cigarettes and booze for lye! Delman straightened up in his seat. Why would Perry favor such a lopsided trade? Then it occurred to Delman: Perry might be getting a rakeoff from the depot's flabby NCO.

"So what if I was getting something in return?" Perry would have said. "That's how you conduct business in the Army and it works. You're only sore, Delman, because you didn't think of it yourself." And Perry would justify that "business": "Every day your convoy's out here, ten more POWs are freezing and starving in the camp. If your job's to get supplies for them, do it. You've got barter, so barter."

But Delman wasn't going to be bamboozled—not now and not in the future. He was convinced his convoy, properly handled, could lead to more convoys. Perry, the old veteran, the careerist, simply was reflecting his heritage: he was a prisoner of the Army's upside-down, you-scratch-my-back-and-I'll-scratch-yours corrupt culture.

"Ever buy a used car?" Delman asked his driver.

"A used car?" Ramer said. "Once and that was the last time."

"Why?"

"Used car salesmen are the worst," the POW said. "Phonies, manipulators, liars. My friends say the same thing. You're always taken by used car salesmen."

Exactly, Delman thought. And when it came to Perry—and the slimy NCO in the depot—Delman felt he was being romanced in a used car lot by manipulative salesmen: the liver-lipped NCO, his patsy of an officer, and smirking Perry. Only, thought Delman, here's one guy who's not buying any piece of junk, regardless of how well it's polished.

"Nice country," the driver said, "but in a different season."

Delman nodded. He might have enjoyed this drive along the Loire but not in wartime, not in the cold of winter. He'd read how the wealthy sent their children on such trips to Europe, following college. And then he thought of going home, of returning to Northwestern. He'd have catching up to do, making up for his lost war years, and, finally, competing with 4Fs and draft dodgers like his stateside friend Larry Bayer. Assuming Delman ever got home.

He looked at the empty countryside and wasn't fooled: it was far from peaceful. He had created his own dilemma. To escape the camp—and his punishment—he had concocted the convoy. But it had evolved into a dangerous mission, thanks to Mueller sneaking Heinrich aboard. The other POWs, like Ramer, were predictable. They were satisfied to sit out the rest of the war. Heinrich, searching for a stooge to help him escape, altered the equation, changed the environment.

Now there was danger within and without. Delman hadn't overlooked the French. What if they discovered their enemy—their conquerors—careening up and down their roads in American trucks to get supplies for POWs? Try running that past a few of deGaulle's vengeful maquis.

When Delman first dreamt up the POW-driven convoy, he thought the worst that could happen would be to return empty. He hadn't considered not returning at all. The war was winding down. Who would try to escape now? And weren't the French our friends? His thoughts now, with Heinrich aboard, were no longer so sanguine.

"Check the convoy again," Delman said.

He wondered why Perry, if he was so experienced, had never insisted the convoy get some walkie-talkies. Maybe his push would have got Mueller to do something; he had refused Delman's several requests or, if he did try, he had never told Delman.

So here they were, wasting time to make sure the convoy

hadn't lost some of its trucks. Delman pulled past the vehicles and counted them off, a school bus driver counting his charges.

"Go back," he ordered quickly, "either some trucks are missing or I can't count."

"Christ," he said after his driver ran the jeep back along the fast-moving trucks and Delman counted for the second time. "Goddamn it, it's getting to be a habit. Six, only six. Where are my missing trucks? Now what's happened?"

CHAPTER 20

"PULL OVER," DELMAN told Ramer.

His driver carefully edged the jeep off the road. Trucks followed. Delman raised the collar of his overcoat, pulled his cap down to his eyebrows, and stepped outside into the sudden heavy surging snow that slammed into his face, momentarily caking his glasses, half-blinding him.

He leaned into the wind, his boots squashing the thick snow, and trudged to the fourth truck. He had to see Clary, his friend, the only remaining guard. Delman slid his gloved hand along his jeep to keep his footing and moved cautiously from truck to truck until he reached the vehicle where Clary was imprisoned with Heinrich. Good going, Delman thought, putting your only friend with your greatest danger.

"Jacques," Delman said, "come back here with me."

Carrying his rifle, Clary pulled up his collar and left his seat next to Heinrich to stand behind his truck. Both men leaned backwards against the heavy wind, trying not to lose their balance.

"Just what we need," Delman said, "a blinding snowstorm." At least I'm warm, he thought, encased in four layers of cotton and wool. "Perry's truck—and Trabert's—are missing. I'm on my way to see what the trouble is. You'll be here alone."

"I'll keep the POWs in their trucks," Clary said. "If they have to piss, they'll piss in their pants."

"We should've had walkie-talkies," Delman said.

"Why didn't we?"

"For the same reason we're on this convoy," Delman said. "Everything we need goes to the front. But Perry or Trabert should have done something—anything—to let me know they were dropping off."

"Like what?" Clary asked.

"How about firing their weapons?" Delman said.

"Maybe they did," Clary said, "but you're driving in a snowstorm with your head buried in your overcoat."

"You better move the trucks closer together, and if you stand across the road you'll be able to see all of them in one glance."

"It had to be something mechanical," Clary said, "or a bad tire. The missing trucks, I mean. You'll find them."

"Perry's an experienced NCO," Delman said, "but he takes off and leaves the rear of the convoy unguarded."

"I don't think he had a choice," Clary said.

"If we lose any trucks it'll be my ass, not Perry's."

"And if you come back with your trucks loaded like the best PX in the world, you'll be the hero, not Perry."

"You guarantee that?"

"Damn right," Clary said. "My money's on Delman."

He smiled, patted his friend on the shoulder, and began the trudge forward to his jeep.

* * *

Delman urged his driver to speed back toward Tours in spite of the almost horizontal snow. They passed a sign: twenty kilometers to Tours. After a short drive, Delman caught sight of farmers—a line of fifteen—slowly advancing across the bare frozen snowy field. Some had rifles; others carried hoes and shovels. Soon he saw where they were going. His two trucks were off to the side of the road. Trabert faced the farmers, some seventy-five yards away, his rifle slung over his shoulder, while Perry and the POW replaced a tire.

"Drive as close to them as you can," Delman told Ramer.

As soon as the jeep stopped, Delman was out of it.

"Stay here," he told his driver, "and keep your motor running." He patted his Luger and shoved an ammunition clip into his carbine. He ran toward the three men.

"Perry," Delman said, nodding toward the farmers, "you've got company."

"I don't know how they spotted us," Perry said.

"How about that civilian at the supply depot?" Delman said. "It's not every day you see POWs driving American trucks."

The farmers kept advancing.

"I guess I didn't hear Trabert fire his rifle," Delman said, "to let me know you were leaving the convoy."

"I ordered him not to," Perry said, "just for the reason you see in front of us. I didn't want to send the French an invitation."

"So you left the rear of the convoy unguarded," Delman said, trying to control his rising voice.

"You're here," Perry said, "aren't you?"

"Stop!" Delman shouted at the French. "Hold it right there." He leveled his carbine at the leading farmer. "You speak English?"

The farmer halted and raised his rifle over his head. Those behind him did the same with their rifles and farm implements. Why the histrionics? To show their cooperation—or to make us feel guilty? It was working, Delman thought. He wanted to lessen the tension, remove the hostility.

"You speak English?" he called again.

"Yes, I speak English," the farmer shouted back.

He tried walking forward.

"Please," Delman shouted, "stay where you are."

Perry quickly took his tools back to his truck and returned wearing his helmet and carrying his M1. He took a position next to Trabert and, like the guard, pointed his rifle at the French.

"That's great," Delman said. "Here I'm trying to get our French leader to relax—and talk to me—and you emerge, helmet and rifle in hand, like some paratrooper looking for trouble."

"Thought it might lessen the tension," Perry said. "It was

supposed to be a gag."

"Not funny," Delman said. "They mean business."

He turned back to the French. "We're on our way to the supply depot in Angers. How far?"

"You have a German," the Frenchman called. "We want him—and the other Germans you have driving your trucks."

"How far to Angers?" Delman called. "This is crazy," he said to Perry and Trabert. "They're our allies. We're pointing our rifles at the wrong people."

"We're doing our job," Perry said.

"Some job," Delman said. "They're right, we're wrong."

"You've got your orders," Perry said. "That's all you have to worry about. You follow your orders and do your job."

"Fuck my orders." Delman said. "I'm not going to shoot the French."

"You're responsible for our trucks," Perry said. "Remember that. The Germans are part of our trucks."

"The Germans are the enemy," Delman said. "This is crazy."

"Your convoy's crazy," Perry said. "It's your crazy idea and you're stuck with it. Don't put our fucking lives in danger because you've suddenly got religion."

"Slowly walk back to your truck," Delman said to the POW driver who was standing behind the two soldiers. "Do it and do it slowly."

The leading Frenchman began to lower his rifle. Those behind him started to do the same until Trabert fired a warning bullet. Everyone froze.

"That was good," Delman said, "but hold your fire unless I give the order."

He said to Perry and Trabert, "The two of you, walk slowly back to your truck, start your engines and be ready to follow me as soon as I take off. And no more firing unless I say so."

The leading Frenchman slowly began to move forward.

"Shoot the son of a bitch," Perry said.

"Go," Delman said. "Return to your truck."

He held his carbine pointed at the French. The farmers resumed their slow advance. Delman continued to point his rifle at them as he edged toward his jeep.

He stepped into it and shouted, "Go!"

The jeep darted away from the fence, turned slightly before it reached the pavement, and screeched away. The two speeding trucks followed closely.

When he reached the convoy, Delman almost fell on the uneven road's narrow icy shoulder as he stepped out of his jeep. He watched the two trucks return to the end of the convoy.

"Everything's fine here," Clary told him. "We kept the POWs in their trucks so we should have a piss call before we leave."

"Now," Delman said.

Clary left to talk to Trabert and then the two guards told the drivers to leave their trucks. As they descended, Clary came over to Delman. "Trabert told me what happened," Clary said, "with the French."

"We got out of there as fast as we could."

"I understand Perry wanted to stay," Clary said.

"He wanted to shoot the French," Delman said. "When I said we don't shoot our allies, he told me my orders were to protect the trucks. The Germans were part of the trucks, he said."

"Figures," Clary said.

The POWs buttoned their coats and jackets and returned to their vehicles. Delman went back to his jeep and returned with a small, wrapped package that he handed to Clary. "I meant to gives this to you earlier."

Clary sniffed it.

"Thank you," he said. "Paté?"

"Jewish paté," Delman said. "Salami. I got a package from home. Is Heinrich still trying to talk to other POWs?"

"All the time," Clary replied.

"Don't let up on him," Delman said, "but be careful. He's

dangerous."

"I know," Clary said. "Isn't that why you put me next to him?"

"Yes," Delman said.

Clary joined Trabert as they hustled the POWs back to their trucks. Delman stared at Perry. He was leaning against a tree, field stripping a cigarette. Delman thought of speaking with him but changed his mind when he heard Ramer turn on the jeep's ignition.

Delman paused, put up his hand to signal his driver, and returned to the middle of the convoy. Clary stepped from his cab.

"A question," Delman said. "Be honest, Jacques. Was I right—in fleeing the French?"

"Trabert said there were fifteen of them," Clary said, "maybe more. They could have killed you."

"I ran," Delman said.

"You're here," Clary said.

"I didn't come here to defend the Germans, but I sure as hell didn't come here to shoot the French."

"But you are trying to save the Germans," Clary said, "the POWs. That's what your convoy's all about."

"We're here to fight the Germans, to defeat them," Delman said, "not to starve them, not to murder them."

"Where's the difference?" Clary asked.

He returned to his truck and Delman to his jeep.

"Let's go," he told Ramer.

Delman shook the caked snow from his coat and turned to watch the trucks follow him.

"Not too fast," he cautioned his driver, rubbing his cold hand over his wet face. "I'm not sure what I'm most worried about—the slippery roads or the angry French."

CHAPTER 21

"SUPER-HONEST COP," NELSON said to Captain Roland, sitting across from him. "That became my label before I made detective."

"A good label," Roland said. "I'm impressed."

"Don't be," Nelson said.

He left his desk to pace restlessly around his office as he spoke. "There was this team of reporters for the *Chicago Daily News*. They were doing an in-depth series on the Chicago police department. They talked to the mayor and all the police bigwigs. Then they decided they had to interview one of the younger guys, a yet-to-be-disillusioned, gung-ho cop. I was selected."

"The token idealistic cop," Roland said.

Nelson returned to his chair. "They got me talking and of course they were taken with a couple of the 'do gooder' cases I got involved in."

"Like what?" Roland asked.

"A couple of kids who were accused of stealing. I didn't think they were guilty. I fought for them and eventually I stumbled on the real thieves."

"What else?"

"A friend of mine, the owner of a gas station near my house, refused to be shaken down by an oil company. He took them to court. I testified as one of his character witnesses."

"The good neighbor," Roland said.

"After that, whenever the press needed quotes about police honesty, they called me."

"You became famous."

"Infamous," Nelson said. "More than a few of the older cops said I was a self-righteous ass. Then the police started to use me as their stalking horse."

"Stalking horse?"

"There was trouble in Cicero," Nelson said, "a notorious Chicago suburb. Police corruption was suspected. So super-honest cop Nelson was sent galloping to the rescue. I didn't like it, the local cops didn't like it, but it played well with the press."

"You found your calling."

"I accepted it. I don't know if I liked it but I got used to it. I did a lot of galloping to the rescue."

"You were your label."

"I tell you, I had my share of problems because of it, especially with the older guys who thought being honest meant you were a queer. After I banged a few heads, I got some respect."

"You and Delman," Roland said. "Is that why you like him?"

"I mention this," Nelson said, "because you can't live with that kind of a label and then accept what's happening around here without reacting."

"You've reacted. You've done all you could. Your memos, your calls, the convoy, your visit to Paris. What's left? An audience with Ike?"

"There's one more thing I can do."

"Drop it. You'll be misunderstood. They'll think you're either looking for a transfer or a Section Eight."

"That's a chance I'll have to take," Nelson said.

*   *   *

With his first sergeant, the Colonel arrived at the camp's railroad station the next afternoon. Two of Roland's security guards were supervising some fifty POWs who were starting to remove the tracks from the railroad spur that curved inside the camp. The Germans carried pickaxes, crowbars, and shovels.

"At the rate they're going," Nelson said, "they'll still be digging up this track when I visit this place with my grandchildren."

"I was here this morning with Captain Roland," Sergeant Bosworth said. "We divided the work force into three groups. One group shovels the snow away from the tracks. A second loosens the rails and ties. A third removes them and piles them off to the side."

"Good planning," the Colonel said, "but not enough manpower. Triple the work force."

"We've got plenty of men," Bosworth said. "It's the tools we don't have."

Nelson said, "I don't think Mueller knows what he's got in his tent. Go over there yourself. Dig through those cartons and crates. I want this track removed this week."

"It's tough work," Bosworth said. "The ground's frozen and so are the POWs. They work and then they go inside to warm up and then they work again."

"More men," Nelson said, leaving, "and more tools. I want this spur gone, removed, out of here, by this week."

When Bosworth arrived at the supply tent, Mueller and his single helper, an old POW, had finished piling up newly found tools. "How did you know," Bosworth asked, "the Colonel needed more tools?"

"I was there this morning," Mueller said, "where they're digging."

"I thought you were out of supplies," Bosworth said.

"I thought so, too," Mueller replied, "but Heinrich had these tools, still uncrated, under a tarpaulin."

"Lucky," Bosworth said.

"Do an inventory, Kiefur," Mueller said to the POW. He signaled Bosworth to follow him to the front of the supply tent.

"Why is the Colonel doing this?" Mueller asked.

"His last ditch effort, he called it."

"Funny," Mueller said. "Only the TPM won't think it's funny when they get wind of it. Does he think moving the tracks out of the camp will stop more POWs from being shipped here?"

"That's what he thinks," Bosworth said.

"What do you think?" Mueller asked.

"It could work."

"You're serious."

"To send POWs here," Bosworth said, "without a track into the camp means they'd be dumped at some other station in Le Mans and then they'd either be trucked or marched over here."

"What's wrong with that?"

"The locals won't be pleased," Bosworth said. "They might even show their displeasure by knocking off a few of the incoming Krauts."

"So?"

"So," Bosworth continued, "rather than assign more security forces here to protect the POWs—and, logistically, that's unlikely—the TPM might decide to send the POWs to some other camp."

"They also might decide," Mueller said, "to transfer the cause of all their problems to some post where he can't cause trouble. Tell me if I'm wrong but isn't the Colonel asking for it?"

"He's asking for a new policy," Bosworth said, "one different from Germany's, one that shows some respect for human life."

"That's bullshit!" Mueller said. "We're here to win the war—and so is Germany. I say the Colonel's looking for a transfer and this little excavation of his could be his way out of here."

*   *   *

Captain Roland left the railroad spur and stopped at the Colonel's quarters.

"You still can call it off," Roland said, sitting across the desk from the Colonel. "It's not too late. At least wait until the convoy returns."

Nelson was happy to see Roland. The Belgian now seemed

comfortable with his American superior. That he could drop in without an invitation was as remarkable as his readiness to be critical of Nelson. "Pomerantz said the convoy's doomed," Nelson said. "The French will attack it."

"Your young sergeant's resourceful," Roland said. "I bet he returns with trucks full of supplies."

"Maybe, and maybe not. He's on a dangerous mission, possibly a wild goose chase, all because I had to assuage my guilt."

"Guilt? What guilt? You're a soldier. You obey orders. You do what you're told. Your war's here. If you believe you're being asked to do the impossible, you're expected to complain. You've done that. If you're still not satisfied, you're expected to show initiative. You've done that. You've done all you can. There should be no guilt."

"You make it sound cut and dried," Nelson said. "Simple."

"It is simple. That's why I like the military. It is simple if you accept authority."

"Accepting authority's one thing. Abdicating independent thought is something else."

Nelson knew what was wrong. He was condemned to ambivalence. That was his assignment. To preserve the same enemy he was supposed to destroy. How could you be untroubled when your mission was diametrically opposed to what you were trained to feel? It's a wonder we're not all Section 8s in this prison, he thought. Especially Delman, cruising around in his crazy convoy, scrounging for supplies to save the Germans he hates.

"It's easy for Pomerantz in Paris, with all the rest of his fat-ass coterie," Nelson continued, "to keep sending us prisoners. So what happens? You feel sorry for them, their deprivation, their suffering, and you start to think of them as human beings, not just as your enemy."

"Is that why you feel guilty," Roland said, "because you think you don't hate them enough?"

"That's what it comes down to."

"What you're doing removing the tracks, whether it works or not, isn't an answer. It will only antagonize Pomerantz."

"That's not why I'm doing it," Nelson said.

"He sounds as angry as you," Roland said, "as obsessive. He'll see it as a protest, an act of defiance. He'll say you're forcing his hand."

"To change his policy," Nelson said.

"No, to change his command here."

"Is that how you see it?" Nelson asked.

"That's how I see it," Roland said, "that's how anyone will see it—and particularly Pomerantz who now must have his eye on you after your face-to-face."

Nelson lifted himself from his chair—with a groan. Arguments increased his weariness. He realized Roland, who always leaned his way, was trying to be helpful. Nelson strode around his office, trying to grasp the mindset of Pomerantz, and then returned to his chair. With another groan, he sat down.

"I'll stop it," Nelson said, "for now. But only for now. If the convoy doesn't work, I'll start it again. That's a promise."

                              *   *   *

When the convoy stopped, Sergeant Perry walked over to Trabert who was watching the POWs leave their trucks. "Come over to my truck for a minute," Perry said. "I've got something to show you."

The guard followed Perry who went to his truck, opened its door, and pulled out a carton.

"Take a look," Perry said.

Trabert opened it and saw walkie-talkies.

"Where did you get these?"

"At the last depot," Perry said. "I know the sergeant there."

"Why didn't you give one of them to Delman?" Trabert asked. "It might have come in handy when we had to drop out of the convoy."

"Delman trusts me as far as he can throw me," Perry said. "And I don't blame him. He might think I was holding out on him, that I had the walkie-talkies all the time and, for whatever reason, didn't want him to know about them."

"I don't know," Trabert said. "Why would you hold out on him?"

"To cause trouble," Perry said. "To make him more anxious. To wear him out."

"Is he that suspicious?"

"If he isn't," Perry says, "he's a jerk and he's not a jerk. Hell, he knows I'm regular Army and that I'm a friend of Mueller, his big enemy."

"But you've proved you're out to help him," Trabert said, "sitting in the last truck, getting out your rifle when the French came closer."

"A mistake," Perry said. "He thought I was wrong doing that—and he was right. I was trying to be funny, the warrior with his helmet and rifle. But it didn't come off."

"Do these work?" Trabert asked, turning over the carton in his hand. He returned it to Perry.

"I should test it," he said. "You take one and we'll see if it works."

"Then what?"

"Then," Perry said, "I'll have to figure out what to do. Maybe you keep one and we give one to Clary. But if I tell Delman we've got walkie-talkies he's going to think I've got it in for him."

"He's smarter than that," Trabert said.

"I think he's plenty smart," Perry said. "This convoy proves it."

"I don't know that this convoy proves anything," Trabert said, "except we're desperate."

"Delman would be cleaning latrines until the end of the war if he hadn't come up with this convoy idea and sold it to the Colonel who's also plenty smart."

"Only Delman's helping the Germans who he says he hates."

"He had to figure out a way to escape from Mueller," Perry said, "from his punishment for slugging two POWs, and he did."

"The POWs will think he's their savior if this works."

"Who cares what they think."

"Doesn't this convoy help them?"

"Doesn't everything we do in our POW camp help them?" Perry said. "It just proves how fucked up this war is. We want to eradicate the Germans but we take prisoners."

CHAPTER 22

WHEN MUELLER ENTERED the Colonel's office, the first thing he noticed was that it smelled musty, stale, and a window should've been cracked. Then Mueller noticed that the Colonel's usual tightly made bed, complete with sharp military corners, was indented. He took cat naps. His musette bag, the one he had carried on their Paris trip, was thrown on top of his crumpled, half-empty duffel. It leaned in a corner like a shrunken torso, headless, armless, forlorn.

The Colonel's had it, Mueller thought. No wonder he didn't react when I sent Heinrich to the convoy.

When the Colonel looked up, Mueller saluted sharply, quickly, with his usual military panache. Only when he was in the middle of it did he realize its near-perfection was a mistake.

The Colonel paused—Mueller thought he'd never get around to it—before he returned the salute. And when he added a grimace to his perfunctory salute—a swat, as if he were fighting persistent, annoying gnats attacking his face—he showed his usual disdain for Mueller's military correctness.

Then the Colonel, suddenly tired, leaned back for an instant, his chin on his chest, his mouth partially open, his hands folded in his lap, as if he were recovering from a five-mile marathon. Mueller, who hadn't examined his commanding officer so carefully or so closely for months, saw he'd aged two years for each of the nine months he ruled the camp. His resemblance to Ike had vanished. The Colonel was thinner, balder, and new wrinkles were under his eyes, on his forehead. He no longer seemed Ike's clone and no longer radiated a suggestion of the General's always energetic, always confident demeanor. Nelson had been relaxed, casual, close to light-hearted, a funny guy if you liked your humor dry. Now, Mueller thought, the Colonel was intense, hypersensitive, ready to take offense. If you didn't know better, you'd look at him and say we've lost the war.

"At ease, sergeant," Nelson said, even his voice subdued. "Sit down."

Mueller had heard that Nelson barely slept at night. He got up four or five times, not because of a growing prostate problem, but because his cot was solitary confinement, a prison within a prison. He needs R & R, Mueller thought; at the least, a weekend pass, at the most, if his conscience would let him, a generous woman. He had even let his dress go to pot. He used to be meticulous, his shirts pressed, his jackets brushed. He had a natural style, a flair, a cavalier appearance, a World War II version of the World War I scarf-around-the-neck, crushed-capped aviator.

No more. Now, he slumped around in ordinary fatigues that weren't so ordinary. They were stained, rumpled, rancid, and repulsive. They looked as bad as he did, slept-in and unwashed. Even his desk was a mess. Mueller traced its pungent odor to a smashed stogie in the overflowing ashtray. It was full of cigarette butts and wads of paper—perhaps attempted letters to his wife—that must have been crushed in despair and frustration.

Mueller always despised dirt and disorder. He traced his hatred to his youthful days when he thought he'd live and die in his family's miserable gas station. In preparation for his life term, he struggled daily to do his father's bidding: keeping the station clean and orderly. After school, he'd attack it with a broom, sponge, soapy water, and a shovel he used to scoop up the ever-present dog shit. Two giant Schnauzers, released at night, insured the station's security, destroyed visiting cats and rats, and kept Mueller humping. After cleaning, he'd align the numerous products—cans of oil and oil additive, batteries, antifreeze—they sold from the office. He'd also try to straighten up the service area. He even prepared open cartons, each carefully marked: "wrenches," "screwdrivers," "hammers."

But the mechanics refused to cooperate. So, every day, Mueller would have to rescue their tools from the floor or from cars that were being serviced. He gathered used rags, supplied clean ones, and spread sawdust on the floor to sop up spilled liquids. Anything to fight the filth.

"I wanted to let the Colonel know," Mueller began, "Delman's convoy's been spotted in the supply depot at Tours."

"And?"

"He took off—without any supplies."

"Why?"

"No idea, sir."

"Maybe," Nelson said, "because he wouldn't pay off someone. That sounds like Delman, doesn't it? He was smart."

Mueller said, "His convoy was attacked when he was leaving Tours. A hundred French farmers went after him."

"Only a hundred?" the Colonel said.

"Delman turned tail and ran."

"Smart again," Nelson replied.

He rose, glanced at Mueller, and began to pace. He made two full circles of his office before he stopped in front of the NCO.

"This comes from your network, right," Nelson asked, "your NCO buddies?"

"Yes, sir," Mueller said.

"Tell me again," the Colonel said, "how your network works."

"I sent a V-mail to my friends, fellow NCOs," Mueller explained, "stationed near the supply depots along the convoy's route. I told them to be on the lookout for a convoy driven by POWs. They made sure anyone leaving their base kept their eyes open."

"Why would anyone bother telling what they saw to his NCO?"

"We reward those who give us reliable information," Mueller said.

"What kind of reward?"

"Cigarettes, chocolate," Mueller replied, "sometimes booze. Depends on the information."

"Then your NCO near a supply depot," Nelson said, "relays the information to you."

"He calls me," Mueller said.

Nelson planted himself in front of Mueller. "What do you want me to do, sergeant, call off the convoy, bring it back here because of your report?"

"Delman's on his way to Angers," Mueller said.

Nelson hastened to the map pinned to his wall. "He should be here," he said, pointing to Angers on his map.

"Just in time," Mueller said, unable to hide a small smile, "to find its depot closed."

Nelson turned to face Mueller. "You sure of that?"

"Yes, sir," Mueller replied.

"Then Delman'll go to Rennes," the Colonel said, running his finger along the map.

Mueller said, "Unless he gives up and . . ."

"Delman!" the Colonel said, back in his chair. "Delman give up!" His voice, his attitude, his posture, suddenly changed. He was the old Colonel, assured, angry, and astounded at Mueller's suggestion.

The Colonel slapped his desk. "You've got the wrong boy, sergeant. Delman'll go back to the states to find a depot with supplies before he gives up. We've got a bulldog in charge of that convoy, Mueller. A bulldog. Jews are bulldogs, Sergeant Mueller, you know that. That's why they've survived—they don't give up. Delman's a bulldog."

"A fucking bulldog, sir," Mueller replied, eyes dead-ahead, seated across from his colonel.

Nelson glared at him. "Delman won't return empty. The convoy was his idea, his first command. He won't let it fall apart. Not even with Heinrich aboard."

Mueller hadn't expected that. He replied in kind. "Unless

Delman punches out another German."

"I wouldn't count on that, sergeant."

"No, sir," replied Mueller, rising, saluting, giving no quarter now, holding it until his tired Colonel, this beat civilian, returned it.

"Maybe, Sergeant Mueller," Nelson said, giving a quick return salute, "you should spend more time investigating what you've got in your supply tent. I hear you discovered a hoard of shovels and pickaxes and crowbars that Heinrich had hidden in some corner, that we used to remove the railroad spur. Now why would Heinrich do that? Certainly not to escape. He wouldn't dig an escape route under one of our fences. Not your valued assistant, the POW you decided had to be sent on the convoy."

Mueller didn't deserve such a reprimand. It was unwise to argue with a superior but an explanation was in order.

"Sir . . ." Mueller began.

Nelson would have none of it; he interrupted.

"Dismissed," he said.

You sloppy, disorganized civilian, Mueller thought. Dismissed! You're the one who should be dismissed! With your wild goose chase to Paris and your dismantling of our railroad track. You're cracking up. Mueller about-faced and left the disheveled, malodorous office that told him all he needed to know about the sorry state of his commanding officer.

*   *   *

Ramer, Delman's driver, nodded at a road sign that showed they weren't far from Angers. For a change, the weather was clear; cold but clear with an occasional shock of sunshine. Now all they had to do was to locate the supply depot and convince its cadre to load the trucks.

Or would Delman face another corrupt NCO who gave left-overs—forget what you really needed—for prized loot? Maybe, he thought, he had acted too fast at the Tours depot. A little less anger and a little more adroitness might have turned the lye into clothes, tents, rations. But Delman showed Perry—and the few POWs who weren't dead on their feet—that their leader wasn't a patsy, about to roll over for a greedy clerk, friend of Perry's or not.

The convoy passed empty farm after empty farm. Some with broken trees, smashed fences, torn silos; more with deep craters where planes and artillery dropped bombs, lobbed shells. Delman ordered his driver to decelerate. He held up his hand to the trucks behind him to slow them down as he saw the spires of Angers through the bare winter trees. He checked his map, looked for the big D he had circled, and knew he was on the right road.

He soon spotted the supply depot to his right. A barbed-wire fence surrounded it, except for its open entrance. Next to the depot were several smaller buildings, probably barracks, maybe a garage for the motor pool and latrines. No soldiers were anywhere.

"It looks deserted," Delman said to his driver. "Damn. Go toward that large door at the end of the depot."

As they approached it, they saw indented tire tracks in the packed ice and snow. Here and there, oil stains—like giant bird droppings—left their black marks. A part of the area—an uneven rectangle between the buildings—was flattened, probably where troops marched in place and shuffled to keep warm while they waited, with packs on, rifles at parade rest, for their orders.

"Stop here," Delman ordered.

His trucks pulled in behind him. Delman slid toward the depot's huge door. Perry helped him slide it open. Inside they found remnants of a fast pull-out: empty cartons, broken crates, putrid garbage pails, acrid jerry cans, shelter halfs, filthy blankets, dented mess kits, broken tables and chairs. Delman kicked at the debris. What now? It was too late in the day to move out and he didn't relish driving in the dark. It would be custom-made for Heinrich.

"I've been here to pick up auto parts," Perry said. "Used to be like ten PXs rolled into one. Squads of GIs along with civilians, mostly old men and young girls, got your stuff for you. Nice looking girls."

"It's warmer in here," Delman said, "and there are only those two big, sliding doors. Windows are too high to climb out of."

"Spend the night here?" Perry asked. "Why not?"

He strolled to a long counter and reached below it. He tugged at something and slowly extracted a stuffed mattress cover.

"I wondered," he said, "if it would still be here."

"Looks well-used," Delman said.

He surveyed the deserted depot. Empty but sturdy. No holes in the walls, no holes in the ground, no ways to escape. They could bring the trucks inside; not a bad idea after what had happened with the French, and be secure. He returned to Perry.

"Move the trucks into the depot," Delman said.

When they were inside, he and Perry pulled the door closed.

"While you take the POWs to the latrine," he told the guards, "Perry and I'll get out the rations."

When the guards returned with the POWs, Delman directed them to put their blankets against a wall equidistant from each door.

"What do you think," he asked Trabert, "a guard at each door?"

"I'll move a truck against one door," he replied, "so they can't open it and Clary and I will take turns guarding the other one."

"I'll ask Perry to watch Heinrich," Delman said.

He could guess what Perry would think: the kid suspects I might've had something to do with Heinrich being here. So I'm going to be the one who's stuck watching him when we're not driving. Cute, very cute.

And even if I had nothing to do with the German, why not stick me with him, even part-time? If anything goes wrong when it's most likely to go wrong—when he's not driving—it'll be my ass, not Delman's. Nice maneuver, kid.

"What d'you say?" Delman asked. "Clary and Trabert'll watch the doors and you'll watch Heinrich. I'll be circulating, checking the other POWs."

"I'm supposed to guard Heinrich?" Perry replied.

"I know you can handle it," Delman said.

He left to tell Clary the security plan, that Perry would be responsible for watching Heinrich in the depot.

"I can watch Heinrich," Clary said.

"You need a break."

"Guards don't get breaks," Clary said.

"Perry has to get more involved in this convoy," Delman said. "Guarding Heinrich's one way to do it. Why don't you give him a hand distributing the rations."

"Before you go," Clary said, "I've got something to show you."

"Christ," Delman said, looking at the walkie-talkie. "Where did you get that?"

"Perry," Clary said, "Trabert has the other one."

"Perry!"

"I know," Clary said. "Perry got them from that NCO at the Tours depot. We tested them and they don't work very well. Perry was afraid if you knew he got them, you'd suspect he got them earlier and then you'd think he was holding out on you. So I said I wouldn't say anything."

"Perry," Delman said.

"Maybe he's one of the good guys," Clary said. "You won't say anything?"

"You say they don't work," Delman said.

"Now and then," Clary said. "Only worth a try if we have an emergency."

"I wonder what else he's holding back?" Delman said.

He slept fitfully, rising at each unexpected sound. Finally, he threw aside his blankets and strode around the empty depot, remarkably bright from the moonlight. He decided to count the bodies wrapped in their blankets. After one turn, he knew something was wrong. Or was it his count? He quickly returned to where he'd started and counted again.

Two people were missing. Delman wiped sudden sweat from his face and felt it drip down his back. Where was Perry and, more important, where was Heinrich?

Delman bent low over every POW, almost knowing them by smell as well as by sight. The masquerading German officer was gone. Vanished. They had to be here. But where? Did they—Perry and Heinrich—go outside together? That was it, Delman thought. Heinrich and Perry had left together to relieve themselves.

A hand touched him. It was Clary.

"What's wrong?" he asked.

"I can't find Heinrich," Delman said, "or Perry."

"I saw Perry leave," Clary said. "He said something to me but I was half asleep. I had just gotten off guard duty."

"Could it have been Heinrich you saw," Delman asked, "and thought it was Perry?"

"It was Perry," Clary said, now standing, holding his rifle. "But maybe when I thought I saw him return it was Heinrich."

"I'll check outside," Delman said. "You stay here."

He slid open the door with Trabert and ran, his fast, heaving breath making a cloud. He circled the depot, doubling back a second time, using his flashlight. No one was outside. He returned to the door where Trabert was standing, re-entered, and helped slide the door shut.

Then, slowly, he walked along the interior periphery of the depot, using his flashlight. Finally, he cut across, going toward the counter. He saw something, maybe a head, going up and down. Closer to the counter, he heard grunting, whispers, heavy breathing almost in unison, and the fleshy smack of two bodies hitting, sliding into one another.

He saw Perry, his pants around his ankles, prone over a woman, thrusting, bouncing. Their groans reached Delman and, without thinking, his breathing started to match theirs. Where did Perry find a woman?

But then his fear returned. Where was Heinrich? He ran back to the sleeping Germans and counted again. Clary joined him. Delman whispered the names of the drivers to Clary as they bent over them and there was Heinrich, curled up in blankets that Delman knew, with absolute certainty, had been empty only minutes earlier.

Had Heinrich been free—even for a few moments? Had he time to plot with one of the other POWs? The important fact was that Perry was occupied with a woman while his charge, his captive, his responsibility, was possibly doing damage.

Delman had stayed in the sleeping area longer than he realized. When he ran across the depot to find Perry, the non-com was leaning against a wall, his pants up, buckled, a cigarette in his mouth. He saw Delman and held his stare as he whipped out his macho zippo and, like some flasher opening his coat, threw back the lighter's cover to flick on its flame.

"You bastard," Delman said, his face an inch away from the burning tip of Perry's cigarette. "You were supposed to watch Heinrich."

"Relax," Perry said. "Heinrich's not going any place. I told Clary to watch him while I was busy."

"When I checked, Heinrich was out of his blankets."

"So maybe he's a fag," Perry said. "He didn't escape, did he?"

"You gave him the chance he wanted—to set up some escape plan with one of the other POWs."

"Says who?" Perry replied. "You're looking for trouble where there isn't any."

"With you here," Delman said, "I don't have to look very far."

The motor pool chief laughed. "You sad sack."

He dropped his cigarette. Slowly, he ground it with his combat boot. Then, calmly, without any urgency, he turned to confront his furious convoy commander.

"Why don't you blow it out your ass, Delman."

Chapter 23

"Jan. 14, 1945—I can't trust Perry. He's with a woman—where does he find them?—when he's supposed to be guarding Heinrich. And the German's too cooperative. The question is not *if* he'll try to escape but *when*.

"Rennes is next, our last chance for supplies. Everyone's on edge. The Belgians take it out on the POWs, Perry takes it out on me, and I take it out on everyone. When this began, I was optimistic. No longer. The convoy's more dangerous than I anticipated, thanks to Mueller."

*　　*　　*

"What the hell did you think you were doing," Sacher whispered to Heinrich, "waking me up in the middle of the night?"

They both were shivering from the cold as they waited in line in front of the outhouse.

"My guard left me alone," Heinrich said. "I had to talk to you."

"I've got nothing to talk to you about," Sacher said, viciously using his elbow to keep Heinrich away. "Stay the hell away from me."

"Take it easy," Heinrich said, rubbing his shoulder where Sacher hit him, keeping his voice low, moving closer. "The guard's watching us. We'll talk later."

"Not to me, you won't," Sacher said, using his elbow again. "You got the wrong guy."

Heinrich had heard about Sacher's outbursts in camp. They'd been covered up. Rumors had it that Sacher, quick to take offense and use his fists, had punched out several fellow POWs.

He always was a hothead, completely irascible. In large part, it was his explosiveness that made him famous.

You're the right man, Heinrich thought. I'll risk your craziness for your skill. After holding his breath in the latrine, he stepped outside and inhaled the cold air before he slid in his truck next to his silent guard. Any minute, Heinrich was certain, he'd feel the Belgian's rifle jab his side.

The convoy sped out of the empty depot. Heinrich rubbed his cracked fingers over his unshaven face, pock-marked with grime. He had to escape, if only to get clean. Even to himself, he smelled repulsive, sour, a walking armpit.

His masquerade, as necessary as it was, had its drawbacks. Most suspected he was an officer so he'd become a target. For Delman's scorn, Perry's amusement and the pleasure of the sadistic Belgians, especially the baby-faced guard next to him with his poking rifle. What was his name? Clary, that was it. Why was Clary constantly jabbing? To show his superiority, to relieve his boredom? All Heinrich knew was that the Belgian had refined his torture: he hit the same exact spot near Heinrich's lower rib, again and again.

He struggled to hide his pain. There'd only be more frequent jabs from his baby-faced persecutor if he didn't. Heinrich forced himself to think about something other than his tender side. He thought about Sacher. At first, Heinrich hadn't recognized him. With his layers of clothes, his wool cap and unshaven face, he no longer resembled the suave, lithe, slick-haired racing driver whose lizard-like face graced, at one time or another, every major European racing magazine.

No wonder his captors never discovered him. Heinrich recalled the name that, in automotive circles, never referred to the Austrian dessert. Heinrich knew Sacher was the lead driver of Germany's most successful racing team.

And he was more than a daring, come-from-behind driver. He worked with several manufacturers to develop innovative sports cars. He became known as much for his knowledgeable, hands-on automotive expertise as for his courageous driving skills, and he was smart, a good businessman. Sacher had formed several corporations, probably to gain tax advantages as well as positions for members of his extended family. Nor had he forgotten his young children. When they matured—if they wished and were capable—they'd have the choice of a variety of jobs, thanks to their father's enterprises, from financial and marketing positions to eventually succeeding him. But to single-minded Heinrich, Sacher's value was immediate. He would make Heinrich's escape plan a success.

Originally, Heinrich had planned to use a second POW as a distraction, as expendable bait to mask his escape. When he found Sacher, Heinrich altered his strategy. They'd escape together. How would he distract his guards? Heinrich would have to devise some ploy, depending upon the opportunity. Perhaps flattening a tire, starting a ruckus, or, least desirable although most pleasurable, killing his jabbing Belgian.

Then, in the midst of the confusion, he and Sacher would take a truck—and the baby-faced guard if still alive—and disappear. Once away from the convoy, Heinrich would find a car, Sacher would start it, and they'd take off, keeping to back roads. The guard? That would depend on what happened. Heinrich learned that plans never worked out; it was better to be flexible. The guard might be most useful as a hostage. If stopped, they'd say they were French laborers foraging for francs.

They'd obliterate the "POW" stigmata on their clothes and Heinrich's fluent French and Sacher's driving and mechanical skill would guide them back to their lines. Heinrich knew getting through France wasn't the problem; it was getting stubborn Sacher to forsake the safety and comfort of the convoy.

At the next stop, Heinrich pretended he had a sudden attack of cramps, a common POW ailment. He moaned, bent over, and clutched his stomach. The guard allowed him to leave his truck and go into the bushes as long as he remained in sight. Heinrich saw Sacher defecating behind a tree.

"Fuck off," Sacher said.

"You're talking to an officer," Heinrich said.

He had heard that Sacher could have become an officer; a commission was offered to him but he rejected it. Instead he enlisted as a private and became a sergeant within one year. He bragged that he was one of the people, not one of the elite. Yet Heinrich knew Sacher owned homes in Germany, Austria, and tax-free Monaco, seven sleek cars, and two airplanes.

"You could be a general for all I care," Sacher said. "Leave me alone."

"You and I," Heinrich said, "are going to escape together."

"Says who?" Sacher answered. "The war's over."

"You know about our offensive," Heinrich said.

"So what?"

"Hitler doesn't waste lives," Heinrich said. "He's prolonging the war for a reason."

"Sure," Sacher said, "to save his ass."

For a moment, Heinrich thought of what he had done to Wanger. He could do the same to Sacher, regardless of his fame. Heinrich would enjoy slamming a board against Sacher's skull and bringing a deserved end to his blasphemous words.

"Hitler's delaying tactics," Heinrich said, "will allow our scientists to perfect the big bomb. And with it, we win the war."

"I've heard that 'big bomb' talk before," Sacher said. "It's nothing but shit." He held up the stained newspaper he used to wipe himself. "Like this."

Heinrich wouldn't let this gross, insubordinate sergeant put him off, celebrity or not.

He'd try a new tactic.

"Give me five minutes," Heinrich said, "to listen to my escape plan. That's not asking too much."

Sacher, speaking slowly, insultingly, pulled together his clothes. "I'm going to say this only one more time—fuck off!"

POW or not, no soldier had the right to speak so flagrantly to a fellow soldier, even if he didn't recognize his superior military rank. Common courtesy demanded no less. Particularly if you were discussing escape—a requisite reaction for any member of the Wehrmacht taken prisoner.

Heinrich realized foul-mouthed Sacher was all ego and had to be shocked into thinking beyond his own emaciated, selfish self. Heinrich knew the process he needed, what he had to do. He recalled how he learned that process during his first experience riding horseback with his elegant, commanding father, who had told his son, "To ride properly, the first thing you must remember is to establish your dominance over your horse. He must recognize you are in charge. To establish your dominance, you first must make certain you have your horse's undivided attention. You don't take it for granted; you must grab it. Giving an animal a command is meaningless unless he is aware of your power, your control."

"How do I get his attention?" Heinrich had asked.

"Painfully," his father had said. "Use your spurs, hard, again and again. Show him you are in charge. Show him you will hurt him unless he pays attention to you. Make him fear you. Then he'll heed what you say."

Heinrich ran to Trabert, the nearest guard, and pointed to Sacher.

"Hit him," Heinrich screamed, "punish him!"

"What?"

"He attacked me," Heinrich said, "when I was squatting over there with my pants down. He's a queer. He went after me."

Delman, nearby, heard Heinrich yelling at Trabert.

"What's going on?" Delman asked.

"This POW," Trabert explained, slowly leveling his rifle at Sacher, "saw Heinrich with his pants down and went after him, like a dog in heat."

"Lower your rifle," Delman said, "and you—POWs. Back to your trucks. Now!"

"Do as I say," Heinrich whispered to Sacher, "or I'll repeat my charge. You won't get off so lucky the next time; I'll make sure the Jew's not around to protect you."

"You're crazy," Sacher said.

"I'll get one of the guards to punish you," Heinrich said. "I guarantee he'll knock you around. All your work, all your efforts, will be sacrificed because you refuse to listen to me. Sacher, now famous, will be forgotten. You'll die in our camp with all the rest of our scared soldiers. There will be no more Grand Prix for Sacher. Five minutes is all I ask."

Sacher stopped. His large hands tightened into fists as he held Heinrich's unwavering eyes. Finally, Sacher's fists uncurled.

"Five minutes," he said. "No more."

*   *   *

Delman withdrew his map from its protective envelope. He checked the distance—using the first joint of his thumb, about one inch, which he measured against the map's scale—from Angers to Rennes. Almost eighty miles. He saw the familiar circled D near the city indicating where a depot was located unless, like the Angers depot, it had been deserted.

I have to get supplies in Rennes, he told himself. There's no way I'll go there and leave with empty trucks. He put his thumb down again on the map. Another ninety miles or so back to Le Mans, two or three hours at the most.

Then he'd be back in prison. But if he returned with supplies, he'd also return with a tested way to take another convoy out of the barbed-wire enclosure. And he'd be able to pretend he was free again.

The awful irony of what he was doing suddenly overwhelmed him. He felt cold, as if a gale had swept across his face. Without thinking, he pulled down his cap, pulled up his collar, thrust his gloved hands into his overcoat's deep unlined pockets. If this, his first convoy, was a success, would he spend the rest of the war protecting POWs? In exchange for his own escape—and it was only temporary, at that—was he turning into a self-indulgent Perry, putting his own comfort first, dismissing what the Germans were, did, could still do?

The convoy rolled through quiet villages, past empty fields, toward Rennes. Delman said little. He kept track of the side-of-the-road Red Ball markers leading to the fall-back depot.

Delman's driver suddenly became alert. He pointed at the familiar barbed-wire fence, the hangar-like buildings, the scarred road and—thank God, thought Delman—American soldiers in overcoats, helmet liners, carrying MI's, manning a gate. What are they guarding? Let it be a supply depot, Delman thought. He returned their salute. I'm an officer again, he thought, probably as short-lived as my freedom. They kept their gate lowered. He handed them Mueller's requisitions. They examined them and went into their small guardhouse.

He could see one soldier on their field phone. Finally, they returned to tell Delman to report to headquarters, the smallest building near the fence. The soldier pointed to it. No salutes this time. They saw my stripes, Delman thought. I've been demoted to flunky.

"You go," one guard explained, "but your trucks stay here."

Whatever you say, Delman thought. You give the orders and I'll do your bidding. All I ask in return are supplies. Inside the headquarters building, Delman saw a strict, by-the-book operation. Mueller would've been proud. Desks were evenly spaced. File cabinets stood, like sentries, in the center of each wall. Even notices on the bulletin board were thumb-tacked symmetrically: charge of quarters, assignments and those receiving daily passes on one side, sick call hours and special assignments on the other.

Three NCOs, two privates and two civilians—both wom-

en—worked at their desks and typewriters. Delman studied the
women. One was a head taller than the other. Both were young,
attractive, full-figured. They wore dark skirts and tight sweaters.
A corporal rose, greeted Delman, and checked his requisitions.
He took them to a captain sitting in an inner office where they
seemed to review each of Mueller's requests, item by item. The
corporal returned to his desk and began to thumb through a
file of index cards.

Delman switched his gaze back to the captain's office where
he now was talking to the taller of the two women clerks. Delman was taken aback; he thought he saw the captain draw her
closer to him. Delman couldn't see what was happening but he
thought he saw the woman suddenly jump, gasp. Was she letting
the captain's hand roam below her skirt? Delman fantasized.
He imagined the clerk's breath becoming louder, quicker; the
captain's hand moving upward, his fingers gently exploring,
touching, entering.

The corporal said, "You can pick up your supplies in the
morning. 0800. Your quarters are the Quonset directly behind
our depot. I understand your drivers are POWs."

It took a moment for Delman to readjust.

"Right," he answered, "POWs."

"You mean you're actually using fucking Germans to drive
your trucks?"

"Fucking Germans," Delman said.

"I'll be damned. Well, how you quarter them's your problem."

"Thanks," Delman said.

"Mess hall's behind your quarters," the corporal continued.
"Hours are posted. Anything you want to know?"

"What about getting supplies tonight?" Delman asked.

"Negative," the corporal replied.

Delman nodded.

"I'll bring my convoy in."

It was going too well, he thought. He looked at the captain's office but he was no longer there. What are they doing now, Delman wondered, as he returned to his jeep, its exhaust steaming in the frigid air, the trucks behind it making their own smoke.

Something had to give. Maybe the corporal would demand a payoff. Or the captain would decide he couldn't part with the requisitioned supplies unless Delman could part with booze and cigarettes. Leading his trucks behind the Quonset, he knew he wouldn't hesitate. He'd happily exchange all his barter—hell, he'd give them his overcoat, his fatigue jacket, you name it—to be able to return with full trucks.

Inside the cold hut, Delman quickly assigned cots. He posted a guard on each end and placed Heinrich and Perry in the center. Delman took the cot closest to the entrance. He told two POWs to start a fire in the stove and ordered the guards to move the POWs into the latrine once they dropped their gear.

Perry approached. "After we eat, what d'you say we blow this place and go into town? I've been here before. I know a couple of local women. Prime pussy. You've been deprived too long."

Perry's offer couldn't have been better timed. Delman still hadn't recovered from what he imagined in the captain's office. He looked at the POWs and figured that, with the Belgians guarding them, he was covered. What's more, the depot was well protected with its own guards.

But why was Perry being solicitous? Why, after their last exchange, was he trying to make amends? Delman wanted to trust him but he'd been conned too many times by the motor pool boss. After all, Delman thought, Perry was Mueller's friend. They were both regular Army, they shared the same loyalty: they came first. Delman distrusted Perry as much as he disliked Mueller.

Delman led the way into the mess hall. Clary and Trabert kept the POWs in single file as they stood in line holding their mess kits to receive stew, beans, cakes, and coffee. When they returned, Delman gave orders to the guards.

CHAPTER 23   225

"Wake us up by 0600," he said. "No later. I want us first in line to get supplies."

He took his toilet kit to the latrine and, for the first time since he left the camp, brought out his safety razor. He missed his POW barber. But, except for two nicks below his chin, he did a passable job. He threw water against his face and hair.

And only then did it occur to him what he was about to do. Deprived or not, Delman realized his leaving would be wrong, an act so blatantly selfish he was stunned that he had even considered Perry's offer. Perry knew what he was doing. He attacked Delman where he was most vulnerable, little different than his earlier ploy, the questionable story about mass sex on Delman's old bunk.

But when you cut through it, maybe Perry, as always, was thinking of Perry. With his commander with him, Perry would be protecting his ass, regardless of where he went, regardless of what happened.

Either way, Delman thought, I'd be properly charged, if something happened while I was gone. And if nothing happened, if I lucked out, I'd still carry the guilt of doing wrong just as I carry the guilt of creating this convoy, this charade that I'm doing something important.

"We'll stay here tonight," Delman told Perry. "No one leaves."

"For Christ's sake," Perry said. "You've got two guards here. There are more guards on the outside. This place is tighter than a virgin's ass. What's your problem, Delman? Did your retreat from the Frogs do you in? You're running scared, Delman, that's what you're doing. Your brains must be in your feet. Or in your ass."

"And yours," Delman said, "must be in your prick."

                              *   *   *

At 0800, Delman had his convoy lined up in the supply depot. He thought of newly born birds in their nest, their mouths agape, waiting for their parents to deposit food in their screaming beaks.

A buck sergeant materialized. Delman gave him the approved requisitions. I'm ready for anything, Delman thought, I know what I'm doing, I've done it before and this time—he repeated to himself—this time, I'll succeed.

The bulky sergeant, bigger than Delman, convinced him his day in the Rennes supply depot would last forever. The shipping clerk was in no hurry. He was precise, exacting, infuriating. He had to be a defensive perfectionist. He triple-checked everything. Delman could feel impatience race through his body. To maintain control, he concentrated on each of his movements, his arm thrusting forward, his hand holding the requisitions, his fingers releasing them when they were accepted by the sergeant.

He kept telling himself to stay calm. He didn't want to do anything to suggest he was desperate for supplies, that getting them wasn't an ordinary, routine, everyday task. He didn't want to provide the sergeant with the slightest reason to interrupt his sluggish behavior that would, sometime, somehow, get Delman's trucks full.

He thought ahead. He believed he was prepared for any eventuality—and had considered every possibility. But he wasn't ready for what happened next.

The sergeant, reading from the first item in the requisition that had been approved by the corporal, called out to his civilian workers in a loud Southern drawl, "Two hundred and fifty shelter halfs."

It's happening, Delman thought: the workers will pull the supplies off their pallets, place them on waiting handcars, and roll them to our trucks. But they remained immobile, as if they had never heard the clerk's raucous voice. The clerk was surprised. He paused, groaned and ambled toward his workers, seven stoic Frenchman. Delman was too far away to hear their complaints.

The NCO paced as they spoke. He didn't interrupt them. When they finished, he stopped pacing and faced them. He appeared to speak quietly at first but, getting no response, became agitated and concluded by waving Delman's requisitions in front of their unflinching faces.

They listened courteously. Finally, they shook their heads and sullenly waited as the NCO, flabbergasted and sheepish, returned to Delman.

"It's your POWs," the sergeant explained. "My workers are civilians. Frenchmen. Some fought the Germans. They say they won't have anything to do with them, POWs or not. They refuse to load your trucks."

Perry stood next to Delman. "I can't believe it," Perry said, "these civilian bastards are as stupid as those fucking French farmers."

Delman understood their dilemma. Maybe you have to be Jewish, he thought, to recognize their thinking—no, their feeling. Their reaction was completely emotional.

"They've had enough," he said. "They've decided that being defeated by them in the war was bad enough, but they'd be damned if they'd forget what happened. And to help them now was too much."

"Except," Perry said, "they're helping us—or supposed to be."

"They don't look at it that way," Delman said. "All they see are their enemies."

"Then they better requisition some white canes," Perry said, "because they're blind."

Delman turned to his drivers. "Out of your trucks," he ordered.

When they were on the ground, he said, "Form two groups. I'll take this one, Sergeant Perry the other. A guard'll go with each group."

Delman told the clerk-sergeant, "We'll do the loading. Take it from the top of the requisitions and point us in the right direction."

"I guess it'll work," the sergeant said.

"Damn right it'll work," Delman said.

The sergeant read and Delman and Perry, dashing from aisle to aisle, helped their groups pull down supplies and pile them on the carts which were then pushed to the trucks. The French civilians watched them. At first, the two groups got in each others' way. But after the first deuce-and-a-half was loaded, a rhythm was established and the trucks were quickly filled. Delman pulled himself up into each one to make sure supplies were well-packed and balanced. When he left the last truck, he heard Perry talking to the clerk.

"Those piles of blankets and tents over there," Perry said, pointing.

"They haven't been sorted," the sergeant said.

"We'll take them the way they are," Perry said.

"I don't know," the sergeant said.

Perry, with two POWs, already started to hoist the blankets and tents into the last truck.

Why this last-minute stunt? What was Perry doing, displaying his independence or his grabbiness? Maybe, Delman thought, he couldn't help himself; he simply was gluttonous, always reaching for a second helping before he finished his first. It was more than that, Delman decided. The motor pool sergeant was a born exploiter, a natural opportunist, compulsive enough to act without considering any of the consequences of his act.

"Hold it," Delman commanded. "Put that stuff back. We take what we requisitioned—nothing more. Then back to your trucks. We're moving out."

After the blankets and tents were removed from the truck and returned to the pile, Delman thanked the clerk and faced the POWs.

"Back to your trucks. Close them up. And start your engines."

He jumped into his jeep, thanked the sergeant again and signaled the trucks to follow him.

"Let's get out of here," he said to his driver, "before Perry pulls something else."

Delman wasn't going to let Perry's last-minute nonsense disturb him. Delman had his supplies. His convoy concept worked. And, before the day was over, he would be leading his trucks through Le Mans on the way to the camp. He tried to anticipate his reception. The Colonel would be pleased, Mueller displeased. He'd probably ridicule the success of the convoy, the amount of supplies it carried.

Delman could hear Mueller asking, "What do we have here, supplies to feed and shelter a hundred POWs for what—two days? Or let's say you even take care of a hundred fifty POWs. That leaves only about twenty-nine thousand of the enemy, cold and starving in our barbed-wired prison. But there'll be more convoys, won't there? Hell, Delman, if the war continues another five years, you'll bring us enough supplies to take care of all of our POWs. If they haven't died first."

CHAPTER 24

MUELLER DECIDED TO pull a Bosworth, to challenge the rakish first sergeant. "You should get the Colonel to request a transfer," Mueller said.

"C'mon," Bosworth replied. "He'd never do it and I'd never do it."

"I saw him yesterday," Mueller said, making sure he was sitting erect so he'd be taller than his adversary. "He's falling apart. He looks older than I do. And his office! It's a mess, a pigsty, it stinks. I mean it reeks. Can't you clean it up?"

"He won't let me," Bosworth said. "I ask him every day."

"It's a disgrace," Mueller said. "Doesn't he know that? It disgraces him and it disgraces our camp. Haven't you told him that?"

"Not in so many words," Bosworth said, "but I ask him every day if I can get his office cleaned. He doesn't hear me."

"He better hear you," Mueller said. "People will start thinking he's bucking for a Section Eight. What's wrong with him?"

"Nothing that a good night's sleep won't cure."

"You know why he can't sleep?" Mueller said. "Because six months running this fucking hole is three months too long. Taking care of thousands of POWs and more coming in every day with a handful of cadre will wear down any man. Enough's enough. Besides, who wants to be an undertaker?"

They were the only ones in the NCO club, working on their third beer. They played with their bottles as they talked. Mueller studied Bosworth. He'd seen it before, a trusted NCO, privy to his commander's inner life—the one he'd never reveal to anyone except his first sergeant—becomes his mother, his defender, his protector.

"I don't tell the Colonel what to do," Bosworth said.

"Maybe you should," Mueller said, "for his own good."

"You want him out," Bosworth said, "so you could get rid of Delman."

"That kike," Mueller said. "How he got the Colonel to approve his crazy convoy scheme beats the shit out of me."

"Kike," Bosworth said. "That's what the POW called Delman, the one he slugged. I wonder who gave him the idea to call Delman a kike."

"I'm not here to talk about Delman," Mueller said. "I'm here to get you to do something about the Colonel—before someone else does."

"Like who?"

"Like the TPM," Mueller said. "They've got their eye on the Colonel, believe me. Our trip to Paris wasn't smart."

Mueller didn't want to go this far. He'd never told a fellow NCO—particularly his unit's first sergeant—what to do. He had always been more subtle. But you never knew where you stood with Bosworth. He was an agitator, a cynic, a perpetual smart-ass. Take his advice to me, Mueller thought. Be decisive he said. So I took him at his word. I acted decisively. I picked Heinrich as a replacement on the convoy without clearing it with the Colonel. And what was Bosworth's reaction? "The Colonel won't like it." First he says to be decisive and then he backs off. A first sergeant should support his men, particularly his NCOs.

And why talk about Delman? It's bad enough the Colonel's hoodwinked by the Jew. If he returns with empty trucks, the Colonel will find some way to justify it. He wants to make Delman a hero, one way or another. There'll be more convoys and pretty soon Delman will be telling me what to do. Over my dead body, he thought.

"You'll be doing the Colonel a favor," Mueller said, "if you get on his back about his office. Believe me."

"You set up Delman," Bosworth said, "didn't you? You got your Germans to set up the kid, figuring if he hit a POW once, he could be set up to do it a second time."

That does it, Mueller thought, that says it all. You're the Colonel's boy all the way. Everything your Colonel does, you approve. One hundred percent. In spades. And there's nothing I can do about it. I'll still have beers with you in the NCO club and we'll still talk, but I'll be on guard and, eventually, you'll become aware I'm on guard and it'll never be the same again.

"I'll get us another round," Mueller said.

*   *   *

"You're a manic-depressive."

Who had said that? Nelson wasn't sure. His wife? Possibly, but he wasn't certain. She never attacked him so directly, so personally. Bosworth? Perhaps. But if it was Bosworth, it was in the early days when he was more outspoken, less concerned about his Colonel's feelings.

Whoever said it, Nelson thought, was right. Only now, where's the "manic"? He could use some of it. He tried not to think about his depression. It would only make it worse. He put down the *Stars and Stripes* he was reading. Not really reading; trying to read. He was so tired his eyes wouldn't focus and they failed to pass on their messages to his weary brain. He was operating by rote. Christ, if he could only sleep.

He stumbled to the closed door separating his office from Sergeant Bosworth's. Someone was complaining so vehemently, so shrilly that Nelson had to find out what was going on. He heard, "I sent it three days ago and I still haven't heard a word." It was Captain Roland. The Colonel was about to open the door when he heard Bosworth reply, "I gave it to him."

"And?" Roland said.

"The Colonel said he'd take care of it."

"Like he takes care of his office?" Roland said. "Does he know about the scuttlebutt?"

Nelson tried to throw open the door and dramatically confront his accuser. But he was so tired, so weak, that he opened the door like an old man, tentatively, slowly, carefully.

"You better come in," Nelson said.

Roland followed the Colonel into his office.

"Sit down," Nelson said, sinking into the chair behind his desk. "Now talk to me."

"I sent you a memo three days ago about guarding train arrivals," Roland began, sitting down and then half-standing so he could remove files and clothes that he'd sat on and put them on the floor next to his chair. "I haven't received a reply."

"Forget the memo," Nelson said. "What about the scuttlebutt?"

Roland hesitated.

"Spit it out," Nelson said.

"The scuttlebutt," Roland replied, "says you're falling apart. It's this filthy office, Colonel. This office suggests . . ."

"That I'm falling apart," Nelson said, sprawled in his chair, looking at his disheveled desk.

"You've got to clean it up," Roland said.

Nelson shuffled paper around his desk until he disinterred a file folder marked "Security." He rummaged through it and handed Roland the memo he'd mentioned.

"Your memo," Nelson said, handing it to Roland, "approved."

"I'd appreciate it," Roland said, putting it back in front of the Colonel, "if you'd stamp it 'approved' and sign it."

"You're a real stickler for detail," Nelson said, stamping it, signing it. "Aren't you?"

Nelson looked across his mess of a desk at Roland, his only friend in the camp. And even he's uncomfortable with me, Nelson thought. And it's not just because he's a stickler for detail. It's because of me. He feels sorry for me. I must look as bad as I feel.

"What else?" Nelson asked.

"Morale's low," Roland said, "as low as it's ever been. You've heard all this before but we're overworked and under-staffed. We abort escapes almost every night. The POWs know about the Battle of the Bulge. They talk about Hitler's secret weapon. And on top of all of this, there's the scuttlebutt about you."

Nelson couldn't think clearly. "What do you want me to do?'

"Get this office cleaned up," Roland said. "And then resume your daily inspections. The troops have to be reassured. They need your leadership. They want to believe you're on top of the situation. The men have to see their colonel."

God, Nelson thought, only a foreigner would talk that way. Old fashioned, Old World, out of some bad World War I novel. And it sounded strange—sentimental, almost a put-on—coming from the young, usually pragmatic career officer.

Suddenly, Nelson felt chagrined and angry. Where did a Belgian captain get off telling an American colonel what to do? Nelson felt betrayed. As if his wife had turned on him and belittled him in public. "I'll think about it," he said. "I know you're trying to help."

When the captain left, Nelson picked up his wife's last letter, really a note. "Hold on" was all she'd written. She had enclosed in the same envelope several newspaper clippings quoting experts who were convinced the war was nearing an end. Why that note, those clippings? He'd been careful about revealing his condition to her. That probably was the giveaway. He was too circumspect, too careful, writing about the weather or not writing at all.

He forced himself to consider Roland's advice. Clean his office. Show himself. That meant he had to maintain the fiction he had everything under control. He had to assume the appearance of a dashing colonel, with all the spit and polish of a Mueller. He had to march through the cages—pushing aside the sick and starving—exuding confidence with a phony grin. Who cared about reality? What was wanted was pretense, make-believe, the projection of what you wanted to believe, not what was. Prevaricate—that was the order of the day. According to Hitler, the bigger the lie, the more likely it would be believed.

So, Nelson thought, that is what Captain Roland—going to the core of his chauvinism—wants me to do. He probably didn't even realize what he was saying. But it came down to that—fake it. Damn the truth. Full prevarication ahead. Everything's either black or white. Put on a happy face.

He picked up his wife's letter again and carried it with him as he rose to study his wall map, to check Delman's route. If he was successful, his return, combined with my visibility, Nelson thought, might give a lift to the troop's morale. The scuttlebutt might even bite the dust. Not bad, Nelson thought, I made a joke. Inadvertently. And it wasn't much of a joke; I could be the only one who thinks it's funny. He returned to his desk and traced his finger across its dusty surface, the source of his sour humor.

But how did the rumor about him get started? He wondered who saw him in his mess of a bedroom-office and transformed his personal sloppiness into a nervous breakdown. Roland? No. He was loyal, a straight arrow. Bosworth? No again. Too devoted. Who else had been in his office? Then Nelson remembered. He could see him sitting there, a fireplug, sturdy, superior. Of course. It had to be Mueller.

He set about cleaning his office. He had to do it himself. He'd be ashamed to let anyone else see the mess, the dirt. He remembered, as a teen, how he'd pile dirty clothes under his bed, throw "A" papers under his desk, and stack magazines in his unkempt closet. He hadn't changed.

He started by shaking out his blankets, turning over his straw-filled mattress, and making up his cot. Next, he found a large carton and used it to hold the files, lists and memos gathered on his desk, the books, letters and photos heaped on chairs, and the stuff he'd tossed carelessly in corners: a duffel, his unpacked musette bag, dirty clothes, two pairs of muddied boots.

Then, with a soapy bucket next to him, he swabbed off every surface, ridding them of paper, rubber bands, paper clips, staples, cigar butts, and a nasty accumulation of putrid ashes. With a broom and then with a sponge and rags, he cleaned the floor, sliding chairs and his desk until, finally, the floor was free of debris. Nelson returned the furniture where it belonged and unpacked his musette bag, relegating to the rubbish his sweaty, dirty clothes.

Rejuvenated, he surged from his office. He took a fast cold shower, donned fresh fatigues, ate a hurried breakfast and, dispensing salutes with new-found vigor, proceeded straight to his barber in Cage 6. "A trim and a shave," he said, and fell instantly asleep.

When he awoke, the barber was sitting in an adjoining chair, writing a letter.

Nelson rubbed his eyes.

"How long?" he asked.

"Two hours," the barber said.

Nelson rushed back to his office and, in spite of the ice and snow and heavy wind, he felt good, better than he'd felt in weeks. When he stepped into his office, he could see Bosworth was surprised at his colonel's appearance.

"Looking good, sir," Bosworth said.

Nelson returned his smile. "We're back in business. Let's start with Mueller."

*   *   *

He never disappointed, thought Nelson. Muscular, shaved and shined, the career NCO always maintained the look and Aqua

Velva smell of a proud and proper drillmaster.

"Sir," Mueller announced.

The click of the heels, the perfect salute, the eyes straight ahead, awaiting his superior's recognition. Nelson wanted to say, "Pack in your shit, Mueller."

But, instead, always slightly wary of the supply sergeant's display of military precision, Nelson flipped a return salute, kept his cynical smile brief and said, "Sit down, sergeant. Let's review how we're getting supplies."

"Sir?"

"Delman's convoy," Nelson said.

"You mean Delman's folly, sir?"

What was this? Mueller brazen and outspoken? Where were his usual careful replies? Had he picked up a dumb draftee's reasoning: if you follow up any comment—regardless of its sarcasm—with "sir," you can get away with it?

"The convoy was Delman's brainstorm," Nelson said, "but I approved it so it's Nelson's folly, sergeant. But that's true only if it's a failure. And I don't believe, with Delman leading it, failure's even a remote possibility. But you know that, Mueller. You're Delman's boss. He works for you."

"Does he, sir?"

A new, pugnacious Mueller had emerged. Or was it the same old Mueller who'd decided to drop his mask and talk to Nelson as he talked to his fellow NCOs, maybe as he talked to everyone except his colonel. Mueller's body language exuded security. In spite of his military bearing, he appeared relaxed, comfortable, cocky. Nelson was intrigued. Why would this careful, correct, almost plodding NCO—at least when it came to his colonel—suddenly let his resentment show?

What was he thinking? That the Colonel, in spite of his clean face and cleaner office, was experiencing only a momentary positive recovery? That, down deep, he was soft, finished, curdled by his command, wrecked because of his responsibility?

Or what about another possibility—Bosworth was in charge.

Nelson's rank was a disguise. His power, once he felt the full
horror of his work, disappeared, like the falling snow trampled
by the POWs. They also trampled his spirit. Perhaps that thinking—as wrong as it was—explained Mueller's unexpected belligerence. It went along with his patronizing attitude toward any
but career soldiers. But why reveal his enmity? Perhaps he was
so angry that his hatred had broken out, uncontrollably, like
sweat disgorged from his body after he'd completed his couple
of hundred daily push-ups.

One more possibility, Nelson thought. Mueller, with all his
sources, with his network of buddies, knows something I don't.
Such as my imminent transfer. The Colonel recalled what Roland
had warned: the TPM, tired of Nelson's continuous barrage of
memos, would relieve him of his command.

Then Nelson thought about the surprising flurry of recent
calls from Colonel Pomerantz. None substantial. All friendly.
Feeling me out? And, if so, for what?

"Where's Delman's convoy?" Nelson asked. "Any idea?"

"Yes, sir."

It must be positive, Nelson thought, or Mueller would've
been breaking down my door, eager to report bad news.

"Well?"

"He's on his way from Rennes."

"And?" the Colonel persisted.

"He got his supplies."

Nelson banged his hand on his desk, his clean, unencumbered desk. Then he ran his hand over its slick surface and swung
around slowly in his chair, making one grand sweep of his office, as if he were presenting it, spruced and sanitized, to take a
much-deserved bow before his disgruntled supply sergeant.

"Dismissed," the Colonel said.

CHAPTER 25

"CONVINCE ME," SACHER whispered.

You sarcastic bastard, Heinrich thought. He'd lost patience with Sacher, but he tried not to reveal his disgust. They stood between two trucks, with the guards off to the side of the road, as they pissed yellow lines in the fresh snow.

I should order you to escape with me, Heinrich thought. But he knew his masquerade created confusion: was he an officer or wasn't he? And, if he was, did that mean Sacher would obey him? From what he heard, Sacher obeyed no one.

The racer had to be suspicious. Add to that Sacher's tempestuous nature—Heinrich recently learned about one of Sacher's more notorious combat feats—and Heinrich doubted if anyone could control Sacher's behavior. He was wild, stormy, unpredictable. Good to have him on your side; dangerous if he wasn't. How could you be sure? But Sacher knew cars, he was a flamboyant artist with cars, and right now for Heinrich that was worth any danger, any trouble, any problem. He needed Sacher.

When he was first attached to a unit, the story went that prima donna Sacher told off an officer because he wasn't immediately assigned to the motor pool. Sacher quickly was given work commensurate with his pugnacious attitude: he was placed before a mountain of stained pots and pans.

That's what he was facing when there was a surprise attack by swarming British troops. A screaming Sacher, already angry, grabbed his rifle and killed two of the attackers. Then, as combat became closer, he switched to a Luger he lifted from a dead officer and felled two more of the enemy. When his ammunition ran out and combat became hand-to-hand, he used pots

239

and pans to smash the English. He left three of them bleeding and immobile. The rest surrendered, fearing, as one put it, "the crazy German." He received his sergeant's stripes on the spot, his resentment of rank notwithstanding.

Whether Heinrich was an officer or not wasn't the point: that he was credible, was. Finally, he had Sacher's attention. Heinrich knew Sacher wasn't intimidated by anything so he would have to be unusually persuasive. Somehow, Heinrich had to discover the right words to influence the edgy racer.

Heinrich believed Sacher was searching for a rationale that would allow him—not propel him—to escape. Heinrich made sure they weren't being watched before he continued his delicate missionary task.

"What made you a successful racing driver?" Heinrich whispered.

"Hunger."

"What else?" Heinrich asked.

"Skill," Sacher replied, "skill and luck. Mostly luck."

"What else?" asked Heinrich.

Sacher stopped to think. That was good. He was an intelligent man and Heinrich waited, hoping for more than an angry reply.

Sacher said, "Organization, selecting the right people, motivating them, rewarding them. And fear. Fear we'd be overtaken by a competitor. And, most of all, my family. Their support."

"What about courage," Heinrich continued, "what about readiness to take a chance?"

"A given," Sacher said, "for any racer."

"A given for any person who tries to escape," Heinrich said. "You won races by taking risks. You became famous for coming from behind. Even when you appeared to be losing, you didn't give up. This is no different. You can't give up because it appears we're losing. We can escape by taking risks. Germany will take risks. And we'll win."

"I didn't take foolish risks." Sacher said.

You arrogant, self-important son of a bitch, Heinrich thought. Who needs this type of discussion now? We should be taking action, not making conversation. But he tried to control his frustration, his irritation.

Should I threaten him again? No, now it wouldn't make sense. Heinrich wanted an eager Sacher, a fully committed Sacher, a Sacher who was willing to court danger, to escape.

Even if Heinrich's earlier manufactured incident worked—when he accused Sacher of a faggish attack so the dumb guard might overreact—it was a dangerous gamble. That it was successful was good; but now Sacher was prone to distrust anything Heinrich did.

"Wouldn't it be more foolish to go back to the camp," Heinrich said, "back to your hole than try to escape? You think with the advance the enemy's making you'll get more food, more medicine, more shelter? If it was bad before, it'll be worse now. POWs are a burden. Better to be rid of them—any way at all. Both sides feel the same way: you fight to destroy the enemy, not save him. Unless we save ourselves, we'll sure as hell be dead tomorrow, one way or another.

"Believe me," Heinrich concluded, "you take a bigger risk in the camp, facing starvation and dysentery, than escaping. Or do you like being pushed around? Do you like being told when to get up, when to piss, when to eat, when to sleep? At least when you escape, you're in control, not some long-nosed bossy Jew, not some bovine trigger-happy Belgian."

"The Jabos," Sacher said.

So that was it, Heinrich thought, that was his fear. Every soldier, high or low, had one. For Sacher, it was the P47s, the Jabos, the always growing number of American hunter aircraft. With their unlimited ammunition and the sad state of the Luftwaffe, the Jabos would go after even one fleeing German.

"They'd be looking for us only if word got out immediately that we'd escaped," Heinrich said. "There's little chance of that. By the time they start searching, we'd have switched to a car."

"Assuming everything goes according to plan," Sacher said, "and it never does."

He's right there. But Sacher, Heinrich believed, was arguing for argument's sake. Emotionally, he was still the hot-headed racer, the competitive overachiever, ready—almost eager—to take a risk.

"When you were racing," Heinrich tried, "you were part of a team. Didn't you think of your team?"

"You always thought of your team."

"We're a team," Heinrich said, "the Wehrmacht, Germany. We're your friends, your family. What about Kameradschaft?"

Heinrich had finished urinating. He repositioned his balls, buttoned his fly, pulled his layers of clothing around his emaciated body. Would he ever be warm again? He studied Sacher. Perhaps he was making a decision. Heinrich looked around; they still weren't being watched.

Finally, Sacher asked, "When do we go?"

Heinrich didn't smile. The wrong reaction, suggesting he defeated or entrapped Sacher, could wreck the fragile relationship he'd so carefully constructed. Instead, he silently met the stare of Sacher's narrowed, still unsure, never-blinking, always belligerent eyes.

"We go now, right now," Heinrich said. "Here's my plan."

"Christ," Sacher said, buttoning his fly, "how many times do I have to hear your fucking plan?"

"Again and again," Heinrich said, "until we both get it right."

If you wanted it right, if you wanted to make sure you remembered every detail, you had to repeat it again and again.

"Repeat it," Sacher said, "repeat it. But get it over with."

"The first thing you do is disable the vehicles closest to my truck," Heinrich said. "To enable us to get a head start on them."

"Repeat it," Sacher said, "but not as if you're instructing some stupid two year old."

Heinrich dismissed the complaint. He wasn't sure about Sacher's mental acuity. If he were the same driver who won so many Grand Prix, fine; but he'd been in combat, he was a POW, and he, like all the rest of the defeated, was desperate. Better to oversimplify and make sure he understood than worry about whether the hypersensitive racer was feeling insulted.

"Look around," Heinrich said. "Go ahead. They're not watching us. The jeep and the truck next to my truck—they're the ones you disable. Then you approach my truck. You wait for the guard to climb in. You pile in next to him and slam the door shut. He'll be startled. That's when you grab his rifle. That's when you push it in his baby face. Then we take off. There's a bombed-out industrial complex not far from here where I fought before. That's our destination."

"To do what?" Sacher asked.

"To take care of our guard," Heinrich said.

"What do you mean, 'take care of our guard'?"

"We tie him up. We throw him in the back of the truck."

"Then?"

"You drive, and I look for a car."

"Your signal," Sacher said, "what's your signal to start our great escape?"

"Watch me," Heinrich said.

He looked around. Why wait? Sacher was buttoned up. The guards weren't attentive. Delman was not nearby. Nor was Perry.

"Follow me," Heinrich said. "Do what I do."

Heinrich hadn't meant that Germany's foremost racing driver, the sports star whose every exploit had been regularly documented in sports media throughout the world, should ape Heinrich's every move. But that's exactly what the stir-crazy POW was doing.

Heinrich thought Sacher's exasperation had reached the

breaking point. He had had it with being a powerless prisoner. He was sick of being subjugated by the enemy and maybe even more sick of being told what to do by another POW who claimed a rank he wouldn't show. Sacher, Heinrich was convinced, believed the war, at least for him, had degenerated into a grotesque circus. So he'd ridicule his state. Why not? Who cared? He'd become a mimic, a clown. If Heinrich could carry out a masquerade, why not Sacher? He'd go him one better—he'd ape the masquerader.

Maybe such a ploy, such a mindset, would keep him sane, at least sane enough to escape. Heinrich had to be careful. Sacher, above all, was touchy. Heinrich had to be careful he didn't push the defiant racer too far. Totally frustrated, his fame forgotten, his status gone, Sacher could be discombobulated by the slightest unintended offense. He could turn on anyone. Including the last person who exploited him once, who could exploit him again.

Heinrich could accept that. He wasn't looking for love. Popularity was never his—and its possibility was even less with the rambunctious racer. But Heinrich recalled Sacher's inadvertent advice: don't take foolish risks. It would be a foolish risk to intentionally antagonize the one person he needed to make his escape—their escape—successful. He didn't care if he was Sacher's friend; what he didn't want was to become Sacher's enemy. His anger undoubtedly made Sacher more alive. He'd become excited, alert. But Heinrich thought that if he challenged Sacher too often—and he might consider each challenge an affront—he was capable of exploding, of aborting their escape.

Heinrich had to be sure of his boundaries. He had to know precisely where the line was between arousing Sacher's competitiveness—his sudden, energetic surges mixed with equal anger—and keeping the purpose of what they were doing clear in the racer's distrustful head. Heinrich wanted to believe that Sacher's pride, his strength, hadn't been totally squeezed out of him by his superiors, his jailers, and now by Heinrich.

"Move closer to the jeep," Heinrich whispered to Sacher as

they shuffled with the other drivers back to their trucks. To slow down their walk, Heinrich beat his hands against his body as if he were warding off the cold. He saw he hadn't fooled Delman. Except for me, Heinrich thought, he may be the only one on the convoy—or in the entire POW complex, for that matter—who is convinced I'd never stop trying to escape.

Delman stayed alert. He was not about to let his mission become a failure, Heinrich thought, because of overconfidence. The obsessively vigilant Jew had glanced at Heinrich, perhaps thinking that if he were the German this would be the perfect time to make his long-delayed break.

Heinrich walked faster. He was directly behind Sacher. "Forget disabling the vehicles," Heinrich whispered, "Delman's watching us."

We'll need some of his endless dumb luck as well as some of his contemptible cleverness if we're to get out of here alive, Heinrich thought. He drifted behind a large pine, watching Delman. Sacher followed.

"Let's move toward my truck," Heinrich said.

He watched Delman and Perry and the Belgians. Heinrich approached the door of his cab. He nodded at his guard, standing on the passenger side of the truck.

Clary reciprocated by stamping out his cigarette with particular glee. His enjoyment of his simple act struck Heinrich. Was it a warning? The tough Belgian had never returned to the vehicle so quickly after a piss stop. Why now? What did he suspect?

Heinrich saw Sacher step behind the guard. Heinrich opened his door and slid behind the steering wheel. Why was Clary moving so slowly? Heinrich rubbed his left arm over his forehead to catch the sudden, unexpected drip of sweat into his eyes. Even his gloved cold hands seemed wet. He heard the passenger door open. Heinrich now was almost sickened by the strong smell of his own sour sweat. To stay calm, he concentrated on the guard's rifle. Heinrich caught sight of it when the door opened and then, almost as if it were self-propelled, the rifle butt rested on the floor.

The Belgian pulled himself into the cab. Why was he moving so carefully? The door was about to shut. But it was suddenly pulled open and Sacher fell against the surprised guard, dislodging his rifle from his grasp.

"What the hell," he said.

Heinrich pressed his hands over the guard's face, twisting his nose, chopping at his throat, remembering Wanger. At the same time, Sacher pressed the rifle muzzle against the Belgian's temple. Clary froze. Sacher closed the truck door.

"Keep it on him," Heinrich said.

"I am," Sacher said. "Let's get out of here."

"Not until I finish with him," Heinrich said, turning to the guard, feeling all over his trembling body, pushing through his heavy clothes.

"What are you doing?' Sacher said. "Are you some kind of pervert?"

"Searching him," Heinrich said.

"You're clawing his privates," Sacher said.

"I found a knife," Heinrich said, "a little knife with a little blade."

The guard forced out a question. "Getting a thrill, Heinrich?"

Sacher pushed his rifle under Clary's chin. His head was tilted up so high he looked like he was studying the cab's roof. Heinrich suddenly leaned over to his right behind Clary, pushing him forward. Clary cried out.

"I stuck him where he stuck me," Heinrich said.

"Jesus," Sacher said, "start the fucking truck!"

Heinrich listened happily to Clary's sporadic breathing, his face creased with pain.

"Make the wrong move," Heinrich said, flipping on the ignition, pushing down the clutch, moving the gear shift, "and you'll be killed with your own rifle. That's what I call poetic justice. Don't you agree that's poetic justice, Sacher?"

"Let's go," Sacher said. "Let's get out of here."

I've reestablished my superiority, Heinrich thought. Sacher may not like what I'm doing but we're where we should be. Masquerade or not, I'm the officer in charge. Heinrich edged the truck forward. When he saw the jeep directly in front of him a new thought occurred to him. He increased his speed. Then, unexpectedly, there was Delman, three truck-lengths from his jeep, looking up. For less than a second, Heinrich stared into the Jew's hate-filled eyes.

Swerve the truck, Heinrich thought, kill him. But the Jew was too quick. He guessed Heinrich's intent. Delman jumped out of the truck's path. That leaves me with a single alternative, Heinrich thought.

"Watch this, Delman!" he shouted.

He pressed his accelerator to the floor and slammed into the left front of the jeep. He saw Delman running toward it.

Heinrich could hear Delman's words as he shouted over the sound of the impact, "They're making a break!"

As he rushed to the road, Heinrich sideswiped the nearest truck. It seemed to totter to one side. He swerved again, missed another truck, and was on the road's narrow shoulder and then on the road itself. His truck wobbled, shook and, like a huge animal, regained its balance and picked up speed.

This was not the break Heinrich had planned. Sacher had not disabled any vehicles. Heinrich tried to—by smashing the jeep and truck—but he didn't know if he'd been successful. They could be following us, he thought. But you did what you could. You stayed flexible. You didn't panic, even when it appeared everything was confused. They'd escaped, they'd left the convoy behind and, Heinrich thought, we may even have surprised them. Except Delman.

At a turn in the road, Heinrich glanced back. No Delman, no jeep, no truck. He was not being followed. Not yet. Whatever happened, he was in the clear, out of sight, in control. He had a truck, he had a hostage, and he had an armed Sacher.

Everything that, for a moment, had seemed to be going wrong was going right. In fact, he thought, what I'm doing now, so close to Delman's final destination, might destroy the Jew, might shatter his smug confidence.

Without reducing his truck's speed, Heinrich hurtled off the main road. He kept his foot down until he saw the deserted group of factories. He bumped over rubble, moving through empty streets. He passed a large complex of bombed-out buildings, careened through an alley and braked to a stop on a damaged incline, probably part of a factory's partially demolished receiving platform. Its downhill slant hid the truck. But where were the cars he remembered from his earlier visit?

"Don't move," Heinrich warned the guard, "not an inch."

Clary leaned to his right. Heinrich wanted to see his face writhing in pain, his mouth downturned, fear in his eyes. So, with his left hand, he reached over Clary's body to strike him with his fist in the wet spot on his right side. This time the Belgian didn't cry out. Perhaps he'd learned to accept his pain, control his reaction, and consider what was happening. Clary regained his composure; he stayed stoic, tough, almost like a German, Heinrich thought.

He had to make a decision. He jumped quickly from the cab, leaving the driver's door ajar. A terrible odor attacked him. He looked around and saw the remains of several German artillery horses, probably hit by shells, still with leather straps over their bloated carcasses. He circled the truck and went to the highest point nearby. There were no cars. His plan had to change. What to do next? Their jackets! They had to hide their POW-stamped jackets. Delman could be charging after him while he was worrying about their disguise. But it was important.

Heinrich reached into his pocket, found the pen knife he had used to stab Clary, and pushed in its blade. He returned to the passenger side of the cab where Sacher held the rifle against

Clary's chin. "I'll cover him while you get the jackets in the back," Heinrich said. "Give me the rifle. Make it fast. We could be followed. Put on one jacket over your coat and bring one to me. We have to cover up our POW markings."

Sacher rummaged through the truck's supplies. He found what he wanted, jumped from the truck, and opened the passenger door. He handed a jacket to Heinrich.

"There are no cars around here," Sacher said. "We'll take this truck. We've got rations, gasoline, more clothes in the back. Here, Heinrich, put on this cap. Now you look like an American. Anyone looking at the three of us will think we're Americans in an American truck."

"There were cars here before," Heinrich said.

"This truck's better than a car," Sacher said. "Besides, to get to our troops we'll have to go through American lines. They won't look twice at one of their own trucks."

"We don't have a choice," Heinrich said.

"He smells," Sacher said, taking the rifle from Heinrich, leveling it at Clary's chest. "He smells worse than those horses. It's the blood dripping from his side."

Heinrich looked at the guard, smiled, and hit his side again. Clary visibly clamped his jaws tighter but a deep groan escaped him.

"God," Sacher said. "You can't stop."

"Something you want to say?" Heinrich asked Clary.

"We don't have time for this," Sacher said.

Heinrich wasn't listening. He was focused on Clary, who refused to beg for mercy. "Should we spare your life?" Heinrich asked him. "What do you think?" Maybe an apology, Heinrich thought, a plea for forgiveness, a cry for his life. "What should I do?"

"Fuck yourself," the Belgian said, "you pig, you German swine."

Heinrich found his knife, opened it, pressed it against Clary's throat.

"No!" Sacher yelled. He pushed the small knife aside. "We need a hostage."

"That was before," Heinrich replied.

"No," Sacher said. "We still need a hostage."

As much as he wanted to dispose of the guard, Heinrich was no longer uncertain about Sacher. He was strong. He could be right. Heinrich would put off killing the baby-faced guard—for the time being.

Sacher had opened the guard's coat, pushed aside two sweaters and a shirt and was powdering the wound, using an envelope he found in a First Aid kit. Then he slapped a bandage over the bloody cut and used tape to fix it to the guard's torn skin.

Heinrich started the truck and slowly backed it up and out of its hiding place. He quickly sped from the complex and came to a two-lane road. There were no tire marks on the fresh snow. He drove into the road without stopping, hoping he wouldn't confront a searching Delman.

"You like the Jew, don't you?" he asked Clary.

He reached behind the guard to hit his wound again.

"Enough," Sacher said.

"When I ask you a question," Heinrich said to Clary, "you answer!"

"The Jew's a dog," Clary said.

"Ha!" Heinrich replied. "Hear that, Sacher? He says the Jew's a dog."

"A bulldog," Clary said. "He won't let you steal a truck and spoil his convoy. He'll find you, you German pig."

"I'll kill him first," Heinrich said, "but not before I kill you."

CHAPTER 26

"JAN. 15, 1945—Clary said he'd spend a year with me at NU. Then I'll spend a year with him, probably studying at Ghent. Assuming we both get out of here alive.

"Perry believes Heinrich's too smart to try anything this close to Le Mans. That's exactly why he will. He's like an experienced fighter pilot: ready to take a risk if he could fake out the enemy.

"Clary and Trabert are on alert. Perry and I have our weapons loaded. Except for Heinrich, we're in good shape. We've got our supplies. The French, after one threat, haven't bothered us.

"Weather has improved. Occasional sunshine. Snow has diminished. If it weren't for the threat of Mueller's boy, our drive to Le Mans could be satisfying, maybe even triumphant."

Perry ran back toward Delman and, together, they circled Delman's smashed jeep, assessing its damage. Perry fell on his knees, threw off his gloves, and ran his hands above the tires on both sides. Then he rolled over on his back and pushed himself under the vehicle.

"It's not pretty," Perry said, "but you can drive it."

"Heinrich's got Clary," Delman said, as he waved Ramer, his driver, into the jeep and leapt in next to him.

"Check the POWs," Delman told Perry. "See if anyone else is missing."

Perry ran to each truck, looked into each cab, and hurried back to a departing Delman.

"Sacher," Perry said. "Heinrich's got Sacher with him."

"Keep the POWs in their trucks," Delman yelled, as he

tapped Ramer to pull away, "and wait for me. Don't leave without me."

"Watch out for an ambush," Perry called.

If he hadn't noticed that Heinrich wasn't around and hadn't seen his truck suddenly turn and charge, Delman was certain he would have been killed. Heinrich wanted Delman dead. The theatrical German couldn't be satisfied with a simple escape. It would have been too ordinary, too gentle, simply closing the door of the home he hated. He had to rattle its windows, shake its foundation and, if he could, blow it up, fire it, wreck it, What better way to celebrate his escape than killing the convoy's arrogant commander?

Delman expected nothing less from the obsessive POW nor was he surprised that Heinrich had convinced another POW to escape with him. Especially Sacher. Delman knew the tough, excitable POW had been a big-name racing driver in Europe and was considered a genius with anything automotive.

Not only would he be able to spell Heinrich as they sped toward Germany but Sacher would keep their stolen truck running. What's more, Delman thought, if they decided to dump it, Sacher would be able to select the right replacement and cross its wires to get it going.

Taking Clary was something else again, nasty and personal. He was more than a hostage, a bargaining chip. Heinrich, who Delman knew was always watching him, had to know the Belgian was Delman's friend. So Clary became Delman's surrogate, the target for all of Heinrich's hatred. Every time he felt like relieving his rage, reinforcing his power or, simply bashing a Jew, even a surrogate Jew, he'd attack his hostage.

Heinrich had another reason to assault Clary. He never let up on Heinrich, bossing him mercilessly, sitting next to him in the truck, constantly poking him with his busy, penetrating rifle.

So Heinrich had a double reason for getting even and Delman was convinced the German would savor it. He was a genuine sadist—he enjoyed inflicting pain, physical and psychological, and now he'd be able to get even with two of his enemies at the same time.

Delman was devastated by Clary's predicament. He couldn't recall when he'd ever felt such frustration, such powerlessness, such guilt. He didn't think he would ever forgive himself for putting the convoy's success above his friend's safety. How could he have been so indifferent to Clary's danger? Or had he thought he was flattering his friend by having him guard the convoy's most dangerous POW, the one most likely to escape?

*   *   *

"Faster," Delman ordered Ramer.

He couldn't trust another POW, regardless of how cooperative he appeared to be, to track down two of his escaped comrades. So he kept pushing his reluctant chauffeur, making certain the jeep sped along the narrow, slippery, poorly repaired road. Suddenly Delman felt a body-racking tremor dropping from his left shoulder to his right groin. His father's gift? Was it caused by the wicked cold or inherited fear? Could genes transfer an emotional state from father to son? I won't let it happen, Delman told himself, not this close to my destination, not this close to success.

He wondered if he'd be facing two of the enemy—or three? He studied his silent driver, Ramer, the enemy next to him. To Delman, POWs were suspect, all of them, even the family men, the drivers he had interviewed so carefully. Unlike some of the cage wardens, Delman refused to fraternize with the POWs, refused to forget they were Germans. He treated them as they treated Jews.

Delman had never let Ramer forget he was a POW, that his sole reason for remaining Delman's driver was his ability to react quickly to Delman's every command—or else. The "or else" may have assured rancor but it also encouraged submission.

Delman had quickly stopped his driver's fawning attempt

to make him feel important. He recalled the plaques Ramer had had made by some of his POW friends, a variation of the insignia—usually stars—some jeeps carried if among their occupants was a senior officer. Placing Delman's insignificant rank on the jeep would have been laughable.

So Ramer went a different route. His plaques read "Convoy Commander." One day, approaching his jeep, Delman caught sight of them, on the front and back of his jeep. He shied away, believing he had approached the wrong vehicle. Then he realized what had been done. He thought it had to be a gag, perhaps something Perry might pull. But when Delman did a walk-around of the jeep and looked at his driver, he realized it was Ramer who thought he'd make points by flattering Delman with the shiny signs.

"Get rid of them," Delman ordered.

He wasn't going to be victimized the way Mueller was victimized by Heinrich's exaggerated servility, his fake respect. Perhaps being friendly with POWs was understandable but Delman found it unacceptable. He rarely conversed with POWs; he gave orders. German soldiers, Nazis or not, did as they were told by Nazis. That was crime enough.

So it was three—Heinrich, Sacher and Ramer—against one. Delman recalled Mueller's remark: "The convoy could be a death trap." Clary's death trap, Delman thought, and mine, too, if, even for a moment, I forget where I am, what I am, and who I'm facing. He checked the magazine in his carbine, patted the weapon in his jacket. Inexperienced or not, he'd show the Nazis that his hatred, nurtured by too many successful Nazi ploys, gave him the courage he needed.

"Slow down," Delman ordered.

Ramer disregarded the order.

"I said to slow down," Delman repeated, not raising his voice, instead pushing his carbine against the driver's face. "Now."

"Wind noise," Ramer said. "I couldn't hear you because of the wind noise."

"They can't be that far ahead," Delman said, "so it must mean they've turned off. Make a right at the next road. We'll examine every turn-off, every lane. They're hiding somewhere and we're going to find them."

They approached a corner and the driver failed to reduce his speed.

"I said to slow down and turn," Delman said quietly. "Do as I say or I'll blow your fucking head off."

The driver quickly turned. But, to irritate Delman, he reduced his speed to five miles an hour. Delman slammed his rifle's barrel into the POW's jaw. In an instant, Ramer's cheek started to redden. Blood began to ooze from a small cut close to his eye.

"One more smart-ass move," Delman said.

The jeep picked up speed. Delman wasn't surprised that Heinrich's power extended to Delman's driver. He was only surprised that Heinrich's influence wasn't seen earlier, that his escape hadn't triggered some type of mass rebellion.

Or had it? Delman might already have been victimized. By rushing after Heinrich and Sacher and their hostage, Clary, Delman had left only the remaining Belgian and Perry to guard seven POWs. Had the sullen drivers refused Heinrich's entreaties to escape—or were they part of a long-delayed secret plot to wreck the convoy?

It was too late—too late to turn around, too late to worry. In thinking about what Heinrich may have done, Delman wasn't focusing on what they were passing. He concentrated on surveying the large, partially bombed-out industrial area.

"Slow down," he ordered, looking up.

It reminded Delman of the factory area in west Evanston where he got lost when he first visited Northwestern. There, three- to five-story buildings, mostly flat-topped, meandered up and down the streets with their narrow parkways and their recently planted thin-trunked trees, battered and weakened by the fumes of laboring trucks. All the Evanston factories seemed the same height. The few that were different were new—their sidings brighter, their entrances glassed. Aside from cosmetic variations, they were as large and ugly and already almost as dirty as their big-windowed predecessors.

The French industrial area, perhaps developed right before the war, seemed little different. Except that most of the buildings had been struck by bombs or shells. Windows were without glass, empty eye-sockets. Those suffering accurate hits had their innards exposed—naked timbers, fallen furniture, vomiting file cabinets, frozen paper. Below their smashed floors were piles of debris, half covered with snow, unexpected reflections revealing glass or glazed bricks or, perhaps—Delman thought—bones. Marauding dog bones, thin deer bones, gnawed human bones.

"Stop!" Delman shouted at Ramer. "Get down, out of the jeep!"

Delman fell out of the vehicle, pressing up against its side. He'd seen a glare from a window. A rifle? Searching eyes? Heinrich? Delman leaned against his car, a perfect target for a grenade. But there were no explosions, no bullets.

"Crawl over here," he called to Ramer.

Delman, his carbine's safety off, watched the POW slither around the jeep. He moved closer to the POW and pressed his rifle against the driver's body. You're my shield, he thought, looking behind, looking up, believing if Heinrich was nearby, he had to be above them.

The upper stories were ideal firing platforms for snipers. The only sound Delman could hear was the occasional crunch of the snow's crust as the two men shifted their weight.

The sun suddenly brightened. A searchlight. Now, Delman thought, I've become a well-lighted target. Am I in the center of Heinrich's sight? Is he in the prone position I learned in basic training, his rifle sling around his arm, elbows braced, head immobile, ready to kill me?

To get closer to his human shield, Delman held his carbine almost vertical, its muzzle against the back of his driver's immobile, capped head. "Let's move out of here," Delman ordered, "now."

The driver's fear was audible. Heavy breathing, an occasional groan as he tripped over a rock, a brick, a hole.

"Go to the next building, then slowly around it," Delman whispered. "Stay close to the wall. Damn it, put your hands down!"

Why did Ramer suddenly raise his hand? Fear? A signal? Delman realized he too, like the POW, was breathing out of his mouth, as if he'd completed a marathon. He clamped his lips shut.

Delman heard a scream, laughter. He looked up. A rock sailed from a window. It bounced once, twice. More laughter. A head appeared, two. Not Heinrich, not Sacher. Kids. Playing in the upstairs rubble, shouting at each other.

"Behind the building," Delman ordered. "Get down! Get on your stomach!"

It could be a ploy. He wouldn't put it past Heinrich. He could have bribed some lost hungry kids, foraging for food among the rubble, with GI rations from his stolen truck.

"Throw stones at the American soldiers," Delman could imagine Heinrich telling the kids. "Do what I tell you and I'll feed you."

Delman stayed on his stomach. He crawled toward the feet of his now fearful driver, who was trembling, prone, at the corner of the bombed-out factory. Delman crawled next to him. He looked around and then, once more, up where he'd seen the stone-throwing kids.

There were no more stones. No truck. No Heinrich. All Delman could see was devastation and then he smelled it, an awful stink. A skunk? No, this was a different odor, higher, sharper, more pervasive. He looked toward its source and saw dead horses, partially covered by snow, leather harnesses on their skeletal heads. Horses! For a moment Delman thought he was mistaken, shaken by his situation, imagining he was his father in World War I. But the horses were there, the harnesses were there, and he was on his stomach searching for his escaped prisoners and their hostage. Then he remembered the Germans used horses to pull their artillery.

He stopped crawling through the snow and saw what appeared to be an inclined driveway, perhaps a receiving platform. He pushed Ramer toward it. They remained on their bellies, feeling pieces of brick—shorn from the building—below their cold gloved hands.

Delman saw tire tracks. Partly covered by snow but clear tire tracks, deep and recent. He tried to reconstruct Heinrich's thought process. He'd seen the incline. He believed it could hide his truck. Not from overhead surveillance but from another vehicle following the same road that Heinrich used.

"Tire tracks," Delman said to his driver.

"Yes, sergeant."

"They look fresh," Delman said, "don't they?"

"Fresh tracks, sergeant, yes."

He was frightened. On his stomach, a rifle pointed at his head, the explosive American sergeant next to him. The POW, Delman realized, would say anything, agree to anything.

"On your feet," Delman said. "Stick close to the wall. We're going back to our jeep, back to the convoy. If you try anything, anything at all, you've had it. No more warnings. Now let's go."

Delman didn't have to tell Ramer to speed back to the convoy.

As they neared it, Delman saw Perry and Trabert waiting for his return in front of the buttoned-up trucks.

Perry couldn't wait until the jeep stopped.

"Any sign of them?" he called.

Delman shook his head. He stepped from the jeep into the stamped-down snow.

"Clary?" Trabert asked.

"I saw fresh tire tracks in a bombed-out industrial complex," Delman said, "but they disappeared on the road."

"They're heading to the front," Perry said.

Trabert, head down, shuffled to the rear of the convoy.

"You've done what you could," Perry said.

The motor pool boss pulled up the collar of his overcoat and pulled down his wool cap. He hadn't shaved since the start of the convoy and his beard looked like a dark hand moving up his face, fingers reaching for his large eyes.

"I haven't done a thing," Delman said. "Nothing. I'm going after them."

"How are you going to find them?" Perry said. "Heinrich can take any number of roads back to the front."

"I know him," Delman said.

"What's that supposed to mean?" Perry asked.

"He has to keep showing how brave he is," Delman said. "My guess is that he'll take the same road we're going to take. He'll pass the camp and then go right through the center of Le Mans."

"Don't you wish," Perry said. "He's not that dumb and not that psychotic."

"He is and I'll get him," Delman said. "I'll track him down."

"If you want to save Clary," Perry said, "you'll stay away from Heinrich. You force Heinrich's hand and he'll kill Clary . . ."

Delman knew Perry was about to say more, about to add, "if he hasn't already," but he caught himself.

Delman wouldn't let him off.

"Clary's alive," he said, "and Heinrich will keep him alive. What's the good of a dead hostage? I'll find them."

"I hope you do," Perry said, "but you better face it—it's a long shot. A very long shot."

"I'm now putting you in charge of this convoy," Delman said. "You lead it back to camp."

Trabert returned and stood next to Perry.

"The Germans will be looking for you," Perry said. "You've got to stay alert, you've got to beware of every side road and make sure you don't let them sneak up behind you."

"Take this," Trabert said. He handed Delman a walkie-talkie. "I don't know if it'll work—or its range. Clary has one too."

Delman grasped the two-way radio in his hand. He consciously tried to dismiss thinking what it would have meant if he had it earlier. He hadn't overlooked it. But it was his urgency to leave the camp—escaping with his POW-driven trucks—that took priority. He had been afraid that if he'd made an issue of the walkie-talkie, Mueller, along with Perry, might've used it to delay—maybe even abort—the convoy. The Colonel never mentioned walkie-talkies but, with all of Delman's planning, he had to assume the convoy's commander wouldn't overlook something so vital.

"Thanks," Delman said, taking the radio. "This could help. And you take Ramer."

He signaled his driver to leave the jeep.

"You sure?" Perry said.

"He pulled a few things when I was looking for Heinrich," Delman said. "I don't want him next to me. He can drive Sacher's truck."

"I would suggest you take Trabert with you," Perry began, "but it would be too risky to leave me alone with seven POWs."

"I'm not suggesting Trabert should come with me," Delman said. "He stays with you, with the convoy. I'll go alone. What I need is rope and tape."

"Rope and tape," Perry said, "for what? If you think you're going to find Heinrich and Sacher, capture them and return them here, tied and taped, you're kidding yourself."

"You never know," Delman said.

"I don't think you've got a chance in hell of finding them," Perry said. "They're miles ahead of you and they'll stay miles ahead of you."

"Maybe," Delman said. "and maybe I'll find them and rescue Clary."

"If you find them," Perry said, "you'll have to kill them. If you don't kill them, Delman, they'll sure as hell kill you."

"Then I'll kill them," Delman said, pulling away in his jeep.

CHAPTER 27

"COLONEL POMERANTZ AGAIN," Bosworth said. "He has to talk to you."

Bosworth placed Nelson's morning coffee on his desk. Nelson had stopped eating breakfast when the convoy left.

"I'm on my way out to inspect the cages," he said. Standing in his baggy winter underwear, he pulled crumpled fatigues and a khaki shirt from his already packed musette bag. "Tell him that."

He dressed and decided to wear his paratrooper boots. Easier to wear them than to pack them. He cared little about clothes, but he liked the high boots with their mirror-like finish—thanks to an energetic POW.

He had the boots only because of Mueller. The sergeant probably hoarded them—no one knew how he got them—and used them for various purposes—in exchange for steaks for his mistress, for new sheets for their bed, and in the case of the Colonel, for simple judicious ass kissing. Nelson knew that the wily sergeant figured that the Colonel, despite his anti-militarism, wasn't above enjoying a little swagger. The boots were a lesser version of Patton's pearl-handled pistols or a chest full of ribbons. At the least, Nelson thought, they might come in handy to slosh through a Chicago winter. Along with his green fatigues. Unless he couldn't bear to have anything around him to remind him of the POW camp.

He usually braced his feet on the end of his bed to lace the boots, but today he used the seat of his desk chair. The bed had already been removed. They wanted him out of the camp today and the fast exit of his cot suggested he himself would follow quickly. Pomerantz had dropped any pretense of civility.

Bosworth returned. "Colonel Pomerantz says to call him immediately."

Nelson, between sips of his black coffee, finished lacing his left boot and brought it down and raised his right one.

"Everybody uses everybody," he said.

"Colonel Pomerantz is well liked," Bosworth said.

Nelson looked up. "No criticism intended."

He still had to be careful with Bosworth. As supportive as he'd been the past few weeks, he still chafed under authority. And that came out whenever he spoke to a superior, any superior. As much as he tried to control his resentment, Bosworth, the best first sergeant Nelson ever had, was as transparent as he was argumentative.

"Don't get me wrong," Nelson said. "I like Pomerantz. He's a likable guy. But he's using me so he can get back to his old unit."

"I guess he's been doing that for a long time," Bosworth said, not backing down. "I mean, trying to get back to his old unit."

Nelson rose and then bent down to blouse his pants over the boots. He realized he'd never told Bosworth, in so many words, why he was delaying his departure. He assumed his first sergeant knew more about Delman's convoy then he did.

"I respect that," Nelson said, "Pomerantz trying to get back to his old unit."

He walked to the window and saw that the weather had turned clear and bright.

"Pomerantz is pretty gutsy," Nelson said, turning to face Bosworth, "willing to risk his neck so he can be with his old unit when it charges through Germany."

"Should I get him for you?" Bosworth asked.

"He's always been up front with me," Nelson continued. "I told him I wanted to stay here until the convoy returned and he said he'd do what he could but he couldn't make any promises."

"He probably figures that, after all your complaints, you'd

be glad to get out of here."

"I am glad to get out of here, but not until the convoy re-
turns. I owe Delman and Perry and the two guards that much.
One more day. Pomerantz knew that. I made that clear. Now he
insists it's because the General wants everything nailed down."
His voice suddenly went up an octave and became louder. "It's
Pomerantz who wants everything nailed down!"

"They think differently in Headquarters," Bosworth said
quickly.

Nelson knew Bosworth was trying to calm him. But he knew
his first sergeant also had a point. Nelson had better understand
Headquarters' thinking. He'd be there shortly: tomorrow if he
had his way, today if he didn't.

"How do they think in Headquarters?" Nelson asked.

"They think about faceless units," Bosworth said, "never
individuals."

Nelson sat down in his chair, leaned back, put both booted
feet on his desk and looked over them at Bosworth. Faceless,
he thought. Bosworth continued to surprise him.

"What else?" Nelson asked.

"The convoy," Bosworth said. "You see it as a way of over-
coming a problem, of keeping POWs alive. The TPM doesn't
even admit there's a problem."

"He's right," Captain Roland said, entering the office.

"Captain," Bosworth greeted him and returned to his desk,
leaving the two officers alone.

"They think you approved the convoy out of guilt," Roland said. "They call it Nelson's guilt trip. They're convinced
you approved it to counter what you see as the POW's—your
POW's—purposeful mistreatment."

"Mistreatment!" Nelson jumped from his chair. "We're
not mistreating them. That would be too decent, too humane.
We're killing them!"

Roland held up his hand. "They say what's happening here
is an inevitable consequence of what happens on the battlefield."

Roland sounded like a simple-minded military primer. Nelson had discussed the rationale behind the care and feeding of German POWs by the Allies too often with too many people. With Pomerantz, with Bosworth, with Mueller, with Delman, and now, again, with Roland. He was tired of it, exhausted by it. He couldn't talk about it anymore.

"Has there been an escape?" he asked. "Is that why the convoy hasn't returned?"

"I don't know," Roland said, "but that's what I suspect."

"So it's become a death ride. Except we don't know who's dead."

"Maybe no one," Roland said.

"Then where are they?"

With his cot removed, Nelson's office was again only that—cold, Spartan, gloomy. His packed duffel in one corner, his musette bag in another. The numerous photos he'd kept on his desk of his wife and kids that relieved the dreariness of the room, had been packed away with books and clothes.

His successor, Major Hughes, had arrived yesterday. At least he'd inherit one good relic: the heavily marked wall map that showed the Allied progress and the location of supply depots. The latest entry was a dotted red line tracing the short route of Delman's convoy.

The Colonel glanced outside one more time. The prediction that heavy snow would create havoc on Le Mans roads leading to Paris had been changed. The winter storm, originally destined for mid-France, had detoured north. So Nelson was stuck with good weather. He'd run out of reasons to delay his exit.

He telephoned Pomerantz.

"Who the hell do you think you are," Pomerantz said, "not taking my calls! The General expects you here today. In St. Cloud. In Headquarters. In my office. No more phony excuses. What do you think's going to happen—that God, in His infinite wisdom, is going to guide your crazy convoy, jampacked with supplies, back to your camp?"

Was He still around? Nelson wasn't sure. He prayed to Him nightly. The same prayer he prayed as a child only he'd added more requests, more names. Not with great confidence but with fear that if he didn't keep praying, something untoward might happen. Like taking over Pomerantz's command without knowing about the convoy.

Delman's trip had become a symbol of everything that was wrong in the war. All Nelson knew was that he had never left a job unfinished. Never as a cop. Never as a soldier. His sense of decorum, of decency, was offended if he left any project, any mission, half-completed. Like the convoy.

Now, because Pomerantz had his own agenda and the ear of the General, Nelson, once denied, would be denied again. He wasn't pleading for supplies, not this time. All he wanted was one more day, one more lousy day in the camp he was eager to leave. Then he would happily relinquish his thankless mission to another officer—with little idea of the horror he'd inherit—who would be dominated by Nelson, the General's new yes man. Nelson, of all people, the constant critic, the chronic memo-writer, would become what he most despised—a bureaucrat, an administrator, a desk-bound authoritarian double-talker who would prolong the inaction he'd fought against for so long. He'd prolong the fiction that POW compounds were nothing more than detention camps.

"All I'm asking for," Nelson said, "is one more lousy day."

"It's that fucking convoy," Pomerantz said, "isn't it? Drop it, Nelson. Its success or failure means absolutely nothing."

"To you," Nelson said. "Not to me."

"You get here today," Pomerantz said. "That's an order. Disobey it and you're in trouble. A car's on its way to pick you up."

Before he could reply, the line went dead. Nelson slammed his hand against the bare top of his empty desk. To depart now, without seeing Delman, was unfeeling, inexcusable, wrong.

Always quick to think the worst of the military, Delman would assume his sole supporter had forgotten him. Or that he had decided that the convoy, now that Nelson had completed his escape from the camp, was only a meaningless gesture waiting to be discarded.

Nelson realized he'd projected the illusion that he made his own rules, that his barbed-wire enclosed world didn't have to abide by West Point behavior, that, in spite of the military hierarchy, he was his own boss. I really believed it, Nelson wanted to shout, but it's false. In spite of my rank, I'm as much as a POW as you are, Delman. As long as you follow orders, endure your endless frustration, pretend your silence means acceptance, you can exist. But do the unexpected, the unconventional—such as your convoy—and you face suspicion, resentment and, worst of all, indifference. What you've done gets lost in the war's chaos. Add to that a new commander who, at least at the beginning, must rely on the Muellers, and your convoy becomes as important as yesterday's skirmish.

I need another day, Nelson thought.

* * *

Mueller, disconsolate, sat in the supply tent he'd just opened. Where was Bosworth? Mueller had told the first sergeant he had to see him immediately but Bosworth, as if he had the whole operation of the camp on his shoulders, had only said he would get there as soon as possible.

Since their last conversation in the NCO club—where they had their dispute about Delman—Mueller hadn't seen too much of Bosworth. Hell, Mueller thought, if he'd asked me I could've helped with some of the paperwork bringing a new commanding officer to replace Nelson, if he'd ever leave.

Life would be so easy, Mueller thought, if the military operated the way it did pre-war, when there were only career soldiers. Now, with draftees infecting the whole system, the real soldiers had to keep glancing over their shoulders to prevent the mess the draftees made from gaining on them.

Mueller pulled himself erect. He discerned a shadow in front of him—and heard Bosworth's basso.

"Little early for a nap," Bosworth said, "isn't it? You've got it made, haven't you? No supplies, no supervision, not even a Delman or Heinrich to get in the way. What's this urgent business we have to discuss?"

Smart-ass, Mueller thought. If he'd been considerate, he'd have made some noise, coughed, anything, instead of stealing up on me as if I was asleep on guard duty. At the worst, I drifted off a moment.

"Delman'll pull in today," Mueller announced, "and—"

"Hold it." Bosworth, sitting across the desk from Mueller, was amazed at his mysterious, usually correct, always-in-action network of buddies. "You sure of this?"

"I've got to figure out how to handle the supplies he's bringing in," Mueller said. "I figure we could pile the stuff in this front tent. Easier to unload, easier to divide. What d'you think?"

"That's your urgent business?" Bosworth asked. "Since when've you ever cleared what you do with me? C'mon, Mueller, what's eating you? Why did I have to drop everything I was doing to rush over here?"

"I hear the Colonel's got his orders," Mueller said. "I hear he's going to replace Colonel Pomerantz, the officer the Colonel and I saw when we made that wild goose chase to Paris."

"The Colonel's got his orders," Bosworth replied.

"His career's on the line," Mueller said. "If he disobeys an order from the TPM, he's had it. He may be the boss here, making his own rules, not saluting, acting the civilian, but he better know his attitude won't wash with the TPM. He has to follow orders."

Bosworth leaned over the desk. "Since when are you so concerned about the Colonel?"

"It's up to you," Mueller continued. "When that car comes

for him, you have to see he's in it."

"You knew about the car," Bosworth said. "I learned about it this morning. You keep ducking my question, Mueller. Why are you so concerned about the Colonel?"

"I like things done right," Mueller said, "that's all."

"Bullshit. It has to do with Delman's convoy. That's it, isn't it? What else have you heard?"

"There's been an escape," Mueller said.

"Heinrich," Bosworth said. He tipped his chair back. "Your boy Heinrich finally escaped."

"I don't know who escaped," Mueller said.

Bosworth brought his chair up and leaned over the desk, his face close to Mueller's. "You're afraid the Colonel won't follow orders and that he'll be brought on the carpet by the TPM and asked some questions. And if that happens, he may talk about the convoy and how you put Heinrich, an officer masquerading as an ordinary POW, on it. And now he escapes.

"So you're afraid you'll be found out. Isn't that it, Mueller? That's why you're so concerned about the Colonel. You'll be found out as the Kraut-lover you are. It'll be revealed that you not only were out to get an American soldier but that you compromised his creation—a convoy approved by your commanding officer—all to benefit a POW."

"Bullshit!" Mueller said.

"You're covering your ass. That's what this is all about. You're always covering your ass."

"Bullshit!" Mueller repeated, with growing anger.

Bosworth persisted. "You don't know where all of this'll lead—so you're covering your ass by making sure the Colonel goes to Paris. Once he's there, you figure you're safe. What you did to Delman and how you helped a POW escape won't come out. All your dirty tricks, your secret plots, won't be exposed."

"I'm thinking of the Colonel," Mueller said.

Bosworth rose. "You're thinking of yourself, Mueller. You're always thinking of yourself."

The first sergeant strode from the desk. He stopped before leaving the supply tent and turned to face his fellow NCO.

"Mueller, I hate to say this but I'm coming to the sorry conclusion that, in spite of all your words to the contrary, you're like Heinrich. You're hiding your true identity. You're pretending to be my concerned buddy when, instead, you're nothing but one lousy manipulative son of a bitch."

CHAPTER 28

DELMAN, HIS NOSE dripping from the cold, his foot pushed all the way down on the accelerator, bounced and slid the jeep on the icy road. He was happy to be alone, without his two-faced POW driver. He glanced at the crinkled map he had spread out next to him. He saw it was a straight run back to the camp, back to Le Mans. As he slid the battered jeep past shell holes and broken pavement, he thought of Perry's warning—kill Heinrich and Sacher or they'll kill you.

No alternatives? Not a single way to do something, anything, to avoid a shoot-out? What about an ambush? A ruse that would surprise Heinrich and Sacher, trap them, get them to surrender? And, equally important, how could he, Delman, avoid being ambushed by them, by the two desperate runaways?

As he passed upended vehicles—dismembered jeeps, bombed-out command cars, burnt-out half-tracks—pushed to the side of the road, Delman knew his enemy had the edge. They knew combat—the kind of fighting that caused pile-ups like those he'd passed along the road's slippery shoulders—and they knew how to kill.

What's more, they were two against one. That didn't seem overpowering when he said it—"two against one, two against one"—but they had twice his firepower, twice his manpower, and they'd have twice as many opportunities to feign and swerve and trick him into defeat. They had deception on their side.

"I better have luck on mine," Delman said.

He wiped his sleeve against his nose and dodged more shell-holes. At least, he thought, he'd prepared the best he could. Every night after the convoy had stopped and he'd made sure his POWs were housed, fed, and guarded, he had continued target practice. He used a carton, a hunk of wood or, as he had several times, created a paper outline of a figure that he stuck on a tree.

Eventually, he felt expert with his weapon of choice, the automatic carbine. It was well-balanced, reliable and, unlike the infantry's omnipresent M1, had little kick. He still remembered how, on the rifle range during basic, the M1's recoil left a nasty bruise on his right cheek. He practiced firing his carbine—and his Luger—endlessly. Finally, he found he could shoot the carbine from almost any angle, any unorthodox position. His favorite—straight from the hip, a Hollywood cowboy discharging his six-shooter.

The Luger was just as flexible, maybe more so. Once Delman got the hang of it, sighting it, he admired its accuracy, its solid feel and, above all, its irony. That's why, of course, Nelson gave it to him. What better way to kill Nazis than with their most famous pistol?

But killing, even killing Heinrich, was a hand pressing hard against Delman's throat, shortening his breath, weakening his knees. He remembered the time he went hunting quail—or was it pheasant?—on a weekend with Larry Bayer and his father in his slick, two-door, red Olds Hydromatic. They drove to a wooded area near the Fox River. Birds, their prey for the day, were everywhere, mostly gathered on the ground. Delman still recalled his shock when Bayer and his father raised their rifles, aiming at the congregating birds, before Delman screamed at them.

"You can't shoot them on the ground—they're sitting ducks!"

They laughed, lowered their rifles and tossed pine cones and stones at the quail until they rose—exploded—and were quickly dispatched. Delman helped. Afterwards, he called it a slaughter, not a sport. He swore he'd never go hunting again. He developed a strong distaste for hunting, fishing, and even—like Schweitzer—hesitated stomping on an ant, whacking a fly. Killing! Where was the satisfaction, the enjoyment? If you had to kill to live—to get food to eat—that was one thing. But recreational killing was an abomination.

But saving his own life—or the lives of the people around him, people he knew—that was a different story. After all, that was why he had joined the Army—to kill Nazis. So why was he worrying about sitting ducks?

His jeep kept sliding on the treacherous road. He brought it about, almost automatically. Now out of nowhere, he remembered he hadn't eaten lately. Perhaps that was the reason for his lightheadedness. He preferred to believe that was what caused his fatigue, his weariness—not his fear. He reached across and down into his musette bag. He felt around to locate the K-ration he'd opened but left uneaten when he'd seen Heinrich make his move. Delman began to nibble at the cheese but it slipped from his trembling fingers.

It shocked him, his inability to hold a wad of cheese in his gloved hand. He thought he was calm, in control. He moved his hand along the floorboard but, with his heavy glove, he couldn't feel anything.

He began to peel off the glove. When he had only the glove's fingers left to remove, he took both hands off the wheel, held the jeep as steady as he could with his right forearm and worked at the right glove's fingers, finally releasing them. With his right hand free, Delman held it in front of him at eye-level, driving with his left hand. His shakiness was unmistakable.

"Damn it!" he said aloud. "Shit!"

His hand was shaking, his fingers quivering. The movement he felt wasn't imaginary. His fear was visible. He was afraid and he was spastic. But he'd control it. He'd practice again with his carbine and Luger and make appropriate adjustments. If he could get Heinrich and Sacher to attack first, he could react unthinkingly in self defense. But he knew it would be too dangerous. He couldn't afford to wait for their attack. He'd have to overcome his fear. He'd have to attack them.

This reminded him of his early football days. He remembered the first game he played in Dyche Stadium against Northwestern's most famous and dangerous opponent, Notre Dame. Delman played both offense and defense. And, as his fellow linemen told him, they counted on him—because of his size, his speed and his endurance—to lead the Wildcats' line in repelling the Irish. But that was not enough. In the last quarter, with Northwestern down a touchdown, it was the line's attack—their attack, not their reaction—that turned the game around. Delman, leading the way, kept Notre Dame from reaching NU's quarterback as he searched and found receivers.

And it was Delman, inspiring the rest of the line, who opened up routes for the Wildcats' runners to gallop toward the Irish goal. Thanks to attack after attack, NU made two touchdowns in the closing minutes of the seesaw battle. They won the game and it was that game that brought Delman headlines, praise and, eventually, awards.

"Attack, Delman, attack!" he said aloud.

He'd have to do it again. Nelson had never mentioned what he undoubtedly realized would have to happen—the killing. He probably thought giving Delman the Luger said it all. But at the time, Delman had only thought about his escape from the camp—his convoy idea had become a reality—and not the convoy's inevitable dangers.

He passed more snow-covered debris on the side of the road—discarded cartons, worn-out tires—and again considered the men he might have to kill, especially Heinrich. From the first moment he met him, he pegged the German as a showboat, a ham, a guy hungry for recognition. Would Heinrich, as Delman had once mentioned to Perry, risk a run past the camp and through Le Mans as a gesture if he does escape? Delman thought so; Perry disagreed.

"He'd have to be crazy," Perry said, "and he has to be stupid and I don't think Heinrich's either."

Now, Delman thought, it depended how the escape was

going. Was Heinrich getting along with Sacher? Was Clary a problem? Was the truck holding up or did they have to look for another vehicle? And the French—their civilians and their rag-tag military—what were they doing?

If all was going well Heinrich's natural arrogance might erupt. He might take chances. If he could escape so close to the camp, why couldn't he speed past it and thumb his nose at the stupid Americans? And, maybe, to distract them and stun them, toss out his battered hostage. Delman glanced at his map and saw he could keep zigzagging—taking different roads to hunt for them—and still keep heading toward Le Mans.

Of course Delman would've liked nothing better than to lead his convoy into camp. Make Mueller eat his "I told you so's." See Colonel Nelson vindicated—establishing Delman's feat as original, creative, and maybe, if it was repeated, practical.

But except for Nelson and a few scoffing NCOs, no one at the camp gave a damn about the convoy. They didn't think about it. They didn't notice when it left and they wouldn't notice when it returned. Perry had been bucking for leadership. Isn't that why he came along without complaint? Take the convoy's command, Delman thought, and enjoy it. Luxuriate in it. It's yours, exploit it, savor it. And choke on it. Delman hadn't forgotten it was horny Perry who opted for a woman over guarding Heinrich. Ordinarily a logical choice, but not this time. Not on convoy, not when Delman assigned the motor pool chief the specific task of guarding Heinrich when they were in quarters. What the bald mechanic failed to do may have given the masquerading German the few minutes he needed to complete his escape plans, to visit Sacher.

Delman concentrated on checking every place—behind clumps of trees, turn-offs near abandoned farms—where Heinrich and Sacher might be hiding. At least my task's clear, he thought. No POWs to watch. No plans to make. No rations to check. All I have to do is to rescue Clary, kill two Germans, and come out alive.

He was glad to be free of Ramer. His tricks became obnoxious. His smart-assed actions—literally obeying Delman's orders—brought him closer to being read his final rites than he realized. Delman had been furious enough to kill him. That feeling made him believe he could kill the escaped POWs if he had to. Delman let up on his accelerator. He realized he could be doing exactly what Heinrich wanted, thinking ahead, overlooking the present. His unstable jeep could hit an icy patch, flip, and the escapees would be free of their only pursuer.

The weight of that, the realization that he wasn't under orders, that he had decided on his own to take the kind of risk that even Heinrich wouldn't take—a lone, inexperienced soldier against two of the experienced enemy—brought a shudder down Delman's spine, into his legs, into his arms. He took a deep breath. And a second one.

"Slow down!" he yelled aloud.

That felt good. He repeated his shout. "Slow down!" He did more: he stopped on the side of the road. He turned on his walkie-talkie and, as he did, told himself it didn't mean anything if Clary didn't answer. He could be out of range. His walkie-talkie could be dead or lost or confiscated by Heinrich. But he still had to try. He had to try to give Clary some hope and he had to try to worry the Germans.

"Jacques, this is Delman. Hold on. Don't give up. I'm on Heinrich's trail. I know where you are. I'll rescue you soon. If you hear this, Heinrich, you won't escape. And when you're captured, your punishment will depend upon how you treat your prisoner. Treat Clary well and you'll be treated well. That's a promise. Clary, don't worry. You'll be rescued. I'll see you soon."

*   *   *

"Your command car's here," Sergeant Bosworth said.

He walked into the office where Colonel Nelson sat reading a history of Paris and began to hoist Nelson's duffel onto his shoulder.

"Not yet," Nelson said. "Put it down. I'm going to wait a while."

"The longer you wait," Bosworth said, "the more difficult it's going to be to leave and Colonel Pomerantz said . . ."

Nelson interrupted. "I don't give a damn what Colonel Pomerantz said. I know what I have to do."

"What's that, sir?"

"To wait until the convoy arrives," Nelson said. "Then I'll leave."

"Major Hughes hasn't moved his things in here, but I'm sure he'd like to get organized and . . ."

"I agreed to leave today," Nelson interrupted again, "and I'll leave today but not until the convoy arrives. Put down my duffel, Bosworth. Is there anything else?"

"How do you know the convoy will arrive today?" Bosworth asked.

"It's overdue," Nelson said, "and I've got a feeling today's the day. There must be some scuttlebutt about the convoy, Bosworth. What do you hear?"

"Why don't I take your stuff outside to your car," Bosworth said, "and the driver of the command car will help me bring in Major Hughes' stuff."

"Not yet. Put down my duffel. Now answer me. What've you heard about the convoy?"

Bosworth took the duffel off his shoulder and set it on the floor.

"There's been an escape."

"Says who?"

"Sergeant Mueller."

Nelson closed his book. He rose from behind the bare desk and walked to the window and back to his chair, all the time looking at his first sergeant.

"How does he do it?" Nelson asked.

"He's regular Army," Bosworth said. "It's like my grandmother's sewing circle. They stay in touch. They know everything that's happening to everyone. They've got a network."

"I don't imagine Sergeant Mueller told you who escaped."

"No, sir."

Nelson sat down. "Take a load off, sergeant. Let's try to figure out what this escape means."

"It's only a rumor, Colonel," Bosworth said, sitting across from Nelson.

"What would you do if you were leading that convoy," Nelson asked, "and there was an escape?"

"We don't know who escaped," Bosworth said.

"I know," Nelson said, "and you know. I bet even Mueller knows. What would you do if Heinrich escaped?"

"It depends."

"It depends if he's alone," Nelson said, "and it depends if he escaped in a truck and it depends if he took someone, like a guard, with him. Is that what you were going to say, Bosworth?"

"If it's Heinrich who escaped, sir, Delman would go after him and let Perry bring in the convoy."

Nelson turned in his chair to glance out the window.

"With this good weather," he said, turning to face Bosworth again, "it shouldn't be too long before the convoy returns."

"Colonel," Bosworth said, beginning to reply but Nelson had returned to his book.

He had trouble concentrating. But he forced himself to pay attention to what he was reading. He found he had to read paragraphs twice to get their meaning. He must have been at it for two hours, maybe more, when Bosworth returned.

"The convoy's pulling in," Bosworth said.

"Delman?" Nelson asked.

"He went after the escapees," Bosworth said.

"Plural?" Nelson said.

"Heinrich," Bosworth replied, "and Sacher."

"Did Perry bring in the convoy?"

"Yes, sir."

"Let's go." Nelson moved quickly from his desk and put on his overcoat.

"With all due respect," Bosworth began.

"What now, sergeant?"

"You're no longer in charge of this camp, Colonel."

"I'm in charge of this camp as long as I want to be in charge of this camp," Nelson replied. "Let's go."

Bosworth threw on his coat as they trotted toward the supply tent where the convoy had stopped. At a distance, Nelson could see Captain Roland talking to Sergeant Perry but before Nelson got closer, Perry had left to enter the supply tent.

"We've got the supplies," Captain Roland said as soon as Colonel Nelson came up. "But they have one of our guards. Private Clary. A friend of Sergeant Delman's."

"That's why he's chasing them," Nelson said.

"Sergeant Perry," Roland reported, "said Delman believes the POWs who escaped may drive past the camp. Perry doesn't agree. It would be a perfect time, a melodramatic time, to release their hostage."

"Bosworth," the Colonel said, "get some trucks over here fast and barricade the road and, captain, I want your best riflemen lined up on either side of the road."

"Yes, sir."

"Did I hear you right, Colonel?"

It was Major Hughes, Nelson's replacement, a tall young unsmiling officer, who had just joined them.

"It's possible that Heinrich," Nelson explained, "the POW who led the escape, might, for whatever reason, pass our camp."

"Do you really believe that, Colonel?" Hughes asked.

"I've heard of crazier things," Nelson replied.

"With all due respect . . ." Hughes began.

Nelson interrupted him. "Fuck due respect, Major."

"Then I'll say it straight out, Colonel," Major Hughes said. "One or two escaping POWs aren't worth jeopardizing the security of this camp by taking away guards for some theory, right or wrong."

"What about the hostage?" Nelson asked.

"We have to be realistic," Hughes said.

"My order stands," Nelson said.

"Yes, sir!" Hughes said, raising his voice. He followed his loud reply with a perfect salute, a brisk about-face, and a hurried exit.

"He and Mueller should get along fine," Nelson said.

"It's getting dark, Colonel," Bosworth said.

"Put my stuff in the command car," Nelson ordered.

"It's already there, Colonel."

Nelson reached out to shake his first sergeant's hand. "You're a good man, Bosworth. I'll miss you. Tell Delman I waited as long as I could. And, Bosworth, when you're in Chicago, look me up."

"Yes, sir."

"I'm not just saying that, Bosworth. I mean it. Look me up. We'll have a lot to talk about."

"I'll do that, Colonel."

Nelson turned to Captain Roland and they shook hands.

"Call me," Nelson said, "as soon as you hear anything, regardless of the time. I have to know what happens here, the POWs, Delman, and your guard, Clary."

As Nelson was about to get into the waiting command car, he stopped, straightened up, and threw a farewell salute to the remaining NCOs and the cold miserable nightmare of a camp he'd never forget and never would want to see again. It was the first time he thought a salute made sense.

CHAPTER 29

HEINRICH, DRIVING THE getaway truck, had had enough of Sacher's belittling sarcasm. He had to reduce the rancor. How could they fight the enemy if all they did was fight each other?

"I'll say it again," Sacher continued. "What you're planning to do is a mistake. It's dumb, driving past the camp. You're speeding right into their trap."

"What trap?"

"Everyone's on to you," Sacher said. "They all know what you want to do. They'll be waiting for you."

Why, Heinrich thought, did I ever suggest driving past the camp? It was obviously dangerous, even reckless. But he knew he had to be dramatic; no, melodramatic. Maybe "theatrical" was a better word. He blamed it on his parents. He was raised to be startling even though he—particularly with his glamorous sister around—was the most reserved, least extroverted member of his extroverted family. His parents never accepted the ordinary; they always opted for the extraordinary.

But there was more to it than that. He saw the military as a way for him to gain recognition on his own if he consciously became more than another cipher, another number, another good soldier. Even as a POW, his masquerade wasn't only to fool the enemy. It was also to reinforce what he saw as his individuality, although he feared he often was the only one to recognize it. He thought his disguise—exchanging custom-tailored uniforms for the ordinary soldier's ill-fitting clothes—set him apart from his fellow officers. He wanted his escape to be equally unusual, equally memorable.

It was not easy to give up his plan to run past the camp and thumb his nose at his captors as he raced to the front to join his unit. But he had to put his escape first. That meant repairing his relationship with Sacher.

"Then I'll surprise everyone," Heinrich said. "I won't drive past the camp. I won't drive into their trap."

Sacher wasn't listening.

"You want everyone to think what a mighty Prussian you are," he said, "and what could be more courageous than this no longer disguised S.S. officer rushing past your former prison on your way to join your unit?"

"You're not listening to me," Heinrich said. He slowed down the truck, turned to Sacher and spoke insultingly slowly, pausing after each word. "What I said is that I will not drive past the camp."

Sacher turned toward Heinrich.

"It's about time," Sacher said, now paying attention, "about time you started to listen to me."

"And it's about time you listened to the engine," Heinrich said. "Hear that? It's not the usual rattling noise. I think we've got a problem."

Sacher listened.

"Pull over," he said. "I'll take a look."

Heinrich knew Sacher didn't appreciate what a sacrifice it was to drop his plan. But perhaps the racer's attitude would become less confrontational. Heinrich pulled over to the side of the road and turned off the ignition.

He watched Sacher slide from the truck's cab. He was now dressed in seedy U.S. Government-issued green fatigues he had found in the truck. With his grimy unshaven face, he resembled nothing more than an American dogface, an ugly cartoon character.

At least he's good for something, Heinrich thought. Sacher could repair the truck. If he failed, Heinrich was already prepared. He'd looked across the road and seen that they weren't too far from an old partially bombed-out farmhouse. A car was behind it. If their truck was in trouble, they'd go to the farmhouse, kill its inhabitants, and take their vehicle.

Sacher came around to Heinrich's side of their truck and tapped on the window.

"Nothing serious," he reported. "I'll get some tools and tighten up a few things. It shouldn't take long."

"While you're back there," Heinrich said, "check the guard."

Returning with his tools, Sacher stopped next to Heinrich. He rolled down the window.

"The guard's not moving," Sacher said. "You better take a look at him. The last time you hit him might've finished him."

Heinrich tightened his jacket and slowly stepped out of the truck. He pressed against it, holding Clary's rifle in front of him, his finger near the trigger. Without moving, he carefully looked up and down the road and only when he was sure it was clear did he edge toward the vehicle's rear.

They were still alone on the road. Sacher was bent over, half-hidden behind the truck's raised hood. Heinrich was certain they were far ahead of Delman but this delay, as brief as it was, had to be in the Jew's favor.

Heinrich climbed over the truck's tailgate and stepped across the tarpaulin-covered platform toward the cab. The Belgian guard was either asleep or dead. Heinrich saw Sacher had tossed a blanket over the prostrate body. Clary's gloved hands were tied in front of him. Frayed rope was pulled tightly around his legs, above his boots. Heinrich pushed at him and the guard grunted. Heinrich pulled up the Belgian's cap and saw his angry eyes drift open.

"Too bad," Heinrich said. "I hoped you were dead."

"You swine," Clary muttered. "They'll get you."

"Well, I've got you," Heinrich said, grabbing the guard's coat, pulling him up, looking into his drawn gray baby face. He dropped him quickly; Clary smelled dead. "I've got you and I don't want you. I've a good notion to get rid of you right now."

"Do it," Clary said slowly, between labored breaths. "Go ahead, do it, kill me, get it over with."

"Not before I do this," Heinrich said, using the guard's own rifle to poke him on the side where blood still was oozing. Clary's breathing stopped and then he exhaled and released, at the same time, a long, awful groan. Heinrich watched the blanket darken.

"Well," Heinrich said and jabbed him again in the same place, "that must be where it hurts."

There was another loud, pained, sustained moan.

"What's going on back there?" Sacher called, staring into the truck's dark interior as he put down the tools he'd used.

Slowly Heinrich moved from his victim but not before he pushed the rifle's butt against the wet spot on the blanket. Clary, startled, cried out. Heinrich left the truck and ambled toward its front where he saw the hood was down. He opened the driver's door and was surprised to find a stolid Sacher camped behind the steering wheel.

"What do you think you're doing?"

"If something goes wrong with the truck," Sacher said, "it's better if I drive."

"If you fixed it properly," Heinrich said, "nothing will go wrong with the truck."

Who did Sacher, this egotistical NCO, think he was! Heinrich never should have agreed not to run past the camp. His change of plans gave Sacher a false sense of importance, as if he were now in charge. Heinrich pointed his rifle at the upstart.

"Out, out, out!" Heinrich commanded. "Get out from behind the wheel and get over to the other side where you belong."

Sacher, hands on the wheel, eyes straight ahead, didn't move.

"Did you kill our hostage?" he asked. "He's dead, isn't he? Or are you keeping him alive so you can torture him? Is that what you do? Torture people? Is that what you did to Delman in the supply tent and what you're doing now to the Belgian? I think you like to torture people. Physically, mentally, any way you can as long as someone suffers. Let me ask you, Heinrich: do you get off when you torture people? Is that it? Is that why you do it?"

Sacher was disgusting, Heinrich thought, repulsive and disgusting. Like Wanger. Heinrich never should have taken Sacher with him. This self-important, uneducated, lower-class greasemonkey—not much better than a Jew—believed his celebrity gave him the right to say anything to anyone, consequences be damned. This time he'd gone too far.

Heinrich used his rifle like a saber. He slashed it across Sacher's hairy cheek, opening a red gash from the tip of his left eye to the end of his busy mouth. Sacher, stunned, grabbed at his face and then, still in shock, examined his wet, bloody glove as if it were a beloved pet mauled by a wild animal. He lifted his head to stare into the muzzle of Heinrich's rifle pressed hard between his eyes.

"You're a pervert," Sacher said, not moving, "a sadistic, fucking pervert. How did you get this way? And why did I ever fall for your 'escape with me' drivel?"

"Get out from behind that wheel," Heinrich said, "and over to your side."

Sacher tottered out of the door to the truck's rear and found the first-aid kit. He tore his gloves off, found another envelope he hurriedly ripped open, moaning all the time.

He tilted his head and poured powder on his open cheek. By feel, he placed a large bandage on his wound. Panting, he replaced his gloves before he walked to the cab's passenger side and climbed into the truck.

"One more remark," Heinrich said, "and that's it. I've taken all I'm going to take from you. Is that clear?"

When there was no answer, Heinrich lifted the rifle and pressed its muzzle against Sacher's temple.

"So you'll kill me." Sacher said, "is that it? You'll kill me if I tell you what an arrogant, perverted son of a bitch you are."

Heinrich flipped off the rifle's safety. He stared at his fellow
POW—the only mistake he had made in planning his escape—
and let his finger touch the trigger. It was so easy, so tempting
but, finally, he pushed the safety back and lowered the rifle.

"My last warning," he said.

Heinrich switched on the ignition and quickly turned it
off.

"What's wrong now?" Sacher said.

"Delman! I saw Delman!"

"Delman?" Sacher looked wildly in the direction Heinrich
was looking. "Where?"

"On the other side of the snowdrift. See that little break
there. I saw him pass it, on the other side. Look over there, by
those trees. That's Delman's jeep."

"Let's go!" Sacher said. "Start the truck. Let's get the fuck
out of here!"

"No!" Heinrich said. "This is what I've been waiting for.
You stay in the truck. I'll crawl toward him and surprise him
head-on. You take the rifle. You'll be able to shoot him from
the truck. We've got him. We'll kill him before he knows what's
happened. We can't miss."

*   *   *

Delman had developed a routine. As he approached each crossroads, he'd stop his jeep behind a snowdrift or a stand of leaf-
less trees, turn off his engine, and begin his silent surveillance.
He didn't want to be seen or heard in case the Germans were
nearby, waiting to ambush him.

With carbine in hand, Delman quietly dropped from his jeep
and, on hands and knees, using his vehicle as a shield, crawled—
as he had learned to snake along in basic training—to check all
the roads. First left and then right, and, finally, forward and back
to see if he could discover the escaped deuce-and-a-half.

His routine—speeding to a crossroads, stopping, surveying—was time-consuming and, so far, fruitless. If the escapees kept driving, never pausing, they'd increase their lead. But Delman counted on their chutzpah, their weak bladders, the cold. They'd slow down and he'd catch up.

He'd marked every crossroads on his map. He kept zigzagging, always going toward the camp. Once he satisfied himself that the stolen truck was not nearby, he placed a checkmark on the map on top of the last crossroads he surveyed, and then moved on to the next one. He believed he'd find Heinrich. In fact, he had the feeling Heinrich wanted to confront him, wanted to prove to his jailer that the Wehrmacht's best always could out-fight, out-think, out-maneuver the enemy, particularly the Jewish enemy.

As Delman crawled at the latest crossroads, he thought of his father's warnings, always the same: don't be a hero, don't take foolish chances, think before you act, be cautious. Cautious! How Delman hated his father's favorite word. Now, sweating on the inside, freezing on the outside, barely moving, Delman was acting like his father's son. He was cautious. On his stomach, using his legs and arms, he pulled and pushed himself along the base of the high snowdrift.

He was so cold and had been so cold for so long he accepted his icy discomfort like another layer of clothing. It was next to his skin, between his skin and his underwear, an everyday part of his everyday uniform—another layer of misery.

He'd crawled past his jeep and, there, on the other side of an indentation in the snowdrift, he saw it—the missing truck, the getaway deuce-and-a-half. It was stopped, empty, hidden as he'd hidden his jeep. He stared at it. Was it real or another mirage, another in the long line of quivering puddles he saw settled on roads but, when approached, would evaporate, leaving not a trace of moisture?

He checked his weapons. His carbine was cumbersome. Holding it with one hand or even cradling it in both arms made it difficult for him to crawl. He didn't want to relinquish it but he did, sliding it behind him. He turned on his back so he could pull out the Luger. He checked to make sure it was loaded, ready to fire. He rolled back onto his stomach and resumed his crawling, edging closer to the truck. They had to be nearby, Heinrich and Sacher. And he had to act quickly.

He rubbed his gloves over his eyes to catch his sweat. How could he be sweating on this cold day, his breath making clouds? Then he thought his crawling body might be leaving a trail, one that could be seen by the Germans behind him. There was no trail; everything was frozen. If he'd pushed the snow or ice down by crawling over it, it wasn't visible. He was safe. Unless, like him, Heinrich was crawling in his direction on the other side of the snowdrift so that momentarily they'd clash, head-on.

Another thought broke through Delman's tension. Clary. Where was Clary? In his eagerness to attack, to get in the first shot, he'd forgotten his friend, their hostage, his rationale for his dangerous tracking. Would Clary be used as a shield? Delman wasn't sure how close he was to the stolen truck. Could he stand up, look over the snowdrift and see it—and would he see their hostage, tied and strapped to it? As eager as Delman was to take the initiative, to get it over with, he had to be sure he wasn't trapped by his own inexperience. What else could they do? Of course! There were two of them. He kept thinking of Heinrich, only Heinrich. He kept overlooking Sacher. Heinrich could approach and, as Delman prepared to shoot, he could be hit by Sacher.

*   *   *

Delman knew the longer he took, the more time he gave them to entrap him and to put Clary in Delman's line of fire. He had to take a risk.

He heard a sound from above. A trick? He looked up. A large bird was circling over him. It kept drifting down, perhaps considering Delman a kind of prey. Its dark, outspread shadow was getting closer. Would Heinrich or Sacher see it and deduce what its prey was and wait for Delman to raise his head? Bird or not, he had to see over the snowdrift. He had to jump up, his gun in hand, ready to fire, and surprise them. But not to hurt Clary if, as Delman suspected, they placed him in Delman's line of fire.

Delman heard heavy breathing, panting, and realized it was his own audible fear. He put down the Luger, whipped off his gloves and thrust them in his pocket to warm them. He withdrew his hands, blew on them and again grabbed the pistol. Now he could feel it, cold and lethal, in his hand. Now he would attack.

"One, two, three," he silently cued himself.

He jumped up. There was a shot. A second one. He dropped. He was breathing hard. Where was he hit? He felt his body, his shoulders, chest, stomach, crotch, legs. No holes, no blood. He moved his head, his hands, his feet and then stopped. He heard someone call in German, then English. Finally, Delman grasped what was being shouted.

"I surrender!"

A trap. That's what it had to be. He slid backwards. He found the carbine. Now he held the Luger in his left hand, the light carbine in his right. He rose quickly, his mouth open, breathing heavily, ready to fire, a weapon in each hand.

But it wasn't necessary. There was a body on the ground and beyond it, not far away, in front of the stolen truck, Sacher, the rifle on the ground in front of him. He waved a shirt and shouted, "I surrender, I surrender, don't shoot!"

Delman ran around the snowdrift and pointed his weapons at Sacher.

"Don't move," Delman commanded.

He put the Luger in his pocket and, pressing the carbine against the German's face, patted him down. Then, facing Sacher, Delman backed toward Heinrich, face down on the icy ground. His jacket was torn and his head was bloody. There was a bloody rock on the ground next to him. Delman used his carbine to jab at the body. It didn't move.

Delman still looked at the other POW, Sacher. He'd dropped the shirt he'd been waving and now stood unmoving, his cap pulled over his shadowed, bandaged face, his hands upraised.

Delman was confused. He hadn't fired his weapons, Heinrich appeared dead, and there was this other unarmed German and—Clary! What had they done to Clary? Where was Clary?

Before Delman could look for him, he had to make sure Heinrich was truly dead. He knelt on the icy ground and examined Heinrich's back. Delman couldn't tell what was flesh or fabric. Heinrich's blood was that pervasive, that heavy. All that was clear was that several shots had gone into Heinrich's back, at least one below his shoulder, another lower down. Delman caught the smell of blood. He gagged and then held his breath as he turned over the body and stared at Heinrich's scraped face, bloody nose, and open eyes.

"Heinrich," Delman said, pushing at his shoulder, staying away from the hole in his chest and stomach where the bullets exited. Delman removed one glove—his other hand still holding the carbine—and searched for a pulse on Heinrich's throat. Then Delman held his fingers in front of Heinrich's parted lips. Delman felt no throb, no breath.

"Good riddance," he muttered.

He replaced his glove and felt relief. The chase was over. But he didn't rejoice. He was stunned by the unexpected, confusing nature of Heinrich's death. Delman pressed his fingers against Heinrich's eyelids to close his eyes.

"Don't move," Delman yelled at Sacher. "Stay where you are. Keep your hands up."

"I'm not moving," the POW said.

"Where's Clary?" Delman asked, taking the rifle that was at Sacher's feet. "I want to see Clary."

"He's dead," Sacher said. "Heinrich tortured him to death."

"Take me to him," Delman said.

They went to the truck.

"Go inside," Delman said, pushing his carbine into the German as they climbed into the truck.

Clary was on his side, his tied legs drawn up to his chest. A blanket was near his feet. Was he dead? Had they killed him?

"Jacques," Delman said, reaching for him and gently turning him on his back. "It's over. Heinrich's dead."

As he spoke, he untied the ropes on Clary's hands and legs. He touched his face. His eyes were closed but he felt warm.

"Jacques," Delman said, "you're free."

Delman reached to embrace his friend and, inadvertently, brushed against the wound on his side. Clary, closed-eyed, open-mouthed, released a long, terrible moan.

"Thank God," Delman said, "you're alive."

Delman examined Clary's wound and remembered how he had incessantly poked at Heinrich, who had returned the favor with fervor. Clary's wound was large and open and smelled.

Delman had seen a first aid kit when he climbed into the truck.

"Bring me that first aid kit," he told Sacher.

Sacher handed it to Delman who rummaged through its contents but all he found were tape and bandages.

He returned to look at the wound. He tried to pull the cloth away from it and saw that a bandage, now in tatters, had been applied. He found some cotton and tried to clean the wound but Clary cried out. Delman put a bandage over the bloody one and used tape to keep it intact.

"Heinrich," Clary muttered, "got even."

"You'll be okay," Delman said.

"The walkie-talkie," Clary said between gasps.

"It worked," Delman said.

"It helped," Clary whispered.

"We'll get you back to the camp," Delman said.

Clary didn't answer.

"Let's go," Delman said to Sacher and they left the truck.

When they were on the ground Delman stood in front of Sacher.

"You shot Heinrich," Delman said, "didn't you?"

"He was crawling toward you," Sacher said. "When he saw you move, he raised himself and that's what killed him. I was firing at you and he took the bullets meant for you."

Delman removed Sacher's cap and saw the bloody bandage on his face partially covering an awful gash.

"Heinrich did this to you?" Delman asked.

Sacher nodded and then he said, "I didn't mean to kill him. He got excited when he saw you move and I fired."

Delman returned Sacher's cap.

"Get Heinrich's body," he said, "and put it in the truck."

Sacher went to the snowdrift and hoisted Heinrich's bloody body over his shoulder; its head bobbed as he carried it to the truck. Delman saw something drop. He leaned down and picked up Clary's small knife.

It was blood-stained. What was Heinrich doing with Clary's penknife? God, thought Delman, putting it together, slowly slipping the knife into his overcoat pocket. He unlatched the tailgate and, with Sacher, dropped Heinrich on the truck's platform.

"You'll drive the truck back to the camp," Delman said. "Follow this road. I'll be in the jeep behind you. Don't leave until I give you the signal."

Sacher nodded and got into the truck.

Delman returned to Clary. He was unconscious. Delman pulled up the blanket over him and placed what appeared to be part of a torn duffel bag under his head. He stepped over Heinrich's body, climbed out of the truck, and raised and fastened its tailgate.

"Drive as fast as you can," Delman told Sacher, "but watch out for shellholes. Clary's been beat up enough. Let's go."

As he followed the truck, Delman took a last glance at the spot where Heinrich had died. He expected to see a bloodstain but there was nothing, no sign that anything unusual had happened on the road to Le Mans.

CHAPTER 30

THE BELGIAN MP manning the camp's front gate was startled to see a truck pull up with a POW driving it. He questioned the scruffy German and then quickly shunted to the jeep behind it.

"Sergeant," the guard said to Delman, "what's going on, a POW driving one of our trucks?"

"We're the last of that convoy that left a few days ago," Delman said. "POWs drove all the trucks. The one in front of me was the one who escaped, who took Clary as a hostage. He's in the back, wounded and unconscious."

"I better see your orders," the guard said.

"Jesus," Delman said, "you know me. We're wasting valuable time. Clary's in bad shape and needs immediate medical attention."

"Your orders," the guard said.

Checking orders—for what? Didn't the Belgian realize his fellow guard could die while he went through his military routine? But he did what his commander, Captain Roland, told him he had to do. Delman hurriedly reached down for his musette bag. He pulled it up on the seat next to him and quickly rustled through it. He finally located his all-important, forgotten orders. "Here," he said, thrusting the typewritten document toward the impassive guard.

Delman impatiently watched him glance at it, saunter back to his post, and use a phone. He finally returned to Delman but not before he stopped at the truck to speak to Sacher.

"You can enter," the guard said to Delman, giving him back his orders. "I told the POW to pull his truck up to headquarters.

An ambulance is on the way."

"Good," Delman said.

He followed Sacher, driving slowly, inside the camp. He left his jeep next to the truck and told Sacher to wait. Not to move from the truck. When the ambulance arrived, Delman spoke to the medic who climbed into the truck, examined a moaning Clary, and came out, stone-faced.

"That's a bad wound," the medic said, "and he's dehydrated. We'll get him to the hospital."

"How bad?" Delman asked.

"Bad," the medic said. "What's with the dead body?"

"You take care of Clary," Delman said, "and I'll take care of the dead body."

He watched his friend transferred in a litter from the truck to the ambulance. Then Delman went into headquarters to see Bosworth and report to the Colonel. Instead, he found only ex-cop Waddell, now a buck sergeant, who had taken over Delman's cage.

"Where's everybody?" Delman asked.

"Big shipment of POWs," Waddell said. "Everyone's at the railroad."

"I'm reporting back," Delman said.

"Back?" Waddell said. "Back from where?"

The phone rang and Delman stepped outside the building. He could see he'd been missed. It was sunny but cold. Delman walked back and forth, flapping his arms, trying to figure out what he should do. Sacher should be placed under guard. Heinrich's body should be seen by the Colonel or Captain Roland. And, most important, Roland should make sure his wounded guard received the medical treatment he needed. Delman returned to Waddell.

"What now, Delman?"

"Captain Roland," Delman said. "I have to see him. Do you know where he is?"

"Look," Waddell said. "I'm in charge of quarters and it's bad enough I'm pulling double duty without keeping track of fucking officers."

"Right," Delman said.

Delman left to go to the railroad spur by way of Roland's quarters. As he jogged, slapping his gloved hands together to warm them up, he felt as if he'd never left the camp. Then he saw the Captain walking toward him. Delman stopped and saluted.

"Sergeant Delman," the Captain said, surprised.

"Private Clary's been wounded," Delman said. "They just removed him to the hospital."

"It's too cold to talk out here," Roland said. "Let's go inside."

When they entered headquarters, Sergeant Waddell rose to salute the security forces' commander.

"We're going to use the office," Roland said, starting to walk into the Colonel's office.

"I'm sorry. sir," Waddell said, blocking his way. "I have strict orders from Major Hughes that no one is to go in there while he's away. I can't even go in to leave stuff on his desk."

"This won't take long," the Captain said, moving forward.

"I'm sorry, captain," Waddell repeated, his large body in front of the slim captain's.

Roland's slit-eyes narrowed.

"Get the hospital on the phone for me," he ordered.

Delman listened to the Captain check on Clary's condition. He hung up and told Delman, "They're getting liquids into him and cauterizing his wound. He'll recover. Let's go to my quarters."

Delman was confused. Who was Major Hughes? What did he have to do with the Colonel's office? And where was the Colonel? When they arrived in Roland's quarters, the Captain threw off his mackinaw and sat at his desk. He nodded for Delman to sit across from him.

"First," Roland said, "you should know you were put up for

a commendation by the Colonel. Now tell me what happened.
I understand there was an escape."

"Heinrich and Sacher," Delman said. He began to explain
about the escape but the Captain interrupted.

"Sacher. He must be Sacher, the racer," the Captain said. "I
heard he was here. Go on."

Delman explained that Clary was taken as a hostage and
Delman's jeep was rammed, that he tracked the escaped deuce-
and-a-half and discovered it on an empty road where Heinrich
was killed.

"You shot him," the Captain said.

"Sacher shot him."

"Sacher!" Roland said.

"Twice in the back."

"What happened?"

"I was following the escaped truck and came to this snowdrift," Delman said. "I heard shots when Sacher fired at me
but got Heinrich in the back. With two shots. At least that's
Sacher's version."

"What's your version?" Roland asked.

"Sacher killed Heinrich intentionally," Delman said. "I think
he may have hit him with a rock before he shot him, and that's
how he got his gun. Heinrich must have attacked him earlier.
You should see Sacher's face. It's split on one side, like somebody
took a hatchet to a watermelon."

"Sacher could think," Roland said, "that his career would
be wrecked if it was revealed he shot a Wehrmacht officer in the
back. He'd rather make you the killer, the hero."

"I'm not a killer," Delman said, "and I'm not a hero."

"You could become a hero. You took after two escaped
POWs, found them, and brought them back here."

"One killed the other," Delman said, "and the one who was
left surrendered."

"They were two against one," the Captain said. "You never
hesitated."

"They took Clary as a hostage. I didn't have a choice."

"You always have a choice," Roland said.

"I was lucky."

"I don't believe in luck," Roland said. "There was a reason why Sacher shot Heinrich. There was a reason why you were there. Luck had nothing to do with it."

"I was lucky to find them."

"You're a hero only when somebody calls you a hero. You have to file a report so it's known what you did."

"I should report to the Colonel." Delman said.

"He's not here," Roland said. "He's been reassigned. He stayed here as long as he could, hoping to see you."

"He's not here?"

"Major Hughes replaced him. You better report to him as soon as possible."

"The convoy. It was the Colonel's as much as mine."

"Nelson's guilt trip," Roland said, "that's what some called it."

"Guilt trip?"

"The Colonel wanted to prove he wasn't running a killing factory, so to prove it he sent out your convoy. Isn't that what you were thinking about when you came up with your convoy idea?"

"I was thinking about escaping from Mueller and Heinrich," Delman said. "Where's the Colonel now?"

"St. Cloud, outside of Paris," the Captain said, "TPM head-quarters. He's in charge of all POW camps in the ETO."

"They got even with him," Delman said.

"He was promoted to full colonel."

"Promoted," Delman said.

"Clary," Roland said. "His wound. How did it happen?"

"He was tortured by Heinrich."

"Tortured?"

"Heinrich was getting even. I put Clary in Heinrich's truck to guard him and Clary had the habit of rifle-jabbing Heinrich on his right side. That's exactly where Clary has his wound, on his right side. Heinrich's body's in the truck. I told Sacher to stay with it."

"I'll take care of them," the Captain said.

"I would like to see Clary," Delman said, "but first I should see Sergeant Mueller."

"And Major Hughes," the Captain said. "You don't want to forget Major Hughes."

Mueller was sitting at his desk when Delman walked into the supply tent. Just as I left him, Delman thought.

Mueller turned around. "Well, if it isn't Sergeant Delman." He swung his chair so he could face Delman. "Perry said I should be expecting you soon."

"I thought I should check in with you," Delman said, "before I report to Major Hughes."

Delman strolled through the tents and then came back to Mueller. "I guess you distributed the supplies we brought back."

"The day they got here," Mueller said.

Delman stood in front of the master sergeant.

"Did you hear about the escape?" Delman asked.

"That's why Perry brought the convoy in," Mueller said, "so you could go after them."

"Heinrich's dead," Delman said.

He watched Mueller's face: there was no reaction.

"Anyone else?" Mueller asked.

"The Belgian guard, Clary, has a hole in his side, thanks to Heinrich. If you hadn't put him on the convoy . . ."

"Don't stick me with that," Mueller said. "Who knew he'd escape?"

"Everyone in the compound," Delman said.

"You better report to the Major," Mueller said, "before we both say something we'll regret."

"Why did you send Heinrich?" Delman asked. "You knew we didn't get along."

"Because I thought he was the best man for the job."

"What job?" Delman asked. "Why?"

"You want some 'why's'?" Mueller said. He stood up to face Delman. "Why did Colonel Nelson approve your convoy? Answer me that. For your supplies, your great haul? They were used up in one day. In one cage."

"It was a beginning," Delman said.

"I don't blame you," Mueller said. "You had an idea and you pushed it. You had enough of your punishment and you wanted out. You saw the convoy as a means of escape. But Colonel Nelson! He should've been objective. He should've known better. He should've weighed what was to be gained against what was to be lost."

"He did," Delman said. "That's why he approved it. But you—to get even, you sent me your favorite Nazi."

Mueller sat down and looked up at Delman.

"To get even," Mueller said, "the Colonel sent out your fucking convoy."

*   *   *

Delman trudged to the railroad spur to report to Nelson's re-placement. He thought about Nelson and wondered how the Colonel could leave the very day he returned. One more day, he thought. But he was being unfair. The Colonel couldn't know how soon Delman would return. At least, unlike everyone else, Nelson didn't take the convoy lightly.

Delman heard someone call his name. He turned and saw Sergeant Perry walking toward him.

"Hey," Perry said, "what happened?"

"I found them," Delman said. "Heinrich's dead, Sacher's in the truck with the body, and Clary's wounded."

"How bad?" Perry asked.

"Bad," Delman said. "But Captain Roland checked on him and said he'd recover. I'll know more when I visit him."

"Your plan worked," Perry said.

"I was lucky."

"I knew you'd get the bastards."

"You brought the convoy in without any trouble," Delman said.

"Straight to the supply tent," Perry said. "Even Mueller was surprised at all we were able to get from depots that never acknowledged his requisitions. I wouldn't be surprised if there are a lot more convoys."

"Not if Mueller has anything to say about it," Delman said.

"Major Hughes thinks a convoy's the way to go."

"I'm going over to the railroad now," Delman said, "to report to him."

"He's in his office," Perry said. "Saw him come in a few minutes ago. He's a lot different from the Colonel."

"So I hear."

"Watch yourself with him," Perry said. "He was drafted and he's more regular Army than Mueller."

Delman was surprised at Perry's friendliness. He had expected the motor pool chief to show the same resentment he displayed on the convoy. But Perry didn't hold grudges. Delman returned to headquarters to see Major Hughes.

"Go right in," Waddell told Delman.

He approached the Major, sitting tall behind the Colonel's desk, and saluted. It was returned briskly.

"At ease, sergeant," the Major said.

Delman saw Nelson's bed was gone as well as his wall map. New photos—all camp commanders must have a wife and kids, Delman thought—had replaced the Colonel's.

Delman remembered the first time he'd been in Nelson's office. He'd been reprimanded for striking a POW. He remembered the bowl made from an artillery shell that contained baby Tootsie Rolls and how he craved one but had never been offered any.

"It's about time you reported to me, Delman."

"I was on the way to report to you, Major, when I bumped into Captain Roland," Delman explained. "I stopped to tell him that I had one of his guards—wounded and unconscious—in the truck I brought back."

"I'm in charge here, sergeant," the Major said. "Captain Roland's under my command. You should've reported to me."

"As soon as I came in," Delman said, "I reported to headquarters."

"And," the Major said, "the charge of quarters told you where I was. You should have reported to me directly before you did anything else."

Delman decided not to repeat what he'd said.

"Yes, sir."

"Am I right, sergeant?"

You're an asshole, Delman thought.

"You're right, sir."

The Major's got all the makings of a Mueller, Delman thought. After Nelson's easy-going style, his replacement was a throwback, probably a shock to everyone.

"First," the Major said, "tell me what happened on the convoy. Sergeant Perry said there was an escape."

Delman gave a full report.

"What's the name of the dead POW?"

"Josef Heinrich," Delman said. "I checked his body. He was shot in the back. Twice."

"You killed him?"

"No, sir," Delman said. "Sacher, the other POW, killed him. He has a huge gash on his face that was put there by Heinrich."

"So you didn't kill Heinrich," the Major said.

"I brought them back, Major," Delman explained. "I followed them, found them, and brought them back. I didn't kill Heinrich. I left that to Sacher."

"He's giving you credit," the Major said.

"He's got his own reasons for that," Delman said. "At least

that's what Captain Roland thinks."

"This convoy," the Major said. "I understand it was your idea."

Was that an accusation? Delman wasn't certain. He also didn't care.

"Sort of," he said.

"What's that supposed to mean?" Hughes asked.

"I had the basic idea," Delman said. "The Colonel improved it, made it practical."

"One day makes a difference," the Major said. "I was ready to ask you to organize another convoy. Now I understand we'll be getting all the supplies we need."

Figures, Delman thought. Colonel Nelson's seeing to that. Which takes care of me. Who needs the only NCO in the ETO who has led a convoy driven by POWs to secure supplies from back-of-the line supply depots? Colonel Nelson inadvertently eliminated my job. Now what? Back to the supply tent? Back working for Mueller? From hero to victim in less than an hour.

"You were originally a cage warden," the Major said, "but all our cages have wardens. And Sergeant Mueller tells me he no longer wants you working in his supply tent. He told me about you striking prisoners and I share his disgust with such behavior."

"I was set up," Delman said.

"Sergeant Mueller told me you'd say that," the Major said. "He also told me you came here as something of a sports celebrity, thinking you were bigger than the Army."

"Sir . . ." Delman began.

"Enough," the Major said. "You've already shown what Sergeant Mueller said is true. Sergeant Perry told me you placed your friend, the guard Clary, next to the POW you said had been killed. If you're a friend, sergeant, I'd hate to have you as an enemy."

He was the best guard for the job, Delman was about to say

but he decided any comment would be meaningless.

"Is Clary the guard who was wounded?" the Major asked.

"He was tortured by . . ."

"The very POW you had him guard!" the Major said, delighted with his discovery.

"The very POW," Delman said, "that Sergeant Mueller placed on the convoy."

"We don't need a cage warden who hits POWs," the Major said, "Sergeant Mueller doesn't need an assistant, and, as I said, we no longer need your convoy."

"Makes sense to me, Major," Delman said.

"I'm not unaware of the commendation Colonel Nelson put in for you," the Major said, "and, from where the Colonel sits, it might be deserved. But, from where I sit, I want you out of here."

"I second that motion, Major."

"That's the kind of smart-ass, insubordinate remark," the Major said, "that allows me to reassign you without any regret in spite of you bringing back the escaped POWs. I've asked Sergeant Bosworth to draw up orders for your immediate transfer."

"Thank you, Major," Delman said.

"I want you out of here, sergeant," the Major said.

Delman straightened up, took one step back, saluted and left the Major's office. Delman was surprised to see Sergeant Bosworth sitting at his desk, waiting for him.

"This is for you, sergeant," Bosworth said. "Your orders."

Delman saw what had been typed: "Report immediately to Colonel Nelson at TPM headquarters."

"You've got the kind of attitude," Bosworth said, looking over Delman's shoulder at the Major, still standing in the doorway to his office, "that we don't want in this compound. You get it, sergeant?"

"I get it, sergeant," Delman said.

He got it. He figured it out. You see a need. You meet the need. You assume command. You use your head. You beat the odds. Then, success or not, you're sent packing. Make sense? Not at all. Then you've got it. At last. You're finally a soldier. You know little is as it appears. Everyone's fighting his own small war plus the larger one. But, thanks to a Bosworth, your escape, maybe your last one, is as unexpected as it is appreciated.

Delman turned to the Major. "I'd like to see Private Clary before I leave."

"I want you out of here now," the Major said.

"He's going to pull through," Bosworth said. "I'll let him know where you are. A jeep's waiting to take you to Paris."

Paris, Delman thought, Paris—with Nelson in charge.

"Good riddance," the Major added.

He said it loud enough for Delman to hear. My very words, he thought, but they were for Heinrich. For a moment, Delman thought of answering. But he decided neither the Major nor Mueller were worth it.

He thought of saluting the camp, giving it the same kind of cynical salute he learned was delivered by the Colonel when he departed, Nelson's final "good riddance." Delman didn't want to do anything to diminish it.

He nodded to Bosworth who, Delman saw, had his gear put in the waiting jeep. Then he remembered and pulled from his right overcoat pocket the bloodstained penknife.

He handed it to Bosworth.

Delman said, "This is Clary's. He might want it."

He saw that the Engineers had arrived. Their convoy of trucks, laden with enough wood and posts and barbed wire to add more cages to the POW complex, pulled up near headquarters. Delman saluted Lt. George Taylor who passed him on his way to report to Major Hughes.

Then Delman stepped into the jeep and, without looking back, told its driver, "Let's get out of here. Go. Wake me up when we get to Paris."